W9-DDE-038

THE RETURN OF

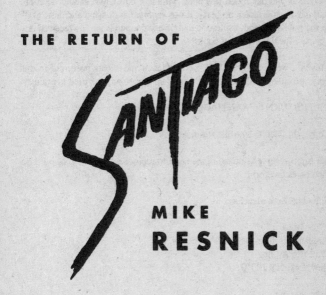

SANTIAGO

MIKE
RESNICK

TOR®

A TOM DOHERTY ASSOCIATES BOOK
NEW YORK

This is a work of fiction. All the characters and events portrayed in this book are either products of the author's imagination or are used fictitiously.

THE RETURN OF SANTIAGO

Edited by Beth Meacham

A Tor Book
Published by Tom Doherty Associates, LLC
175 Fifth Avenue
New York, NY 10010

www.tor.com

Tor® is a registered trademark of Tom Doherty Associates, LLC.

ISBN 0-765-34146-8
EAN 978-0-765-34146-4
Library of Congress Catalog Card Number: 2002075660

First edition: February 2003
First mass market edition: April 2004

Printed in the United States of America

0 9 8 7 6 5 4 3 2 1

TO CAROL, AS ALWAYS

AND TO THE MEMBERS OF THE RESNICK LISTSERV
(JOIN IT AT WWW.MIKERESNICK.COM), WHO KEEP ME
AMUSED, STIMULATED, ALERT, AND REASONABLY SANE

CONTENTS

PROLOGUE

SOME PEOPLE SAY HE WAS killed by the Angel. Others say that Johnny One-Note gunned him down. Most think he died at the hands of Peacemaker MacDougal.

Nobody knows exactly when he met his fate, or where. It just slowly began dawning on his enemies—he didn't have any friends, not that anyone knew about—that he hadn't made any trouble for some time.

Now, that doesn't mean men weren't still killed and banks weren't still robbed and mining worlds weren't still plundered. After all, Santiago wasn't the only outlaw on the Inner Frontier; he was just the biggest—so big, some say, that his shadow blotted out the sun for miles around.

Long after the Angel and Johnny One-Note and Peacemaker MacDougal had all gone to their graves, men and women—and aliens—were still arguing about Santiago. Some held that he was just a man, a lot smarter and more ruthless than most, but a man nonetheless. Others said that he was a mutant possessed of extraordinary powers, or else how could he have held the Navy at bay for so many years? There were even a few who thought he was an alien, with undefined but awesome alien abilities.

There was no known holograph of him, no retinagram or fingerprint anywhere in the Democracy. There were a few eyewitness accounts, but they differed so much from each other than no one took any of them seriously. A long-dead thief who called himself the Jolly Swagman swore he was eleven feet three inches tall, with orange hair and blazing red eyes that had seen the inner sanctum of hell itself.

A preacher named Father William claimed he was an alien who always wore a face mask because oxygen was poison to his system. Virtue MacKenzie, who wrote three books about him, never described him, and the only holograph she took was of the S-shaped scar on the back of his right hand. According to one description he was a purple-skinned alien with four arms. Another had him a mechanized, gleaming metal cyborg, no longer capable of any human emotion.

There was even a school of thought that argued that there never was a Santiago, that he was a merely a myth—but there were too many graveyards on too many worlds to lend any credence to that belief.

They say that Black Orpheus, the poet and balladeer who wandered the spaceways, writing his endless epic of the larger-than-life heroes, villains, adventurers and misfits that he found there, spent half a dozen verses of his *Ballad of the Inner Frontier* describing Santiago in detail, but those verses were never codified and were lost to posterity.

The one thing everyone agreed upon was that the last time he had manifested his presence was in the year 3301 of the Galactic Era, and with the passing decades it was generally assumed that Santiago, whoever or whatever he may have been, was dead.

Which simply goes to show, as has been shown so many times in the past, that a majority of the people can be wrong.

For in 3407 G.E., 106 years after he vanished, Santiago returned to the Inner Frontier, to once again juggle worlds and secrets as in days of old, to bring death to his enemies, to stride across the planets in all his former glory.

This is his story. But to fully understand it, we must begin with Danny Briggs (who is not to remain Danny Briggs for long), a simple thief, physically unimpressive, artistically wanting, morally ambiguous, a young man of seemingly unexceptional gifts and abilities, and yet destined to play a central role in the return of Santiago. . . .

PART I

THE RHYMER'S BOOK

1.

SOME SAY THAT HE'S A HUNDRED,
SOME SAY THAT HE IS MORE;
SOME SAY HE'LL LIVE FOREVER—
THIS OUTLAW COMMODORE!

THAT WAS THE LAST VERSE ever written by Black Orpheus, the Bard of the Inner Frontier. Though Santiago's name doesn't appear in it, it is generally considered to have been about the notorious King of the Outlaws.

And with that, Black Orpheus' history of the Frontier was done. Not finished in the sense that it was complete, but done. Shortly after writing those words he disappeared forever. Some say he found an idyllic world on which to live out his life. Others say that Santiago himself gunned him down. A handful believe that he found the task of codifying the entire history of the Inner Frontier in verse too daunting, and that he simply gave it up and went off to live out his years in solitude.

At the moment that he became a catalyst for history, Danny Briggs knew little of Santiago and even less of Black Orpheus. Like most kids, he'd grown up thrilled by legends about both, but that was the extent of his knowledge and his interest. On the third night of the fifth month of the year 3407 of the Galactic Era, Danny Briggs had other things on his mind as he scaled the end of a long, low building, a cloth bag slung over his right shoulder.

He moved slowly, carefully, trying not to make a sound—but then the wind shifted, carrying his scent to the creatures below, and all his precautions were for nothing. A huge Moondevil, two hundred pounds of muscle and sinew, saw him creeping across the roof and began howling. A Polarcat, glistening white in the moonlight, leaped up from its own enclosure and tried to dig its claws into Danny's leg.

As the young man sidestepped the Polarcat, two more animals of a type he'd never seen before launched themselves toward him, falling back as they hit the edge of the gently pitched roof.

Danny cursed under his breath. There was no sense moving cautiously any longer. The only way to shut all the animals up was to get out of their sight as quickly as possible. He raced the length of the roof, ignoring the increasing din, and finally jumped down to a small atrium. He adjusted his pocket computer to set up a signal that disrupted the security cameras, found the door he was looking for, used the code he had stolen months earlier, and entered the office.

He ignored the safe and instead activated the computer. In seconds he had accessed the data he needed. He pulled out his tiny scanner, transferred the data to it, and put it back in a pocket. Then he deactivated the computer. The entire operation took less than a minute.

He considered killing the security system and just walking out the front door, but that would have given away the fact that he'd been there, and all his efforts would be wasted if the police suspected that anyone had invaded this particular office—especially when they discovered that no money had been taken.

Instead he went back the way he'd come. The animals were silent now, but he knew they wouldn't stay that way for long. Choosing speed over stealth, he climbed onto the roof of the long, low building again and raced the length of it in the face of the ever-increasing howls, growls, and screams. When he came to the Moondevil, he reached into his cloth bag, withdrew a small dead animal, and tossed it into the Moondevil's enclosure. Now if enough neighbors reported all the noise and the police investigated, they'd find the remains of the animal and assume that it had somehow wandered into the kennel and caused all the commotion.

An hour later he was sitting at his usual table at the Golden Fleece, a tavern on the outskirts of New Punjab, a small city that had nothing in common with the original Punjab except the subjugation of its natives, in this case the orange-skinned humanoids of Bailiwick. The world wasn't a very large or very important one: it held no fissionable materials, few precious stones or metals, and the farmland wasn't the best. But it did have two million natives—it had had close to five million before the Navy pacified them—and three human cities, of which New Punjab, with almost forty thousand residents, was the largest.

It was said that Black Orpheus had once spent a night on Bailiwick, but there were no holograms or other records to prove it. Bailiwick's main claim to fame was Milos Jannis, who had been born there and was now the Democracy's middleweight freehand champion. Two minor actors and a second-rate novelist were the only other things Bailiwick had to brag about.

Danny Briggs didn't want to add to that total. He was content to remain relatively unknown and unapprehended. He shunned publicity the way bad politicians seek it out. Even when he turned a profit at what he considered to be his business, he always made sure to deposit and spend it offworld.

He ordered a drink and sat there, staring at himself in the mirror behind the bar. He wasn't thrilled with what he saw: He stood a few inches under six feet in an era when the average man stood two inches over six feet. He was thin; not emaciated, but somewhere between slender and wiry. His head was covered by nondescript brown hair. He didn't like his chin much; too pointy. For the hundredth time he considered growing a beard to cover it, but his mustache was so sparse he hated to think of what a beard would look like. His ears stuck out too far; he figured one of these days he was going to lose one or both in a fight.

No, on the whole, there wasn't much about Danny Briggs that he liked. Hell, he didn't even like the way he made his living. He didn't believe in God, so he didn't believe that

God had some nobler purpose for him. He had no fire burning in his belly, but rather a certain unfocused dissatisfaction, a desire to make some kind of mark, to scratch his name on the boulder of Time so people would know he'd been here. Not that he was a hero, because he wasn't; not because he would someday make a difference to the handful of misfits and criminals that formed his circle of friends, because he knew he was incapable of making one; but simply to show those who came after him that once upon a time there was a man named Danny Briggs, and he had lived right here on Bailiwick, and that, just once, he'd done something worth remembering.

Except that everything he'd done up to now was aimed at letting no one know he'd been here, and far from remembering him, he wanted nothing more than for the police and the Democracy to completely ignore his existence.

Interesting conflict, he thought wryly. The urge to be known versus the need to be hidden. Perhaps someday he'd resolve it, though he doubted it.

A grizzled, white-haired man with a noticeable limp entered the Golden Fleece, looked around, and walked directly to Danny's table.

"I'm not too early, am I?" he asked.

"No, I've got it," said Danny.

"The usual price?"

"Three hundred Maria Theresa dollars up front and twenty percent of whatever you make."

"It was two hundred fifty last time," grumbled the man.

"Success breeds inflation."

"You sure you won't take Democracy credits?" asked the old man.

"I don't want anything to do with them," said Danny. *Besides*, he added mentally, *you start spending too many Democracy credits, you start attracting a little too much Democracy attention—but I guess you haven't figured that out, have you?*

"Okay, okay," said the old man. He removed a prosthetic hand, pulled a wad of money out of it, counted out three hundred Maria Theresa dollars, and pushed them across the table.

"Thanks," said Danny. He pulled out a tiny computer, retrieved an address, and transferred it to a hologram for the old man to study. "This is it."

"You're sure?"

"Have I ever been wrong yet?" asked Danny, nodding to another client, who had entered the Golden Fleece and caught his eye.

"No, you never have been," said the old man. "I don't know how you do it."

That's because you and every other fool I deal with would have broken into the kennel's safe tonight and come away with a couple hundred credits if you were lucky. Not one of you would ever think of stealing a list of the animals' owners, complete with their addresses and the dates that they're gone.

"Memorize it," said Danny, indicating the hologram that the tiny computer was projecting.

The man studied it, then nodded his head. Danny wiped the information from the machine and deactivated it.

"Thanks, Danny," said the old man, getting to his feet. The next client sat down opposite him.

Jesus! I rob the data from that computer every three or four months and don't take any other risks, and I get twenty percent of three hundred robberies a year. It's almost too easy. Doesn't anyone else on this dirtball have a brain?

Their negotiation completed, the man got up and left, and Danny was alone with his drink once again. A redhead, a bit overweight but still pretty, smiled a greeting at him from a nearby table.

"Hi, Danny," she said.

"Hi yourself, Duchess," said Danny. "I just finished tonight's business. Why don't you come over and join me?" He flashed a wad of money. "I'm solvent tonight."

"You never give up, do you?" she said, amused.

"Of course not," replied Danny. "You don't hit the moon if you don't shoot for it."

"Am I the moon?"

"You'll do."

"Boy, you sure know how to turn a girl on," she said sardonically.

He smiled. "It works with all the other girls."

"So turn your charm on one of them."

"Anything worthwhile takes effort," he replied. "*You* take effort."

"I suppose I'm flattered," said the Duchess.

"So join me."

"I said I was flattered, not interested."

"One of these days you're going to say yes, and it'll be a race to see which of us drops dead from shock first."

"One of these days you'll get an honest job, and maybe I'll say yes."

"If I had an honest job, I couldn't afford you." He smiled. "I'm sure someone somewhere has based an entire philosophical system on a paradox just like that one."

"Not funny, Danny."

"Look, some people are great rulers of men, some are great cleaners of stables. I found out what I was good at early on."

"I think it's criminal that you feel that way."

He smiled again. "Criminal's the word. Still, I'm willing to be shown the error of my ways. Come have a drink."

"No, thanks."

"You really won't join me?"

"I really won't."

"But your heart would be broken if I hadn't asked, right?"

"Try not asking some night and we'll see."

"You drive a hard bargain, Duchess," said Danny. "But one of these days you'll see me as I really am."

"Maybe I already do."

"Fate forfend," he said in mock dismay.

A moment later he got up and made his way to the men's room. As he was washing his hands the door dilated and two burly men entered the small cubicle.

"Hi, Danny," said the taller of them.

"Hi, Mr. Balsam," replied Danny, trying to hide his apprehension. "Hi, Mr. Gibbs."

"That's *Commander* Balsam."

"And *Lieutenant* Gibbs," added the shorter, wider man.

"That's only when you're on duty," said Danny. "And if you were on duty, you wouldn't be drinking in a tavern."

"We're not drinking," said Balsam. "And it's still Commander."

"Whatever makes you happy," said Danny. "Good evening, Commander."

"Well, it didn't start out that way, but it's improving," replied Balsam. A grin that boded no good spread across his face. "You fucked up big time tonight, Danny."

"I don't know what you're talking about. I've been in the bar all night."

"No, you've been swiping data from a kennel. We've got you cold."

"You have holograms of me breaking into a kennel? I doubt that."

"Of course we don't have any holos, Danny. You disabled the cameras, remember?"

"Fingerprints, then? Or maybe voiceprints, or a retinagram?" suggested Danny.

"We know you've wiped your prints, and you've got contacts that give a false retina reading," said Gibbs.

"Well, you're certainly welcome to search me for this mysterious data you're referring to."

"You're a bright lad, Danny," said Balsam. "You've either got it hidden away or committed to memory."

"I wish I could help you," said Danny with a smile, "but aren't you supposed to have evidence before you start making accusations?"

"Oh, we've got it, Danny. Holograms, retinagrams, voiceprints, everything."

Danny frowned. "But you just said—"

"We didn't get it at the kennel," said Balsam. "We got it at the market."

"What market?"

Balsam grinned again. "For a smart guy, you did a really dumb thing, Danny. You went to the biggest, best-protected market in town, and you bought a dead *minipor* to feed the animals if they got noisy."

"I assume you're going to get to the point sometime this evening," said Danny, already scanning the room for some means of escape.

"The *minipor*'s a rare item, Danny. And the reason it's a rarity is because it comes from Churchill II. The store has security cameras showing you buying the only *minipor* imported to Bailiwick in the past half year—and there was enough of its skeleton left in the Moondevil's enclosure so that we could identify it." He paused. "It was a nice scam, Danny. Of all the scum I deal with, only *you* would have figured out there was a hundred times more profit in a list of empty houses than in the kennel's cash box."

Danny glanced at the small window on the back wall of the washroom.

"Don't even think of it," said Gibbs. "You'd never fit through, and we'd tack on another two years for trying to escape."

"Who's escaping?" said Danny pleasantly. "I hope you have a comfortable cell. My lawyer doesn't like getting up before noon, so I'll be spending the night with you."

"This night and the next thousand," said Balsam. He withdrew a pair of glowing manacles. "Hands behind your back, Danny."

"Can I get a drink of water first?"

"Okay, but no funny stuff."

"You tell me what's funny about a glass of water," said Danny, pulling a cup out of the wall and holding it beneath the faucet. "Cold," he ordered.

Cold water filled the cup, and Danny drank it down.

"One more?"

"Come on, Danny. You had your drink."

"You know what the water's like in jail," said Danny. "Let me have one more drink. How can it hurt?"

Balsam shrugged. "Yeah, okay, go ahead."

"Thanks," said Danny. He turned to the sink and held the glass under the tap as the two officers relaxed and waited for him.

"Hot!" he croaked.

Boiling hot water filled the glass, and in a single motion he hurled it in Balsam's face, grabbed the manacles, connected Gibbs' wrist to the sink, and raced out the door.

Danny had a three-step lead on Balsam as he raced to the door of the Golden Fleece. The commander pulled out a screecher, a sonic pistol that would put him out for the rest of the night and give him a headache for a week, but as he was running after Danny and taking aim, the Duchess stuck out a foot and tripped him. He fell with a bone-jarring thud.

Danny raced back to the table, took her hand, and began pulling her toward the door.

"I didn't mean to do that!" she said, panic-stricken. "It was instinct! I just didn't want him to shoot you!"

"I believe you!" said Danny urgently. *"He* never will! Come on! He's not going to stay down forever, and he's got a partner!"

Suddenly Gibbs, the manacle hanging from his wrist, burst into the tavern.

"Now!" said Danny urgently. The Duchess took a quick glance at Gibbs, screamed, and actually beat Danny out the door.

"Left!" he whispered as he caught up with her. They reached the corner and had just turned out of the line of sight when the two policemen emerged, weapons in hand, from the tavern.

"Now they're going to kill us!" whispered the Duchess, terrified.

"They're never going to find us," answered Danny. "Just trust me and do what I say."

They ran through the streets, turning frequently, never seeing any sign of their pursuers, always moving farther and farther from the center of the small city. After a few minutes the buildings took on new and different shapes: some were triangular, some trapezoidal, some seemed to follow no rational plan at all.

"Where are we?" asked the Duchess, as Danny led her down narrow winding streets that seemed totally pattern-less.

"The native quarter," he said. "They won't follow us here."

"Is it dangerous?" she asked, looking around.

"It is if they know you work for the Democracy. They'll leave us alone."

"How do you know?"

"I've spent a lot of time here," said Danny, nodding to an orange-skinned being who stared right through him as if he didn't exist. "They know I won't do them any harm."

"You have alien friends?"

"They're not aliens, they've natives," answered Danny. "And yes, I have friends here."

She began looking panicky again. "I can't believe it! I'm a fugitive, and I'm hiding out in the alien quarter!"

"Calm down," said Danny. "You're safe now."

"*You* calm down!" she snapped. "Maybe you're used to having the police after you, but it's a new experience for me, and I don't like it very much!"

"They won't come to the quarter," he said confidently.

"Are we going to spend the night here?"

He shook his head. "We'll give the police half an hour to figure out where I went, and another couple of minutes to decide it's not worth the effort to search for us here."

"Then what?"

He smiled. "Then we have our choice of fifty-three empty houses."

She lit a smokeless cigarette. "So it's not enough that I helped a criminal escape capture," she said bitterly. "Now the police can add breaking and entering to the charges."

"I'm grateful that you stopped my friend Commander Balsam from shooting me," said Danny, "but no one asked you to. It was your choice to hinder a police officer in the pursuit of a criminal, so don't blame me."

"I told you: I wasn't thinking clearly," she said. "I was just reacting."

"Believe me, no one's going to arrest you," Danny assured her. "Any red-blooded man who was at the tavern will swear that Balsam tripped over you."

"Do you really think so?"

"I do. Besides, if *I* don't know your real name, neither do they. If you choose to stay with me, all they know is they're after someone who called herself the Duchess. Correct me if I'm wrong, but I'll give plenty of ten-to-one that that's not the name on your ID disk or your passport."

"It isn't. I didn't like my name, so I changed it."

"They do that on the Inner Frontier, not here on the Democracy worlds. How can the government keep tabs on you if they don't know who you are?"

"I never thought of it that way," she said, "but maybe choosing a new name wasn't a bad idea."

"Beats the hell out of being a Myrtle."

"Do I look like a Myrtle to you?"

He stared at her and shook his head. "You look like a Duchess who saved my life. Of course, you won't drink with me, but if I have to choose between your doing one or the other . . ." He ended with a smile.

"Well, you look exactly like a Danny Briggs."

"That bad, huh?"

"If you don't like the name, change it like I did."

"What would I change it to?"

"That's for you to decide."

"I never had a hero," he admitted. "I guess I'll keep it and stay who I am."

They stood in silence for a few more minutes, engulfed in angular shadows. Then Danny checked his timepiece.

"We've been here almost an hour," he announced. "I think we can start hunting up a place to stay while we figure out our next move."

"Where are we going?" she asked as he began walking back toward the city.

"Where do you want to go?"

"You know that little hill at the south end of town, the one overlooking Lake Belora?" she said. "Have you got anything there?"

"I've got two houses in the area," he replied. "I won't know if either of them has a lake view until we get there."

The first house was actually in a valley just beyond the hill, but the second, still luxurious but less impressive, looked like they would be able see the lake from the second level.

"It's too bad I didn't know this would be happening," remarked Danny. "There's an empty villa fronting the lake. It even has a dock and a couple of boats."

"So let's go there."

He shook his head. "It's going to be robbed sometime tonight. We don't want to be anywhere near it, just in case."

"How will we get in?" asked the Duchess as they approached the front door of the house they had chosen. "I don't know *how* to break into a house. Won't it have a security system?"

"Have a little trust in the man whose life you saved," he replied, kneeling down to study the computer lock. *"Shit!"*

"What is it?"

"I can crack the combination in a couple of minutes, but it's got a bone reader."

"A bone reader?"

"Yeah. I can get around almost any retina ID system, but bone readers are tough. They scan your skeleton and compare it to anyone who the computer's been programmed to accept. I've got a couple of healed fractures that won't match up against anyone else's."

"Then we'll do without our lake view and go to the other house."

"Give me a minute," he said. "There's never been a security system that couldn't be penetrated."

"By you?"

"By somebody." He flashed her a smile. "I am but a talented amateur."

"Sure," she retorted. "And I'm a millionaire virgin."

"That gives me all the more reason to find a way into the house."

He touched the lock, and a holographic screen appeared in the air, filled with dozens of icons. His fingers began moving expertly over the lock, and the icons began racing across the screen in near-hypnotic patterns.

"How's it coming?" asked the Duchess after a few minutes.

"Oh, it's been unlocked for a while," he said.

"But you can't hide your fractures."

"I'm not trying to."

After another minute he stood up. "Okay," he said. "I'm done."

The door dilated, and she began to step through it. He grabbed her arm and held her back.

"Gentlemen first," he said, stepping through.

The door slammed shut in her face. He disappeared for a moment, then opened the door and invited her in.

"What was that all about?" she said, entering the house.

"I fed the computer the data about my skeleton and told it I'd been approved. But I didn't know what your skeletal history might be, so after I went in I deactivated the security system." He paused. "I also ordered all the windows to polarize. We can see out, but no one on the outside can see in, even if we have the lights on."

"Do you do this kind of thing often?" she asked.

"Certainly not," he replied. "I get people who are hungrier than I am to do it for me."

She stared at him with an expression that was a cross between concern and admiration. "There's a lot more to you than meets the eye."

"Thank you," said Danny. "I won't even offer an obscene rejoinder." He looked around. "So what do you think of our new quarters?"

"Elegant," she said, walking through the entry room. The

carpet anticipated her steps and thickened as she walked, and the mural on the wall slowly, almost imperceptibly, began turning into a three-dimensional scene, then gradually added motion. It went back to being a flat painting as they passed into the next room.

"This is some house!" she said. "I've never been close to anything like this!"

"Yeah, a person could get used to this without much effort," agreed Danny, as a chair positioned itself to accommodate him.

"As long as we're going to be stuck here for a day or two, let's go upstairs and see if we can see the lake," suggested the Duchess.

"Why not?" assented Danny, following her to a staircase. As they put their feet on the first wide stair, it metamorphosed into a carpeted escalator, totally silent, and gently transported them up to the second floor.

They walked to a window and stared out.

"You can *almost* see it," she said. "If we were even one floor higher we'd have a magnificent view."

"I saw a third level of windows when we were outside," said Danny. "There's probably an attic above us somewhere. We should be able to see it from there."

They searched through the rooms, and finally came to an airlift next to a storage closet.

"This has got to be it," said Danny. "It's the only thing leading up."

"What do we stand on?" asked the Duchess nervously as she looked down to the basement some thirty feet below.

"Just step into the shaft," explained Danny. "It'll sense your presence, and you'll stand on a cushion of air that'll take you up to the attic."

"You're sure? I've never seen one of these things before."

"They're all the rage on Deluros VIII and the bigger worlds," said Danny. "Give it another twenty years and they'll be just as popular here."

She looked skeptical, so he stepped into the shaft first.

When she saw him standing on air she joined him, and they floated gently up to the attic.

"Lights," he ordered, and suddenly the attic was illuminated with soft, indirect lighting. As tidy as the house had been, the attic was that chaotic. Books, tapes, disks, and cubes were stacked awkwardly on the floor; paintings were piled against a wall, each leaning on the next. Piles of old wrinkled clothes sat beside piles of unmarked plastic boxes.

"Take a look, Danny!" she enthused, staring out a window. "You can see the whole lake. It's gorgeous!"

"Just a minute," he replied, walking to another window. He knelt down, pushing a few plastic boxes aside. One of the ancient boxes literally cracked open and fell apart.

"Don't you just love the way the moonlight plays on the water?" said the Duchess.

"Oh, Jesus!" whispered Danny.

"I didn't hear you."

There was no answer, and she turned to him.

"I thought you were looking out the window," she said, staring at him as he fingered through a stack of ancient, crumbling papers. He paid no attention to her. *"Danny!"* she said irritably. "What's the matter with you?"

Finally he looked up, the strangest expression on his face. "Who'd have guessed it?" he whispered. "I mean, this is just another house. Nothing special, nothing to indicate . . ." His voice trailed off.

"What are you talking about?" she demanded.

He held up a sheet of paper.

"We just hit the mother lode," he said in awed tones.

2.

COME IF YOU DARE, COME BUT BEWARE,
COME TO THE LAIR OF ALTAIR OF ALTAIR.
OFFER A PRAYER TO THE MEN FOUL AND FAIR,
TRAPPED IN THE SNARE OF ALTAIR OF ALTAIR.

THAT WAS THE FIRST THING Danny read. Soon he was making his way through the thousands of verses.

"They don't even know what they've got here!" he said excitedly. "If they did, it would be under lock and key in a vault, not out in the open in a plastic box that's falling apart."

"What is it?" asked the Duchess.

"Listen," said Danny. He picked up another page and read to her:

> *They call him the Angel, the Angel of Death,*
> *If ever you've seen him, you've drawn your last*
> *   breath.*
> *He's got cold lifeless eyes, he's got brains, he's got*
> *   skill,*
> *He's got weapons galore, and a yearning to kill."*

"Is that supposed to mean something to me?" she asked.

"That's the Angel he's writing about!" enthused Danny. *"The Angel!* Haven't you heard of him?"

She shrugged.

"He was the greatest bounty hunter of them all! They say he killed more than two hundred men!"

"So you found a poem about the Angel," said the Duchess, her interest fading. "So what?"

"You don't understand!" said Danny. He held up a sheaf of papers with the same scrawl on all of them. "This isn't just *any* poem! This is Black Orpheus' original manuscript!"

"Yeah?" she said, walking over to look at it. "What makes you think so?"

"The verses themselves. They're all about the characters he met on the Frontier. And I've heard about these characters—Altair of Altair and the Angel. Heard about them, read about them. They've even made some videos about them."

"But anyone could write a few verses."

He opened three more ancient boxes, and pulled verse-covered pages from each. "A few verses, sure. Ten thousand verses, I don't think so. This is *it*!"

"What's it worth?" asked the Duchess.

"Who knows? Ten million, thirty million. What's history worth to a people who don't have any?"

"I don't know what you're talking about," she said.

"He was the Bard of the Inner Frontier. There's no law on the Frontier, no government, and there's sure as hell no historians. He was all they had, him and this poem. Bits and pieces have been printed here and there, but no one's ever seen the whole thing." He patted the pile of papers. "Until tonight."

"Who would buy a bundle of crumbling old papers?"

"Every museum and every library in the galaxy," answered Danny. "And probably every collector." He held up a long, thick feather. "This is the quill pen he wrote with. This alone ought to bring half a million."

"You're kidding!"

"The hell I am. All I have to do is check through the whole manuscript and make sure it's authentic."

"And you can really auction it for that much?"

"Not publicly," he said. "I'm stealing it, remember?"

"Well, if the people who own this place don't know what they've got . . ."

"It makes no difference. The bidders—well, the *legitimate* bidders, the ones I plan to avoid—will want to know how I got it. They'll want to take it away to authenticate it, and once it's out of my possession, I can't control what happens to it."

"So it'll be a private sale?"

"A very limited auction, let's call it," he corrected her. "Market value could be fifty million credits. I'll take twenty million and be happy with it."

"I hear a lot of 'I's," she said suddenly. "What happened to 'we'?"

"I thought you didn't want to be a criminal."

"I'm *already* a criminal. I might as well be a rich one."

"I'll take care of you," promised Danny.

"I don't want to be taken care of," complained the Duchess. "I want to be a partner—an *equal* partner."

"I don't have equal partners," said Danny.

"You'd never have found it if I hadn't wanted a view of the lake," she persisted.

"And you still wouldn't know what it was if I hadn't told you," retorted Danny. "I said I'd take care of you and I will. Now get off my back and let me look at what we've got here."

"We should pack it up and leave Bailiwick tonight," said the Duchess.

He shook his head. "Too soon. They'll have men posted at the spaceport, and I don't own a private ship."

"What makes you think they won't still have men posted in another day or two?"

"Look, I embarrassed them, but it was a small-time crime. Pretty soon there'll be a nice juicy murder or two, and they'll decide to go after bigger fish."

"You'd better be right," she said.

"You're free to leave any time you want," said Danny. "But I stay here, and so"—he patted the boxes—"do *these*."

She stared at him sullenly for a long moment, then walked to the air shaft. "I'm going down to the kitchen to see what kind of food they've got." She paused, then added reluctantly, "Do you want anything?"

"Yeah. Bring me back a beer if they have any."

She disappeared down the shaft, and returned five

minutes later with a pair of beers. She walked across the cluttered floor to hand one to Danny.

"Listen to this," he said excitedly:

> *"The Songbird stalks, the Songbird kills,*
> *The Songbird works to pay his bills.*
> *So, friend, beware the Songbird's glance:*
> *If you're his prey, you'll have no chance."*

Danny looked up, his face aglow with excitement. "You know what I think? I think he's writing about Sebastian Cain!"

"Never heard of him," said the bored Duchess.

"What kind of education have you had?" he said contemptuously.

"Math, science, computers, literature—the usual."

"Sadly lacking."

"Not everyone studies killers and cutthroats," she shot back.

"They should. They're much more interesting than vectors and angles."

"So who was the Songbird?"

"I told you: Sebastian Cain."

"That's what I meant: who was Sebastian Cain?"

"Another bounty hunter. And a revolutionary early in his life."

"Why is he the Songbird?" she asked. "And don't tell me something silly like he whistled whenever he killed a man."

"His full name was Sebastian Nightingale Cain. I think Orpheus took it from his middle name."

"And everyone knew him as the Songbird?"

Danny shook his head. "No, I don't know if anyone did." He paused and stared at the paper in his hand. "I could be wrong, but I'd bet the farm that the Songbird was Cain!"

"Why is that so important?"

"Cain was a major figure on the Frontier a century ago.

There's nothing written about it here, but I've got a feeling he's the one who killed the Angel."

"You got all that from a few verses?" she asked skeptically.

"Like every kid, I grew up learning everything I could about the Inner Frontier. *That's* where the action was, where all the bigger-than-life heroes and villains lived and died. I'm just adding what I already knew to what I've read here." He paused. "Black Orpheus hid a lot of things inside those verses. It's like putting together a very complex jigsaw puzzle."

"Well, you play detective," said the Duchess, making no attempt to feign interest. "I'm going to find a bedroom."

"Fine, you do that," he said, never looking up from the manuscript.

When she awoke in the morning, she went up to the attic and found him still sitting there, poring over the manuscript.

"I take it you haven't been to bed yet," she said.

He looked up, his face aglow with excitement. "Listen to this:

> *"His name is Father William,*
> *His aim is hard to ken:*
> *His game is saving sinners;*
> *His fame is killing men.*

"Father William was a preacher. They say he tipped the scales at more than four hundred pounds. According to legend, he was also a bounty hunter."

"It sounds like your friend Black Orpheus went to a bounty hunters' convention," she observed.

"That's all the law there was on the Inner Frontier," replied Danny. "All the law there is even today." He looked up from the papers. "I've been piecing things together all night, and you know what I think?"

"What?" she asked in bored tones.

"I think Father William actually worked for Santiago. In

fact, I think he was a conduit for most of the money that Santiago stole."

"That doesn't make any sense," said the Duchess.

"Why not?"

"Santiago was the greatest outlaw in the galaxy, right? Why would he use this preacher as a conduit to move money he stole? Move it *where*? You don't steal money just to give it away again. You keep it, or else you spend it on yourself. So it makes no sense." She made no attempt to hide her annoyance.

"I've still got thousands of verses to read," said Danny, "but there's something very strange about this manuscript, and it has to do with Santiago. I'm not sure what, but I'll find out before I'm done."

"Well, at least you know now that Santiago existed."

"I always did."

"You took it on faith," she said.

"And now my faith has been rewarded."

"Good. Now let's pack up and get the hell off the planet and sell the damned thing."

"Too soon," said Danny. "We'll give Balsam and Gibbs another day to get tired of looking for us."

"Just one day, and then we go!"

"Probably."

"What's this 'probably' shit?" she demanded. "One day and we're out of here!"

"There's no rush," he replied. "The owners aren't coming home for two more weeks."

"I'm not staying here two weeks!"

"Just a day or two."

"*One* day. And even so, I don't like it."

"You're free to go any time you want," said Danny. "But the manuscript stays with me."

"Don't get so cocky," she warned him. "I might leave right now and turn you in for the reward."

Danny smiled. "You might, but you won't."

"Why not?"

"Because whatever the reward comes to, it's peanuts next

to what I'll give you once we've sold the poem." His smile vanished. "Now leave me alone and let me get back to work."

He spent the day poring over the manuscript. At sunset the Duchess insisted he come down to the kitchen for dinner. He ate quickly and unenthusiastically, then went back to the attic to continue reading.

She heard a loud *thump!* in the middle of the night and went upstairs to see what had happened. Danny had been sitting on the floor, reading, and finally fell asleep. He had fallen over on his side, and now lay, snoring gently, a page still clutched in his hand. She figured he was out for the next twelve to sixteen hours, but when she checked on him again in the morning he was up and reading.

"Danny!" she insisted. "Put it down for a few hours. You'll kill yourself!"

"I didn't know you cared."

"I don't want you dying before we sell the poem. I wouldn't begin to know how or where to do it."

"You sure know how to flatter a guy," he said.

"So are you going to get some sleep?" she said, ignoring his remark.

"Not right away," he said. "I'm getting close."

"Close to what? Finishing?"

"To understanding."

"What's to understand? They're all just four-line verses. There's nothing very difficult about them. In fact, I thought Black Orpheus would be a better poet. The things you've read to me sounded wimpy and literary and kind of lame."

"It's *what* he says, and what he *doesn't* say, not *how* he says it," replied Danny. "This thing is nothing short of the secret history of the Inner Frontier up to a century ago."

"Everything's a mystery," she said with no show of interest. "Why does it have to be a *secret* history? Why not a public one? After all, the public read it."

"The men and women and aliens he wrote about were alive when he wrote these verses. Many of them had prices on their heads. Still more confided in him, told him of deeds, some good, some bad, that no one knew about. You have to understand: Black Orpheus was the Bard of the Inner Frontier. He was welcomed everywhere he went. No one ever turned away from him—but to earn that kind of trust, he couldn't openly say anything more than you might find on a Wanted poster." Danny paused, his eyes still bright with excitement. "So he found secret ways to say what he wanted to say. This manuscript is to the Inner Frontier what, oh, I don't know, what Homer was to the Trojan War. Except that Homer exaggerated like hell and told everything out in the open, and Orpheus is concealing things all over the place. Including something huge, right in the middle."

"You said that yesterday. What is it?"

"I don't know. I think I'm getting close to piecing it together, but I won't know what it is until I'm done. It's as if he were holding someone for ransom, and I had the money, and he wanted to make sure the police weren't tailing me, so he ran me all over the city to make sure I was clean." He emitted an exhausted sigh. "He's running me all over the history of the Inner Frontier before I can discover what he's hiding."

"Maybe you're not supposed to find it."

"That would make a mockery of the whole thing. No, it's there—but he didn't want it to be easy." Danny looked at her. "That means it's something *big*. Otherwise, he wouldn't have taken such trouble to hide it. I spotted Cain and some of the others right away, but this whatever-it-is is taking a lot more work. Still, another few hours, another day or two, and I'll have it."

"Hey!" she shouted. "We're leaving today, remember?"

"We'll see."

"You promised!"

"You *wanted* me to promise," answered Danny. "That's not the same thing."

"Every day we stay here we increase our risk. A neighbor could report us. The police could find us. The owners could return early. We've been pushing our luck, Danny. Why can't we leave?"

"I'm still piecing things together," he said. "I don't want to stop, not even for a day."

"You act like it's some kind of treasure map."

"I doubt it. Legend has it that Orpheus died broke on an uninhabited world that he named after his dead wife, Eurydice."

"He doesn't sound all that brilliant to me," said the Duchess. "He writes little rhymes that anyone can do—"

"I *told* you—" Danny interrupted her.

"I know what you said. But you haven't discovered any deep dark secrets yet, so maybe there aren't any. He's famous all over the Frontier, all over the Democracy too, and he died penniless." She snorted contemptuously. "Some genius."

"Most poets die penniless," said Danny. "Anyway, I envy him."

"Why?"

"He traveled the Frontier, saw a new world every few days, lived every kid's dream, every romantic's dream. He did important work—and look at the people he got to meet, men and women like the Songbird, Father William, the Jolly Swagman, Peacemaker MacDougal, Johnny One-Note, the Angel, the Sargasso Rose. Just the names alone conjure up such fantastic pictures." He picked up another sheet and began reading:

> *"Moonripple, Moonripple, touring the stars,*
> *Has polished the wax on a thousand bars,*
> *Has trod on the soil of a hundred worlds,*
> *Has found only pebbles while searching for pearls.*

"Listen to her name: Moonripple. A girl named Moonripple, who's been to a hundred worlds. Now, *that's* evocative—especially when you live on a dirtball like"—he grimaced—"Bailiwick."

The Duchess was unimpressed. "Read the rest of the

verse. She found only pebbles while searching for pearls."

"She found a lot more than that," said Danny. "You just have to know where to look and how to read it."

"It sounds to me like she died as broke as Orpheus," said the Duchess with finality, walking to the shaft. "I'm not kidding, Danny. I want to leave here today. I keep looking out the windows every five minutes, expecting to see the police surrounding us."

"Soon," he said distractedly, his attention already back on the manuscript.

Two hours later he went down to the kitchen and made some coffee.

"Well?" she demanded.

"I just need a little time away from the poem, time to think."

"To think about what, or am I going to be sorry I asked?"

"There's stuff there even Orpheus didn't know about," said Danny. "He was too close to the forest to see the trees."

"Whatever *that* means."

"I don't know what it means." He paused, swaying slightly from lack of food and sleep. "But I *will* know," he promised as he downed his coffee and went back up to the attic.

He was back down an hour later, a triumphant smile on his face.

"All right," he said. "Now we can leave."

"Why now?" she asked. "What do you think you've learned?"

"*The* secret."

"This is about the poem?"

"This is about the Inner Frontier," he replied. "It's all there in the poem, but even Black Orpheus didn't know how to interpret it." He shook his head in wonderment. "The greatest character of all, and he never knew!"

"Orpheus was the greatest character?" she asked, puzzled.

"No," he said distractedly. "I'm talking about Santiago!"

"*That's* what you learned?" she said incredulously. "Everyone knows that Santiago was the greatest outlaw in the history of the Inner Frontier."

"But he *wasn't*," said Danny, still smiling. "*That's* what I learned."

"What are you talking about?" demanded the Duchess.

"Santiago," explained Danny. "He wasn't an outlaw, not in the normal sense of the word. Oh, he did illegal things, but he was actually a revolutionary. I knew that yesterday afternoon."

"That's rubbish! Everything I've ever heard about him—"

"—was what he *wanted* people to hear," concluded Danny. "You asked once about bounty hunters. Here's your answer: if the Democracy had known he was a revolutionary, they'd have sent the whole fleet, five billion strong, to the Inner Frontier to hunt him down—so he made them think he was an outlaw, and all he had to deal with was a handful of bounty hunters. Orpheus guessed at that, but he never knew for sure."

"So Santiago killed all the bounty hunters?" she said.

Danny smiled again. "He tried, but he didn't always succeed—and *that's* the secret that's hidden in the poem, the secret even Orpheus didn't know."

"You're not making sense. How could he have stayed in business if he *hadn't* killed them?"

"There wasn't just *one* Santiago!" said Danny, unable to contain his excitement. "There was a series of them! I'm sure Sebastian Cain was one, and I think his successor was Esteban Cordoba." He paused for effect. "There were at least six Santiagos, maybe as many as eight!"

"You're crazy!"

"I'm right! Virtue MacKenzie, his biographer—she tried to hide it, but she was so sloppy that scholars never put much stock in her books, even though they sold tens of millions of copies." His arms shot up in a sign of triumph. "The most important single thing in the history of the Inner Frontier, and we're the only two people who know it!"

"So now we can leave the planet and then sell the manuscript?" she asked with a look of relief.

"We'll leave the planet," he agreed.

"And sell the manuscript."

He shook his head. "I'm not selling anything, not yet."

"Then what are you going to do with it?" she demanded.

"Add to it."

"What are you talking about?"

"Maybe it's time for the Inner Frontier to have a chronicler again."

"You?" said the Duchess incredulously.

"Why not?"

"I thought you were a criminal."

"I've *been* a criminal. I've never tried being a poet or a chronicler."

"What does the job pay?"

"What's the going price on immortality?"

"Immortality?"

"I plan to create something that outlasts me, just as Orpheus did." He looked off into the distance, at some exotic place only he could see. "Think of all those worlds I've never seen—Serengeti, Greenveldt, Walpurgis III, Binder X, the Roosevelt system, Oceana . . . worlds I only heard about and dreamed about when I was a kid. You know," he added confidentially, "this is the first time I've been excited—really *excited*—about anything since I was that little kid, dreaming of those worlds."

"You're really considering it, aren't you?" she said.

"I'm done considering it," he said with a sudden decisiveness. "I'm *doing* it."

"But why?" she demanded, as visions of the auction receded into the distance.

"There are hundreds of thieves here on Bailiwick. There are millions in the Democracy, dozens of millions in the galaxy. But there was only one Black Orpheus, and there will be only one me. A century after I'm dead, someone will read my poem the way I'm reading *his*, and I'll have made my mark on the universe. I'll have done something that outlasts me. People will know I was here."

"And is that so important to you?"

"It always was."

"And what about me?" she said bitterly. "Three days ago I was a law-abiding citizen. Three minutes ago I was a fugitive, but one who'd been promised a substantial amount of money from selling Orpheus' poem. Now I'm still a fugitive, but with no financial prospects again! You owe me something!"

"I said I'd take care of you. I will."

"How?"

"I don't know yet—but a million opportunities are opening up, and one thing I've always been good at is seizing opportunities."

"You'd damned well better be," the Duchess shot back. "In the meantime, you'd better work at making the name of Danny Briggs worth something."

He shook his head. "That's no name for a Bard."

"Did you have one in mind?"

"Give me a few minutes," he said, walking to a computer and activating it.

She went to the kitchen to pour herself a beer, and she drank it before returning. When she entered the room he looked up at her, a happy smile on his face.

"You found one," she said.

"We may be going to worlds that seem like paradise, and we may be going to worlds that reek of hellfire. Now I'm prepared for both." He paused. "From this day forward, my name is Dante Alighieri."

3.

> THEY CALL HIM THE RHYMER, A WORDSMITH
>   BY TRADE,
> HE CAN BRING YOU TO TEARS OR USE WORDS
>   LIKE A BLADE.
> HE ROAMS THE FRONTIER WRITING DOWN
>   WHAT HE SEES,
> AND HE MAKES MEN IMMORTAL, DOTTING I'S,
>   CROSSING T'S.

THAT WAS THE FIRST VERSE Dante Alighieri ever put to paper. Internal evidence suggests he wrote it while still on Bailiwick, though of course that is impossible to prove.

It wasn't true when he wrote it. No one had yet called him the Rhymer (or even Dante), and he had never been to the Inner Frontier. But before long the verse would gain an aura of absolute truth, and eventually it was so widely accepted that people forgot that it was merely a prediction when it first appeared.

Finding Black Orpheus' manuscript may have given him his initial impetus to go to the Frontier, but it was the arrival of the police that gave him a more immediate reason.

"Hey, Danny!" hissed the Duchess, staring out the kitchen window.

"I keep telling you," he replied irritably, looking up from his coffee cup, "the name's Dante."

"I don't care what the name is!" she snapped. "Whoever you are today, you'd better know a way out of here!"

"What are you talking about?" asked Dante.

"Take a look," she said. "We've got company."

"You must be mistaken. The owners aren't due back for almost two weeks!"

"These aren't the owners! They're the police!"

He raced to the window and saw two policemen standing

about fifty feet away, staring at the house and speaking to each other. *"Shit!"*

"I thought you told me no one could see in!" said the Duchess accusingly.

"They can't," answered Dante. "But I should have figured once Balsam knew what I'd stolen from the kennel, he'd put a lookout on every house that was boarding an animal there."

"So they're just going to set up shop out there and watch the house?" she asked.

"Probably," he said. "But we can't count on that. They might decide to check and see if anything's been stolen."

"They don't seem to be moving any closer."

"They could be waiting for orders to enter, or for a backup team, or for some heat and motion sensors that will tell them we're here." He stepped back from the window. "We're not going to wait for that."

"What will we do?"

"Leave, of course."

"You're crazy!" she said. "It's broad daylight, and neither of us is armed."

"I don't like guns. If you carry one, sooner or later you have to use it. I'm a thief, not a killer." He paused. "By nighttime they'll definitely have the place under electronic surveillance. We're better off leaving right now."

"You think we can just go out the door and wave to them as we walk past?" she said sardonically.

"They're both in front," said Dante. "We'll go out the back. With a little luck and a little maneuvering, we can keep the house between us and them until we make it to the next street." He saw the doubt on her face. "Trust me. I've gotten out of worse scrapes than this."

He walked to the airlift.

"What are you doing?"

"I've got to get the manuscript."

"Five boxes? Do you know how heavy that will be?"

"Then you can help me carry it."

"What if we have to run?" she persisted. "I know what

you think it's worth—but it's not worth a thing to us if they throw us in jail."

"I'm not leaving without it. Look through the closets and see if there's something we can carry it in. Most of the boxes it's in now are falling apart."

He returned a moment later, and found her waiting for him with a small overnight bag.

"You're going to look damned silly walking through our neighbor's yard and down the street carrying that," she noted.

"Not as silly as I'd look carrying three thousand pages in busted boxes," he replied, transferring the manuscript to the bag. "One thing I've learned over the years: act as if whatever you're doing, no matter how aberrant, is normal, and nobody will give you a second glance." He examined the bag. "Has this thing got a strap?"

"I didn't see one."

"Then let me rig something with one of our host's belts. I'll be a lot happier if I can sling it over my shoulder and have both hands free."

"Why bother? As you pointed out, you're unarmed."

"Don't get too melodramatic," he said. "I'm more likely to need my hands to solve a computer lock or even hold a sandwich than to shoot anyone."

She walked to a closet, found a belt, and tossed it to him. "You got me into this," she said. "I hope to hell that you can get me out."

"Just don't lose your head and you'll be fine."

He connected both ends of the belt to the bag, slung it over his shoulder, was surprised at how heavy it was, and walked to the back door.

"Okay," he said. "Take one last look to make sure they haven't moved, and then we'll leave."

She walked to the window, peered out, then turned to him. "They're in the same place," she informed him.

"Good," he said. "It's less than one hundred feet to all that shrubbery our neighbor planted at the back of his yard. See the tallest bush there? Just walk to it in a straight line from the back door, and I guarantee that no one on the street will be able to see you."

"And when I get there?" she asked, staring at the bush.

"I think there's room to walk around it on the left without getting tangled up in any thorns. Then walk straight through, and if anyone sees you just act like you've got a perfect right to be there. I promise no one will challenge you."

"What if someone does?"

"Not to worry—I'll be right behind you."

"Then what?"

"Then we walk to the nearest public conveyance, take it to the spaceport, and figure out a way to get the hell off this dirtball."

"Have you got any money?"

"You know I do. You saw me getting paid at the Golden Fleece."

"Then let's take a private aircab to the spaceport," she said. "For all you know, our faces are plastered all over the public transports."

He considered her suggestion, then nodded his assent. "Yeah, probably we're safe either way, but there's no sense taking chances."

"If we're safe, why are the police watching the house?"

"If they thought there was even a one-in-a-hundred chance that Danny Briggs was in the house, they'd have blown the door away and come after me," answered Dante confidently. "They're the crime-prevention unit, not the criminal catchers." He opened the back door. "Now let's go."

The Duchess walked out into the warm dry air and he followed her. They made it to the largest shrub undetected, then circled it, walked through the neighbor's yard—not undetected, but unhindered by an orange-skinned native gardener who stared at them for a moment and then went back to work—and then they were on the next street.

They walked to a corner and summoned an aircab, then rode in silence to the spaceport. Dante waited while the robot driver scanned the cash he'd given it and made change. He looked around for the Duchess and saw that she was walking toward the spaceport's entrance. He quickly caught up with her, linked his arm with hers, and turned her so they were walking parallel to the large departure building.

"What's the matter?" she complained.

"If they're watching houses, they're watching the spaceport too," he said. "Don't be in such a hurry to walk right into their hands."

"You've spotted them?" she asked as they walked past an upscale luggage store flanked by a pair of restaurants, one catering to humans, one to aliens.

"I don't plan to get close enough to spot them. It's enough that I know they're there."

"Then how are we going to get on the spaceliner that takes us away from here?" demanded the Duchess.

"We're not going to take a spaceliner."

"We're not?"

"We never were," said Dante. He glanced carefully around to make sure they weren't being followed. "It's too dangerous to book passage on it—and why tell them where to find us? Even if God drops everything else and we make it out of here on a liner, they'll simply signal ahead to wherever it's bound and have their counterparts waiting for us."

"I thought most Frontier worlds don't have police forces," she said.

"So you'll be met by a couple of bounty hunters," he replied with a grimace. "Is that any better?"

"Come on, Danny," she said, annoyed. "Why are you trying to scare me? You know we didn't do anything to put a dead-or-alive price on our heads."

"You know it and I know it, but I don't think they're real fussy about that on the Frontier. If the reward isn't big enough, it's not cost-effective to keep you alive and deliver you back into the Democracy. That's another reason we want a private ship: we don't want anyone knowing where we're going."

She frowned as the logic of his answer registered. "What the hell have you gotten me into?" she asked in panicky tones. "All I did was trip a man—and suddenly we're leaving Bailiwick and you're telling me that bounty hunters may want to *kill* me!"

"*I* didn't get you into anything at all," said Dante. "I'm grateful that you tripped Balsam, but it was your idea. I think it was a fine idea, and it kept me out of jail, but it wasn't mine." He paused. "Try to calm down. Neither of us was doing all that well here. Maybe it's time to go to the Frontier and start over."

"I was doing just fine!" she snapped.

"Well, you can stay if you want . . ."

"*No!*" she shouted.

"Well, *that's* settled."

"Some hero!" she muttered.

"I'm no hero. I'm just a guy who's trying to get the hell off the planet before the police catch up with me." He spotted a small hotel that catered to travelers who were changing flights on Bailiwick, and began walking toward it. "And it's time I started putting the wheels in motion."

"What are you going to do?" she asked, unable to slow down while their arms remained linked.

"I thought I'd warn the spaceport that we're coming in," he said with a smile.

"You're kidding, right?"

"I was never more serious in my life."

They reached the hotel, and Dante approached the front desk.

"May I help you?" asked the robot clerk in obsequious tones.

"Yeah. I want to contact the spaceport about my connecting flight. Where's a communicator?"

"There is a row of communication booths on the west wall, sir," said the robot. "Allow the booth of your choice time to scan your retina and verify your credit rating, and then follow the instructions."

"I know," said Dante. "I've done it before."

"In that case, have a most pleasant day, sir," said the robot as Dante walked to an empty booth.

"Wait here," he said to the Duchess. "There's only room for one in a booth."

He went in and emerged less than a minute later.

"Okay, that takes care of Step One," he announced.

"What did you do?"

"I reserved two seats on the spaceliner to Far London. It leaves in about two hours."

She frowned, trying to comprehend. "Correct me if I'm wrong, but I thought we were trying to escape from Bailiwick. Why did you announce our presence?"

"So that every spaceport official, every security guard and policeman, will be alerted that we're going to show up in the next hour or so and board the liner." He smiled. "I didn't stay connected long enough for them to trace my location."

"Okay, so now the spaceport is swarming with men and women whose sole desire is to capture us. Now what?"

"Now, while they're all all trying to hide themselves near Passport Control or the boarding gate and appear unobtrusive, we choose a private ship to steal." He looked out the window. "You'll notice that they're all at this end of the spaceport."

Suddenly she smiled. "Maybe you should stay a thief. I don't know how good a poet you'll be, but you were born to be a thief."

"Well, it's still not that simple. We won't move until dark."

"Why not? By then they'll know we're not showing up for the Far London flight."

"We've got them all tense. The next step is to make them relax so they don't react as quickly."

"I'm not following you at all."

"In about an hour and a half, I'm going to cancel Far

London and book us on a flight to Deluros VIII. Then I'll cancel that and book One to Sirius V. By the time I've changed flights six or seven times, they'll be convinced we're just having fun with them, and most of them will go home. The ones who are left behind will assume we're not showing up, and if anything alerts them, they'll be reasonably sure it's not us."

"So we're staying here for what, another eight or nine hours?" she asked.

"Yeah, about that. I don't know what the robot's programmed to think of as unusual behavior, so I think we'd better rent a room for three or four days."

"Three or four?"

"Right. We're not going to pay for it regardless, but I'm sure the police are monitoring every hotel desk. If someone takes a day room, or even a room for one night, anywhere near the spaceport, alarms are going to go off in every police station within fifty miles."

"All right, that makes sense," she agreed. "Now, how do we know which ship to take?"

He handed her his pocket computer. "I've put all the proper codes in for you to get past any security walls. Find out which ships have been fueled in the past six hours. Then check the registry; we're not interested in any ships that are owned by citizens of Bailiwick."

"Why not?"

"Because they have to file new flight plans, so if we take one we'll run a pretty fair chance of getting shot out of the sky. But a ship that's just stopped for fuel, or business, will already have a flight plan filed. They might *think* it's been stolen, but unless the owner reports it within two minutes of our taking off, they won't *know* it before we're at light speeds and out of the system, and they really aren't about to blow away a ship on a suspicion."

Dante approached the desk and rented a room, then went up to the fourth floor with the Duchess. A moment later they were inside the room, and she was starting to assemble her list of possible ships on Dante's computer while he stood by the window, looking out at the rows of private ships across the street. There was a sparkling force field surrounding the area, but he spotted the entrance, recognized the locking mechanism, knew he could break its code, and nodded in satisfaction.

Then he walked over to the large bed and lay down on it, cupping his hands behind his head. He wanted to read more of the poem, but he knew it would only annoy the Duchess, so he simply stared at her as she worked. Finally she put the computer down and turned to him. "I've got the perfect ship," she announced.

"Perfect in what way?" asked Dante.

"It's a six-man ship, so there will be plenty of room. Three sleeping cabins and a fully-equipped galley. Owned by a mining baron from Goldstrike, which is way into the Inner Frontier. Refreshed its atomic pile this morning, but it's not due to leave until tomorrow afternoon." She paused. "And best of all, it's *close*! You can see it from the window!"

He walked over.

"See that row?" she continued. "It's the fourth one back from the fence. We won't have to walk a hundred yards once we're inside the fence."

"Okay," said Dante. "Let's go for a walk."

"Now? I thought you wanted to steal it after dark."

"I do. But if I can disable that lock on the fence right now, it'll be even easier tonight."

"You can't just kneel down and work on a computer lock in broad daylight!" protested the Duchess.

"I don't plan to," he said. He walked to the door and ordered it to open. "Come on."

They emerged in the lobby a moment later. He stopped by the desk to speak to the robot clerk, then rejoined her.

"What was all that about?" she asked.

"I told it we're going shopping."

"Why does a robot care?"

"It doesn't—but if the police start searching all the hotels near the spaceport, and it won't be too long before the thought occurs to them, I don't want it to respond that it doesn't know where we are. It should take them a day to figure out that I used a phony ID to register—but if they have a reason to want to learn more about us, they'll break that identity in five minutes." He looked out into the street, then slung the bag containing Orpheus' poem over his shoulder. "Okay, let's go."

"Are you planning on stealing the ship now?" she asked, indicating the manuscript.

"No, I'm just not willing to leave it in a spaceport hotel."

They walked out, arm in arm, and began window-shopping up and down the street. Dante kept looking for an excuse to cross to the spaceport's side of the thoroughfare if anyone was watching them. He needed a stray animal, a child who might step into traffic while his parents were concentrating on each other, anything like that—but nothing turned up.

"Okay, we'll do it the bothersome way," he said after about ten minutes.

"What way is that?"

"We walk about a mile down the road, far enough that no one from the spaceport is still watching us, and then cross the street and walk back. We're no longer window-shopping; now we're taking our afternoon constitutional."

They walked away from the spaceport for ten more minutes. Then, as they reached the outskirts of the small city, they crossed the street and began walking back.

As they neared the spaceport, Dante, looking straight ahead, said, "When we get opposite the entrance through the force field, twist an ankle."

"What?"

"Twist an ankle. Fall to one knee. Make a bit of a fuss about it. I'll kneel down and examine it."

"What does this have to do with the lock?"

"Just trust me."

They walked another two hundred yards. Then, when they were within five yards of the door, the Duchess lurched forward, fell to her knees, and began holding and massaging her left ankle.

Dante knelt down beside her, his back to the entrance, his hands shielded from any onlookers by her body.

"What's that?" she asked as she heard a faint beeping.

"Quiet!"

She fell silent, and concentrated on her ankle.

More beeps, and suddenly he looked at her and grinned. "Okay, we can walk through it any time we want."

"You could do that with your pocket computer?" she asked, surprised.

"Well, it's not an ordinary computer. It's been jury-rigged by experts. Well-paid experts, but on days like today I decide they were worth the money."

"Why don't we walk through right now? We could be at the ship in less than a minute."

He shook his head. "If anyone's been watching, your being able to walk or run without a limp will be a dead giveaway."

"So I'll limp."

He looked up and down the force field. "We'll wait until dark."

"But the place is deserted."

"It's *too* deserted," he said. "I haven't made any more reservations yet. They're all still here. *Someone's* got to be watching the private ships."

"Why? They're waiting for us to show up for the spaceliner to Far London."

He shook his head. "It's already taken off. Besides, *most* of them will be there, but the bright ones—and that includes Balsam—will know we'll never show up at the public terminal, and the only other way off the planet is to swipe a ship."

"But there's no one here! *Now* is the perfect time. We don't have to take off until you want, but they're more likely to search our room than the ship."

"It's too easy," he said, frowning. "I don't see a single guard. Do you?"

"No. That's why—"

"It's wrong," he said. "It's almost as if they're inviting us to try to steal a ship." He helped her to her feet. "Come on, lean on me and limp back to the hotel. I'll start making some more reservations."

"I don't want to," said the Duchess. "You've unlocked the entry, and there's no one around. I say we go to the ship. Even if they know we're there, we can take off before they can do anything about it."

"They'll blow us out of the sky."

"It's owned by Schyler McNeil. Just call the tower and tell them you're McNeil and you've got an emergency back on Goldstrike. They may not believe you, but they'll hesitate about destroying the ship until they find the real McNeil."

Dante studied the area once more, then shook his head. Something felt wrong, and he always listened to his instincts.

"Tonight," he said, still scanning the spaceport. "Now let's go back to the hotel."

She made no reply, so he turned back to her—and found that she was gone.

"*Shit!*" he muttered, trying and failing to grab her arm as she darted through the entrance and raced toward the private ships.

He didn't know how they would stop her, but he knew in his gut that she'd never make it to McNeil's ship. Then he heard a hideous roar, and he turned to see a huge animal, almost four feet at the shoulder, not canine and not feline but clearly a predator, racing toward the Duchess.

"Get into a ship now!" he yelled, breaking into a run.

The Duchess turned back to him, startled, then saw the creature bearing down on her. It was possible that she couldn't even have made it into the ship she had just passed, but she didn't even try. She screamed and raced toward McNeil's ship, and the animal swerved to run her down.

Dante saw that he couldn't reach her in time, even if he

hadn't been carrying the huge manuscript. He looked for a weapon, even something as primitive as a club, as he ran, but the spaceport was neat as a pin, and he couldn't see anything he could use. Then he saw another motion out of the corner of his eye—the animal's keeper.

It made sense. Someone had to be able to control it, or it might savage someone with a legitimate reason for being there. The keeper, armed with a pulse gun, was walking leisurely after the animal, obviously in no hurry to call it off. Dante raced to him, knocked him down just as the creature reached the Duchess. It took about ten seconds to wrestle the pulse gun away from the keeper and crack him across the head with it—and those were ten seconds the Duchess didn't have.

Dante whirled and fired at the animal, killing it instantly—but it fell across the Duchess's torn, lifeless body.

"Damn you!" yelled Dante at the senseless body by his feet. "She didn't do anything worth dying for!" He stared at the main terminal. "Damn you all!"

He knew he couldn't stay where he was or return to the hotel. A sweeping security camera or another beast and keeper would spot the Duchess in a matter of seconds. He tucked the gun into his belt and ran to McNeil's ship.

He followed the Duchess's instructions, claiming to be McNeil. That bought him enough time to reach the stratosphere. Then came all the warning messages, which meant they'd either found the Duchess or McNeil or both. He alternately lied and threatened for the next thirty seconds, spent another fifteen seconds admitting that he was Danny Briggs and promising to return to the spaceport—and while they were debating whether to shoot him down his ship passed through the stratosphere and reached light speeds.

And because he was Dante Alighieri and not one of the larger-than-life characters he planned to write about, he did not vow to avenge the Duchess. *Someone* would avenge her; that much he *did* promise himself. When he found the right person, he would tell him the story of the Duchess and point him toward Bailiwick, and he would enjoy the results every bit as much as if he had physically extracted his vengeance himself.

Then he was on his way to the Inner Frontier, where he would assume his new identity and his new career among legendary heroes and villains who, he suspected, couldn't be any more dangerous than the Democracy's finest.

4.

HAMLET MACBETH, A WELL-NAMED ROGUE,
LOVES THE WOMEN, WHEN IN VOGUE.
LOVES THE GENTS WHEN NO ONE CARES,
GETS RICH OFF HIS PERVERSE AFFAIRS.

THAT WAS THE FIRST POEM that Dante Alighieri wrote once he reached the Inner Frontier. There was nothing very special about Hamlet Macbeth except his name, which fired Dante's imagination. He decided he couldn't leave anyone named Hamlet Macbeth out of his history, so he began finding out what he could about the man.

What he found out was a little embarrassing to both parties, because it turned out that Hamlet Macbeth was a gigolo who rented himself out to both sexes. The people of Nasrullah II, his home world, didn't much give a damn what Macbeth did as long as he didn't do it to or with them, but some of the men who were just passing through found that they were expected to pay not only for Macbeth's sexual skills, but also for his silence.

Nasrullah II was the first world that Dante touched down on. He stayed only long enough to refuel his stolen ship and have a drink in a local bar, which was where he heard about Macbeth. He didn't write the poem until he had landed on New Tangier IV, in the neighboring system, where he proceeded to recite it in a couple of taverns.

He spent a couple of days on New Tangier, a dusty, ugly reddish world with nothing much to recommend it except one diamond mine about ten miles east of the planet's only Tradertown. There was one hotel—a boardinghouse, actually, since not enough people visited New Tangier to support a hotel; one casino, which was so obviously rigged that the humans gave it a wide berth and the only players were the Bextigians, the mole-like aliens that had been imported to work the mine; and the two taverns.

Dante was standing at the bar in the larger of the taverns, sipping a beer and idly wondering how Orpheus had been able to spot colorful people when they weren't doing colorful things, when a slender man with sunken cheeks, dark piercing eyes, and braided black hair sidled up to him. Everyone else instantly moved away.

"Hi," said the man, paying no attention to anyone but Dante.

"Hi," replied Dante.

"I heard your little poem yesterday. Have you written any others?"

"Some," lied Dante. "Why?"

"Just curious. I like poems. Especially erotic ones. You ever read anything by Tanblixt?"

"The Canphorite? No."

"You should. Now, *there's* someone who truly understands the beauty of interspecies sex."

"If you say so."

"I also like epic poems of good and evil, especially if Satan himself is in them." He smiled. "It gives me someone to root for."

"You have interesting taste in poetry."

"I have interesting taste in everything." The man paused. "What's your name, poet?"

"Dante. But people call me the Rhymer."

"They do?"

"They will."

The man smiled. "I think I'll call you Dante. We were made for each other."

"Oh?"

"I'm Virgil Soaring Hawk." He paused, waiting for the connection to become apparent. "Dante and Virgil."

"Virgil Soaring Hawk—what kind of a name is that?"

"It's an Injun name."

"Okay, what's an Injun?"

"It takes too long to explain. But once, when we were

still Earthbound, white men and Injuns were mortal enemies—or so they say."

Dante frowned. "White men? You mean albinos?"

"No," replied Virgil with a sigh. "The Injuns were red-
skins, except that our skins weren't really red. And the
white men weren't really white, either—they ranged from
pink to tan. But a lot of people died on both sides because
of what they thought their color was."

"You're making all this up, right?" said Dante.

"Yeah, what the hell, I'm making it all up." Virgil signaled to the bartender. "Two Dust Whores."

"What's a Dust Whore?" asked Dante.

"You're about to find out."

"I don't understand."

"You've got Democracy written all over you, poet," said
Virgil Soaring Hawk. "Virgil was Dante's guide through
Heaven and Hell. I figure a new Dante needs a new Virgil
to show him the ropes. Right now I'm going to introduce
you to one of our local drinks."

"What the hell, why not?" agreed Dante.

"Let's go sit at a table," suggested Virgil.

"What's wrong with standing here at the bar?"

"I don't like turning my back to the door. You never
know what's going to come through it."

"Whatever you say," said Dante, walking to a table in
the farthest corner of the tavern.

"Glad you agree," said Virgil, sitting down opposite him.
The men at the two nearest tables immediately got up and
moved to the other side of the tavern.

"Why does everyone move away from you?" asked
Dante.

Virgil sighed deeply. "They don't like me very much."

"Have they got some reason?"

"Not any that I agree with," said Virgil.

"What the hell did you do?" asked Dante.

"I don't think I'm going to tell you."

"Why not?"

"I don't want you making a rhyme out of it and reciting it in bars all over the Frontier."

"I can always ask someone on the other side of the tavern," said Dante.

"You'd do that to the only friend you've made on the Frontier?" asked Virgil.

Dante stared at him in silence for a long moment. Virgil stared right back.

The bartender dropped off the drinks and left immediately.

"What goes into them?" asked Dante, staring at the purple-green liquid that was smoking as if on fire. "They look like they're going to explode."

"It varies from planet to planet," said Virgil, taking a long swallow of his own drink. When he didn't clutch his throat or collapse across the table, Dante followed suit, and promptly grimaced.

"Jesus! This stuff'll take the enamel off your teeth!" He paused. "Still," said Dante at last, "it's kind of warming. Got an interesting aftertaste." He frowned. "I don't know if I like it."

"After you've had a few more, you'll know," said Virgil with conviction.

"All right," said Dante. "Now the drinks are here and I've had half of mine. So why did you approach me and what do you want to talk about?"

"I want to talk about you."

"Me?" repeated Dante, surprised.

"And me."

"So talk."

"What are you doing out here?" asked Virgil. "Why have you come to the Inner Frontier? You're no settler, and you don't strike me as a killer. No human comes to New Tangier IV to play at the casino, so I know you're not a gambler. You haven't offered to trade or sell anything. So why are you here?"

"Did you ever hear of Black Orpheus?"

"Everyone out here has heard of Black Orpheus," answered Virgil. He grimaced. "He was probably about as black as you are white."

"I'm here to finish his poem."

Virgil Soaring Hawk stared at him expressionlessly.

"Well?" said Dante.

"Why not choose something easy, like going up against Tyrannosaur Bailey?"

"Who's Tyrannosaur Bailey?"

"It doesn't matter. Black Orpheus was one of a kind. He was unique in our history. What makes you think you can be another Orpheus?"

"I can't be," admitted Dante. "But I can follow in his footsteps." He paused, then added with conviction: "It's time."

"What do you mean?"

"I take it Tyrannosaur Bailey is a formidable figure?"

"He's about fifteen formidable figures all rolled into one ugly sonuvabitch."

"You make him sound fascinating—but I've never heard of him until just now. No one in the Democracy has, and probably ninety percent of the Inner Frontier hasn't either." Dante took another sip of his drink. "The Democracy is so damned regimented! All the really interesting characters are out here on the Frontier. It's time someone wrote them up the way Orpheus did, before they're gone and we have no record of them."

"You don't think the Secretary of the Democracy is interesting? What about Admiral Yokamina, who has six billion men under his command?"

"They got where they are by following the rules and fitting the mold," replied Dante. "All the men who broke the mold are out here, or on the Outer Frontier."

"Or dead," said Virgil.

"Or dead," agreed Dante. "Killing is one of the Democracy's specialties. They killed a friend of mine as we were preparing to come here."

"Did he have it coming?"

"Nobody has it coming—and it was a she."

"What was her crime?"

"She tripped a man," said Dante.

"That's all?"

"That's all," repeated Dante. "The Democracy doesn't seem to care who trips it these days."

"What uniquely individual crimes did you commit?" asked Virgil.

"Nothing that deserved that kind of retaliation."

"They obviously saw it differently."

"They always do. That's why I'm here. The Democracy stops at the borders to the Inner and Outer Frontiers."

Virgil stared at him as one would stare at a child. It was a look that seemed to say: *If you're that dumb, is it even worth the effort to set you straight?* "The *law* may stop," he said at last. "But the *Democracy* doesn't."

"What are you talking about?"

"They come out in force and take what they need," said Virgil, "whether it's fissionable material, or food for newly colonized worlds, or conscripts for the military. Any Man or planet that objects gets the same treatment that any alien or alien planet would get."

"I didn't know," admitted Dante. "None of us do."

Virgil shrugged. "Maybe I'm being a little hard on them. Sometimes they pay for what they take, though it's never what it's worth. And if they come to a mining world with, say, thirty miners working it, and grab a couple of hundred pounds of plutonium, well, they'll probably use it to fight off some alien army that would otherwise subjugate a planet with ten million Men on it." Virgil paused. "But we don't *know* that. We just know they come and they take and they leave and no one can stand up to them. So maybe it's comforting to think they have some noble purpose for plundering the Frontier whenever they want."

"Are they on New Tangier IV?"

"The Democracy?" Virgil shook his head. "You might go years without running into them. Or you might run into them three times in a month. It depends on where you are and what they want at the moment."

"Okay, forewarned is forearmed. But in the meantime, I still need material for my poems, so I still plan to travel the Frontier."

"I was hoping you'd say that."

"Why?"

"Because we're going to make a deal," said Virgil. "You'll need a guide, and I've worn out my welcome in the New Tangier system."

"How?" asked Dante.

"How," replied Virgil, holding up his right hand in a sign of greeting.

"I beg your pardon?"

"An old Injun joke. Forget it."

"How did you wear out your welcome?"

"How can I put this delicately?" said Virgil. "I indulge in certain, shall we say, unmentionable acts with members of . . ."

"The opposite sex?" Dante offered.

"The opposite species," Virgil corrected him.

"Is that against the law?"

"We don't have too many laws on the Frontier," answered Virgil. "It's against at least four hundred laws back in the Democracy."

"What species do you perform these unmentionable acts with?" asked Dante.

"Why should I limit myself to one species?"

"So what's you're saying is . . ."

"What I'm saying is that I've worn out my welcome," answered Virgil. "We'll talk about it more after you've adjusted to the Frontier."

"Okay—but I'll probably spend all my spare time wondering who you did what with."

"It'll give you something to do while we're traveling between planets."

Dante finished his drink and slapped some bills on the table. "I'll have another one of these."

"Credits," noted Virgil. "They'll take them here, but

most Frontier worlds don't have much use for Democracy currency."

"Speaking of Frontier worlds, where are we going next?"

"As I remember my *Inferno*, I guide you through the nine circles of hell." Virgil paused. "Of course, you were in hell when you lived in the Democracy. You just didn't know it."

"I knew it. That's why I came out here."

"Oh, you're still in hell. It's just a less structured, less orderly one."

At that moment a tall, burly man appeared in the doorway. He was covered with reddish dust, which he brushed from his heavy coat.

"I'm looking for the poet," he announced.

"You mean the Rhymer," Dante corrected him.

The tall man glared at Dante. "I'm Hamlet Macbeth," he said furiously. "Does that mean anything to you?"

"I know who you are."

"Have we ever met before?"

"No," answered Dante.

"Then why are you spreading lies about me?"

"What I wrote was the truth and you know it," said Dante.

"Hi, Hamlet," interjected Virgil. "Come join us."

Hamlet stared at Dante. "You're with *him*?" he demanded, jerking a thumb in Virgil's direction.

"That's right," answered Dante.

"You don't choose your friends any more carefully than you choose your subject," said Macbeth. He stepped into the tavern, and two more men entered with him. "How many worlds have you been kicked off of, Injun?"

"I stopped counting when I ran out of fingers and toes," replied Virgil easily.

"I hear tell you turned a couple of your mutant ladyfriends into corpses," added one of the other men, staring at Virgil through narrowed eyes.

"That's a lie," replied Virgil. "They were corpses *before* I met them."

"Did you hear that?" roared the man. "Did you hear what he just said?"

"Excuse me for a moment," Virgil said softly to Dante. "I'll be back as soon as I clear up this little misunderstanding." He got up and began walking toward the three men. "I know you don't mean what you say, but I wish you wouldn't embarrass me in front of my new friend."

"Your new friend ain't gonna be around that long, Injun," said Macbeth. "We got nothing against you, at least not today. If you're smart you'll keep out of our way."

"Come on over to the bar," said Virgil. "I'll buy you a round of drinks, and then maybe we can all be friends."

"Keep your distance, scumbag!"

"You really shouldn't call people names like that," remarked Virgil, still approaching them. "Even scumbags have feelings."

"What are you going to do about it?" demanded Macbeth pugnaciously, his right hand resting on the butt of his holstered burner.

"This," said Virgil softly.

His hands moved so fast that Dante couldn't follow them, but suddenly he had a knife in each, and an instant later all three men lay writhing on the floor, gagging and clutching their necks as blood spurted forth. None of them had had a chance to draw a weapon.

Virgil calmly walked back to the table, paying no attention to any of the other patrons, who stared at him but made no move to stop him. By the time he rejoined Dante, all three men had stopped thrashing and were still, each lying in an widening pool of his own blood.

"You killed them!" exclaimed Dante, staring in fascination at the corpses. "All three of them!"

"They would have killed you," said Virgil. "And me, too, if they thought they could get away with it."

"You just walked right over and killed them!" repeated Dante. "In front of witnesses."

"So what?"

"So they'll report what they saw."

Virgil stared at him. "To who?"

Dante blinked rapidly. He tried to come up with an answer but realized he had none.

"Welcome to the Inner Frontier, poet."

"Just who the hell are you?" demanded Dante.

Virgil got up to leave. "You're the new Bard of the Inner Frontier," he said. "I'm sure *you'll* tell *me* before we hit the next world."

5.

THE SCARLET INFIDEL IS ODD—
HE HAS NO QUALITY OF SHAME.
HE SPITS INTO THE EYE OF GOD,
AND COMMITS SINS THAT HAVE NO NAME.

VIRGIL SOARING HAWK'S SKIN WASN'T really red, but Dante decided to exercise some poetic license, especially since Virgil kept referring to himself as a redskin.

Besides, the Scarlet part didn't interest Dante anywhere near as much as the Infidel part. Virgil would never discuss any details, but from what Dante heard on his first few worlds, the poet concluded that if a race of oxygen breathers—*any* race—was divided into sexes, Virgil had spent a night or two with a female member of that race and another night with a male. There were a few races that boasted more than two sexes, and Virgil had sampled some of their wares as well.

Virgil also didn't speak much about his other areas of physical prowess, but Dante noted that most people were content to disapprove of the Scarlet Infidel from afar, that no one wanted any part of him in a fight.

As for Virgil, he was thrilled to be written up by the new Orpheus, and was constantly nagging Dante to give him more verses.

"Come on, now," he was saying as Dante's ship neared Tusculum II. "Orpheus gave Giles Sans Pitié nine verses. Giles Sans Pitié, for Christ's sake! Take away his metal hand and he was nothing, a second-rate bounty hunter. I mean, really, who the hell did he ever kill?"

"Who did you?" asked Dante.

"I'm not a bounty hunter, so I'm not in a position where I can brag about it without certain legal repercussions. But the things I've done, the places I've been, surely they're worth as many verses as Giles Sans Pitié!"

"He only gave one verse to the Angel," Dante shot back. "And Peacemaker MacDougal and Sebastian Cain got just three apiece. Are you sure you *want* all those verses?"

Virgil grimaced. "Well, I was sure until about twenty seconds ago. Now I have to think about it."

"While you're thinking, suppose you tell me why we're going to the Tusculum system?"

"You said you wanted to meet Tyrannosaur Bailey."

"What makes you think he'll be on Tusculum II?"

Virgil smiled. "He owns it."

"He owns the whole world?"

"Well, there's not that much to own—a couple of Trader-towns and a landing field."

"How did he get to own a world?" asked Dante. "Did he win it in a card game?"

"Nothing so romantic," replied Virgil. "He killed the man who owned it before him."

"I take it the laws of inheritance don't work quite the same out here as in the Democracy."

"Well, yes and no."

"What does that mean?"

"It means they might very well work the same, but no one felt compelled to argue the point with Tyrannosaur."

"No one hired any mercenaries?" asked Dante. "I mean, hell, with a whole planet at stake . . ."

"Tyrannosaur Bailey eats mercenaries for breakfast," answered Virgil.

"Has he got a price on his head?"

"A big one," said Virgil. He smiled. "He eats bounty hunters for lunch."

"How did you get to know him?"

"I met him at a gaming table out on the Rim, years ago. One of the players accused him of cheating, and he killed him. Literally ripped his head off his body."

"*Was* he cheating?"

"Absolutely."

"But you didn't complain?"

"I don't have that kind of death wish," said Virgil.

"So you just kept playing?"

"For another hour or so," replied Virgil. "I won forty thousand New Stalin rubles. He asked me if I was cheating, and I said of course I was, that after playing a couple of hands I just naturally assumed everyone at the table was supposed to cheat. Well, he could have killed me for that, but instead he laughed so hard I thought he'd bring down the ceiling, and we've been friends ever since."

"How many men has he killed?"

"You'll have to ask him. First, I don't know, and second, even if I *did* know it's been better than a year since I've seen him, and he's probably added to his total since then."

"If he's such a fearsome killer, why does anyone else live on Tusculum II?" asked Dante.

Virgil stared at him. "The Bard of the Inner Frontier doesn't ask stupid questions."

"*Was* it a stupid question?"

"Figure it out."

Dante considered it for a moment, then nodded. "Of course. They're there for protection." He paused. "How does it work? They pay him a fee to live there, and he doesn't allow any bounty hunters to land?"

"Well, you got the first part right. They pay for the privilege of living on Tusculum. But Tyrannosaur will let anyone land. He owns a casino, and he doesn't much care whose money he takes. He just makes it clear that if you kill a resident, one of his 'children,' as he calls them, you won't live to enjoy the reward."

Dante chuckled. "I take it Tusculum II is a pretty peaceful place."

"So far. But you never know what'll happen tomorrow."

"You made it sound like no one could kill this Tyrannosaur."

"You're on the Inner Frontier now, where just about every man and woman carries a weapon and can be hazardous to your health."

"What are you getting at?"

"If they're alive and they're carrying weapons, what does it imply to you?"

"Stop with the guessing games," said Dante irritably. "What is it *supposed* to mean to me?"

"That every last one of them is undefeated in mortal combat," said Virgil. "They don't all have big reputations. In fact, mighty few have reputations to rival Tyrannosaur's. But there's fifty, maybe sixty million people out here, all of 'em undefeated. It seems unrealistic to assume a few dozen of them couldn't kill Tyrannosaur if push came to shove." He paused. "That's why you have to be a little cautious out here. You know the odds, but you never can tell *which* of those nondescript men has it within him to be the next Santiago."

"Hey, I'm just a poet and an historian," said Dante. "I don't plan on challenging anyone."

"And I'm a lover," said Virgil wryly. "Problem is, you don't always have a choice."

"As far as I know, no one ever called Black Orpheus out for a duel to the death."

"Yeah—but he was the real thing. You're just an apprentice Orpheus."

"Keep talking like that and I may tear up your verse," said Dante.

"Keep thinking you're above the fray and you may not live long enough to write a second one."

The ship jerked just then, as it entered Tusculum II's stratosphere at an oblique angle.

Dante stared at his instrument panel. "Now what?"

"Now you land."

"But no one's fed any landing coordinates into the navigational computer."

"You're not in the Democracy anymore," said Virgil. "Have the sensors pinpoint the larger Tradertown, and then find the landing field just north of it."

"And then?"

"And then tell it to land."

"Just like that?" asked Dante.

"Just like that."

"Amazing," said Dante after issuing instructions to the sensors and the computer. "Have you ever been to Deluros VIII?"

"Nope."

"It's got more than two thousand orbiting space docks that can each handle something like ten thousand ships. There are dozens of passenger platforms miles above the planet, and thousands of shuttles working around the clock, carrying people to and from the surface. I don't think a ship has actually landed *on* Deluros VIII in two millennia." He shook his head in wonderment. "And here we just point and land."

"You'll get used to it."

"I suppose so."

The ship touched down, and the two men soon emerged from it.

"I assume there's no Customs or Passport Control?" asked Dante.

"You see anything like that?" responded Virgil, walking over to a row of empty aircarts. "We'll take one of these into town."

"Fine," said Dante as he climbed in.

"Uh . . . you want to let it read your retina?" said Virgil.

"Is something wrong with your eye?"

"Something's wrong with my credit. It won't start until the fee has been transferred to the rental company's account."

"No problem," said Dante, walking up to the scanner. His credit was approved in a matter of seconds, and shortly thereafter they were skimming into town, eighteen inches above the ground.

"Tell it to stop here," said Virgil as they cruised along the Tradertown's only major street.

"Why don't you tell it yourself?"

"Your credit, your voiceprint. It won't obey me."

Dante ordered the aircart to stop. "The casino's up the street."

"Yeah, but we need a place to stay. We'll register at the hotel first, and then go hunting for dinosaur."

They entered a small hotel, and Dante ordered two adjacent rooms, both of which were to be billed to his account.

They decided to stop at the hotel's restaurant for lunch before going to the casino, and they emerged half an hour later, ready to meet Tyrannosaur Bailey.

A nondescript man of medium height and medium build was standing outside the hotel, leaning against a wall. As Dante and Virgil emerged, he stepped forward and faced them.

"You're Danny Briggs, right?" he said.

"I'm Dante Alighieri."

"Well, yeah, you're him, too," agreed the man. "But it's Danny Briggs I want to speak to."

"Never heard of him," said Dante, trying to walk past the man, who took a sidestep and blocked his way again.

"That's too bad," said the man. "Because I have a business proposition for Danny Briggs."

"I know who you are," said Virgil. "Get the hell out of our way."

"Now, is that any way to talk to a businessman?" asked the man. His hand shot out and pushed Virgil backward. The Scarlet Infidel took a heavy flop onto the street, and his hand snaked toward his pocket.

"Don't even think about it, Injun!" said the man harshly. "If you know who I am, you know I don't die as easily as those assholes you took out on New Tangier."

Virgil tensed, then looked into the man's eyes, and slowly, gradually relaxed again.

"Good thinking, Injun," said the man. "You get to live another day and deflower another corpse." He turned to Dante. "My name is Wait-a-bit Bennett. Does it mean anything to you?"

"No," said Dante.

"We have something in common, Danny. You come from the Democracy, and I work for the Democracy. On a freelance basis, anyway."

"Get to the point."

"The point is that the bank account the aircart computer okayed was in the name of Danny Briggs, not Dante Alighieri." Bennett smiled. "It seems that the Democracy has issued a fifty-thousand-credit reward for you, dead or alive."

"Bullshit!" said Dante. "That dead-or-alive crap is for killers. I never killed anyone."

"Sure you did," said Bennett. "You killed Felicia Milan, alias the Duchess, back on Bailiwick."

"*I* didn't kill her!" snapped Dante. "The police did!"

"The Democracy says you did," replied Bennett. He smiled. "What's a poor bounty hunter to believe?"

"You're going to believe whoever's offering the money, so why are you wasting both our time talking about it?"

"I do believe you've got a firm grasp of the situation, Danny, my boy," said Bennett. "I always believe the man with the money. That could be you."

"What are you talking about?" demanded Dante.

"A business deal," said Bennett. "A transaction, so to speak." Suddenly he turned to Virgil. "Keep those hands where I can see 'em, Injun!" Then back to Dante: "Before I can get paid, I have to take your body back to the Democracy for identification, or to one of the Democracy outposts, and I think the nearest one is fifteen hundred light-years away. That's a lot of bother."

"My heart bleeds for you," said Dante.

"It doesn't have to. Bleed, I mean."

"So what's the deal?"

"Pay me the fifty thousand credits and I let you walk."

"When do you need an answer?" asked Dante.

"I'm a reasonable man," said Bennett. "If I wasn't, you'd be dead already." He looked up toward the sky. "It's getting toward noon. I'll give you until noon tomorrow. Either you hand me the money then, or I'll kill you and your pal."

"Why Virgil?"

"I don't like him very much."

"He hasn't done anything to you."

"No corpse is safe around him. That's reason enough." He turned to Virgil. "I'm going into the hotel now. I think it might be a good idea for you to stay where you are until I'm inside."

He turned and walked through the hotel's doorway and vanished into its interior.

"Wait-a-bit Bennett," said Dante, staring after him. "You never mentioned him to me."

"I didn't know he was in this part of the Frontier."

"Tell me about him."

"There's not much to tell," said Virgil, finally getting to his feet. "He's a bounty hunter. A good one. He's up around twenty kills, maybe twenty-five."

"Then let's go meet Tyrannosaur Bailey and get the hell off the planet before morning," said Dante.

Virgil shook his head. "You're fifty thousand credits on the hoof. You don't think he's going to let you walk just because you can't pay him the reward, do you?"

"He can't watch us forever."

"Forever ends tomorrow at noon."

"I meant that he's got to sleep sometime. We'll sneak out tonight."

"He knows that nobody comes to Tusculum without a reason. He's gone off to take a nap while you take care of whatever business brought you here. He'll be awake by dinnertime, and he'll seek out your ship and wait there until noon, just in case you're thinking of leaving."

"This is ridiculous!" said Dante. "I came here to get *away* from the Democracy and now they're paying bounty hunters to kill me!"

"The only difference between here and where you came from," said Virgil, "is that out here there are no voters and no journalists to restrain the Democracy's worst instincts."

"Is Wait-a-bit Bennett as good at his trade as he thinks he is?" asked Dante.

"Better," answered Virgil. "You didn't see me move when he told me to be still, did you?"

"How am I going to get fifty thousand credits to buy him off by noon?"

"You've got a bigger problem than that."

"Oh?"

Virgil nodded. "Even if you get the money, you don't think he's the only bounty hunter who reads Wanted posters, do you?"

Suddenly Dante's stomach began to hurt.

6.

WAIT-A-BIT BENNETT, CALM AND COOL,
SIPS HIS DRINK BY THE SWIMMING POOL.
HIS PREY APPEARS, ALL UNAWARE;
HE'LL WAIT A BIT, AND THEN—BEWARE!

VIRGIL SOARING HAWK HIT THE roof when he sneaked a
look at the poem. Here was this bounty hunter who had
already manhandled the notorious Scarlet Infidel himself
and was preparing to extort money from the poet in the
morning or (more likely) kill him, and Dante was actually
writing him into the poem.

Even worse, he gave three verses to Bennett—but of
course, Bennett was the first man on the Frontier to threaten
Dante's life, so Virgil reluctantly admitted that it made
sense in a way.

Bennett had threatened a lot of lives, and had taken more
than his share of them. Rumor had it that he'd been a hired
killer before he started doing his killing for the Democracy.
They said he'd been shot up pretty badly on Halcyon V,
but he certainly didn't move like a man who was suppos-
edly half prosthetic, and he never ducked a fight.

Somewhere along the way, he'd decided that it was easier to make money for not killing men than for killing them,
and from that day forward, he always offered to let a
wanted man walk free if the man paid him the reward. And
he was a man of his word: more than one man paid the
price, and none of them were ever bothered by Bennett
again. (Well, none except Willie Harmonica, who went out
and committed *another* murder after buying his way out of
the first one. He refused to pay Bennett the reward the
second time, and wound up paying with his life instead.)

And now Dante Alighieri had less than a day to raise
fifty thousand credits or somehow escape from one of the

deadlier bounty hunters on the Inner Frontier.

"I can't spend all day working on the poem," he announced after giving Bennett his third verse. He put down his quill pen and got up from the desk in the corner of his room. "Let's go visit your friend."

"I've been ready for an hour," remarked Virgil.

"I had to write those verses," explained Dante. "Who knows if I'll be alive to write them tomorrow?"

"Son of a bitch doesn't deserve three verses!" muttered Virgil, ordering the door to dilate.

"Kill him tonight and maybe I'll give you four," said Dante, stepping through into the hallway.

"Mighty few people out here can kill him," answered Virgil. "And I'm honest enough to admit I'm not one of them."

"I saw what you did to those three guys in the bar back on New Tangier."

"Those were two miners and a gigolo. This guy is a professional killer. There's a difference."

"He didn't look that formidable."

"Fine," said Virgil. "*You* kill him."

"I'm no killer," replied Dante. "I'm a poet. I can outthink him, but I have a feeling that won't help much in a pitched battle."

"Look around the galaxy and you'd be hard-pressed to prove that intelligence is a survival trait," agreed Virgil.

They reached the street and walked out of the hotel, turned right, and headed to Rex's, which was the name Tyrannosaur Bailey had chosen for his establishment.

"Anything else I should know?" asked Dante as they reached the door to the casino.

"Yeah," said Virgil. "No dinosaur jokes."

"I don't know any."

"Good. You'll live longer that way."

They entered, and Dante was surprised at the level of luxury that confronted him. From outside, Rex's seemed like every other nondescript Tradertown building. Inside it was a haven of taste and money. The floors gripped his feet, then released him as he took another step, and another. The gaming tables were made of the finest alien hardwood, meticulously carved by some unknown race, while the matching chairs hovered a few inches above the floor, changing their shapes to fit each player's form—and the players were not merely men, but giant Torquals, tripodal beings from Hesporite III, Canphorites and Lodinites and a couple of races that Dante had never seen before.

Atonal but seductive alien music filtered into the casino, and nubile young men and women dressed in shimmering metallic outfits ran the tables.

Sitting alone in the farthest corner was a huge man, easily seven feet tall, muscled like an athlete. His hair was the color of desert sand, and tumbled down to his shoulders. His nose had been broken at least twice, maybe more, and looked irregular from every angle. One ear was cauliflower; the lobe of the other was stretched enough that it was able to hold an unwrapped cigar that had been placed in an exceptionally large hole there. When he smiled, he displayed a mouthful of ruby and sapphire teeth, all carefully filed to dangerous-looking points.

His shirt was loose-fitting, which added to the impression of enormous size. Dante couldn't see his legs or feet, but he managed to glimpse the tops of three or four weapons stuck in the man's belt.

The man looked up, saw Virgil, and smiled a red-and-blue smile.

"Virgil, you corpse-fucking old bastard, how the hell are you?"

"Hi, Tyrannosaur. I've got a friend who'd like to meet you."

Tyrannosaur Bailey studied Dante for a long moment. "You're the one that Wait-a-bit Bennett is after?"

"How did you know that?" asked Dante.

"This is *my* world," answered Bailey. "Not much goes on here that I *don't* know."

"Then you know who I am and why I want to see you," suggested Dante.

"I know who both of you are," laughed Bailey. "You're Danny Briggs, a thief from the Democracy, and you're Dante Alighieri, the self-proclaimed successor to Black Orpheus." He gestured to a pair of chairs. "Have a seat. You too, Virgil."

"*He's* the one who wants to speak with you," replied Virgil. "I could go spend a little money at your gaming tables, if you wish."

"You don't want to gamble," said Bailey.

"I don't?"

Bailey shook his head. "No, you don't. What you want is to get my Stelargan bar girl into the sack while I'm paying attention to your friend."

"What a thing to suggest!" said Virgil with mock outrage.

"Virgil, the last time you were here, two of my human girls and one of my Tilarbians had to seek psychiatric help to get over the experience. Next time it happens, you pay the bill."

"It was worth it."

"That's it!" snapped Tyrannosaur. "You sit here or you wait outside. There's no third way."

"I thought we were friends."

"We are—but we're not close friends. Now make your choice."

"I think I'll get a breath of air," said Virgil with all the dignity he could muster. He turned and slowly walked out into the street.

"Have a seat, poet," said Tyrannosaur after Virgil had left the casino.

"Thank you," said Dante, sitting down opposite the huge man.

"I approve of what you're doing," continued Bailey. "That poem is all the history we've got—and there's tens of millions of us out here. It's time someone added to it. I'm just as loyal to the Frontier as all those people we left behind are to the Democracy."

Dante didn't quite know what to say except to thank him again, so he remained silent.

"Interesting friend you've picked up," continued Bailey. "They're going to have to write two or three books just to cover the new perversions he's invented." He paused. "How many verses did you give him?"

"One."

Bailey nodded thoughtfully. "Who else have you written up?"

"Not too many," said Dante noncommittally. "I'm still getting my feet wet, so to speak."

"Well, assuming you live past tomorrow, you should find it a pretty easy job."

"Being the only historian for a third of the galaxy isn't all that easy. I suspect it can be quite a burden from time to time."

"I'm sure it was a burden for Orpheus," agreed Tyrannosaur. "But that's because someone had to be first. He paved the way. It should be a cakewalk for you."

"It'll be harder for me."

"Don't have the talent, huh?"

"I don't know. That's for others to judge. But Orpheus had a unifying theme."

"What theme was that?" asked Bailey.

"He had Santiago."

"Santiago wasn't a theme. He was a man."

"He was both. Everyone in the poem is valued based on how he related to Santiago."

"What are you talking about?" said Bailey. "I grew up on that poem! I can quote whole sections of it to you, and we both know that most of them never even knew Santiago!"

"The outlaws were compared to him, never very favorably. The bounty hunters and lawmen were measured based on how close they got to him. Preachers, thieves, aliens, even an itinerant barmaid, they all formed a kind of nebula around him. They were caught in the field generated by his strength and his charisma; Orpheus knew it, even if they didn't."

"So who's *your* Santiago?" asked Bailey.

"I don't have one . . . yet." The poet sighed. "That's why my job's harder."

"And you may not live past noon tomorrow."

Dante smiled ruefully. "That's another reason why my job's harder."

"So what's your name—Danny or Dante?"

"Dante Alighieri—but they call me the Rhymer."

"Who does?"

Dante made a grand gesture that encompassed half the universe. "Them."

"Them?"

"Well, they will someday."

"We'll see," said Bailey dubiously.

"What makes you an expert on poetry?" demanded Dante.

"I'm not," answered Bailey. "I'm an expert on survival." He stared at Dante. "You've already made a lot of mistakes. You're lucky you're still alive."

"What mistakes?"

"You hooked up with my friend Virgil, who attracts outraged moralists everywhere he goes. You made some kind of mistake at the spaceport, or Wait-a-bit Bennett would never have spotted you. You made a third mistake by sticking around after he made you that offer. He probably has a confederate watching your ship, but by tonight he'll be there himself, and I guarantee he's more dangerous than anyone he might hire." He paused. "How long have you been on the Frontier, poet? A week? Ten days? And you've already made three fatal blunders. Tomorrow you'll probably make a fourth."

"I don't know what I can do about it," said Dante. "I can't raise fifty thousand credits by tomorrow morning."

"Sell your ship."

"Uh . . . it's not exactly *my* ship," said Dante.

"Make that *four* fatal blunders. The spaceport's got to

have reported the registration back to the Democracy. You'll have another warrant out on you by dinnertime, and you've almost certainly got a squad of soldiers already flying out here to reclaim the ship—after they kill you for putting them to the trouble."

"So what do you think I should do?"

"I thought you'd never ask," said Tyrannosaur with a grin. "What you should do is hire a protector, someone who can stomp on Wait-a-bit Bennett as easily as you stomp on an insect."

"If I can't afford to buy him off, I can't afford to pay you to protect me," explained Dante.

"I don't want your money."

"What do you want?"

Bailey learned forward. "How many verses did you give Bennett? I want the truth, now."

"Three," said Dante.

"Then the man who kills him ought to get at least four, right?"

"At least," agreed Dante.

Tyrannosaur extended an enormous hand. "You've got yourself a deal, poet."

Dante shook the giant's hand. "Call me Rhymer," he said with a smile.

"Rhymer it is!" said Bailey, gesturing to the purple-skinned Stelargan barmaid. "This calls for a drink!"

This calls for more than that. It calls for some serious thought. Here I am, the objective observer, the nonparticipant, the man who reports history but doesn't make it, and I've just commissioned a man's death. Sure, it's a man who's planning to kill me, but that's his job, and he did offer me a way out.

And then:

I'm the only historian out here, as well as the only poet. What I write will become future generations' truth. Is Tyrannosaur Bailey worth five verses? Was Bennett worth three? What criteria do I apply—who saves me and who threatens me? Is that the way history really gets created?

And because he was nothing if not a realist, he had one last thought:

What the hell. Orpheus didn't leave any guidelines for the job, either. I'll just have to play it by ear and do the best I can—and how can I serve history or art if I die tomorrow at noon?

"Here you are, Rhymer," said Tyrannosaur, taking a drink in his massive paw and handing another to Dante.

"Thanks."

"Here's to four verses!"

"You've got 'em, even if he runs."

"Bennett?" asked Tyrannosaur. "He won't run."

"But he can't beat you." Suddenly Dante frowned. "Can he?"

"Not a chance."

"Well, then?"

"A man in his profession can't run," said Bailey. "He's got to believe he's invincible, that nothing can kill him, even when he knows better. Otherwise he'll never be able to face a wanted killer again. He'll flinch, he'll hesitate, he'll back down, he'll run, he'll do *some*thing to fuck it up."

"But *if* he wants to back down, if it's his last day as a bounty hunter, let him walk," said Dante. "You'll get your verses anyway."

"Whatever you say," agreed Tyrannosaur. "But he won't back down."

"Against a monster like you?" said Dante, then quickly added: "Meaning no offense."

"None taken," said Bailey. "But size isn't everything. They say the guy who killed Conrad Bland wasn't much bigger than you are. And I know the Angel was supposed to be normal in size, maybe even a little undernourished. Men have developed more than two hundred different martial arts, and we've picked up dozens more from aliens. Those are great equalizers." He uttered a sigh of regret. "Size just isn't what it used to be."

"Then why does everyone come here to live under your protection?"

"Because I've mastered seventy-two of those martial arts, and I'm the best shot you ever saw with a burner or a screecher."

"Yeah, those are good reasons," agreed Dante. "And the fact that half the guys you fight can't reach your head probably doesn't hurt either."

"Neither does spreading the word."

"I beg your pardon?"

"When I was a young man, I was an adventurer," answered Bailey. "I wanted to pit my skills against the best opponents I could find. I was a mercenary, and for two years I was the freehand heavyweight champion of the Albion Cluster, and I even put in some time as a lawman out in the Roosevelt system. But eventually a man wants to settle down."

"What does that have to do with spreading the word?" asked Dante, confused.

"I still needed an income, so I passed the word that anyone who was willing to tithe me ten percent of their income and their holdings could live here under my protection. My reputation drew more than a thousand immigrants to Tusculum II and kept an awful lot of bill collectors and bounty hunters away."

"I see."

"You're a man of letters," continued Bailey, "so let me ask you your professional opinion about something."

"Shoot."

"I think Tusculum II is a really dull name for a world. I'm thinking of changing it."

"To what?"

"I don't know. Tyrannosaur's World, maybe." He looked across the table. "You don't like it."

"It's a little too, well, egomaniacal."

"I'm open to suggestions."

"How many planets are there in the system?"

"Six."

"Okay," said Dante. "As long as you're a Tyrannosaur, name them after periods in Earth's prehistory."

"I *like* that. What are the periods?"

"Damned if I know—but there were dozens of them. Have you got a pocket computer?"

"Sure. Don't you?"

"No."

"How do you write?"

"With a quill pen, just like Orpheus."

Bailey withdrew his computer and slid it across the table to Dante, who instructed it to list the various prehistoric eras.

"All right, this should work," announced Dante. "Call the first planet Cambria. This world is Devonia. The next four, in order, are Permia, Triassic, Jurassic, and Cretaceous. If any of them have moons, name the moons after the animals that existed in their eras."

"You've got a head on you, Rhymer!" enthused Bailey. "It would have been a shame to let Wait-a-bit Bennett remove it from your shoulders." He paused. "What'll we call the star?"

"Well, it's on all the charts as Tusculum, but that shouldn't matter. The planets are Tusculum I through VI, but if you're giving them names that appeal to you, there's no reason why you can't do the same to the star. How about Dinosaur, since that's the idea that gave birth to all the names?"

"Sounds good to me," said Bailey. "Tomorrow I'll have the spaceport computer start signaling ships that we're Dinosaur."

"Make sure it adds that you were formerly Tusculum or you'll drive 'em all crazy."

"Right. I'm sure glad I ran into you, Rhymer."

"Not half as glad as *I* am," said Dante as Wait-a-bit Bennett entered the casino.

Bennett saw Dante and walked over to him.

"Got my fifty thousand credits yet, Danny?" he asked pleasantly.

"No."

"Well, you've got a little over half a day left. I'm sure a bright young lad like you can come up with the money." Bennett paused. "But until that happy moment occurs, I'm not letting you out of my sight."

"You've made two mistakes, Wait-a-bit Bennett," said Tyrannosaur.

"Oh?"

"First, his name's Rhymer, not Danny, And second, no one's laying a finger on him as long as he stays on Devonia."

"Where the hell's Devonia?" asked Bennett.

"You're standing on it."

"You don't have to stand up for him, Tyrannosaur," said Bennett. "The kid's not worth it."

"This is *my* world!" bellowed Bailey, getting to his feet. "I'm the only one who decides who lives and who dies!"

"I have nothing against you," persisted Bennett. "My business is with Danny Briggs and no one else."

"You have no business on Devonia."

"Like I say, my business is with Danny here . . . but if you try to hinder me in the pursuit of my legal livelihood, I'll have to kill you too."

Tyrannosaur smiled. "Is that a threat?"

"You may consider it such," acknowledged Bennett.

His hand moved slowly down toward his burner, but before he could reach it Tyrannosaur's hands shot out with blinding swiftness, one grabbing him by the neck, the other holding his hand away from his weapon.

Bailey lifted Bennett straight up two, then three, then four feet above the ground. The bounty hunter struggled to free himself. His free hand chopped at Tyrannosaur's massive arm. He landed a pair of devastating kicks in his attacker's stomach. Bailey merely frowned and began squeezing.

Soon Bennett was gasping for air. He landed two more kicks, and poked a thumb at Bailey's right eye, but Bailey simply lowered his head, and Dante could hear the bounty hunter's thumb break with a loud cracking sound at it collided with Bailey's skull.

Bennett's struggles became more desperate, and finally Bailey released his grip on Bennett's arm, used both hands to lift the bounty hunter above his head, and hurled him into the wall. There was a strange, undefinable sound as all the air left Bennett's lungs, and he dropped to the floor, where he lay motionless.

Suddenly a cheer went up from the assembled gamblers and drinkers.

"What the hell are they applauding?" asked Dante, staring at the dead bounty hunter.

"They're paying for my protection, remember?" said Bailey, who wasn't even panting from his efforts. "They're cheering because I've just shown them they're getting their money's worth. Bennett came after you, but he could have been *any* bounty hunter coming after any of *them*."

Virgil stuck his head in the door in response to the cheering, and gazed impassively at Bennett's corpse.

"Couldn't wait till tomorrow, huh?" he said.

"Out!" ordered Bailey, and Virgil removed himself from the doorway. Tyrannosaur then ordered two of the men on his staff to remove the body and dispose of it.

"The usual method, sir?" asked one of the men.

"Unless you've got a better way," answered Bailey. He turned back to Dante, who was staring at him intently. "I thought I just solved your problem. Suddenly you look like you've got another one?"

"No." *Just a question.*

"Good. And don't forget our bargain: I get four verses."

"At the very least," said Dante.

Who knows? You may get a hundred or more. It's become clear to me that I can't be an Orpheus without a Santiago. Could I possibly have found you this soon?

7.

TYRANNOSAUR, TYRANNOSAUR,
WHATEVER YOU GIVE HIM, HE WANTS MORE,
THE WORLD IS HIS OYSTER, THE STARS ARE
    HIS SEA;
HE FISHES FOR SOULS, A MAN ON A SPREE.

THAT WAS ABOUT AS POLITICAL as the Rhymer ever got
to be.

The first three verses were about Bailey's size, his
strength, his mastery of martial arts and martial weapons.
It glorified his fighting abilities, and in time it made his
name a household word.

But it was the fourth verse, the one you see above, that
was written with a purpose, for the new Orpheus sought a
new Santiago, and the mythic proportions he drew—"the
stars are his sea" and "He fishes for souls"—were written
expressly to get Tyrannosaur Bailey thinking along those
lines, to consider himself as something unique and special,
a man not so much on a spree as on a holy mission.

"I like it," said Bailey enthusiastically after Dante had
read it aloud to him the morning after he killed Wait-a-bit
Bennett. "I don't know that I understand it, especially that
last bit, but I like it. You've fulfilled your end of the bargain, Rhymer."

"Maybe I could explain the parts you don't understand,"
offered Dante.

"Sure, why not?"

"It means you collect lost souls, just as you've been doing here on Devonia. But you don't just collect them here;
like the poem says, the stars are your sea."

"Well, that's right," agreed Bailey. "They come from all
over."

"I don't see you being so passive, just sitting here and

waiting for them to come to you," said Dante, selecting his words carefully. "As a matter of fact, I can see you going out and recruiting them."

"Devonia can't support that many more people," Bailey pointed out.

"Then you'll leave Devonia," said Dante. "Maybe you'll come back here from time to time for spiritual refreshment, but you'll find you have a greater purpose and you'll have to go abroad to fulfill it."

"I doubt it," said the huge man. "I'm happy with the purpose I've got."

"The choice may not be yours. It may be thrust upon you by powers that are beyond your control."

"I still don't know what you're talking about, Rhymer," said Bailey. "You almost make it sound like I'll be recruiting an army."

"Not the kind anyone else would recruit."

"We've already got the Democracy protecting us from the rest of the galaxy."

Dante leaned forward. "Who's protecting you from the Democracy?"

Bailey stared at him for a long moment, then laughed. "You're crazy!"

"Why?" demanded Dante. "Exceptional times call for exceptional men. You're an exceptional man."

"I'm a *live* man. I plan to stay that way." The huge man paused. "And you'd better get off the planet soon if *you* want to stay a live man. The Democracy's got to have traced your ship by now."

"Send them packing when they show up."

"Me? Take on the whole Democracy?"

"Just one squad. How the hell many men are they going to send to find a thief and his ship?"

"You don't understand much about geometrical progressions, do you, Rhymer?" said Bailey. "Say they send ten men, and I kill them all. Next week they'll send fifty to exact revenge. Maybe I'll hire some help and kill *them*, too. Then they'll send five hundred, and then thirty thousand, and then six million. If there are two things they can spare, they're men and ships—and if there's one thing they can't tolerate, it's having someone stand up to them."

"There are ways," said Dante.

"The hell there are!" growled Bailey.

"It's been done before."

"Never!"

"It has!" insisted Dante.

"By who?"

"Santiago."

"Come off it—he was just an outlaw!"

"He was a revolutionary," Dante corrected him. "And what kept him alive was that the Democracy never understood that he *wasn't* just an outlaw."

"What do you know about it?"

"Everything! If the Democracy had ever guessed what his real purpose was, they'd have sent five billion men to the Frontier and destroyed every habitable world until they were sure they'd killed him. But because they thought he was just an outlaw—the most successful of his era, but nothing more than that—they were content to post rewards and hope the bounty hunters could deliver him."

"Let me get this straight," said Bailey. "You're saying that you want me to pretend I'm Santiago?" He snorted derisively. "They may be dumb, Rhymer, but they can count. He'd be close to a hundred and seventy-five years old."

"I don't want you to *pretend* anything," said Dante. "I want you to *be* Santiago!"

Tyrannosaur Bailey downed his drink in a single swallow and stared across the table. "I never used to believe all artists were crazy. You've just convinced me I was wrong."

Dante was about to argue his case further when Virgil Soaring Hawk burst into Rex's and walked directly over to him.

"Time to go," he said, a note of urgency in his voice. "Say your good-byes, pay your bar tab, and let's get the hell out of here!"

"What's your problem?" asked Dante irritably.

"You haven't paid any attention to the news, have you?" said Virgil.

"What news?"

"Remember New Tangier IV, that pleasant little planet where you and I met?"

"Yeah. What about it?"

"It's become a piece of uninhabited rock, courtesy of the Democracy."

"What are you talking about?" demanded Dante.

"They sent a Navy squadron to find you and your ship," explained Virgil, fidgeting with impatience. "No one there knew where you'd gone. The Navy didn't believe them, so to punish them for withholding information they dropped an exceptionally dirty bomb in the atmosphere." He paused. "Nothing's going to live on New Tangier IV for about seven thousand years."

Dante turned to Tyrannosaur. "Did you hear that? The time is ripe!"

"The time is ripe to get our asses out of here, and to lose that fucking ship as soon as we can," said Virgil.

"*Shut up!*" bellowed Dante, and Virgil, startled, fell silent. "It's time for him to come back."

"The Democracy does things like that all the time."

"Then it's time to stop them."

"Maybe it is," agreed Bailey reluctantly. "But I'm not the one to do it."

"You've got all the attributes."

"You don't even know what his attributes were," said Bailey. "And neither do I. No one does."

"Someone has to stand up to the Democracy!"

"And have them do to Devonia what they did to New Tangier IV?" snapped Bailey irritably. "How do you stand up to a force like that?"

"*He* found a way. *You* will, too."

"Not me, Rhymer. I'm no revolutionary, and I'm no leader of men."

"You *could* be."

"I've *done* my time in the trenches. You'd better listen to the Injun and get the hell out of here, because if it comes to a choice between fighting the Navy or telling them where you've gone, I'll be the fastest talker you ever saw."

Dante stared at him, as if seeing him for the first time. "You mean it, don't you?"

"You bet your ass I mean it. *You* may have a death wish; *I* don't."

Dante blinked his eyes rapidly for a moment, as if disoriented. Then he sat erect. "I'm sorry. I was mistaken. You're not the one."

"I've been telling you that."

"But I'll find him."

"If he exists."

"If the times call exceptional men forth, they're practically screaming his name. He exists, all right—or he will, once I find him and convince him of his destiny."

"I wish you luck, Rhymer."

"You do?" said Dante, surprised.

"I live here. I know we need him." Bailey paused. "Are you going to keep my four verses?"

"Yes."

"Even that last one?"

"Even the last one," replied Dante. "It's not your fault you're not Santiago."

"Okay," said Bailey. "You played square with me. Maybe I can do you a favor."

"We're even," said Dante. "You killed Bennett, I gave you four verses."

Bailey shook his head. "A couple of hours from now the Navy is going to show up and ask me what I know about you, and I'm going to tell them. So I owe you another favor."

"All right."

"If you want to find a new Santiago, you'd better learn everything you can about the old one."

"I know everything Orpheus knew."

"Orpheus was a wandering poet who may never even

have seen Santiago," said Bailey dismissively. "If you really want to know what there is to know about Santiago, there's a person you need to talk to."

"What's his name and where can I find him?"

"He's a she, and all I know is the name she's using these days—Waltzin' Matilda. She's used a lot of other names in the past."

"Waltzin' Matilda," repeated Dante. "She sounds like a dancer."

Bailey smiled. "She's a lot more than a dancer."

"Where is she?"

"Beats me. She moves around a lot."

"That's all I have to go on—just a name?"

"That's better than you had two minutes ago," said Bailey. Suddenly he looked amused. "Or did someone tell you that defeating the Democracy was going to be easy?"

The giant's laughter was still ringing in Dante's ears as he and Virgil left the casino and hurried to their ship.

PART II

WALTZIN'
MATILDA'S BOOK

8.

MATILDA WALTZES, AND SHE GRINDS.
MATILDA GETS INSIDE MEN'S MINDS.
MATILDA PLUNDERS AND SHE ROBS;
MATILDA'S PULLED A THOUSAND JOBS.

IT WAS AN EXAGGERATION. At the time Dante found her, Matilda had pulled only 516 jobs, which was still sufficient to make her one of the most wanted criminals on the Frontier.

Her specialty was that she didn't specialize. Gold, diamonds, artwork, fissionable materials, promissory notes, she stole them all. She'd done two years in the hellhole prison on Spica II, and another four months on Sugarcane. She escaped from both, the only prisoner ever to break out of either penitentiary.

She was a lot of things Dante wasn't—skilled in the martial arts, skilled in the ways of high society, exceptionally well read—and a few things that Dante was, such as an outlaw with a price on her head. It didn't bother her much; she figured that if she could survive Spica II, she could survive anything the Democracy or the Frontier threw at her.

The most interesting aspect of her past was that she came from money, and had every whim catered to. At eight she was so graceful a ballerina that her family mapped out her entire future—and at nine she proved to be even more independent than graceful by leaving the Democracy forever. She stowed away on a cargo ship bound for Roosevelt III, somehow made her way to the carnival world of Calliope, bought a fake ID with money she'd stolen from her brother, and soon found work dancing in various stage shows.

As she grew older she learned every dance from a tango to a striptease, and made her way from one world to another as an entertainer, dancing solo when possible, with partners when necessary. She changed her name as often as most people changed clothes, and changed her worlds almost as frequently—but she never left a world without some trinket, some banknote, some negotiable bond, *something*, that she hadn't possessed when she arrived.

Just once she made the error of stealing within the Democracy's borders. That was when she was apprehended and incarcerated on Spica II. She never went back again.

No one knew her real name. She liked the sound of Matilda, and used it with half a hundred different surnames. She was Waltzin' Matilda just once, on Sugarcane, but that was where she was arrested the second time, and after she escaped from jail, that was the name that was on all the Wanted posters.

She still used a different name, sometimes more than one, on every world, but she was resigned to the fact that to most of her friends and almost all of her enemies she had become Waltzin' Matilda, despite the fact that she could not recall ever having performed a single waltz onstage.

It was a pleasant life, punctuated only by the occasional narrow escape from the minions of the Democracy or those bounty hunters who wished to claim its reward. She liked appearing onstage, and she found her secret vocation as a thief sexually exciting, especially when she knew that her movements were being watched.

Like tonight.

Dimitrios of the Three Burners was in the audience. He hadn't come to Prateep IV to find her—he was after other prey—but he had a notion that Matilda Montez was really Waltzin' Matilda, and since he hadn't turned up his quarry yet, he'd dropped in to check her out, maybe keep an eye on her in case she was up to her usual tricks.

She watched him out of the corner of her eye as she spun and dipped, jumped and pirouetted. It was Dimitrios, all right, with two of his trademarked burners in well-worn holsters and the handle of the third peeking out from the top of his boot. He seemed relaxed, sipping his drink, staring at her with the same appreciative smile she'd seen on so many other men in so many other audiences.

Well, you just keep drinking and smiling, bounty killer, because before you leave here I'm going to be two million credits richer—and even you, who's seen it all and heard it all, won't believe the only eyewitness.

She spun around twice more, then stopped and bowed, perfectly willing to let the audience think her smile was for them. They were informed that she would take a twenty-minute break, and then return for the evening's finale.

She waited for the applause to die down and bowed one last time, then began making her way to her dressing room. A drunken man jumped up from his chair and tried to climb onstage. She dispatched him almost effortlessly with a spinning kick to the chest, and got another standing ovation as she finally left the stage.

Once there, she locked the door behind her, peeled off her clothes, and donned a thin robe. She picked up a tiny receiving device and inserted it in her ear, then hit the control on her makeup table.

"Twenty minutes . . . nineteen minutes fifty seconds . . . nineteen minutes forty seconds . . ." droned a mechanical voice.

She slid her feet into a pair of rubber-soled shoes, then ordered her window to open. She climbed up onto the ledge and leaped lightly to the roof of the adjoining brokerage house with the grace of an athlete. A cloth bag was suspended on a very thin line from her room. She walked over to it, removed a pint of hard liquor from the neighboring system of Ribot, walked to a door leading to the building's interior, whispered the code that opened it, and stepped inside.

"Eighteen minutes, thirty seconds . . ."

She removed her shoes, took off her robe, and unstrapped the shocker from her leg. Then, totally naked, she descended two levels on the airlift.

A middle-aged man, dressed in a guard's uniform, suddenly looked up from the musical holo he had been watching on his pocket computer. His jaw dropped when he saw Matilda.

She smiled at him and began walking straight toward him.

"My God!" muttered the man. "Who . . . what are you doing here?"

Her smile widened, promising no end of wonders as she approached him, her hands behind her back.

"You . . . you . . . you shouldn't be here!" he stammered.

She considered replying, but decided that total silence would be more effective as she continued walking toward him.

"This is . . ." he began, and then seemed to run out of words for a moment. He blinked his eyes. "Things like this don't happen to me!"

Her left hand held the whiskey. She stretched it out to him, offering it, and as if in a dreamlike trance, he took a step toward her and reached out his arms.

And then, before he quite knew what hit him, she brought the shocker out in her right hand, aimed it at him, and felt it vibrate with power as it sent its voltage coursing through his body. For a moment he seemed to be a life-sized puppet dancing spasmodically on strings; then he fell to the floor in a silent heap.

She knelt down next to him, poured as much of the whiskey as she could into his mouth without choking him, spilled the rest on his clothes, and, after carefully wiping her fingerprints from the bottle, tossed it onto the floor, where it broke into pieces. She then raced to his desk and began manipulating his pocket computer.

"Fifteen minutes, ten seconds . . ."

She was still trying to find what she needed five minutes later. Then, finally, she broke through the encryption, found the code words she needed, walked to the safe, uttered the words in the proper order, and a minute later was thumbing through a score of negotiable currencies. She finally settled on New Stalin rubles and Far London pounds, since they were the largest denominations, took two huge handfuls, and raced to the airlift. Once she reached the third level she donned her robe and shoes and walked out onto the building's roof.

The guard would be out cold for at least five more hours. More to the point, he'd stink of booze, and no one on this or any other world would believe his story about a gorgeous naked woman entering the building and turning a shocker on him. It sounded too much like a drunken fantasy—and the remains of the drink were there to prove it.

She went to the bag that was suspended from her window, the one where she'd found the whiskey, and put the money into it. Then she tested the line that held it to make sure it was secure. It was, and a moment later she scrambled up the wall, feet on the slick metal exterior, hands on the line, until she reached her window.

She climbed back into her dressing room, raised the line high enough so that in the unlikely event someone else were to walk on the brokerage house's roof, they wouldn't be able to reach the bag, then removed her shoes and robe, put them in a closet, and began climbing back into her costume.

"Four minutes, twenty seconds . . ."

She felt proud of herself. She didn't believe in repeating her methods—that was the quickest way to give the police and the bounty hunters a line on you—and she thought tonight's job was one of her most creative to date. She'd stolen the equivalent of two million credits in currency that would be almost impossible to trace, and the only witness was an old man stinking of alcohol and raving about a naked lady. It was beautiful.

"Two minutes, thirty seconds . . ."

She took the receiver out of her ear, deactivated it, and placed it in a jar of face cream, covering it so no one could see it—not that anyone had a reason to look for it, but she hadn't made it this far by not being thorough.

Then, nineteen minutes after she left the stage, she walked out again and stood in the wings, waiting to be introduced, her take suspended from a window where no one could see it, and another perfect crime to her credit. If she was a little flushed from her efforts, well, that could be written off as excitement at appearing onstage, or satisfaction at the wild applause she generated.

She waited for the emcee to run through her intro, then stepped out and faced the audience, smiling and bowing before beginning to dance again.

Yes, he was still there: Dimitrios of the Three Burners. *I pulled it off right under your nose, bounty killer, and it's almost a pity that I did it so well you'll never know what happened. That's the only part of this business I don't enjoy; I can never let anyone know how good I am at what I do.*

She was on such an adrenaline high that she gave them not only a five-minute dance but a four-minute encore, and then another four minutes in which she and the band improvised wildly but in perfect harmony. When it was finally over, she bowed again, gave Dimitrios a great big smile, and returned to her dressing room—and found a small, slightly-built man sitting there on her chair.

"Hi," he said. "My name's Dante Alighieri. We have to talk."

"Who let you in here?" she demanded.

"I let myself in. It's one of the things I do really well."

"Well, you can let yourself right out!"

"Look," he said, "I'm not a bounty hunter, I'm not a security guard, I don't work for the Democracy or any police agency. I don't give a damn that you robbed the office next door."

Her eyes widened. "How . . . ?" She forced herself to stop in midthought.

"Because robbery is another of the things I do really well. I have nothing but professional admiration for you." Suddenly he smiled. "I wonder if Dimitrios knows how close he is to a *real* outlaw?"

"Probably not," she said, still eyeing him suspiciously.

"Where are my manners?" said Dante, suddenly getting to his feet. "This is your chair."

"I'd prefer to stand."

"All right," he said. "But hear me out before you start hitting and kicking. That's *not* one of the things I do well—though I'm learning."

"Just what the hell is it that you want?"

"I told you—I want to talk to you."

"If you think I'm going to pay you to keep quiet about tonight, you can forget it. They can question that old man all they want, his story will never hold up."

"I don't care about him or about what you stole."

"Then what *do* you want to talk about?"

"Santiago."

9.

HE WAS A COP ON THE MAKE, A COP ON
   THE TAKE,
AS CORRUPT AS A COP GETS TO BE.
THE VERY SAME MEN THAT HE SAVED FROM
   THE PEN
ARE NOW OWNED BY SIMON LEGREE.

HIS NAME WAS SIMON LEGREE, and he'd been after Matilda for a long, long time. She was the One Who Got Away, and it was a point of honor with him that he bring her to the bar of justice—or at least threaten to do so.

For Legree had his own profitable little business, not totally dissimilar from Wait-a-bit Bennett's. It was trickier, because he didn't have the advantage of a price on his prey's head—but when it worked, it was far more lucrative.

Oh, he took bribes, and he always managed to stuff a few packets of alphanella seeds in his pocket for future resale when there was a major drug bust—but what Simon Legree lived for was to catch a criminal in the act of committing a crime. Then it was a choice between jail and turning over a third of their earnings for the rest of their lives—and Legree had enough working capital to hire agents to make sure his new partners fulfilled their obligations.

He made millions from Billy the Whip, and millions more from the New Bronte Sisters, and he had almost fifty other partners out there earning money for him—but the one he wanted the most, the one he was sure had amassed the greatest fortune, Waltzin' Matilda, had thus far eluded him. Oh, he knew where she worked and where she lived, and whenever she changed planets—which she did on an almost weekly basis—his network of informants always let him know where she came to rest. But she was so damned creative in her lawlessness that he had yet to catch her in a compromising position, and she remained his Holy Grail.

He knew she was on Prateep IV. He knew she was dancing at the Diamond Emporium. He knew that she had signed a six-day contract, and had already been there five days. He knew that this was the night she figured to strike. He knew that by morning someone would be short hundreds of thousands, maybe even millions, of credits, and that her alibi would be airtight.

He tried to think like her, to predict what she might do, but he had nothing to go on, no past performance, no modus operandi. The damned woman never operated in the same way twice, and trying to predict and outthink her was driving him to distraction.

He sat in the audience, aware that Dimitrios of the Three Burners was there too, and wondered if Dimitrios had come for Matilda. He had no desire to go up against Dimitrios—no one in his right mind did—but he wasn't going to give Matilda up without a fight.

So Simon Legree sat there, silent, motionless, going over endless scenarios and permutations in his mind, and wondering how long it would be before Matilda emerged from her dressing room and returned to her hotel.

But Matilda had more important things on her mind—or confronting her from a few feet away. She stared curiously at the young man who knew she had just plundered the brokerage house but wanted only to talk about Santiago.

"He's been dead for more than a century," she said at last. "What makes you think I know anything about him?"

"Tyrannosaur Bailey seems to think you know more about him than anyone else alive," answered Dante.

"Probably I do," she agreed. "So what? He's still been dead for over a century."

Dante met her stare. "*All* of them have been," he said.

She looked her surprise. "I thought I was the only one who knew!"

"You were, until a few weeks ago."

"What happened a few weeks ago?"

"I found Black Orpheus' manuscript."

"The whole thing?"

Dante nodded. "Including a bunch of verses no one's ever seen or heard."

"Okay, so you know there was more than one Santiago," said Matilda. "So what? That was *his* secret, not mine."

"Tell me about them," said Dante. "And tell me why you're the expert."

"I'm the only living descendant of Santiago."

"*Which* Santiago?"

"What difference does it make?"

"It would help me to believe you."

"I don't give a damn if you believe me or not."

"Look, I have no reason *not* to believe you, and I want very much to. It's in both of our best interests."

"Why?" she insisted. "Who the hell are you, anyway?"

"My name is Dante Alighieri. The name I plan to be remembered by is the Rhymer."

"So you're the new Black Orpheus."

"You're very quick, Miss . . . ah . . ."

"Matilda." She frowned. "Okay, you're Orpheus. That's doesn't change anything. Santiago still died more than a century ago."

Dante stared at her for a long minute. "I think it's time for him to live again," he said at last.

Her eyes widened, and a smile slowly crossed her face. "Now, *that's* an interesting idea."

"I'm glad you think so."

"Just a minute!" she said. "I hope to hell you're not thinking of *me*!"

"I'm not thinking of anyone in particular," said Dante. "But if we can talk, if you have any memorabilia, anything at all, I might get a better idea of what I'm looking for. As far as I can tell, of them all only Sebastian Cain could be considered truly skilled with his weapons, so they obviously had other qualities."

"They did."

"Qualities such as you exhibited tonight."

"I told you—I'm not a candidate for the job!" she snapped. "I'd like a Santiago, if only to take some of the pressure off me and give the law and the bounty hunters an even bigger target—so why in the world would I volunteer?"

"All right," he said. "I won't bring it up again." He paused. "*Do* you have any records or other memorabilia—letters, holograms, anything at all?"

"My family has lived like kings for three generations on what he chose to leave us—probably about two percent of what he was worth—but whatever we started with, it was converted into cash over a century ago. I've never seen any documents or anything like that."

"Did they ever speak of him?"

"How else would I know I was his great-great-granddaughter?"

"What did they say?"

"When people were around, the usual—that he was the greatest bandit in the galaxy, that he was a terrible man, that he might not have even been a man at all."

"And when people weren't around?"

She studied his face again, then shrugged. "What the hell. Who cares after this long?" She leaned back against a wall. "They told me that he was a secret revolutionary, that he was trying, not to overthrow the Democracy, but to hold it in check, to stop it from plundering the human colonies on the Frontier when there were so many alien worlds to plunder." She paused. "Does that agree with what Orpheus said?"

"No," replied Dante. "But Orpheus didn't know. It agrees with what I pieced together after reading the manuscript. Orpheus was too close to things. He studied all the people, but he never stepped back and really looked at the picture." He looked at her. "What else did they tell you?"

"That he had to do some morally questionable things, that he killed a lot of men because he felt his cause was just. Since it was essential that the Democracy think of Santiago as an outlaw rather than a revolutionary, almost everyone who worked for him was a criminal. Some looted and murdered on their own and let him take the blame—and some did terrible things on his orders." She paused. "They all served his cause, one way or another."

"Sounds about right. He came into existence because we needed him. I think we need him again."

"And if you and I select him and train him and control him, there's no reason why we shouldn't get a little piece of the action," she agreed.

"I don't want it," said Dante. "I just want *him*."

She looked at him like he was crazy. "Why?"

Dante shrugged. "It's difficult to explain. But he helps define me: there can't be an Orpheus without a Santiago. And God knows the need still exists. I've seen more brutality practiced in the name of the Democracy than I've ever seen practiced against it. Nothing's changed. They still don't seem to remember that they're in business to protect us, not plunder us."

"They would say they're doing just that."

"They're doing that if you're a citizen in good standing," replied Dante. "But out here, on the Frontier, they prevent alien races from running roughshod over us only so they can do it themselves. It's time to remind them just what the hell the Navy is *supposed* to be doing out here."

"What makes you think one man can stand up to them?" asked Matilda.

"Your great-great-grandfather did."

"*They* didn't know that, or they'd have used the whole Navy to hunt him down," she replied. "I know he robbed a lot of Navy convoys, and I know he ran the Democracy ragged trying to hunt him down—but what good did it do? All the Santiagos are dead, and the Democracy's still here."

"They stopped it from being worse," said Dante. "They built hospitals, they misdirected the Navy, they saved some alien worlds from total destruction. That's *some*thing, damn it."

"And who knows it besides you and me?" said Matilda.

"Everyone he fought for thought he was a criminal out for *their* property."

"You know who knows it?" shot back Dante. "The *Democracy* knows it. They were scared to death of him—of them—for more than half a century . . . and if Santiago comes back, they'll be scared again."

She grimaced. "You know why there are no more Santiagos?"

"Why?"

"Because the Democracy blew Safe Harbor to smithereens when they got word that an alien force was hiding there. They never knew it was Santiago's headquarters, or that they'd killed him and his chosen successors. We live out here on the Frontier, so we think of him as King of the Outlaws—but if you're the Democracy, he's no more than a bothersome insect that's hardly worth swatting."

"You're wrong," said Dante. "I've studied it. The Democracy had eleven different agencies charged with finding and terminating him. Even today there's still one agency whose job is to find out who he was, how he got to be so powerful, and to stop history from ever repeating itself."

"Really?" she asked, interested.

He nodded. "Really." He paused. "So are you in or out?"

"Like I told you, I could use a Santiago to take the heat off me. Hell, I could use a couple of dozen. I'm in. Now what do I do?"

"Now we pool our knowledge and try to find the next Santiago."

"We could do a lot worse than the Tyrannosaur," she suggested.

"He's out. Doesn't want any part of it—and he's not what we need anyway."

"Why not? He's well named."

"Santiago wasn't just a physical force, or even primarily one," answered Dante. "He was a *moral* force. Men who never gave allegiance to anyone laid down their lives for him." He paused. "Do you see anyone giving up their lives because Bailey tells them to?"

"If that's your criterion, we'll never find a Santiago," she complained.

"We'll find him, all right," said Dante firmly. "The times will bring him forth."

"They haven't brought him yet."

"He's out there somewhere," said Dante. "But he doesn't *know* he's Santiago. It was easier for most of the others, all of them except the first one; they were recruited by the man they succeeded. *Our* Santiago doesn't know that the Santiago business still exists."

"All right, we'll proceed on that assumption," said Matilda. "I'll see what I can remember from my childhood." She paused. "I'm leaving Prateep tomorrow, for New Kenya. What should I be looking for?"

"I don't know. They were all different. Reading between the lines, I figure the original collected animals for zoos, and he was followed by a chess master, a farmer, a bounty hunter, and a bank robber. You'll just have to use your judgment, look for the kind of qualities you think he should have."

"That's not much to go on."

"We're planning to take the Frontier back from the Democracy. We can't put too many restrictions on the man who will lead us."

"All right," she said. "Where will you be? How can I contact you?"

"*I'll* contact *you*." She stared at him curiously. "I'm a little hotter than you are right now," he explained. "I've got to keep moving."

"What did you do?"

"Nothing," he said wryly. "*That's* one of the things I have against the Democracy."

"I saw Dimitrios in the audience," she said. "Is *he* looking for you?"

"I doubt it," answered Dante. "If he was, I'm sure he'd have found me by now."

"He's one hell of a bounty hunter," Matilda noted. "You don't seem very worried about it."

"I'm not without my resources."

"They must be formidable."

"They're okay." He got to his feet. "I think I'd better be going now. I'll contact you again before you leave New Kenya."

"I don't know where I'll be staying yet."

"I'll find you."

He turned toward the door, which opened before he could reach it—and Simon Legree, dressed in his trademark navy blue, entered the dressing room, a burner in one hand, a screecher in the other.

"What have we here?" he said. "A carnival of thieves?"

"Go away," said Matilda contemptuously. "You don't have anything on me."

"I will soon, Tilly," he said.

"The name's Matilda, and you can tell me about it when you have it. Now get out of my dressing room."

"When I'm ready," he said with a smile. "As it happens, I didn't come for you." He turned to Dante. "Hello, Danny Briggs, alias Dante Alighieri, alias the Rhymer."

"All three of us bid you welcome," said Dante with no show of fear or alarm.

"Got a nice price on your head, Danny Briggs," continued Legree. "I could blow you away right now and take what's left to the nearest bounty office for the reward."

"The nearest office is halfway across the Frontier," said Dante. "I'd spoil."

"That wouldn't do either of us any good," said Legree. "Perhaps we should consider alternatives."

"I'm always happy to consider alternatives."

"What do you do for a living, Danny Briggs?"

"My name's Dante, and I'm a poet."

Legree made a face. "Poets don't make any money, Danny. You're going to have to learn another skill if you want to live." He paused. "Do you rob or kill?"

"I write poems about colorful characters like you before history has a chance to forget them."

"Damn it, I'm trying to give you a chance to buy your

way out of this!" snapped Legree. "Usually I take thirty percent of your earnings for life—but what the hell does a poet earn?"

"I'm rich in satisfaction," replied Dante. "I love my work and I have loyal friends. What more does a man need?"

Legree shook his head. "No good, Danny. If you know a short prayer, you've just got time to say it."

Danny looked him in the eye. "I pray that you die quickly and painlessly," he said.

And before the words were out of Dante's mouth, Simon Legree blinked and frowned, as if he couldn't quite understand what had just happened. His weapons fell from his hands. He cleared his throat and opened his mouth to speak; nothing came out except a stream of blood.

"I *told* you I have loyal friends," said Dante, just before Legree fell to the floor with a knife protruding from his back, and Virgil Soaring Hawk entered the room, stepping over the lawman's corpse.

"Ma'am," said Virgil, staring at her with unconcealed lust, "you are unquestionably the most gorgeous creature to grace this forsaken world since the Maker of All Things set it spinning in orbit."

"Matilda, this is Virgil Soaring Hawk," said Dante.

"Dante's Virgil at your service." The Injun bent low in a stately bow. "Or the Scarlet Infidel, if you prefer."

"The Scarlet Infidel?" she repeated.

"It's a long story, ma'am," said Virgil. Suddenly he smiled. "But it's an interesting story, if you've got time to hear it over a couple of drinks."

"Leave her alone," Dante said. "She's one of us."

"What better reason to initiate her?" said Virgil.

"Don't," said Dante, and something in his voice made the Injun back off. The poet jerked his head toward Legree. "Get him out of here before someone sees him."

Virgil smiled apologetically at Matilda. "If you'll excuse me, ma'am, I'll just pick up this poor gentleman's body and put it somewhere where it won't bother anyone." He lifted Legree's corpse to his shoulder. "If you need anything, ma'am, now or anytime I'm around, just holler."

Dante stared at him for a moment, then turned back to Matilda. "If he lays a hand on you, tell me."

"I'm not the complaining type," she said. "Anything either of you try to do with me, you do at your own risk."

"Fair enough," said Dante.

Virgil vanished into the hallway.

"He seems to work for you."

Dante shrugged. "He attached himself to me the moment he heard my name. He insists that Dante needs a Virgil to get through the hell of the Inner Frontier." He smiled wryly. "So far he's been right."

"Does he do anything you ask, or is it limited to killing and disposing of bodies?"

"I don't know. I suppose I'll find out someday."

An uneasy silence followed, broken at last by Matilda.

"I'm sure you have things to do," she said. "You'd better be going."

"I will be. We can cover twice as much territory and consider twice as many candidates if we split up. I'll be in touch every week or two until we've finally found our Santiago." He paused. "I'm just giving the Injun a couple of minutes to get the body safely away. Don't let me keep you from doing whatever it is you have to do."

"You're not."

"Of course not." He smiled, walked over to the window, opened it, and pulled up the bag containing the currency. Matilda surreptitiously picked up a nail file from her vanity and held it behind her back as she watched the poet. He hefted the bag without opening it, then tossed it on her dressing table. "You can drop the knife," he said. "We're partners now—and partners don't rob each other."

She placed the file back on the vanity, opened the bag, pulled out the money, checked to see that it was all there, then turned to him.

"How did you . . . ?" she began—but Dante Alighieri was already gone.

10.

HE HAS NO FUTURE, HE HAS NO PAST,
HIS EYE IS SHARP, HIS GUN IS FAST,
HE LIVES FOR THE MOMENT, HE LIVES FOR
  THE KILL,
HE'S DIMITRIOS, AND HE'S ANGRY STILL.

MEN AREN'T ALL CUT FROM the same cloth. Many bounty hunters started out as lawmen, and when they decided they were good enough, they went out to the Rim or one of the Frontiers to ply their trade for far more money than a lawman makes.

Some were outlaws who decided that killing other outlaws was far more profitable than killing the agents of the law who pursued them.

And then there were men like Dimitrios of the Three Burners. No one knew his last name. No one knew where he came from. Some said he grew up on a small world in the Spiral Arm, others say he spent his youth on the Outer Frontier. There was one point where the speculation ended, and that was the day Johnny the Wolf shot his wife and infant daughter. He wasn't aiming for them. In fact, he probably never even knew they were there. He had just finished robbing the bank of Marcellus III, and they blundered between him and the law.

Dimitrios had never fired a hand weapon in his life, but he bought a matched set that afternoon, and spent the next hundred days working from sunrise to sunset at becoming proficient with them. When he felt he was ready, he went out hunting for the Wolf, and finally caught up with him in a casino on Banjo, an obscure little world in the Albion Cluster.

That fight was the stuff of legends. Dimitrios walked right up to Johnny the Wolf as he sat at a table playing cards, placed the muzzle of his burner in Johnny's ear, and fired. Johnny never knew what hit him—but six of his hired killers did, and Dimitrios shot four of them down before one of his burners shorted out and the other was blown out of his hand. He began throwing whiskey bottles, chairs, spittoons, anything he could get his hands on. The two men were no cowards. They fought back gamely, but they were no match for the vengeful Dimitrios, and within a few minutes of Dimitrios entering the casino the Wolf and all six of his men were dead.

Most men would have considered themselves lucky to have survived and returned to their normal lives, but Dimitrios had nothing to return to. He also had the feeling that for the first time in his life, something he'd done had made a difference, that given the geometrical permutations involved, he might have saved as many as a hundred lives by killing those seven murderers, and he decided then and there to go into the bounty-hunting business. The first thing he did was buy an extra burner to stuff in his boot, just in case one of the two he wore in holsters should ever short out again, and since he never offered his last name to anyone, before long he was known simply as Dimitrios of the Three Burners.

He didn't talk much, socialized even less, rarely drank, never drugged. If he ever felt like hanging it up and going back to his former life, he just forced himself to remember how it felt when he learned his wife and child had been killed, and he rededicated himself to preventing others from sharing that terrible, aching emptiness, that undirected hatred at the universe.

He wasn't interested in bringing anyone back alive. If the rewards didn't specify dead or alive, he ignored them. He was even particular about the types of killers he went after. He much preferred to go after those who had killed unarmed women and defenseless children, and he frequently passed up closer, easier, and far more lucrative prey to go after the ones who fit his criteria.

He lived very simply. His clothes were commonplace;

even his weapons were not of the best manufacture. His ship was old and unimpressive. Most people felt he was hoarding his rewards. They would have been surprised to know that he kept only enough to live and travel on, and sent the rest to handpicked charities that gave help and comfort to women who had survived violent attacks and children whose parents had been murdered.

He was on Prateep because he'd been given a tip that Hootowl Jacobs was there, but he hadn't seen any sign of him. He'd heard about this new character called the Rhymer, but when he looked into it, he found it far more likely that the Democracy had killed the Duchess than that the young poet had.

He knew all about Matilda, too, but he had no interest in bringing her down. In fact, he admired her. He liked the way she drove the Democracy and the Frontier's authorities crazy. He knew that she plundered every world she visited; what impressed him the most was that everyone else knew it too, and no one had been able to prove a thing. He'd stopped by the Diamond Emporium to watch her dance— he'd seen her before, and was intrigued by her combination of grace and athleticism—and to see if there was anyone in the crowd who might point him in the direction of Hootowl Jacobs. As usual, he didn't socialize; there was no one there that he either trusted or respected—there were mighty few of either in the galaxy—and so he simply relaxed and enjoyed his drink.

When the show was over, he got to his feet. He'd seen the Rhymer sneak into Matilda's dressing room, but that was no concern of his. He walked two blocks to his hotel, stopped at the bar for a nightcap, and went up to his room.

A few minutes later he heard a single knock at the door. He was still dressed, but his weapons, all three of them, were on the dresser. He quickly walked over, grabbed one, and trained it on the door.

"Come in," he said, uttering the code words that unlocked it.

"Thank you," said Matilda, entering the room. "I think it's time we met."

He shrugged. "I know who you are—and I know what you're supposed to have done. Makes no difference to me. As far as I'm concerned, you're free to keep on doing it."

She smiled. "That's very comforting."

"Is that what you came to find out?" asked Dimitrios.

"No."

"Then have a seat. Can I get you something to drink?"

"No, thanks."

"I don't do drugs, and I don't let anyone around me do them," he said.

"That's all right. I don't drug."

"You're a cheap date," he said, finally lowering the burner and stuffing it in a boot.

"I believe in making every credit count."

"Really? I've heard that you've got money you haven't even counted yet."

"Oh, no—I always count it. How else would I know that I'm not being ripped off?"

"I like you, Waltzin' Matilda," said Dimitrios. "I like the way you dance. I like the fact that you drive the Democracy crazy. And now I find that I like your wit." He paused. "But I still don't know what the hell you're doing here."

"I want to get to know you."

"That's a line I usually hear from some floozy the hotel manager sends up to make sure I don't shoot up the place," he said.

"I'm sure it is," she replied. "But I really *do* want to get to know you."

"Why?"

"Because from everything I hear you're an honorable man, and they're pretty rare."

"All right, I'm an honorable man. Now what?"

"Now I want you to tell me about the other honorable men you know: who they are, what they do, what they believe in?"

"You want to talk to a minister, not a bounty hunter."

"I know what I want to talk to," said Matilda. She sighed. "Okay, forget honorable. Who's the most formidable man on the Inner Frontier?"

"*I* am," he said, and when she made no comment, he continued: "I know it sounds egomaniacal, but if I didn't think so, if I didn't truly believe it, then I'd never be willing to go up against some of the men I have to face."

"Who else?"

"There are a lot of formidable men out here," answered Dimitrios. "Hootowl Jacobs, for one. I've heard about a character called Silvermane, out in the Quinellus Cluster. There's the Plymouth Rocker, there's Mongaso Taylor, there's the Black Death, there's a woman they call the Terminal Bitch who's supposed to be as deadly as any of them." He lit a thin smokeless cigar. "And there are some mighty formidable aliens too. From what I hear, there's a pair named Tweedledee and Tweedledum that might be deadlier than any of them."

"Well, that's a start," said Matilda. "How many of them are honorable?"

"Maybe one, maybe none, who knows? Mind if I ask you a question?"

"Go ahead."

"Why is the most accomplished thief on the Inner Frontier looking for an honorable man? That's kind of like mixing oil and water, isn't it?"

She laughed. "I don't think you'd believe me if I told you."

"Probably not, but why don't you tell me and I'll decide for myself."

"Fair enough. I'm looking for an honorable man to train and finance."

"What will you train him to be?"

"A dishonorable man."

He stared at her for a long minute. "That's an interesting notion. What are you looking for—a bodyguard or a partner?"

"Something much more than that," said Matilda. "I'm looking for a leader."

"Leaders are in short supply these days," replied Dimitrios.

"That's why we need one so badly."

"We?" he repeated. "As in you and me?"

"As in the whole Inner Frontier."

"We've never had one."

"Yes we have," said Matilda.

He stared at her curiously. "You're getting at something. I wish you'd come right out and say it."

"It's time for Santiago to return."

He chuckled. "You wouldn't like it much. He's been a rotting corpse for over a century."

"Maybe not," she said.

"Oh?"

"Maybe I'm looking at him right now."

"You've got me all wrong, Waltzin' Matilda," said Dimitrios. "Santiago was the King of the Outlaws. That's just the kind of person that I'm in business to hunt down and kill."

"What if I told you he wasn't what you think?"

"I'd ask what special insight you had into him."

"I'm his granddaughter."

He stared at her, then shook his head. "The numbers are wrong."

"All right," she said with a shrug. "His great-great-granddaughter."

"And you want me to go out and pillage and steal and kill for you?"

"No, I want you to do it for *us*."

"You and me?"

"The entire Inner Frontier."

"You keep saying that, but it doesn't make any sense."

"Have you got any coffee?" she asked. "Because what I have to tell you is going to take a while."

He ordered the kitchenette to prepare it, then handed her a cup and finally sat down on a chair that hovered a few inches above the ground, and changed its shape to accommodate his long, lean body.

"All right," he said. "I'm listening."

She proceeded to tell him about Santiago—everything she knew about him, everything her family had said when no one was around to overhear, everything Dante Alighieri had found hidden in the pages of Black Orpheus' poem. It took her close to two hours. When she was done she stared at him, waiting for a reaction.

"I believe you," he said at last.

"Good. That means I haven't wasted either of our time."

"Let me finish," he said. "I believe what you said. I believe Santiago was a secret revolutionary. I'm even willing to believe there was more than one Santiago." He paused, considering his words. "I believe that the time is right for another Santiago. But I'm not your man."

"Why not?"

"I'll help you look for him," continued Dimitrios. "I'll work for him and I'll fight for him." He stared unblinking into her eyes. "But I won't *become* him."

"Think of the difference you could make."

"Someone else can make it. Not me."

"But why?" she insisted.

"Because I'm not willing to do the things Santiago has to do if he's to *be* Santiago. I won't give orders to kill innocent men and women. I won't be the one who sends out men to kill young soldiers who are only trying to protect the Navy's payrolls or weapons. I understand why it has to be done, but it's contrary to everything I believe in, everything I *am*. I'll help you as far as I can, I'll protect you while you and the Rhymer are searching for the next Santiago, I'll never betray you—but I won't be Santiago, not now, not ever."

"You're sure?"

He smiled again. "Santiago is capable of lying. I'm not."

"But you *will* help us?"

"I said I would."

"Have you any suggestions where we should go next?"

"It'll take some thought," answered Dimitrios. "Santiago has to be able to lie, as I said. He has to send men to their deaths. He has to commit enough crimes to convince the Democracy that he's a criminal and not a revolutionary, and he has to be brutal and efficient enough to discourage any criminals on the Frontier from trying to take over his operation." He shook his head and added wryly, "He could be every scumbag I've ever hunted down."

"But he's not," she pointed out. "With him, it's a facade."

"I know. But they're not traits you're likely to find in a minister."

"That's why we decided to start with lawmen or bounty hunters," said Matilda.

"Maybe," said Dimitrios dubiously. "The question is who you trust more: a man who's been an outlaw all his life, or a man who's willing to become an outlaw on five minutes' notice."

"I see your point."

"Tell me about the one they call the Rhymer," he said. "I know he spent some time in your dressing room on Prateep. What's *his* interest in all this?"

"He's the one who sought me out in the first place."

"Why?"

She shrugged. "He wants to write poems about Santiago."

Dimitrios considered her answer for a moment, then nodded his head. "I suppose Orpheus needs a Santiago as much as Santiago needs an Orpheus."

"And what do *you* need?"

"I need men who deserve to die for what they've done. Right now I need one named Hootowl Jacobs. I heard a rumor tonight that he might have gone to Innesfree II. That's where I'll be heading tomorrow."

"If he's the one we're looking for, you won't kill him, right?"

"If he's the one you're looking for, I'll have to reevaluate my pledge to you," said Dimitrios.

"What has he done?"

"You don't want to know."

"Whatever it was, he did it to a woman," she said. "I know that much about you. That's why I was willing to come alone to your room."

"I saw you take that drunk out with a spinning kick," said Dimitrios. "You handle yourself just fine."

She got to her feet. "Tell me where your ship is and I'll meet you there in the morning."

"You're coming along?" he said. "Don't you have any professional engagements?"

"I'll cancel them and pick up work wherever you're going."

"We might do better going in three directions—you, me, and the poet."

"I'm coming with you," she said adamantly.

He shrugged. "Suit yourself."

"So where's your ship?"

"There's only one spaceport. Be there an hour after sunrise."

She got to her feet and walked to the door, then turned back to him. "I can't help thinking it should be you. You're such a goddamned moral man."

"You don't want such a goddamned moral man," he assured her. "You want a man who understands his purpose and will do whatever he has to do to succeed. I'm not that man."

"Well, you might at least look a little sad about it."

"Why?" he said. "Whoever he is, he is—or soon will be—the most important man on the Inner Frontier. We both know he's out there somewhere. What could be more challenging than finding him?"

"Convincing him that he's Santiago?" she suggested.

"When we find him, he'll know," said Dimitrios with certainty. "Hell, he's probably busy *being* Santiago right now. All we have to do is find him and tell him what his true name is."

"You really believe that, don't you?"

"If he's Santiago, the one thing he's not is a fool. If he's got the abilities we're looking for, he's been honing them, getting ready to meet his destiny. Our job is to point it out to him and convince him we're right."

"Do you really think we will?" asked Matilda.

"As sure as my name is Dimitrios of the Three Burners."

11.

HOOTOWL JACOBS LOVES HIS LIFE.
HOOTOWL JACOBS TAKES TO WIFE
A WOMAN HERE, A WOMAN THERE—
A BIGAMIST, BUT ONE WITH FLAIR.

DANTE WROTE THAT VERSE ABOUT Hootowl Jacobs, but he was still new at the job, and he made a major mistake, one Black Orpheus never made: he relied upon other people's descriptions and recollections. He never met Hootowl Jacobs himself, and that was the real reason the verse was so flawed.

Hootowl Jacobs loved his life, all right, and he certainly was a bigamist from time to time, but therein lay the rub: Hootowl tended to fall in love only with ladies of property, and since he was aware that he wouldn't be awarded that property in a typical divorce proceeding, he "divorced" his wives in his own unique way: with a serrated hunting knife across their windpipes.

No one knew how many wives he had taken, though there were doubtless records of it somewhere. No one knew how many he had dispatched either, but he came to the attention of Dimitrios of the Three Burners when the total reached double digits.

Dimitrios was nothing if not thorough—it was the best way to keep alive in his line of work—so he began checking up on Jacobs. The man had killed women on Sirius V and Spica VI in the Democracy, on Silverblue out on the Rim, and on Binder X, Roosevelt III, Greenveldt, and at least four other worlds of the Inner Frontier.

His method was always the same. He'd show up on a world, a well-to-do widower (as indeed he was), and because of his economic and social station he tended to meet more than his share of well-to-do widows. He wasn't all that much to look at, and his manners weren't the type that would sweep a woman off her feet . . . but he would stress what they had in common, which was money and loneliness, and it wasn't long before wedding bells would be ringing and Hootowl Jacobs (who, after the deaths of his first three wives, never used his own name again) was a husband again.

He never rushed into his "divorces." The fastest was five months, the slowest almost three years. But sooner or later it was inevitable. A distraught, hysterical Jacobs would seek out the authorities, claiming some passing stranger had killed his wife. She was always missing some jewelry, so the motive was apparent. The legalities were usually concluded in two or three weeks—a new John Doe warrant, and a quick property settlement in favor of the grieving widower.

Hootowl Jacobs was not just the kind of man that Dimitrios longed to catch, he was the kind that the bounty hunter wanted to kill slowly and painfully with his bare hands. He knew that he was unlikely to get the opportunity, but he could hope.

It took two days for Dimitrios and Matilda to get to Innesfree II. She had wanted to question him further about potential Santiagos, but he had his own priorities and preferred to go into Deepsleep, which would eventually extend his life by two days provided he beat the odds and lived to an old age. And as he explained, "If I didn't plan to live my full span of years, I wouldn't be in this business to begin with."

To which she thought, *The hell you wouldn't*—but had enough tact to keep her mouth shut, and after reading the opening chapters of an exceptionally unthrilling thriller she climbed into her own Deepsleep pod, awakening when the ship went into orbit around Innesfree II.

"Get up," said Dimitrios, who was already awake and alert.

"I'm starving!" said Matilda.

"Of course you are. You haven't eaten in two days. We'll eat when we land."

She climbed out of the pod, amazed at how stiff her joints could become in just two days.

"Any messages for me?" she asked.

"Yeah. The ballet doesn't need a prima ballerina, stripping is outlawed on Innesfree, but if you can dance the flamenco, whatever that is, there's a joint that can give you four days' work." He paused. "Four days is plenty. If Jacobs is here, I'll find him in less time than that."

"Okay, I'll take it."

"Don't tell *me*," said Dimitrios. "Send a message to *them*."

"I will," she said. "Give me a minute to wake up."

"All right," he said. "I've booked two rooms for us at a hotel in the center of what seems to pass for the planet's only city."

"Fine. I hope they have a restaurant."

"I hope Hootowl Jacobs is staying there."

"You act like it's a personal vendetta," said Matilda. "Have you ever met him?"

"No. He deserves to die; that's all I need to know."

"How many women has he killed?"

"Too many."

"You know," she said, "I could represent myself as a wealthy widow, or an heiress . . ."

"Forget it. There's a price on his head. We don't need to set him up."

"I thought it might draw him out."

"If he can find a wealthy widow on Innesfree before I find him, then it's time for me to retire."

"Do you even know what he looks like?" asked Matilda.

"Computer, show me Hootowl Jacobs," ordered Dimitrios.

Instantly a life-sized holographic image appeared. It was a man with bulging blue eyes, a widow's peak of brown hair, an aquiline nose, medium height, medium weight, dressed expensively.

"That's him," said Dimitrios.

"He's certainly distinctive," she said.

"If you mean easy to spot, yes, he is."

"I gather he's inherited a number of fortunes," said Matilda. "What the hell is a man with that kind of money doing on a little backwater world like Innesfree II?"

He shrugged. "Who cares? It's enough that he's here—*if* he is."

"If I were you, *I'd* care. He might have hired a small army."

"What for? He's never killed anyone but middle-aged women."

"Aren't you even curious?"

He shook his head. "Not a bit."

Santiago would be curious, she thought. *And cautious. He'd want to know what business Hootowl Jacobs had on this world. You're so intent on killing him that you're not even interested in what makes him tick, and yet that knowledge could be the advantage you need. I know, I know, all he kills are his wives, but you still should look for any edge you can get. This is life and death, after all.*

She began to appreciate the problem of finding Santiago. He was one tiny needle in the haystack of the Inner Frontier, and he probably had no idea of who and what he was to become. Just finding him could take a few lifetimes; convincing him to fulfill his destiny could take almost as long.

She was still considering her problems when the ship touched down. Shortly thereafter they passed through Customs—they had to purchase one-month visas for fifty credits apiece—and Dimitrios rented an aircar, which skimmed a foot above the ground and got them from the spaceport to the city in a matter of a few minutes.

"Here we are," said Dimitrios, deactivating the aircar. "The Shaka Zulu Hotel."

"Who or what was Shaka Zulu?" asked Matilda.

"Who knows? Probably some politician or poet." He paused. "Let's check it out before we unload our luggage."

The doors faded into nothingness as they approached the entrance, and a moment later a small, rotund purple alien was escorting them to their rooms. He stopped when he reached the end of the corridor. For a moment Matilda thought he had forgotten where to take them, but then Dimitrios flipped him a coin, which he caught in his mouth, and he toddled away.

"I'd have asked him if Jacobs was here, but I don't think he speaks Terran," said the bounty hunter.

"Why not ask at the front desk?"

"Clerks don't keep their jobs long if they reveal their guest lists to bounty hunters." He smiled. "Some of them don't live long, either."

She turned to the doors. "Which is mine?"

"Whichever you want. Just let it read your handprint and retina once, and it'll be programmed for you for the next four days."

"I don't know which one I want until I see them both."

"They're identical."

"Okay, this one is fine then," said Matilda, letting the security system scan her readings. The door dilated a moment later and she passed through it. "Not bad," she said. "Larger than I expected."

"Space isn't at a premium on Innesfree," remarked Dimitrios.

She walked back out into the corridor. "It'll do. Now I have to pop over to El Gran Señor and see about a job."

"I'll come with you," he said.

"Why don't you just stay here and relax? I'll be back in a few minutes."

"I didn't come here to rest."

They walked back to the front of the hotel, where Dimitrios brought their luggage in from the aircar and tossed another coin into another blue alien's mouth after telling him their room numbers.

"I hope he understood," she said as the walked out onto the street.

"They wouldn't let an alien hang around the lobby and collect tips if he couldn't."

They walked two blocks north to El Gran Señor. It was closed for the afternoon, but a doorman let them in. The interior was starkly decorated, with a bar in one corner, a number of tables with uncomfortable-looking chairs, and a small stage. A second, even smaller stage held a single stool, obviously for the guitarist.

"Good afternoon," said a balding, pudgy man with a reddish face. "My name's Manolete. You must be my new dancer."

"Matilda," she said, extending her hand.

"Got a last name?" he asked as he took her hand and shook it.

"Not lately," said Matilda with a smile.

"No problem. Just need something for our records."

"Pay me in cash and use any last name you like."

"Done." He turned to Dimitrios. "*You're* sure as hell no dancer," he said, staring at the bounty hunter's weaponry.

"Just looking for a friend," said Dimitrios.

"Well, I'm as friendly as they come," said Manolete. "What can I do for you?"

"You're not the friend I'm looking for," said Dimitrios. "I hear that Hootowl Jacobs is on Innesfree."

"Could be," said Manolete. "What do you want with him?"

"I'm his attorney, here to deliver an inheritance."

"I hear tell he's had his share of them."

Dimitrios nodded. "Poor fellow *does* seem unlucky," he agreed.

"Not as bad as his luck is now, Dimitrios of the Three Burners," said Manolete with a grin. "I've heard about you. They say you're one of the best."

"So is he on Innesfree?"

"He is."

Dimitrios stared coldly at Manolete. "You wouldn't be so silly as to warn him?"

"Me?" laughed Manolete. "Hell, no! I want you to take

him out right here in El Gran Señor! We can use the publicity. Maybe I'll even catch it on my holo cameras." He
outlined the entertainment with his hands. "Last show each
night. For an extra two hundred credits, watch the fabled
Dimitrios of the Three Burners take out that notorious ladykiller Hootowl Jacobs! Now, why the hell would I warn
him away?"

Dimitrios was silent for a long moment. Finally he
spoke: "Draw up a contract."

"A contract?" repeated Manolete. "What for?"

"*If* Hootowl Jacobs shows up here, and *if* I kill him, and
if you capture it on your holo cameras, and *if* you start
charging customers to watch it, then I want fifty percent of
the gross to go to these two charities." He wrote the names
down on a counter, then looked up. "Is it a deal?"

Manolete sighed. "Okay, I'll have a contract ready tonight."

"If I should ever find out that you were cheating my
charities," said Dimitrios, "I would be seriously displeased
with you. Do we understand each other?"

Manolete nodded, and Dimitrios turned and walked back
out into the street. The club owner turned to Matilda.

"Nice company you keep."

"We get along."

"I hope Jacobs kills *him*!" said Manolete passionately.
"Hootowl would never charge me half just for showing
holos of it." He paused. "Where does he get off, charging
me for showing holos of what happens in my own club?"

"It hasn't happened yet."

"It will."

"Probably," agreed Matilda. "Killing's *his* job. Mine is
dancing. Where's my costume?"

"In your dressing room," said Manolete, getting to his
feet. "Come on, I'll show you." He escorted her backstage.
"We haven't got time to teach you a number. I hope you
can improvise."

"I usually do."

"We've got a Borillian playing the guitar," continued Manolete.

"A Borillian?" she repeated. "Why?"

"It's a fourteen-string guitar, and he's got seven fingers on each hand. You won't believe the music he can make."

"As long as it's flamenco, we won't have a problem."

"Here we are," he said as they reached a small dressing room. "Usually we have two or three women backing up the lead male, but that asshole went and got himself shot last week."

"And the other women?"

He shrugged. "You know how women are."

"No," said Matilda. "How are we?"

"Easy come, easy go."

"Right," she said. "We're so flighty we don't hold still long enough to get shot like your male dancers."

He glared at her, but made no reply. She looked around the room, checked out the costumes to make sure they'd fit her, examined the vanity, and finally nodded. "All right, I've seen it. When do you need me?"

"We're pretty informal here. Show up after you've digested your dinner. You'll do three shows, maybe four." He paused. "Don't you want to try on the shoes?"

"I'll wear my own."

"They won't match."

"But they'll fit."

"You know," said Manolete, "you're as disagreeable as *he* is."

"I'm not here to be agreeable," said Matilda. "You wanted a dancer. You've got one."

"As long as you're hired, I'd better tell you the rules."

"There's only one rule," said Matilda. "No one enters my dressing room when I'm in it."

"There's no drinking, no drugging, no—"

"You'll get your money's worth," she said, walking to the exit. "I'll see you later."

Before he could say a word, she'd shut the door in his face and headed out to the street. Once she was outside she

looked around for Dimitrios, couldn't spot him, and walked
back to the hotel. She checked the bar before going to her
room, and saw him sitting there, the only customer in the
place in midafternoon, a tall cold drink on the table in front
of him.

"Don't drink too many of those," she said, sitting down
opposite him. "I've got a feeling Jacobs will show up tonight."

"There's no alcohol in it," he replied. "I don't indulge
when I'm working. You want one?"

"Sure. What is it?"

"I don't know what it's called. It's a mixture of three or
four citrus fruits native to Innesfree. Nice tang to it."

She signaled the bartender, yet another rotund blue alien.
"I'll have one of those," she said, pointing to Dimitrios'
glass.

"Yes, Missy," growled the alien.

"Are those creatures the original inhabitants of Innesfree?" she asked. "They seem to be omnipresent."

"Only in the hotel," answered Dimitrios. "They're native
to Halcyon II. The ones you see are indentured servants,
working off their debts."

"How do you know that?"

"I've been to Halcyon II, and I know the policy of the
corporation that owns this chain of hotels."

"And you put up with it?"

"It's not up to me," said Dimitrios. "They sign the papers, they work off their debts. It's the law."

"Didn't you ever want to break a bad law?"

"Lady, I represent the law out here. If you don't break
it, you'll never have a problem with me."

"And good or bad law, it makes no difference to you?"
she persisted.

"You're looking for Santiago," he said. "I've got my own
priorities."

"I know," said Matilda. The alien arrived with her drink,
set it down, and scuttled away. "Strange little beasts, aren't
they?"

"Not to a lady Halcyoni," said Dimitrios.

"Point taken." She sipped the drink. "It's very good."

"Most fruit drinks are," he said. "I don't know why, but the human body seems to metabolize alien fruits and vegetables easier than alien protein."

"Are you saying you're a vegetarian?"

"No, I like meat. But I try not to eat it on days that I'm likely to work. Wouldn't want to get stomach cramps or worse at the wrong time."

"You keep saying it so impersonally: 'days that I'm going to work.' "

"You can't humanize these bastards," answered Dimitrios. "You can't ever do anything that'll make you pause, or hesitate, or listen to a plea or an explanation or an excuse. They killed the innocent and the helpless; they have to die."

"Do you ever have second thoughts, or regrets?"

He shook his head. "I might have, about a man who killed another man in a fair fight. Or a man who robbed a bank and killed a guard who was trying to kill him. Or about you. But not about the men I go after."

"So you never feel remorse, or regret?"

"Only satisfaction." He paused. "Why do you care?"

She shrugged. "I don't know. I'm trying to make a list of traits I need to find in Santiago."

He laughed softly.

"What's so funny?" she asked.

"If you get close enough to ask 'em, he's probably not Santiago."

They spent the rest of the afternoon in the bar, sipping fruit drinks and waiting for night to fall. When it had been dark for more than an hour, she got up and made her way back to El Gran Señor.

"You're early," said Manolete. "I like that in a performer."

"Not much to do in this town," she replied.

"And I like *that* in a town," he said. "This is the only excitement there is." He paused. "We should be full all night long. Everyone knows Dimitrios of the Three Burners plans to kill Hootowl Jacobs here tonight."

"Just how many people did you tell?"

"Enough."

"If word reaches Jacobs, you'll be in for a disappointing evening."

"You don't know the Hootowl," said Manolete. "He doesn't back down from anything."

"I thought all he didn't back down from were middle-aged wives who trusted him."

"That's because you've been listening to Dimitrios."

She considered sending a warning to Dimitrios, then changed her mind. His rejection of her offer hadn't discouraged her, but failure to take Hootowl Jacobs would decide it once and for all: if he couldn't kill Jacobs, then he could never be Santiago.

She changed into her costume, put on her makeup, then sent for the Borillian guitarist. His name could not be pronounced by any human, so she decided to call him José. He seemed friendly enough, and spoke in tinkling chimes, which his T-pack translated into a dull monotone. After learning the extent of his repertoire, she felt confident that she could improvise to anything he chose to play.

She had some time to kill, so she left her dressing room and began wandering around the building, trying to acquaint herself with it. She found the staff's bathroom and kitchen, and a small room with a card table, then went out front. A few men and women were already sitting at tables, drinks in front of them, and a hologram of a quartet of guitarists was projected on the stage, with the music coming from everywhere, or so it seemed.

"You look good," said Manolete, approaching her.

"Thanks."

"I mean really good."

"I mean really thanks," she said.

"You know, maybe we could work a little something out here," he continued.

"I doubt it."

"It would mean more money for you."

"It'd mean a quick kick in the balls for you," said Matilda. "Are you sure you want to pay me extra for that?"

He glared at her. "Maybe I'll just turn you over to Hootowl."

"First, I'm not rich enough for him, and second, his life expectancy is probably about an hour."

"We'll see," said Manolete, walking off.

She walked over to the bar, introduced herself to the two bartenders, and sat on a stool for a while listening to the recorded music.

A few moments later a man with bulging blue eyes and a distinctive widow's peak entered and took a table in the farthest corner, his back to a wall, and she knew Jacobs had arrived. Before long the room was full and she went back to her dressing room, awaiting her signal to perform.

It came after another half hour, and shortly thereafter she was dancing to the music of José, her fourteen-fingered Borillian guitarist. He took it easy on her, building his speed and rhythm slowly until he saw that she could keep up with him.

She spun around as José reached the final few bars of his song, then stopped and bowed to mild applause. As she looked up, she saw that Dimitrios had entered the room and was walking calmly toward Hootowl Jacobs. She began stamping her feet and whirling around again, with no accompaniment, hoping to attract Jacobs' attention, to keep him looking toward the stage.

She dared a glance in his direction, and saw that he was indeed watching her. Then Dimitrios was next to him, placed a burner in his ear, and fired.

There was a shrill scream from a nearby table as Hootowl Jacobs pitched forward on the table, blood pouring out of his ear.

"There's no cause for alarm," said Dimitrios in a loud, clear voice. He held up a small titanium card. "I am a licensed bounty hunter. This man was wanted for a minimum of ten murders. I'm sorry to have disrupted your evening.

I'll have him out of here as soon as possible."

A man at a nearby table stood up.

"You didn't even give him a chance!"

"This is a business, not a sporting event," answered Dimitrios.

"But you just walked up to him and shot him!"

"He was wanted dead or alive. Given the crimes he had committed, I prefer dead."

"I wonder how good you are against someone who knows you're there and can fight back." The man pulled his jacket back, revealing a matched pair of screechers in his gunbelt.

"Well, friend," said Dimitrios, "I'm about to show you. Keep your hands away from those pistols."

Dimitrios whirled and fired three blasts into the upper corners of the room, and three holographic cameras melted.

"Do you still want to see how good I am against someone who knows I'm here?" asked Dimitrios.

The man held his hands out where everyone could see them and then sat down.

"Hey!" yelled Manolete, approaching the bounty hunter. "You destroyed three very expensive cameras."

"You didn't prepare the contract we discussed," said Dimitrios. "I told you I wouldn't let you make those holos if you didn't turn half over to the charities I named."

"You said I couldn't *show* them."

"Well, now you can't."

"I'm going to remember this!" promised Manolete.

"I hope so," said Dimitrios. "And the next time you promise a contract to someone, you'd better deliver it."

Some of the customers began leaving, giving Dimitrios a wide berth.

"Look at this!" growled Manolete. "Now all my clients are leaving! Get that body out of here!"

"You didn't mind that body when you thought you could rerun his death every night," said Dimitrios.

"Just get him out of here and don't come back!" yelled

Manolete. He turned to Matilda. "*You* get out of here too! You're fired!"

Matilda climbed down from the stage and approached Manolete. "Why are you firing me?" she asked.

"You're connected with *him*!" he said, jerking a thumb toward Dimitrios. "That's reason enough."

"Well," she said, "as it happens, I would have quit tonight anyway. He's going on to another world, and I'm going with him, so I don't mind being fired. But I mind your reason for it, and I mind your attitude."

"What are you going to do about it?" demanded Manolete pugnaciously.

"I'm going to give you a present."

He frowned in confusion. "What present?"

"Remember the trade we talked about earlier?" she said. Before he could react, she kicked him hard in the groin. He groaned and dropped to his knees. "You don't even have to pay me extra for that."

She turned her back on him and walked to the door, then waited for Dimitrios to sling the corpse over his shoulder and join her.

He summoned a robot car, loaded Jacobs into the back, and ordered it to take them to the spaceport.

"You know," she said, "that's just the way I think Santiago would dispatch an enemy."

He shook his head. "What I did was legal and moral. You've watched too many bad holodramas. I don't know how good Jacobs was with his weapons, so why give him a chance to prove he's better than me?" He paused. "Or take that man who got up and half-threatened me. It's easier to frighten him off with a display of marksmanship than kill him to prove a point."

"Yeah, I suppose so," she said.

"Don't look so depressed," he said. "I *told* you I'm not a candidate for the job. You ought to be pleased that I'm good at what I do, and that I'm willing to join your army."

"I am," she said. "But . . ."

"But what?"

She signed deeply. "But I still need to find a general."

"Finding him won't be so hard," replied Dimitrios. "Recruiting him will be the difficult part."

Which was as wrong a pair of predictions as he'd ever made.

12.

HE USED TO BE A LAWMAN, A MASTER OF
 HIS TOOLS;
HIS NAME WAS THE ROUGH RIDER, HIS GAME
 WAS KILLING FOOLS.
HE USED TO BE A HERO, BACKING UP HIS
 BOASTS—
BUT NOW HE LIVES A PRIVATE LIFE, HIDING
 FROM HIS GHOSTS.

HIS REAL NAME WAS WILSON Tchanga, and there was a
time when he was the most feared lawman on the Inner
Frontier.

They tell the story of the day he followed eight members
of the notorious Colabara Gang into a small warehouse on
Talos II, and less than a minute later he was the only living
soul in the building.

They talk about the evening he saved an entire Tradertown from Pedro the Giant, a nine-foot mutant who had
gone on a rampage with a laser pistol and was in the pro-
cess of burning the place down when Tchanga showed up
to stop him.

It was when he rode an alien steed halfway across Gal-
apagos V to hunt down an escaping killer that he picked
up the sobriquet of the Rough Rider, for the terrain was
positively brutal. Men envied him, women loved him, children worshipped him, and criminals all across the Frontier
feared him.

He never did become a bounty hunter, because he wasn't
in the game for the money. He believed that when you saw
Evil you stood up to it, and for twenty years he never
flinched, never backed down, never once worried about the
odds before he marched into battle, burners blazing,
screechers screaming.

And then one day Varese Sarabande, who was only twenty-six at the time, called him out, just like a cowboy in the Old West, and because he was the Rough Rider he stepped out into the street the way Doc Holliday or Johnny Ringo might have done a few millennia earlier. They went for their guns together, but Varese Sarabande was faster, and a moment later Tchanga lay writhing in the street, blood spurting from an artery in his neck.

They saved him—barely—but as he lay in the hospital recuperating, he finally came to the realization that he was mortal, and that whatever guardian angel had been protecting him over the years had taken up residence on some other lawman's shoulder. He was forty-three years old, and he had painful proof that he couldn't outgun a twenty-six-year-old outlaw like Sarabande. And he knew in his gut that he couldn't beat a strong young man—or woman—in any kind of a fair fight, with weapons or without.

His body, which had resisted age for so many years, suddenly felt decades older as he lay there. He was just a day from being released when a gang of three men burst into the hospital, shot two security guards, and began robbing the pharmacy of its narcotics. A young nurse suddenly entered his room, tossed him a burner, and told him what was happening.

He refused to leave his bed.

They almost had to pry him loose from the hospital the next morning. He resigned his job before noon, withdrew his savings—he didn't transfer them to another world, because he didn't want anyone to know where he was going—and left before the day was over.

He set up housekeeping under a new name on Bedrock II, but the Spartan Kid found out he was there and went gunning for him to pay him back for killing his father and two brothers.

He ran.

He wound up on Gingergreen II. No one knew who he was, no one bothered him, and he lived in total obscurity for three years. Then a thief tried to sneak into his house under cover of night, and he killed him. Shot him dead as he stood there, then shot him thirty or forty more times. And since he was using a burner, he inadvertently set the house on fire.

They saw the blaze and found him still firing into the charred, unrecognizable corpse. He went berserk when they tried to take his weapon away, threatened to kill them all, and finally collapsed as he was about to turn the burner upon himself.

He spent a year in an asylum, and when he came out he was fifty pounds lighter and his eyes were still haunted by visions that no one else could see. This time they knew who he was, but even the young toughs who wanted to make a reputation knew that they couldn't make one by killing this emaciated, fear-ridden old man, and so he was left to live out his years in a kind of peace.

The Rhymer heard about him and was touched by his story, and even though they never met, no one who knew Tchanga ever argued with the truth of the poem.

"So what makes this Rough Rider so special?" asked Matilda as Dimitrios directed their ship to Gingergreen II after dropping Jacobs off at the nearest bounty station. "The word I get is that he's lost his nerve."

"He was my hero when I was a kid."

"That was a long time ago."

"The qualities that made him a hero haven't changed," said Dimitrios.

"But other things have changed *him*," she said. "So why, of all the people you might have suggested, are we seeing the Rough Rider?"

"To give him a chance to save his soul."

"We're not in the salvation business," said Matilda.

"Really?" said Dimitrios wryly. "I thought Santiago was going to be the salvation of the Inner Frontier."

"You know what I mean."

"Yeah, I know."

"Then why him?"

"When I was a kid, I wanted to grow up to be the Rough

Rider," said Dimitrios. "A man who couldn't be bought off or scared off. A man who knew that the humanists are wrong, that there is good and there is evil, and both are abroad in the galaxy, and that someone had to confront evil and destroy it. You slept better knowing there were men like Wilson Tchanga."

She got to her feet and walked to the small galley. "I'm getting hungry. Do you want anything before we land?"

"Yeah, might as well," he said, joining her.

"I hope this Tchanga is everything you think he is."

"He was once."

"That's not much of a recommendation," said Matilda. She sighed. "I've never recruited a Santiago before. I don't know if I'm doing it right." She ordered beer and sandwiches for both of them. "I hope you've got the right man, but somehow I can't believe it's this easy."

"We'll know soon enough," said Dimitrios. "And don't forget, all but the first Santiago had an advantage ours won't have—a ready-made organization. Maybe they had to take it over, convince it, mold it to their needs, but it was there. Our man will have you, me, and the poet. That's not much of an army to stand against the Democracy."

"Then we'll get more."

"Where?"

She shrugged. "Where we got you."

"Bounty hunters?" he replied. "There aren't that many of us, and most bounty hunters don't have any reason to be unhappy with the Democracy."

"No, not bounty hunters," answered Matilda. "Just men and women who know the time has come for Santiago to walk among us again."

"When you describe him like that, he sounds bigger than life," noted Dimitrios.

"He is."

"That's a lot to ask of one man."

"Maybe that's why it's been a century since he last manifested himself."

"You make him sound like he's still alive."

"He is," said Matilda. "He's an idea—and it's harder to kill an idea than a man."

Dimitrios took a bite of his sandwich, then tossed the rest of it into the atomizer. "Next big one I bring in, I'm using the money to buy a ship with a better galley," he announced.

She stared at her sandwich. "It's not spoiled."

"No. It's just not good enough. Like most of your candidates for Santiago. They won't be evil, and they won't be stupid. They just won't be good enough."

"Well, *I* like it," she said, taking another bite.

"I hope you're choosier when it comes to Santiago."

"You worry about your Rough Rider; I'll worry about my decision."

"Fair enough."

They finished their beer and returned to the control cabin just as the ship went into an elliptical orbit around Gingergreen II. A moment later they received their landing coordinates from the sole spaceport, and shortly thereafter they were on the ground.

"So where do we find the Rough Rider?" asked Matilda when they had cleared Customs.

"I've got directions to his place," answered Dimitrios. "It's out in the country."

She looked around. "Except for maybe a square mile, the whole damned planet's out in the country."

"It's an agricultural world," said Dimitrios. "They grow food for seven nearby mining worlds."

"They don't need a whole world for that. Most of the mining's done by machine."

"Then they sell what's left to the Navy at rock-bottom prices . . . or maybe they just give it to them in exchange for being ignored."

"Ignored?" she repeated.

"At tax and conscription time."

"Were you ever in the Navy?"

"The Army."

"For how long?"

"Fifty-three days."

"And then what?" she persisted.

"And then I wasn't in the Army anymore," said Dimitrios, and for the first time since she'd known him, she felt a trace of fear.

She followed him in silence to a ground vehicle, and a moment later they were speeding out of the planet's only town, skimming a few inches above a dirt road that took them through blue-tinted fields of mutated corn. Finally, after about twenty miles, Dimitrios instructed the vehicle to take the shortest route to a location that consisted only of numbers, no words.

It turned onto a smaller, narrower road, bore right through two forks, and finally came to a halt before a small one-story home. Dimitrios and Matilda got out of the vehicle and approached the front porch.

"That's far enough!" said a voice from within the house. "Who are you?"

"I'm Dimitrios of the Three Burners," said the bounty hunter, holding his hands out where they could be seen. "This is Waltzin' Matilda, a dancer."

"What's your business here?"

"We want to talk to you."

"What about?"

"Why don't you invite us in and give us something to drink and we'll be happy to tell you," said Matilda.

"The man drops his burners where you stand," said the voice.

Dimitrios unfastened his holster and let it fall to the ground.

"And the one in your boot."

"Good eyes for an old man," said Dimitrios with a smile. He removed the third burner and placed it atop the other two.

"You got any weapons?"

"I just took them off," said Dimitrios.

"Not you. The lady."

"None," said Matilda.

"You'd better be telling the truth. You'll be scanned when you walk through the door, and I'll have the punisher set on near-lethal."

"Well, let me check and make sure," said Matilda. In quick order she found two knives and a miniature screecher and left them next to Dimitrios' pile of weapons. "I must have forgotten about them," she said with an uneasy smile.

"Can we come in now?" asked Dimitrios.

"Yes—and keep your hands where I can see them."

They obeyed his instructions, got past the scanner without incident, and found themselves in a small, modestly furnished living room. Standing against the far wall was a tall black man, his face ravaged by illness and inner demons, his body emaciated, a pulse gun in his right hand.

"Sit down," said Wilson Tchanga.

They sat on a couch, and he seated himself on a chair about fifteen feet away.

"Why don't you come a little closer?" suggested Matilda. "We're not here to harm you."

"I'll be the judge of that," said Tchanga. "Now talk."

"Do we call you Wilson, or Mr. Tchanga, or Rough Rider?" asked Dimitrios.

"You know who I am?" said Tchanga.

"Why else would we be on your doorstep?" said Dimitrios. "Before we begin, let me tell you that you've been my hero since I was old enough to *have* a hero. Meeting the Rough Rider is quite an honor, sir."

"I haven't been the Rough Rider in a long, long time."

"You're my hero just the same."

Tchanga stared at him, his face expressionless, for a long moment. "What did you say your name was?" he said at last.

"Dimitrios of the Three Burners."

"Lawman?"

"Bounty hunter."

"I suppose you have your reasons."

Dimitrios nodded his head. "Valid ones."

Tchanga turned to Matilda. "And you are?"

"Matilda."

"Got a last name?"

"Got a couple of dozen of them," she said.

He smiled. "*You're* no lawman or bounty hunter."

"No, sir, I'm not."

"All right, now we know who we are," said Tchanga. "Why have you sought me out?"

"I want to see if you're the man I'm looking for," said Matilda.

"If you're looking for Wilson Tchanga, I'm him." He smiled grimly. "If you're looking for the Rough Rider, I used to be him."

She shook her head. "I'm looking for Santiago."

He stared at her curiously. "Santiago's been dead for a century or more—if he ever really existed in the first place."

"He was my great-great-grandfather," said Matilda.

"I know I've aged," said Tchanga, "but do I look like anyone's great-great-grandfather?"

"No," interjected Dimitrios. "But you might look like Santiago."

Tchanga frowned. "I think I'm missing something here."

"Santiago is more than a name or a person," continued Dimitrios. "It's an idea, a concept, maybe even a job description. And the job has been open for a century. We're looking for someone to fill it."

"He was the King of the Outlaws," said Tchanga. "I was an honest lawman. I may not be much these days, but I'm still honest."

"We wouldn't be speaking to you if you weren't," said Dimitrios.

"Then I'm still missing something."

"You're missing a lot," said Matilda. "Sit back, relax, and make yourself comfortable, because I'm going to spend an hour or more filling you in."

Dimitrios studied Tchanga intently as Matilda explained who and what Santiago really was, what he had done, how he had hidden his true purpose from the Democracy, and why the string of Santiagos had ended the day the Navy "pacified" Safe Harbor.

"It's time to call him forth again," concluded Matilda. "The time is ripe for him to return. The Democracy is abusing and plundering the Inner Frontier again, colonists have almost no rights, aliens have even less. The Navy goes where it wants and takes what it wants. It protects us from a hostile galaxy, but there's no one to protect us from *it*."

There was a long silence. Finally Tchanga spoke.

"I'm more honored than you can imagine that you came to me. But I'm a used-up old man whose time is past. I'm no hero, no leader of men. I'm still holding a pulse gun, but if either of you made a sudden motion, I'd be more likely to duck than to fire it." He paused. "There was a time when I might have been the man you seek, but that time is long gone."

"You don't have to be a hero," said Dimitrios. "There's no holograph or video of Santiago anywhere in the Democracy's records. *He* didn't go out on raids, or face Democracy soldiers himself. He ordered his men to do those things."

Tchanga shook his head. "That may be so, but he *might* have gone with them from time to time. He *could* have. I can't. And I can't order men to do things I myself won't do."

"Generals don't fight in the front lines," said Dimitrios.

"They also don't run and hide when the shooting starts," replied Tchanga. "You need a Santiago who commands respect, and I am no longer that man. I wonder if I ever was."

"You were," said Dimitrios with certainty. "And you can be again. You can redeem your life and your reputation through the single act of becoming Santiago."

"I appreciate your words," said Tchanga, "but Santiago is too big. He blots out the stars. The ground trembles when he walks. He does not exist for me to redeem myself. You belittle him by suggesting that."

Dimitrios turned to Matilda. "Aren't you going to say anything?"

"What is there to say?" she replied. "I agree with him."

"Perhaps Santiago isn't a man at all," suggested Tchanga. "Perhaps Santiago is a woman."

"It's possible," she agreed. "But not *this* woman. I'm just someone who needs a little more protection from the Democracy than I've been getting."

"I hope you find your Santiago and get your protection," said Tchanga. He got to his feet and walked to the door. "You'd better be going. If he's as hard to find as I think he'll be, you haven't any time to waste."

They arose and walked out the door.

Dimitrios pointed to the pulse gun. "Is that thing even charged?"

Tchanga looked out across the vast field of mutated corn. "You see that scarecrow?"

Dimitrios squinted into the distance. "That one about five hundred yards off to the left?"

Tchanga nodded. "That's the one." In a single motion the old man spun, aimed his pulse gun, and fired. The scarecrow burst into a ball of flame.

"My God!" exclaimed Dimitrios. "That was more than a quarter mile away! I couldn't do that on the best day I ever had!" He turned to the old man. "Can you hit it every time?"

"Just about," said Tchanga. He paused, and a look of infinite sadness crossed his face. "Unless I thought it might fire back at me."

"Jesus!" said Dimitrios as he and Matilda walked toward their vehicle. "What he must have been as a young man!"

"He still is."

Dimitrios shook his head. "No. Like he said, he's all used up."

"Don't look so sad for him," she said. "He'll be all right."

"I was feeling sad for *me*, not for him," Dimitrios corrected her.

"For *you*? Why?"

"Because that's my fate, probably the fate of every

bounty hunter, if we live long enough." He paused. "I hope I don't."

"Don't what?"

"Live long enough."

They reached their vehicle, and neither of them saw the tear that rolled down the Rough Rider's withered face as he tried unsuccessfully to remember what it felt like to face an armed man with no more fear than he felt when facing a scarecrow.

13.

ALIEN FACE AND ALIEN WAYS,
ALIEN THOUGHTS AND TRIBAL LAYS.
ALIEN APPETITES, STRANGE AND COLD,
BLUE PETER'S SINS ARE MANIFOLD.

THE RHYMER ACTUALLY MET BLUE Peter before Matilda did.

He was on Bowman 17, which was actually the third planet circling its star but the seventeenth opened up by a member of the Pioneer Corps named Nate Bowman, who exercised his Pioneer's privilege of naming it after himself. It was an outpost world, with a single Tradertown consisting of a bar, a brothel, a weapon shop, an assay office, and a jail. That last was unusual for any Frontier world, especially one as underpopulated as Bowman 17.

Dante Alighieri was sitting in the bar, relaxing with a drink, when Virgil Soaring Hawk approached him and asked for a loan.

"What for?" replied Dante. "There's nothing to spend it on."

"I have to make a friend's bail."

"You've got a friend locked up on Bowman 17?"

"Yes."

"Who is it?"

"He's more of a what than a who," answered Virgil.

"Worth a verse?" queried Dante, suddenly interested.

"Maybe two or three."

"Santiago material?"

Virgil chuckled. "Not unless the job description has changed in the last couple of minutes."

"All right," said Dante. "Tell me about him."

"You ever hear of Blue Peter?"

"No."

"He an alien," said Virgil. "I have no idea where his home world is. He's the only member of his race I've ever met."

"He's blue?"

"Skin, hair, eyes, teeth, probably even his tongue."

"How did you meet him?"

"It'll just embarrass you," said Virgil.

"Jesus!" muttered Dante. "Is there anyone on the Frontier that you *haven't* slept with?"

"You."

"Thank heaven for small favors." Dante finished his drink and lit up a smokeless cigar. "What's your friend in jail for?"

"Unspecified crimes against Nature," answered Virgil.

"What does he do when he's not assaulting Nature?"

"You mean for a living?"

"He's got to pay to feed himself, and to get from one world to another. How does he make his money?"

"He does whatever anyone pays him to do."

"Outside of being a rather twisted gigolo, what does that entail?"

"Robbery. Extortion. Murder. Things like that."

"Sounds to me like he's right where he belongs," said Dante.

"You won't loan me the money?"

Dante shook his head. "We have no use for him."

"*I* do."

"I don't want to hear about the use you'll put him to."

"You really mean it."

"I really mean it."

Suddenly Virgil smiled and picked up a chair. "Well, if you can't bring Mohammed to the mountain . . ."

He hurled the chair through a window, then threw two more out into the street before the Tradertown's solitary lawman came over from the jail, trained a screecher on him, and escorted him to the jail. Dante had seen Virgil in action before, and never doubted for an instant that the Injun could disarm the lawman any time he wanted—but of course he didn't want to.

Dante made a very happy Virgil's bail the next morning, spent a few minutes visiting with Blue Peter, and left the jail feeling uncomfortable that something like Blue Peter would soon be free. He wrote the poem that afternoon, and didn't see Blue Peter again.

But Matilda did.

It was on Gandhi III, which wasn't as peaceable a world as its name implied. Dimitrios was there on business—another ladykiller with a price on his head—and Matilda had accompanied him. She had no reason to be there . . . but then, she had no reason to be anywhere in particular. She was looking for a perhaps nonexistent man who embodied a complex concept, and there was no more reason to search for him anywhere else than here, and at least here she was under the protection of Dimitrios of the Three Burners.

Dimitrios spent the day gathering information about Mikhail Mikva, the man he was after, while Matilda stayed in her room watching the holo and catching up on the galaxy's news. The Democracy had opened up nineteen new worlds. The Navy had been forced to pacify the native population of Wajima II, which had been renamed Grundheidt II after the commander of the Sixth Fleet. Contact had been made with four new species of sentient life; three had joined the Democracy, and the fourth was learning just how effective a quadrant-wide economic embargo could be. The Democracy had moved the planetary populations of Kubalic IV and V and their attendant flora and fauna to new worlds before the star Kubalic went nova. Lodin XI had voted to withdraw from the Democracy, but its resignation had not been accepted and the Fifteenth Fleet was on its way to Lodin to "peacefully discuss our differences." Five new cross-species diseases had been discovered; medical science announced that they would have vaccines and antidotes for all five within one hundred days.

She deactivated the holo at twilight, wondering why she ever bothered with the news. All it did was reinforce her decision never to visit the Democracy again.

The door opened and Dimitrios entered.

"Any luck?" she asked.

"If he's here, he's well disguised. No one's seen him."

"Could they be lying to you?"

He stared at her.

"No, of course not," she said. She got to her feet. "Shall we go out for dinner?"

"Yeah. I won't start searching the bars and drug dens for another couple of hours."

They left the hotel and went to one of the small city's half-dozen restaurants, one that advertised real meat rather than soya products (though it didn't say what kind of animals supplied the meat).

They had sat down, ordered, and begun chatting about the news from the Democracy when they became aware of a blue alien standing outside and staring at them through the window.

"You'd think he'd never seen a Man before," grumbled Dimitrios when the alien kept watching them.

"That can't be it," said Matilda. "There are thousands of Men on Gandhi."

"Then what's his problem?"

"I think he's about to tell you," replied Matilda as the alien suddenly walked to the door of the restaurant, entered, and began approaching their table.

The blue alien stopped a few feet from them.

"May I join you?" he asked.

"Do you know Mikhail Mikva's whereabouts?" asked Dimitrios.

"No."

"Then no, you may not join us."

"But you *are* Dimitrios of the Three Burners, are you not?"

Dimitrios stared at him. "What's it to you?"

"We are in the same poem."

"Do you know the Rhymer?" asked Matilda suddenly.

"I know Dante Alighieri, who calls himself the Rhymer. It is he who put me in his poem."

"Sit down," said Matilda, ignoring Dimitrios' obvious annoyance.

The alien pulled up a chair and sat on it.

"Who are you?" asked Matilda.

"My name when I walk among Men is Blue Peter. And who are you?"

"My name is Matilda."

Blue Peter stared at her. "Waltzin' Matilda?"

"Sometimes."

"How very interesting that three of us from what is, after all, an obscure little poem so new almost no one has encountered it should find ourselves on the same planet."

"Dimitrios is here on business. May I ask why *you* are here?"

"I was requested to leave Bowman 17, and since most of your spaceliners will not carry non-Men, I booked passage on a cargo ship. This was as far as my money took me."

"So you're stuck here?" asked Matilda.

"Until I obtain more money."

"How will you do that?"

"There are ways," said Blue Peter. He turned to Dimitrios. "I am pleased to make your acquaintance."

Dimitrios stared at the alien with an expression of distaste, then got to his feet. He turned to Matilda. "I'm going back to the hotel for a couple of hours before I make my rounds."

He walked out of the restaurant.

"He does not like me," said Blue Peter.

"He doesn't like most aliens."

"He has much in common with the rest of your race."

There was a momentary silence.

"I hope you're not waiting for me to apologize for him," said Matilda at last.

"No. I am wondering why you are here, since none of the establishments has advertised the presence of a dancer."

She looked at him, then shrugged. "What the hell, why not tell you? I'm looking for someone."

"You have become a bounty hunter too?"

She shook her head. "No."

"Who do you seek?"

"I don't know."

Blue Peter stared at her expressionlessly, his deep blue alien eyes unblinking. "That *does* make it harder," he said.

"You've seen many men on the Frontier," she began.

"That is true."

"Which of them is the most dangerous?"

"I am not sure I understand," said Blue Peter.

"The most deadly. The one man you would fear to fight more than any other."

"I fear to fight all men," said Blue Peter with an obvious lack of sincerity. "I fear Dimitrios. I fear Tyrannosaur Bailey. I fear Trader Hawke. I fear Mongaso Taylor. I fear Jimmy the Nail."

She sighed deeply. "Forget it. I'm sorry I asked."

"I fear the Plymouth Rocker. I fear Deuteronomy Priest."

"You can stop now," said Matilda.

"But above all others," continued Blue Peter, "I fear the One-Armed Bandit."

"Oh?"

"Yes. He is the most terrifying of all Men."

"Why do you think so?"

"Because he is the deadliest."

"Tell me about him."

"I just did," said Blue Peter.

"Do you know where he is?"

"I know where he is when he is not elsewhere."

She frowned. "You mean his headquarters—his home planet?"

"His headquarters," agreed Blue Peter. "I do not think anyone except the One-Armed Bandit himself knows his home planet."

"And of all the men and women you've seen on the Inner Frontier, you consider him the most dangerous?"

"Yes."

"Even more dangerous than Dimitrios?"

"There is no comparison. If Dimitrios is your friend, pray that he never has to face the One-Armed Bandit in combat."

"He sounds interesting," said Matilda.

"He is deadly."

"The man I'm looking for must be deadly."

"You are already traveling with a deadly man," noted Blue Peter.

"Still, I'd like to meet this One-Armed Bandit."

"I will give you the location of his headquarters," said the alien. "I will not accompany you there. He has promised to kill me the next time he sees me."

"Why?"

"I did something to Galpos that he disapproved of."

"Galpos? Who's he?"

"Galpos is a world," said Blue Peter. "Or, rather, it was."

She stared at expressionless alien and decided she didn't want to know the details. "Where can I find him?"

"If he is not elsewhere, he will be on Heliopolis II."

"Thank you, Blue Peter. Can I buy you a drink?"

"My metabolism cannot cope with human intoxicants." He got to his feet. "There is a tavern that caters to non-Men. I was on my way there when I recognized Dimitrios of the Three Burners."

"I'm sorry you have to go alone," said Matilda.

"I will not be alone for long," Blue Peter assured her.

He stood up and walked to the door. Matilda was about to follow him out when she realized that she'd been left with the check. She placed her thumb on the table's computer, waited for it to okay her credit and transfer payment, and then returned to the hotel.

Dimitrios was sitting in the lobby when she arrived. She walked over and stood in front of him.

"What did the little blue bastard want?" asked the bounty hunter.

"He just wanted to meet us," she replied. "He's all alone here."

"Don't go feeling too sorry for him. He was kicked off Bowman 17, in case that got by you."

"I know." She paused.

"And he had two, maybe three, screechers hidden under that baggy outfit he was wearing."

"I know. I spotted them all."

"Five'll get you ten there's a price on his head."

"Probably," agreed Matilda. She paused. "What if you don't find Mikva tonight?"

He shrugged. "There are four more cities on Gandhi III. I'll check them out, one by one."

"That could take a while."

"I've got plenty of time."

"I don't."

Dimitrios looked up at her curiously. "What are you getting at?"

"I'm leaving here first thing in the morning," answered Matilda.

"Where to?"

"Heliopolis II."

"That's a couple of hundred light-years away—and you came here in my ship," he noted. "Just how do you plan to get to the Heliopolis system?"

"I'll get as close as a spaceliner will take me, which is probably the mining colony on Gregson VI."

"And then?"

"Then I'll rent or charter a small ship," said Matilda.

"You think you've found a candidate?"

"I've found one worth looking at."

"Care to tell me who it is?"

"The One-Armed Bandit."

"Yeah, I figured you'd go out after him sooner or later," said Dimitrios.

"Do you care to tell me anything about him?"

"I never met him. But they say he's formidable."

"So I hear."

"Well, as soon as I find Mikva, I'll hook up with you again."

"I'll look forward to it," she said, knowing full well that even if he found the man he was hunting for, some new ladykiller would take precedence over his joining her on Heliopolis.

Still, it didn't really matter. The Frontier needed a Santiago more than she needed a traveling companion. Maybe this would be the one.

14.

HELIOPOLIS IS ITS NAME;
DEATH AND MAYHEM IS ITS FAME.
DEATH OF HOPE AND DEATH OF DREAMS,
DEATH OF MEN AND ALL THEIR SCHEMES.

THAT VERSE WAS TRUE A thousand years before the first man set foot on Heliopolis II. It was true when Matilda arrived there. It was true when Dante Alighieri visited the place. It would be true a thousand years after both were dead. That's the kind of world it was.

To begin with, it was hot. The daytime temperature often reached 135 degrees Fahrenheit. At night it cooled done to a bone-melting 100.

It was heavy. At 1.18 Galactic Standard gravity, it meant you felt like you were carrying an extra eighteen pounds for every hundred pounds of actual body weight.

It was thin. The oxygen content was eighty-seven percent of Galactic Standard. Even strong, fit men often found themselves gasping for breath, especially after exerting themselves in the Heliopolis II gravity.

It was dusty. The wind whipped across the barren surface of the planet, causing dust devils to rise hundreds of feet high as they swept through human and alien cities alike.

It was dry. Oh, there was *some* water, but hardly enough for the planetary populace. The natives made do with what was there; a water ship landed twice a week to make sure that the Men didn't run out of the precious stuff.

It was hostile. The native inhabitants, a humanoid race known as the Unicorns, doubtless owing to the single rudimentary horn that grew out of each forehead, didn't like each other very much, and they liked Men even less. Almost everything Men did seemed to give offense, and no matter how often they lost their battles against the humans, they never tired of regrouping and fighting again.

So why did Men risk their lives and sacrifice their comfort to stay on Heliopolis II?

Simple. It possessed two of the most productive diamond pipes in the galaxy. The diamonds couldn't be mined with water, of course, not on Heliopolis II, but they could be separated from the rocks in which they were embedded by carefully focused bursts of ultrasound. It was a delicate operation: not enough strength in the bursts and nothing was accomplished, too much and even the diamonds could be shattered.

It never occurred to the miners that the ultrasound, which was beyond human hearing, might be what was driving the Unicorns to such violent states of aggravation—and, in truth, it probably wasn't, since they were a violent sort even before Men began mining. Probably the ultrasound merely served to remind them that Men were still working on the planet, and that knowledge was more than enough to work them into a killing frenzy every few weeks.

Matilda hadn't spent as much as five minutes researching Heliopolis II before she decided to rent a ship. It was more expensive than chartering one, but at least she would have the comforting knowledge that the ship was there if she needed to leave in a hurry.

As she approached the planet, she wondered why the One-Armed Bandit was there. Was he there to rob the mines? Well, if he was, she had no serious problem with that. The Democracy owned the mines, which meant he'd be robbing the Democracy, just as Santiago had done so many times more than a century ago.

Of course, if he was there to rob the mines, he'd probably accomplished his mission already and gone on to some other world. After all, her information wasn't current; all she knew was that he'd been on Heliopolis II six days ago.

On the other hand, the mines could be so well guarded that he was still casing the job, still studying the opposition. If that was the situation, she'd have a chance to see how he performed against overwhelming odds.

She was still considering all the possibilities when her ship touched down and she approached the robot Customs officer.

"Name?" asked the machine.

"Matilda."

"Last name?"

"No."

"Matilda No, may I please scan your passport?"

She held her titanium passport disk up to its single glowing eye.

"Your passport is in proper order, but your name is not Matilda No. Please step forward so that I may scan your retina."

She stepped forward and looked into its eye.

"Thank you," said the robot. A swordlike finger shot out, and its needle-thin extremity touched her passport. There was a brief buzzing sound. "I have given you a five-day visa. If you plan to stay longer, you will have to go to the Democracy consulate and have it renewed."

"Thank you," said Matilda, starting to step forward. The robot moved to its left, blocking her way.

"I am not finished," it said, and she could have sworn she detected a touch of petulance in its mechanical voice. "The world of Heliopolis II accepts Democracy credits, Far London pounds, New Punjab rupees, and Maria Theresa dollars. There is a currency exchange just behind me that can convert eighty-three different currencies into credits."

"I have credits and Maria Theresa dollars," replied Matilda.

"You will almost certainly be using personal credit for your larger expenses," continued the robot. "The machines at all the commercial ventures on Heliopolis II are tied in to the Bank of Deluros VIII, the Bank of Spica, the Roosevelt III Trust, and the Far London Federated Savings Bank. If you have not established credit with one of these banks through their thousands of planetary branches, you will be required to spend actual currency. Should you try to leave Heliopolis II without settling all your bills, your ship will be impounded and you will be detained by the military police until a satisfactory settlement has been arranged."

"Is that all?" asked Matilda.

"No," said the machine. "Will you require adrenaline injections while you are here?"

"No," she said. "At least, I don't think so."

"Do you wish to have your blood oxygenated?"

"No."

"Will you require intravenous injection of fluids?"

"No."

"Should you change your mind, all of these services are available, for a nominal fee, at the military infirmary. I am required to warn you that Heliopolis II, while habitable, is considered inhospitable to the race of Man."

She waited for the robot to continue, but it fell silent and moved back to its original position.

"Is there anything else?" she asked after a minute had passed.

"I am finished."

"What do I do now?"

"Pass through the disease scanner just beyond my booth, and then arrange for your accommodation."

"I'd rather go into the city first and see what's there."

"You will not want to walk from one hostelry to another. You can examine three-hundred-and-sixty-degree holographs of all of them right here in the spaceport. Then you will hire a vehicle, enter it, instruct the governing computer where to take you, and emerge only after the vehicle is inside the climate-controlled hostelry. After that you are free to do whatever you wish, but I am programmed to warn you not to go outside unless it is essential."

"Thanks."

She walked to the disease scanner, passed through it without incident, checked the holograms of the human city's seven hotels and chose one called the Tamerlaine, then walked to a row of vehicles. The first in line opened its doors as she approached. Once she was seated it slid the doors shut, asked her if she was the woman who had booked her room at the Tamerlaine, and then raced forward. Just as she was sure it was going to crash into a wall the entrance irised just long enough to let the vehicle through, then snapped shut behind her.

They sped across the dry, dusty, reddish, featureless countryside. As they circled a small hill a heavy rock, obviously thrown, probably by an irate native, crashed down on the windshield and bounced off without leaving a mark. She suspected that nothing short of a pulse gun could put a dent in the vehicle, and relaxed during the rest of the ten-minute trip. The vehicle approached the Tamerlaine, and just as at the airport, the wall spread apart at the last instant to let it enter, then shut tightly behind it.

She emerged into the cool, dry air of the Tamerlaine's garage, instructed a liveried robot to carry her luggage to the front desk, then fell into step behind it. She found the gravity oppressive, but manageable.

The reception clerk was ready for her. He'd already run a credit check through the spaceport, and had assigned her a room overlooking the garden behind the hotel.

"Have my bags put in my room," said Matilda. "I'm going to take a look around first."

"Outside?" said the clerk. "I wouldn't advise it."

"I won't be long," she assured him.

She walked to the elegantly designed airlock that passed for the front entrance, and found she couldn't get the outer door to open until the door behind her had sealed itself shut.

Two steps outside the door she knew why. The heat was oppressive, the air almost unbreathable. Her dancing had kept her in excellent shape, but she found herself panting before she'd walked thirty paces. The air was as thin as mountain air at three thousand meters, the heat was like an oven, and the gravity pulled fiercely at her.

Still, while Heliopolis II was horribly uncomfortable, it wasn't deadly. After all, she told herself, men worked here every day. (Between the conditions and the Unicorns, she hoped they were getting hazard pay.)

She decided to continue her tour of the small city while she was still relatively fresh, turned a corner—and found out what a Unicorn looked like close up.

There were eight of the creatures walking in her direction. Each stood about seven feet tall, though they were so stocky and muscular that they looked shorter. Their arms were jointed in odd places, but bulged with muscles. Their thighs were massive, as they would have to be on beings that had evolved in this gravity. Their heads were not quite humanoid, not quite equine, ellipsoid in shape, each with a rudimentary horn growing out of the forehead. They didn't wear much clothing, but they were loaded down with weapons: pistols, swords, daggers, a few that she'd never seen before but that looked quite formidable.

She stepped aside to let them pass. They paid her no attention—until one of them brushed against her shoulder as he walked by. He immediately halted and spoke harshly to her in his native tongue.

"I can't understand you," said Matilda.

He said something else, louder this time.

"I left my T-pack at my hotel," she replied. "Do any of you have a Terran T-pack?"

Suddenly the other Unicorns joined the one that was yelling at her. Three of them began talking at once.

She pointed to her ear, then shook her head, to show she couldn't understand what they were saying.

This seemed to anger them. One of them approached her ominously, growling something in his own tongue. When she made no response, he reached out and shoved her. She gave ground, barely keeping her balance in the unfamiliar gravity.

She looked up and down the street. There were no Men in sight.

Another alien pushed her.

This is ridiculous. I'm going to die on this godforsaken

*world, not because I'm a thief with a price on her head,
but because I left my T-pack in my room.*

They formed a semicircle around her and began approaching her again—

—and suddenly a man she hadn't realized was there
stepped forward and stood in front of her, pushing her gently behind him.

"Stand still, ma'am," he said.

"It's all a misunderstanding," said Matilda. "I left my T-
pack in my room, and they don't understand me."

"They understand every word you're saying," said the
man. "Please step back a couple of feet. If they charge, I
may not be able to hold my ground." He looked at the
Unicorns. "But I'll kill the first three or four of you who
try."

Matilda noticed that the man was unarmed.

*Great! I'm being attacked by aliens and protected by a
lunatic.*

"You've had your fun," said the man. "Now get the hell
out of here."

The Unicorns didn't move—but three other Unicorns,
seeing the tense little scene, came over to join their breth-
ren.

"What will you do now?" grated one of the Unicorns in
a guttural Terran.

"We will kill both of you!" growled another.

"And when we are through, we will find more Men to
kill."

"No you won't," said the man, never raising his voice.
"You'll disperse right now, or the survivors will wish you
had."

"Death to all Men!" screamed one of the new arrivals.

"Don't let them frighten you, ma'am," said the man
softly. "If you're carrying a weapon, don't let them see it.
It's better that they concentrate on me."

*I have no problem with that. But what am I going to do
after they kill you?*

"Move to the right, ma'am," he continued without ever

taking his eyes off the Unicorns. "The one on the left looks the most aggressive. He'll be the first to charge."

And almost as the words left the man's mouth, the Unicorn on the far left, the one who had initially yelled at Matilda, launched himself at the man.

The man pointed a finger at the Unicorn—and suddenly the Unicorn literally melted in midcharge. The other Unicorns began screaming, and two more charged. The man pointed again; this time energy pulses shot out of his hand, embedding themselves in the Unicorns' chests.

Then the man was striding among them. Two fell to sledgehammer blows, another to a karate kick. He simply pointed to all but one of the remainder and fried them instantly.

He walked up to the last Unicorn, planted his feet firmly, and looked into the creature's eyes.

"I'm letting you live," he announced. "Go tell your friends that this lady is under my protection. To offend or threaten her is to offend or threaten me, and you saw what happens when you offend or threaten me." He paused. "Nod if you understand."

The Unicorn nodded.

"Now go back to your people and give them my message."

The Unicorn literally ran down the street and disappeared around a corner, as the man turned back to Matilda.

"Are you all right, ma'am?" he asked solicitously.

"I'm fine," she said. "You were awesome!"

"All in a day's work, ma'am," he replied.

"My name's Matilda," she said, extending her hand. "I want to thank you for saving my life."

He took her hand and shook it. "I'm glad I was here to do it." He gestured to the restaurant behind her. "I saw them harassing you from in there. By the way, my name's—"

"I know who you are," she said. "The One-Armed Bandit."

He smiled. "You're well informed, ma'am."

"What should I call you?"

"I've got more names than I can remember," he said. "Why not just call me Bandit and be done with it?"

"I'll be happy to." She stared at him. "That's some set of arms you have!"

He flexed his right arm. "This one's real." He tapped his left arm with the fingers of his right hand; it made a drumming sound. "This one's the fake. I lost the original arm in the war against the Sett."

" 'Fake' is a feeble word for it," enthused Matilda. "It's the most impressive weapon I've seen! What can it do?"

"I don't like to talk about it," he said uncomfortably. "Most people think I'm some kind of freak."

"Not me," Matilda assured him. "And I do have a reason for asking."

He shrugged. "All right, ma'am," he said. "Depending on how I manipulate my wrist and fingers, it can be a burner, a pulse gun, a screecher, or—if I'm carrying the proper munitions—even a laser cannon."

"Amazing!" she said. "And you act as if the heat and gravity don't even affect you!"

"Oh, I feel 'em, ma'am," he said with a smile. "I just don't like to let *them* know it."

She looked at the bodies littering the street. "I'm surprised the law hasn't shown up yet."

"They don't have any reason to," said the Bandit. "Someone'll be along presently to do a body count and dispose of them."

"A body count?"

He nodded. "It's really quite oppressive out here, ma'am," he said. "You may not be aware of it, but I can see that you're gasping for air and having trouble swallowing. Let's go back into the restaurant and get you something cold to drink."

"Yes," said Matilda, suddenly dizzy. "I think that would be a good idea."

She turned to open the door and found herself falling. The Bandit caught her in his arms, set her back on her feet, and escorted her into the restaurant.

"Ah, that's much better!" she breathed as they sat at a table. Not only was the temperature comfortable, but she could tell that the oxygen content of the air had been increased.

"Your eyes look like they're focusing again," he noted.

"Yes, they are." A robot waiter brought two glasses of water to the table. She took one, soaked her napkin in it, dabbed her face and neck, and then took a sip of what was left. "Aren't you having any?"

"I'll get around to it," the Bandit assured her. "Right now I'm more concerned with you."

"I'll be fine."

"I don't know how long you plan to stay on Heliopolis II, ma'am," he said, "but if I were you I'd be very careful about going outside until I'd adjusted to the air and the heat."

"And the gravity," she added. "Am I that obvious a newcomer?"

He smiled. "I'd remember anyone as pretty as you."

She returned his smile, then took another sip of water. She could almost feel the precious liquid spread through her body. Finally, when she felt certain that she wasn't going to black out again, she looked across the table at the Bandit.

"You mentioned something about a body count?" she said.

He jerked a thumb out the window, where a pair of robots were picking up each Unicorn corpse and placing it carefully on a gravity sled. "They'll report it to the authorities."

"And then what?"

"And then I'll get paid."

"They pay you to kill the native inhabitants of Heliopolis II?" she asked, far more curious than shocked or outraged.

"A diamond for every Unicorn," said the Bandit.

She let out a low whistle. "You must have quite a pile of diamonds."

"A few."

"Why don't you just turn your laser cannon on their cities, or wherever it is that they live?"

"I don't believe in genocide," he answered. "I'll protect the men who work the mines, and I'll keep the streets safe, but I'm not going to wipe out an entire race, not even for diamonds."

All good answers so far. You have the greatest arsenal on the Frontier, you don't believe in genocide, you even protect damsels in distress. Maybe, just maybe, you could be Him.

"Why are you called the One-Armed Bandit?" she asked. "I understand the One-Armed, but why the Bandit?"

"It was a term for a type of gambling machine. A few people still use it."

"So are you a gambler?"

"No. I work too hard for my money to lose it at a gaming table."

"Then are you a bandit?"

"I won't lie, ma'am. I've been a bandit in the past. I may be one again in the future. But I've never robbed anyone who came by their money honestly. At least, I've tried not to."

Better and better. You're willing to be an outlaw under the right circumstances.

"And," he continued, "sometimes it's just practical. I'd have no moral qualms about robbing the diamond mines here, given all the abuses the Democracy has committed."

"Then why don't you?" she interrupted.

He smiled guiltily. "I wouldn't know how to find a diamond in a mine, or how to extract one. And why should I want the Democracy after me when it's so easy to let them pay me for killing Unicorns?"

"Your logic is unassailable," agreed Matilda. She paused. "How long is your contract for?"

"Contract?"

"For, how shall I phrase it, policing the planet?"

"I can leave whenever I want," he answered. "As a matter of fact, I was thinking of leaving in the next week or two. A month in this hellhole is plenty." Suddenly he smiled at her. "But I'm willing to stay here as long as you need protection, ma'am—and on Heliopolis II, that translates to as long as you're on the planet."

"I appreciate that, Bandit," she said. "Where were you planning to go next?"

"I don't know. Wherever they might need someone like me."

"I might be able to help you out with that," said Matilda.

"Oh?"

"I have to speak to a friend first."

"Is he here?"

"No—but he can get here in a day or two."

"Well, I'll look forward to meeting him," said the Bandit. He pushed his chair back and got to his feet. "And now, if you'll excuse me, ma'am, I think it's time for me to go collect my commission." He paused awkwardly. "Perhaps you'd like to have dinner tonight?"

"I'd enjoy that very much," said Matilda. "I'm staying at the Tamerlaine."

"Fine. I'll call for you about an hour after dark. It'll still be oppressive, but it'll be a little more tolerable."

"I'll see you then," said Matilda.

He left the restaurant, and she ordered a very tall very cold drink, then another. Finally ready to face the planet again, she paid her tab and passed through one of the airlocks that seemed omnipresent on all the human buildings on Heliopolis II, walked back to the Tamerlaine, and went right to the bar for another cold drink the moment she arrived.

Finally she went up to her room, filled the tub with cool water, got out of her sweaty clothes, and carried the subspace radio into the bathroom. She set it down on a stool right next to the tub, then climbed in and luxuriated as the water closed in around her body.

After a few minutes, feeling somewhat human again, she put through a call to Dante Alighieri. It took about ten minutes for him to answer, and there was static whenever he spoke, but she was able to converse with him.

"How are you doing?" she asked.

"All right, I guess. I've incorporated eight more men and women into the poem. How's Heliopolis?"

"It's enough to make you get religion and walk the straight and narrow," said Matilda. "Now that I've experienced Heliopolis II, I don't ever want to go to hell."

He chuckled. "So where are you and Dimitrios going next?"

"Dimitrios isn't with me, and I'm not going anywhere."

"Oh?"

"But you are," she continued. "You're coming to Heliopolis II as soon as you can."

"Why, if it's that horrible a world?"

"There's someone I want you to meet."

"And who is that?" asked Dante.

"Santiago."

PART III

THE ONE-ARMED BANDIT'S BOOK

15.

FROM OUT OF NOWHERE THE ONE-ARMED
  BANDIT
BUILT HIS LEGEND, HONED AND FANNED IT.
IN THE BOOK OF FATE HE BURNED IT—
WATCHED IT SPREAD TILL ALL HAD LEARNED IT.

"I'VE HEARD ABOUT THE ONE-ARMED Bandit," remarked
Virgil Soaring Hawk as their vehicle sped toward the city.

"So you've said," answered Dante Alighieri. "Why do
you seem so unhappy about it?"

"What I've heard doesn't jibe with Matilda's description
of him."

"Well, we'll meet him in a few hours and make up our
own minds," replied Dante. "In the meantime, I've scrib-
bled down a tentative verse about him."

"Let's hear it."

Dante read it to him.

"What's the Book of Fate?" asked Virgil.

"Poetic license."

"Read the first two lines again."

"From out of nowhere the One-Armed Bandit built his
legend, honed and fanned it."

Virgil frowned. "The meter's wrong. You got too many
syllables in that opening line."

"Orpheus never worried about meter when it interfered
with truth."

"That was Orpheus," said the Injun. "And besides, you
don't know what the truth is."

"Well, if it's anything remotely like what Matilda thinks
it is, I'll polish the verse and maybe fix the meter." He
looked out at the bleak landscape. "Considering that she
didn't call me to check out Dimitrios of the Three Burners

or the Rough Rider, this guy must be something very special."

"The Rough Rider?" repeated Virgil, surprised. "Is he still alive?"

"After a fashion."

"Damn! I'm sorry I missed him."

"One of your childhood heroes?" asked Dante.

"After a fashion." Suddenly Virgil grinned. "I always wondered how he'd be in bed."

"If he doesn't share your unique sense of adventure, I imagine he'd be quite deadly."

"Yeah, probably. Still, it would have been fun to find out for sure."

A couple of rocks bounced off the vehicle.

"Stop!" commanded Dante.

The vehicle stopped.

"Open the doors!"

"My programming will not allow me to open the doors when doing so might put you at risk," answered the mechanical chauffeur.

"We're all at risk right now!" snapped Dante. "If someone's going to try to kill me, I want to be able to shoot back."

"Correction, sir," said the chauffeur. "This vehicle is impregnable to any weapon currently in the possession of the Unicorns. You are *not* at risk, and will not be unless you step outside."

Dante alternated his glare between the chauffeur and the shadows on the nearby hills.

"May I proceed, sir?"

"Yeah, go ahead," muttered Dante. "No sense staying here."

"What would you have done if it had let you out?" asked Virgil. "There could be a hundred of them up in those hills."

"And there could be two."

"Even so, do you think you're capable of taking even two of them?"

"Maybe not," admitted Dante. "But *you* are."

"I've got nothing against the Unicorns," said Virgil. "Besides, I'm a lover, not a fighter."

"Is that so?" responded Dante irritably. "You've killed four people since you hooked up with me."

"But I've been to bed with eleven of various genders and species," answered Virgil, as if that ended the argument.

Dante stared at him for a long moment, couldn't think of a reply, and realized with a wry smile that the argument was indeed over.

The rest of the journey to town was unremarkable. The landscape appeared dull, but from the comfort of their vehicle they could only guess what it felt like to walk through that heat and gravity while breathing the thin oxygen.

"I wonder what the hell he's doing here," remarked Dante.

"The place is supposed to be lousy with diamonds," said Virgil. "What better reason is there?"

"You know, I could get awfully tired of you and your worldview."

"You just don't like the fact that it's so defensible," answered the Injun.

"Maybe I'll change my name back to Danny. Then I won't need a Virgil at all."

"But your Santiago, when you anoint him, is going to need a Virgil, a Dante, a Matilda . . . all the help he can get."

"It's not up to me to anoint him," said Dante.

"Sure it is," replied Virgil. "If you write him up in your poem, he's Santiago, and if you don't, he isn't."

"It's not that simple."

"It's precisely that simple."

Dante was about to argue, realized that he didn't really give a damn what Virgil thought, and fell silent. They reached the city in another minute, and were soon climbing out of the vehicle in the Tamerlaine's basement.

"Well, let's go get our rooms," said Virgil, walking to the airlift as the vehicle turned and sped through the garage doors and began racing back to the spaceport.

"Not just yet," said Dante as they floated up to the hotel's lobby.

"Why not?"

"Matilda sounds more than impressed with the One-Armed Bandit," said Dante. "She sounds half in love. It may be coloring her judgment, so I want you to nose around and see what other people have to say about him. And find out where he's staying, if you can, just in case I want to speak to him alone."

"You might have told me before the fucking vehicle left," muttered Virgil.

"Yeah," agreed Dante. "But then you'd be so fresh and full of energy that you wouldn't do what I asked until you'd bedded half a dozen men and women and probably tried to make it with the robot chauffeur as well."

Virgil frowned. "I think I liked you better when you were an innocent."

"I was never an innocent," the poet corrected him. "I just didn't know you as well as I do now."

"Comes to the same thing," grumbled Virgil, walking through the airlock as Dante went up to the desk to register.

"Mr. Alighieri, right," said the clerk. "Two rooms?"

"That's correct." He paused. "Do you have any rules about visitors in your rooms?"

"No."

Dante tossed a twenty-credit cube on the desk. "Tell my friend you do."

"Yes, sir, Mr. Alighieri," said the clerk, pocketing the cube. "Will there be anything else?"

"You're got a guest named Matilda. I'd like to know what room she's in."

"That's against the regulations, sir."

Dante tossed another twenty-credit cube on the desk. "She's expecting me."

"What is her last name?" asked the clerk, pocketing the cube.

Dante frowned. "I'll be damned if I know," he admitted.

"I don't know how I can help you, then, Mr. Alighieri."

"Check your guest list for a single name: Matilda. If she didn't give her last name to me, she sure as hell wouldn't give it to you."

The clerk checked his computer, then looked up, surprised. "She's in 307."

"Let her know I'm on my way up," said Dante, walking to the airlift. He got off at the third floor, followed the glowing numbers that seemed to float a few inches in front of each door, and stopped when he came to 307. He was about to knock when it slid away from him.

"Come in," said Matilda, sitting on a chair by the window.

"Thanks."

"Did you have a good trip?"

"That depends."

"On what?"

"On whether you've found our Santiago."

"I think I have," she replied.

"I've heard of him here and there," said Dante. "I thought he was an outlaw."

"His name," she said, nodding.

"So you're saying he's *not* a bandit?"

"He's been an outlaw," she answered. "He's not one right now."

"What's he doing on Heliopolis II?"

"Providing protection to the miners."

"If these mines are so damned valuable, why doesn't the Democracy protect them?"

"Because he's better at it."

"Than a whole regiment?"

"Probably. And he's very reasonable." She smiled. "He charges them one diamond per Unicorn."

"Let me get this straight," said Dante. "He kills Unicorns and gets a diamond apiece?"

"Yes."

"That's very much like murder, isn't it?"

"He only kills those who attack or harass miners or other humans," she said.

"From what I understand, that could be a lifetime's work," remarked Dante. "What makes you think he'd quit to become Santiago?"

"Have you been outside yet?" asked Matilda.

"No."

She smiled. "Go outside for half an hour and then ask me that question."

"Point taken," he conceded.

"He's a wonderful man," said Matilda. "Just the kind of man Santiago should be."

"So when do I get to meet him?"

"Well, I was hoping we could have a drink right now—I knew you were due in early afternoon—but the Unicorns killed a miner this morning, and he's out there making sure they think twice before they do it again." She paused. "I don't know how he puts up with the conditions. I can barely walk a block. He goes for miles, and fights at the end of it."

"He's a formidable man."

"And at the same time he's the gentlest, best-mannered man I've come across on the Frontier," she enthused. "It's hard to believe those manners can go with those accomplishments."

Dante stared at her, trying to assess just how much her emotions had influenced her. She stared back, and it was as if she could read his mind.

"It has nothing to do with my feelings for him," she assured him.

"I didn't say that."

"But you were thinking it."

"I was wondering how detached your judgment was. There's a difference."

"He should be back before dark," said Matilda. "We'll meet him for dinner and you can make up your own mind."

"Fair enough." He walked to the door. "I might as well take a nap until then."

"Where's Virgil?" she asked. "Didn't he come with you?"

"He's out enjoying the climate."

"Good God, why?"

"There were a couple of things I wanted him to do." He grimaced. "I just hope he does them before he makes a pass at a Unicorn."

"You told me how you hooked up with him," said Matilda. "But for the life of me, I can't understand why you let him stay with you. You may have needed him the first few days you were on the Frontier, but surely you don't need him any longer."

"That's true."

"Well, then?"

"When we find our Santiago, he's going to need all the help he can get. Including Virgil."

"What makes you think he'll obey Santiago's orders?"

"He obeys *me*, and I'm no Santiago," answered Dante. "He needs an authority figure."

"He needs to be castrated and lobotomized!" said Matilda passionately.

"Well, that too," agreed Dante with a smile.

"He makes my skin crawl."

"He'll leave you alone."

"What makes you think so?"

"I told him to."

"And that will make him leave me alone?" she said dubiously.

"I told you: he obeys me."

"Why?" persisted Matilda.

Dante shrugged. "Who knows? Maybe he's really hung up on this Virgil/Dante thing. Or maybe he just wants a couple of more verses in my poem."

"Wait'll you meet the Bandit!" she said, her enthusiasm returning. "You'll give him a dozen verses!"

"I already wrote one," said Dante.

"May I see it?"

"Not until I've met him. I wrote it based on your messages. I may want to change it."

"You won't," she said with absolute certainty.

"I hope you're right," he said, walking to the door, then turned back to face her.

"But?" said Matilda. "There's an unspoken 'but' there."

"But I can't believe finding Santiago will be this easy."

He walked to the airlift, went up to the fifth floor, found his room, notified the desk that the robot bellhop had mixed his luggage up with Virgil's, waited a few moments until the problem was sorted out, and then lay back on the bed. It seemed that he had just closed his eyes when the desk clerk called to tell him that Matilda was waiting for him in the lobby.

He got to his feet, walked to the sink, muttered "Cold," and rinsed his face off. He considered changing clothes, but he didn't have anything better than he was wearing, so he left the room and took the airlift down to the lobby.

"Is he here?" asked Dante he approached Matilda.

"We're meeting him at the Golden Bough," answered Matilda. "It's a restaurant three blocks from here."

"From everything I've heard about this world, it ought to be the Diamond Bough." He stopped by the desk. "Has my friend checked in yet?"

"Virgil Soaring Hawk?" responded the clerk. "No, Mr. Alighieri."

"Thank you." Dante escorted Matilda to the airlock. "Well, either he's dead or he's shacking up with a Unicorn. We'll find out which tomorrow."

They emerged from the hotel, and he noticed that the gravity had become much heavier.

"I hadn't realized just how much the Tamerlaine had spent to approximate Standard gravity," he remarked. "Why don't we ride instead of walking?"

"The Democracy gets fifty percent of the take from the vehicles that go to and from the spaceport," she explained. "They want the same from city transportation, and so far no one's been willing to give it to them. A couple of men

set up a taxi business a couple of years ago; the Democracy
came in and turned their vehicles to rubble. I think they
killed one of the men, too. Anyway, since then, we walk.
It's reached the point where the miners are proud of being
able to cope with the climate and the gravity."

"Every goddamned Frontier world I've been to has a
story like that," said Dante. "I hope to hell you've found
our man." He grimaced. "Damn! It feels like each foot
weighs fifty pounds."

"I don't mind the gravity as much as the thin air," she
said.

"I don't think I'm especially enamored of the temperature, either," he added.

"It's much better now. Before sundown it's a lot hotter."

"And the Bandit fights Unicorns out here?"

"That's right."

"Well, he's Santiago or he's crazy," said Dante. "I vote
for the latter."

"The conditions don't seem to bother him," said Matilda.
"He's not like us."

"I'll vouch for that. Let's step it up a little and get out
of this goddamned heat and gravity."

She locked her arm in his and gently restrained him.
"You don't want to exert yourself in this thin air. You could
black out before we reach the restaurant."

Dante slowed down and didn't admit that he was just a
bit dizzy. "And he chases Unicorns up and down those
hills! Amazing!"

"Don't keep talking," she instructed him. "Save your
strength until we're inside the restaurant."

His limbs felt heavier with each step, and he fell silent
and walked at her pace. The blocks seemed longer than they
were on most Frontier worlds, but that could simply have
been because he wanted them to be shorter.

Finally they came to the Golden Bough, and he gratefully
entered the airlock with her. His lungs filled with oxygen,
and the temperature dropped until it was comfortable if not

cool—but his arms and legs still felt like the floor was tugging at them.

"There's no artificial gravity in here," Matilda noted. "I suppose it must cost too much for anything smaller than a hotel."

"Remind me not to order a soufflé," he replied wryly.

They were escorted to an empty table by the robotic headwaiter.

"So where's the Bandit?" asked Dante as they sat down.

"He'll be here."

"Yeah, I don't suppose you can kill Unicorns by the clock." He touched a small screen and summoned a waiter.

"How may I help you, sir?" asked the robot in a grating monotone.

"I'd like a beer. A very cold one." He turned to Matilda. "How about you?"

"Make it two," she told the robot.

"Would you care to order?" asked the waiter.

"No, we're waiting for a friend to join us."

The waiter walked to the bar, returning a moment later with their beers.

"You could work up one hell of a thirst walking around this town," commented Dante. He took a long swallow, closed his eyes, and sighed. "God, that's good! I don't think I ever appreciated beer before this evening."

"You'll find you need twice as many fluids as usual if you're going to spend any time outside," said Matilda.

Dante suddenly became aware of the fact that they were no longer alone. A tall man with wavy black hair, his clothes covered by red dust, stood next to their table. Matilda smiled when she saw him.

"Dante Alighieri," she said, "I'd like you to meet the man who saved my life—the One-Armed Bandit."

Dante stood up and shook the man's massive hand. "I've heard a lot about you," he said.

"Ditto," said the Bandit. "Matilda's told me all about you, Mr. Alighieri."

"Won't you sit down?"

"Thank you," said the Bandit. He signaled to the waiter. "Iced water, please—in the tallest glass you've got."

"How did it go today?" asked Matilda, lowering her voice enough so none of the other diners could overhear her.

"It went all right."

"That's all you've got to say?" she demanded.

"I wouldn't want Mr. Alighieri to think I was a braggart, ma'am."

"I won't," Dante assured him. "And I'd also like to hear what happened."

"There's really not much to tell," said the Bandit. "I took a land vehicle out to the mine, and when I didn't see any Unicorns there, I just went farther and farther into the desert until a few of them started throwing rocks at me the way they do. I waited until one of them charged, and before he could reach me I took out the hill where his friends were hiding so there was nothing left of either—the hill *or* the Unicorns. Then I melted the sand between the one surviving Unicorn and me, so he couldn't walk across it, and I told him that what I'd done was retribution for their killing that miner this morning. Twelve of them for one of us. I told him next time it'd be thirty for one, and then I let him go to spread the word." He paused uncomfortably. "I'm sorry I'm late, but the Democracy won't take my word for how many I killed, so I had to load them onto a couple of airsleds and attach them to the back of my land vehicle."

"And you did that in this gravity and heat!" said Dante admiringly.

"The trick is to not let them see that it bothers you, Mr. Alighieri," said the Bandit.

"Please, call me Dante."

"All right."

"And you killed twelve of them?"

"That's right, Mr. Alighieri."

"Dante."

"I apologize," said the Bandit. "That's the way my

mother brought me up, and those early lessons stay with you even out here on the Frontier."

Dante seemed amused. "You don't have to apologize for being polite."

"Thank you," said the Bandit. "I'd call Matilda Miss something-or-other, but she won't tell me what her last name is."

"Welcome to the club," said Dante wryly.

"Dante has become the new Black Orpheus," said Matilda.

"So you told me, ma'am."

"Maybe if you'll tell him about some of your more exciting exploits he'll put them in his poem."

"Oh, I don't think any of 'em are worth putting in a poem," said the Bandit. "Certainly not the kind Orpheus used to write. Those verses were about important people."

"*You're* important," said Matilda.

"Thank you for saying so, ma'am, but I'm really not."

"You *could* be," said Dante meaningfully.

"I don't think I follow you, Mr. Alighieri," said the Bandit.

"I'm here on Heliopolis II for a few days," said Dante. "We'll talk about it before I leave. Tonight let's just get to know each other."

"Whatever you say, Mr. Alighieri."

"Dante."

"I'm sorry," said the Bandit. "Sooner or later I'll get it right."

The robot waiter trundled up and took their orders.

"Matilda's told me all about that arm of yours," said Dante as the waiter glided away. "It's quite a weapon. What made you decide to create it?"

"My father was a successful banker back on Spica II," said the Bandit. "He died just about the same time that I lost my arm in the Sett War. I suppose I could have just packed it in and lived on the interest from my inheritance, but I wasn't ready to retire from living yet. The war had kind of aroused my interest in seeing new worlds, so I took every last credit my father left me and found a team that could create this arm for me. I field-tested it in the Canphor VII rebellion, and then came out to the Inner Frontier."

"Why did you leave the Democracy?" asked Dante.

"I felt . . . I don't know . . . *constricted*. Too many rules and regulations, and I didn't like the way the Democracy enforced them, so I decided to come to where there weren't any rules at all."

"And now *you* enforce them," said Matilda. "That really does belong in Dante's poem."

"I never looked at it that way, ma'am," admitted the Bandit. "Still, I think Mr. Alighieri should stick to the important people, the ones who make and shape the Frontier."

Dante stared at him. *Can you be for real, or is this all just an act?*

Their dinner arrived, and they spent the next few minutes eating, while Matilda tried to make small talk.

When the meal was done, Dante lit a smokeless cigar and offered one to the Bandit, who refused.

"What are you doing tomorrow?" asked the poet.

"I won't know until tomorrow happens," said the Bandit. "I don't have any definite route or anything like that. If the Unicorns don't bother anyone, I'll stay in my hotel most of the day."

"If you're available, I'd like to have a serious talk with you."

"Sure."

"Aren't you curious?"

"You'll tell me when you're ready to," said the Bandit.

"Where are you staying?"

"Over at the Royal Khan."

"Fine. I'll be there about noon."

They got up to leave. As they walked past the bar, they came to a man whose face was swathed in bandages.

"Hello, Mr. Durastanti," said the Bandit. "Welcome back."

"They let me out this afternoon," said the man, his voice

muffled by the bandages. "Lost an eye, and they're going to have to build me a new nose."

The Bandit reached into his pocket and pulled out twelve perfect diamonds. He took hold of the man's hand and carefully placed the diamonds in it.

"What's this?" demanded the man.

"Just in case the Democracy doesn't cover all your medical expenses, Mr. Durastanti," said the Bandit.

"You don't have to—"

"It's an honor to, Mr. Durastanti," said the Bandit, gently closing the man's hand on the diamonds and then guiding it to his pocket. "Don't drink too much tonight, and take those to the assay office in the morning. I'm sure there are identifying marks on them, but I'll stop by first thing and let them know I gave them to you . . . that you didn't steal them."

"As if I could!" said the man with a dry, croaking, humorless laugh.

"Take care, now," said the Bandit, accompanying Dante and Matilda out into the hot, uncomfortable night.

"What was that all about?" asked Dante.

"That's Mr. Durastanti," explained the Bandit. "He's a miner. The Unicorns killed his partner and laid a false trail for me to follow. By the time I realized it and doubled back, they'd already ripped half his face off."

"That's hardly your fault."

"I was supposed to protect him, and I failed." He paused, then continued with genuine regret. "I spoke to the doctors. He inhaled a lot of dust and he lost a lot of his face. They don't think he'll ever work again."

"Were those the diamonds you picked up for the Unicorns you killed today?"

"Yes."

"That's a lot of diamonds to give away."

The Bandit shrugged. "He needed them more than I did."

By God, thought Dante, *we* did *find Santiago after all!*

16.

HE COUNTS OTHER PEOPLE'S MONEY,
HE MOUTHS OTHER PEOPLE'S WORDS,
THE GRAND FINALE HATES HIS LIFE,
AND ENVIES THE FREE-FLYING BIRDS.

DANTE HAD BEEN SO FASCINATED by the One-Armed Bandit that he completely lost track of Virgil Soaring Hawk. That lasted until the middle of the night, when Virgil lurched into his room and poked him in the ribs.

"What the hell is it?" demanded Dante, sitting up.

"It's me," slurred the Injun. "I'm a he, not an it."

"Go away," said Dante, lying back down. "You're drunk."

"What's that got to do with anything?" retorted Virgil. "I've got a recruit."

"Who are we at war with?" muttered Dante, covering his head with a pillow.

"The Democracy."

"Go recruit eighty billion more and maybe you'll stand a chance," said the poet. "Now go away and leave me alone."

Virgil poked him in the ribs again.

"What the hell is the matter with you?" snapped Dante.

"I told you: I've got a recruit."

"All right, you've got a recruit," said Dante, now thoroughly and grumpily awake. "So what?"

"So I think you should talk to him."

"In the morning?"

"Now. He's downstairs in the hotel bar. And he wants to meet you."

Dante got up and started getting dressed. "This recruit of yours—does he have a name?"

"Probably. Hell, he's probably got a bunch of them.

These days he calls himself the Grand Finale."

"Sounds like an actor with an inflated ego," said Dante disgustedly.

"He's waiting."

"I know. You told me." Dante slipped into his shoes and ran a comb through his hair.

"He's a gray-haired guy. Smaller than you. Kinda skinny. White mustache. You can probably find some of his dinner in it."

"Why are you telling me this?" said Dante. "We'll see him in just a minute."

The Injun lay down on the poet's bed. "I thought now that you know what he looks like, I'd take a little nap."

He was snoring by the time Dante reached the door.

Dante went down to the lobby, then turned to his left and entered the small bar. There was only one customer, and he looked exactly as Virgil had described him.

Dante walked over the stood in front of him. "You're the one who calls himself the Grand Finale?"

The old man looked him over critically. "So you're the new Orpheus?"

"So to speak. I gather you want to meet me?"

"Not as much as you want to meet me," said the old man. "Have a seat, Rhymer."

Dante sat down and ordered a beer.

"I'll have another," said the Grand Finale to the mechanical waiter. He turned to Dante. "I'm charging my drinks to your room. I hope you don't mind."

"I'll let you know after you tell me why I want to meet you."

"Because even Santiago can't function without a man like me," said the Finale.

"You don't look that formidable to me," remarked Dante.

"That's because you're thinking along the wrong lines, Rhymer," said the old man. "You don't need another soldier half as much as you need someone to pay for the bullets."

"Keep talking."

"I used to be a banker. A very exotic one: I arranged financing for terraforming worlds. I helped the Democracy bring recalcitrant worlds to their economic knees and helped rebuild them once they'd fallen into line. And I was *good*, Rhymer—there wasn't a trick I didn't know, a law I couldn't circumvent." He paused. "I was too good to stay in a legitimate business. It wasn't too long before the Kalimort bought me off."

"The Kalimort?" repeated Dante.

"They were a planetary criminal organization on Pretorius III that was about to expand to half a dozen other worlds. They needed financing, and they needed to know how to double their money while they were preparing to move."

"And you showed them how?"

"For a few years. Then they were absorbed by Barioke, one of the major warlords on the Rim, and I went to work for him. Over the years I've worked for half a dozen organizations that needed to hide and, at the same time, maximize their resources." He smiled. "The one you dubbed the Scarlet Infidel tells me you may be putting together another one."

"It's possible," said Dante. "Who are you working for now?"

"I'm between jobs," said the Grand Finale, looking uncomfortable for the first time.

"They caught you with your hand in the till," said Dante. It was not a question.

"Why should you think so?"

"Because we're as far from the Rim as it's possible to get. There's the Rim, then the Outer Frontier and the Spiral Arm, then the Democracy, and then the Inner Frontier and the Core. Why else would you be a couple of hundred thousand light-years from your warlord? How much did you run off with?"

"Not enough," admitted the Finale, unable to hide his bitterness. "I thought I'd never have to work again. I forgot how much it costs to live when you're in hiding."

"Yeah, it gets expensive," agreed Dante. "How long have you been the Grand Finale?"

"A few months." He grinned guiltily. "I saw a bakery on Ribot IV called the Grand Finale."

"Silly name."

"Well, I'm hardly likely to call myself the Banker or the Accountant when I'm trying to hide my identity."

"True enough," said Dante. "What's your real name?"

"Wilbur Connaught."

"If we decided to invite you to join us, Wilbur, what is it going to cost us?"

"It varies."

"Explain."

"I don't work for a salary. I'll take some living expenses as a draw against what I earn, but you'll pay me three percent of the profit I make with the money you give me to work with."

"Three percent doesn't seem like very much for a man with your credentials," said Dante. "What's the catch?"

"No catch. After a couple of years, you'll find yourself resenting how much you pay me."

"Give me an example of what you do."

"Let's say you give me a million credits, to name a nice round number," said Wilbur. "And let's say you don't need it for a year."

"Okay, let's say so."

"I'll use my sources to find those planets that are suffering from hyperinflation. They can't be just *any* planets; their economies have to be backed by the Democracy." He paused. "With more than fifty thousand worlds to choose from, it won't be too hard to find three worlds that are returning one hundred percent per annum on deposits, again using a nice round number."

"Okay, so you can double the money."

Wilbur snorted contemptuously. "Any fool can double the money. Just for the sake of argument, let's say each world has a twenty-four-hour day. I'll set up a computer program that transfers the money to each of the three worlds every eight Standard hours. Figuring simplistically, this will quadruple your money in a year, but actually, given compounded interest, it'll come much closer to quintupling. There's no stock market in the galaxy that can guarantee you an annualized five-hundred-percent return, and we'll do this with the full faith and backing of the Democracy. If any of those banks fail, the Democracy will step in and make good their debts."

"Very interesting," said Dante. "I'm impressed."

"That's kindergarten stuff," said Wilbur. "I just used it for a simple-to-understand example. There are investments and machinations that can give you a tenfold return in half the time. You'll need to pay an army, to supply them with weapons and ships, to keep lines of communication open. It all costs money. You need *me*, Rhymer."

"I'm sold," said Dante. "But it could take a while before we're ready for you, before we have anything for you to invest."

"I'm not going anywhere," said Wilbur. "I hate Heliopolis, but I'm probably safer hiding out in this hellhole than anywhere else." He sighed. "Almost makes me wish I'd stayed a banker."

"And we won't have an army, not in the normal sense of one."

"Neither did the Kalimort—but they sure killed a lot of people."

"That doesn't bother you?"

"My job is making money. I'm not responsible for what you do with it."

"That's a refreshing attitude," commented Dante.

"But if you use it against the Democracy, I won't be unhappy."

"Why should that be?"

"There's been a price on my head ever since I worked for the Kalimort," said Wilbur. "I've got two grandchildren in the Deluros system that I'll never see. That's reason enough."

"How will I get in touch with you?"

"I'm at the Royal Khan." The old man looked at him. "Have you found your Santiago yet?"

"I'm interviewing a very promising candidate tomorrow," said Dante.

"I didn't know they could apply for the job."

"They can't."

"But you just said—"

"He doesn't know what I want to talk to him about," said Dante.

"Well, if you're here for anyone, it's got to be the One-Armed Bandit," said Wilbur.

"What's your opinion of him?"

"You could do worse."

"That's all you've got to say?"

"My job is making money," said Wilbur. "Your job seems to be deciding who I make it for. I wouldn't let you tell me how to go about my business; I don't propose to tell you how to go about yours."

"You're going to be a pleasure to work with, old man."

"If you really think so, Rhymer, you might put me in a verse or two next time you're working on your poem."

"I might, at that."

The Grand Finale got to his feet. "I'm going back to my room now. No sense waiting til the sun starts coming out. It's hot enough as it is."

"We'll talk again soon," promised Dante.

"Not necessary," replied Wilbur. "I've told you what I can do and you've agreed to hire me. Contact me again when you're ready for me."

He walked out of the bar, crossed through the lobby, and went out the airlock while Dante sipped his beer and watched him bend over as the force of gravity hit him.

The poet considered going back to sleep, but decided that he didn't feel like wrestling the Injun for his bed, so he activated the bar's holo set and watched news and sports results from back in the Democracy until the first rays of the huge sun began lighting the streets.

He checked his timepiece, decided it was still a couple

of hours too early to visit the Bandit, and walked out to
the lobby.

"May I help you, sir?" said the night clerk.

"Yeah. Where do I go for breakfast around here?"

"We have our own restaurant."

"I know. But it doesn't open for another hour, and I'm
hungry now."

"It's against our policy to recommend any other restaurants, so I am not permitted to tell you that the Deviled
Egg is an excellent establishment and is located sixty yards
to your right as you leave the Tamerlaine," said the clerk
with a smile. "I hope you will forgive my reticence, sir."

Dante flipped him a coin. "All is forgiven and forgotten,"
he said, walking to the airlock.

The heat hit him the second he stepped outside. So did
the gravity. He had a feeling he was adjusting to the thin
air, because he walked the block to the restaurant without
panting.

He walked through the near-empty Deviled Egg, found
a table in the corner where he could look out through the
front window and observe the few people who were out on
the street, and ate a leisurely breakfast.

He sipped his coffee, checked his timepiece again, and
decided that it was almost time to leave for the Royal Khan.
He wondered if he should have Matilda come with him,
but decided against it. He couldn't help feeling that she was
a little bit in love with the One-Armed Bandit, and while
he had no problem with that, he felt he'd rather present the
proposal alone, with no emotional undercurrents distracting
the Bandit.

He paid his bill, got up, and walked back into the hot,
humid, thin Heliopolis air. The Royal Khan was half a
block away, and he headed toward it.

A young woman was walking in his direction. As they
passed each other she veered slightly and brushed against
him. He thought nothing of it until he reached the lobby of
the Royal Khan. A human waiter seemed to be charged
with the task of bringing every person who entered the

lobby a cold drink, and Dante reached into his pocket to grab a coin and tip him. Instead, he found a folded piece of paper, which the woman had obviously placed there. He unfolded it and read it:

> *I know why you are here. The Scarlet Infidel thinks you will be raising an army, but that's not the way Santiago fought in the past, and it's not the way to fight now.*

"That goddamned Injun's got a big mouth," muttered Dante. He continued reading.

> *I have no love for the Democracy. If you would like to discuss matters of mutual interest, fold this up and put it back in your pocket, and I will contact you after you speak to the man you came to Heliopolis II to see.*

Virgil hadn't known he'd be seeing the Bandit this morning. Which meant she'd figured it out herself. It didn't make her a genius, but it made her bright enough to talk to. Dante carefully folded the note and replaced it in his pocket.

He looked around to see who was watching him. The lobby was empty and there was no one in the street outside, but somehow he knew that his action had registered with *someone*.

He tipped the waiter, who had waited impatiently while he'd read the note, and then went to the airlift. He was going to the Bandit's room as the successor to Black Orpheus; he had every hope that he would leave as the creator of Santiago.

17.

A BLOSSOM, A PETAL, AN ODOR SO NICE,
THE FLOWER OF SAMARKAND'S SUGAR AND
   SPICE.
SHE ESCHEWS THE MORAL AND PRACTICES
   VICE,
WITH A PASSION THAT'S HOT, AND A HEART
   COLD AS ICE.

THE DOOR SLID OPEN AND Dante entered the room. It was a little larger than his room at the Tamerlaine, but the air-conditioning didn't seem to be working as well. Then he found himself gasping for breath, and he realized that the window was half open.

"You sure you want the bring the outdoors in?" he asked, pointing to the window.

The One-Armed Bandit, who was floating a few inches above the ground on an easy chair that constantly remolded itself to his body's movements, glanced at the window.

"You can shut it if you like, Mr. Alighieri."

Dante walked over and commanded the window to close. It sealed itself shut an instant later.

"Don't you find the heat uncomfortable?" asked Dante curiously.

"Of course I do."

"Then why—?"

"Because then I find the outdoors a little less uncomfortable, and that's where I do most of my work."

"Makes sense," said Dante. He looked around and saw an empty chair by the desk. "Do you mind if I sit down?"

"You're my guest, Mr. Alighieri," said the Bandit. "You can have *this* chair if you like."

"The desk chair will be fine," said Dante, as he walked over and sat down. "I take it you're free for the day?"

"My services aren't needed." The Bandit paused. "So far, anyway."

"I think you're wrong," said Dante. "I think your services are needed more than you can imagine."

"Have the Unicorns—?"

"This has nothing to do with the Unicorns," said the poet. "Shall I continue?"

The Bandit nodded.

"What do you know about Santiago?"

"Not very much," admitted the Bandit. "They say that he was King of the Outlaws, and that he died more than a century ago. Why?"

"He was an outlaw, all right," said Dante. "But what if I told you that it was just a cover?"

"A cover?" said the Bandit, frowning. "For what?"

"That's what we're going to talk about," said Dante. "You want a cold drink? This is going to take some time."

"Later."

"Good. Now let's talk about what Santiago really was, and why he lasted so long."

Dante spent the next two hours giving the Bandit the full history of Santiago as he understood it. He explained in detail how Santiago made war against the excesses of the Democracy, but always hid it behind a cloak of criminality, because while the Democracy was content to send bounty hunters after the King of the Outlaws, they would have spared no expense hunting him down had they known he was actually a revolutionary. He explained that the first Santiago had trained his successor, and the next three had done the same, that the various Santiagos had included a farmer, a bounty hunter, a thief, even a chess master. Finally, he told the Bandit how the last Santiago and his infrastructure had been wiped out by the Democracy, which didn't even know he was on the planet of Safe Harbor when they turned it to dust.

"All that happened more than a century ago," said the Bandit. "It's interesting, Mr. Alighieri, but what does it have to do with me?"

"More than you think," said Dante. "The Democracy's abuses have grown since Santiago vanished. They confiscate property, they illegally detain and kill men and women, they destroy planets that pose no threat to them."

"I know all that," said the Bandit. "That's why I'm here on the Inner Frontier."

"But the Democracy's forces are here on the Inner Frontier, too."

"True."

"Well?"

"What do you expect *me* to do about it?"

Dante smiled. "I thought you'd never ask."

The Bandit stared at him. *"Me?"* he said at last.

"Why *not* you?" Dante shot back. "You're as decent a man as I've met out here. You're absolutely deadly when you feel you must be, yet you're not bloodthirsty or you'd have wiped out the Unicorns. You disapprove of the Democracy. You're generous to a fault; I saw an example of that last night. I have a feeling that you've never met anything that frightens you."

"That's not so," admitted the Bandit uncomfortably. *"Failure* frightens me."

"So much the better," said Dante. "I consider that a virtue."

"But—"

"We've been waiting a hundred and six years for Santiago to reappear. Are you going to make us wait even longer?"

"I wouldn't know how to go about *being* Santiago."

"That's what you'll have me and Matilda for, at least until you're comfortable with it."

"Just the three of us against the Democracy?" asked the Bandit, looking at him as if he was crazy.

"There's more. I found us a financial wizard last night."

"Why?"

"Money is the mother's milk of revolution. We'll need this man to set up and fund a network throughout the Fron-

tier. Dimitrios of the Three Burners will work for the cause.
So will Virgil Soaring Hawk."

"I've heard of Dimitrios."

"Virgil's in the poem as the Scarlet Infidel."

"Well, if you thought enough of him to write him up . . ."
said the Bandit.

"There are more. And that's without any of them knowing we have our Santiago."

The Bandit was silent for a long moment, then another.
Finally he looked up at Dante, his face filled with self-
doubt. "What if they won't follow me?"

Dante smiled. "Why wouldn't they?"

"I'm just . . . just *me*," said the Bandit. "I'm nothing special, that men should die for my cause."

"It's the cause that's special, not its leader," said Dante.
"Though he's special too," the poet amended quickly. "He
has to be a man of his word, a resourceful man—and he
has to be a man who won't back off from doing what's
necessary. He has to know that if his cause is just, it doesn't
matter that every citizen of the Democracy thinks he's an
outlaw or worse; in fact he has to strive for that to protect
his operation and his agents." Dante paused. "I think you're
such a man."

"I think you're wrong."

"Santiago must also be a modest man, even a humble
one—a man who *thinks* he's nothing special, when it's apparent to everyone else that he's very special indeed."

"I'll have to think about it, Mr. Alighieri."

"Think hard," said Dante. "Think of the difference you
could make, the things you could do." He paused. "I can't
rush you. There are no other candidates for the job. You're
the man we want. But the sooner you agree, the sooner we
can put everything in motion."

"I understand, Mr. Alighieri."

"Dante."

"I appreciate your confidence in me," said the Bandit.
"I'll give you my answer tonight."

"When and where?"

"Meet me back here at the hotel for dinner, an hour after sundown."

"I'll see you then," said Dante. He walked to the door, then turned back. "Do you want me to open the window again?"

"No," said the Bandit. "I'm going down to the lobby to have some coffee."

"I'll join you."

"I'd rather you didn't. I've got a lot to consider, and I do my best thinking when I'm alone."

"Whatever you say," replied Dante. He turned and walked out the door, then took the airlift down to the main floor.

A very pretty woman was smiling at him. It took him a moment to place her; then he realized that she was the same woman who had bumped into him and placed the note in his pocket.

He walked over and stood in front of her. "Good morning," he said. "My name is—"

"I know who you are, and I know why you're here."

"Of course you do," he said. "But I don't know who you are or why you're here. Perhaps you'd care to enlighten me?"

"First things first. Did he agree?"

"I think he will."

"Good. Let's go back to your hotel."

"Why?"

"So we don't distract him," said the woman. "I've been studying him for weeks. Whenever he needs to think out a problem, he comes down here and drinks coffee."

"All right, let's go," said Dante, leading her to the airlock. He took two steps outside and felt like melting. "My God, it's even worse than yesterday."

"If you plan to stay here for any length of time, you really should go to a doctor for help or acclimatization—adrenaline, blood oxygenating, muscle stimulants, the whole works."

"I have high hopes of leaving Heliopolis II in a day or

two and never seeing it again," Dante assured her as they began the seemingly endless two-block walk to the Tamerlaine. "And now, who are you?"

"My name is Blossom."

"Very pretty name," said Dante. "Where are you from?"

"Samarkand."

"Where the hell is Samarkand?"

"It was a city back on old Earth, or so they tell me," she replied. "In my case, it's a planet in the Quinellus Cluster."

"Okay, Blossom," he said, and found himself gasping for breath again. "I'll wait until we're at the hotel to talk to you. I think I'm going to need all my oxygen just to get there."

"I could give you a pill."

"Don't bother," he rasped. "We'd be at the hotel before it had a chance to take effect."

They trudged down the block in silence. Dante stopped at a corner, leaned against a building until his head stopped spinning, and then walked the rest of the way to the Tamerlaine without any further incident.

"The Bandit must keep some doctor in business, considering how much time he spends outside," said Dante when they'd passed through the hotel's airlock and were back in comfortable gravity and temperature.

"He doesn't take any medication," answered Blossom. "He doesn't believe in it."

"He doesn't believe it works?"

"Oh, he knows it works. He doesn't believe in putting any foreign substances in his body."

"Better and better," muttered Dante, taking her to one of the lounges and collapsing in a chair. She sat down opposite him. "All right, Blossom—suppose you tell me why you sought me out and what this is all about?"

"I had a long talk with Virgil Soaring Hawk last night," she began.

"I didn't know he *talked* to women," interrupted Dante. "I thought he just pounced on them."

"He tried." She showed off a steel-toed boot. "He'll be walking bowlegged for the next few days."

Dante smiled his approval. "Good for you."

"Anyway, he told me that you found Black Orpheus' manuscript, and were taking his place."

"I'm continuing his work," Dante corrected her. "That's not quite the same thing."

"Close enough," said Blossom. "Anyway, he mentioned that you were looking for a new Santiago to write about."

"I'm looking for a new Santiago because the Inner Frontier is in desperate need of him," said Dante, idly wondering if he was telling the truth, and then wondering if all writers had that particular problem. "My being able to write about him is very unimportant compared to that."

She stared at him for a moment, making no effort to hide her disbelief, and finally shrugged. "Your motivation is no concern of mine," she said at last. "I just want to know when you've found him."

"Why?"

"Because I want to offer him my services."

"And just what *are* your services?" asked Dante.

"Whatever the job requires."

"We're not dealing with nice people."

"I know that," said Blossom.

"The job could require you to sleep with some men you can't stand the sight of, or perhaps even kill them."

"As long as it hurts the Democracy, I'm in."

"Just what do you have against the Democracy?"

"My parents were missionaries. The Democracy had a chance to evacuate them before they pacified Kyoto II. They didn't. The first attack killed them." She lowered her voice, but continued talking. "My husband's mother was a diplomat; he grew up on Lodin XI. His closest friend was a Lodinite. They were like brothers. During the Lodin insurrection, the Democracy killed my husband's friend for unspecified crimes, none of which he had committed, and then they executed my husband for being a collaborator." She paused, her jaw set, her face grim. "You just tell me what I have to do, and if any member of the Democracy suffers because of it, I'll do it."

"It's not up to me to tell you anything," replied Dante. "I'm just a poet. Santiago will decide what needs to be done, and by whom."

"You'll tell him about me?"

"Of course."

"Do you think he'll let me join him?"

"We're just starting out. He'll need all the help he can get." He sighed. "Hell, he'll need all the help he can get fifty years and a hundred victories from now. This is the *Democracy* we're going up against, even if they're not allowed to know it." He pulled out his pocket computer. "Where can I get hold of you, Blossom?"

"As long as you've assured me that Santiago will be giving me my orders, I'll reserve that information for him."

"But—"

"Don't worry," said Blossom. "Neither you nor he will leave Heliopolis before I speak to him—but there's no sense doing that until he makes it official, is there?"

"It might help him decide."

"If I'm what it takes to make him decide, then you picked the wrong man for the job." She got to her feet. "I'll be watching, Rhymer."

"It shouldn't be long," said Dante.

She turned and left, and he watched her make her way through the lobby and the airlock. It seemed difficult to believe that such a gorgeous woman could have suffered so much—and then he realized that he was thinking in stereotypes. Santiago would know that it was the suffering that mattered, not the appearance of the sufferer.

Hurry up and make up your mind, Bandit. The Frontier is filled with Flowers of Samarkand. Someone has to step forward and make sure that the Democracy doesn't make any more of them suffer as this one has.

18.

> HE'S THE KING OF THE OUTLAWS, THE CRÈME
>   DE LA CRÈME,
> HE'S CLEVER, HE'S DEADLY, HE'S KNAVERY'S
>   GEM.
> HE SUPS WITH THE DEVIL, HE REVELS IN PAIN.
> HE KILLS AND HE PLUNDERS—HUMANITY'S
>   BANE.

DANTE WROTE THAT VERSE JUST before he went to visit the One-Armed Bandit and learn his decision. Black Orpheus had never mentioned Santiago by name; he simply assumed that no one else could possibly fit the verses he wrote about the King of the Outlaws and that his readers would know that.

Dante followed suit for a number of reasons, not the least of which was that he wasn't at all sure that the Bandit would agree to become Santiago. He was so moral, so out-and-out *decent*, that there was some doubt in Dante's mind that he could do all the unpleasant things that were required of him.

Dante tried to visualize the Bandit ordering his men to wipe out a Navy convoy filled with brave young men whose only crime was that they had been drafted to serve the Democracy. He tried to imagine the Bandit ordering Blossom to sleep with a degenerate man who had information Santiago's organization needed. He knew that Santiago would have to commit some actual crimes, some robberies and murders, if only to leave a false trail and convince the Democracy that he was an outlaw and not a revolutionary. All the previous Santiagos had blended in, had been able to hide out in the middle of a crowd—but none of them had the Bandit's reputation, or his easily recognizable prosthetic arm.

So do I want him to say yes or don't I?

Yes, he realized, of course he wanted the Bandit to say yes. There would be problems—but that was precisely why there was a need for Santiago. *I need you, yes,* thought Dante, *but the Frontier, maybe even the galaxy, needs you even more. I could look for a couple of lifetimes and not find a better candidate than you, so please, please say yes.*

He checked his timepiece, decided it was time to get his answer, and walked out into the crushing gravity and hot, thin, dusty air.

The first thing we do when we get the Democracy off our backs is get some public transportation here.

He stopped halfway to the Royal Khan to buy a cold drink, then forced himself back outside to complete the journey. Once inside the Bandit's hotel he found that his shirt was drenched with perspiration, and he stopped by a public bathroom to dry himself off. He looked at his face in a mirror, marveled at how tanned he'd become from the few days in which he'd been exposed to the blazing red sun, and finally, feeling a little more comfortable, went to the airlift and rode it up to the Bandit's floor.

As usual the door slid open before he could knock. This time, instead of using the floating, formfitting easy chair, the Bandit was sitting on a window ledge, his shoulder pressed against it, glancing out to the street every now and then.

"Good evening, Mr. Alighieri."

"Dante."

"I'll get it right sooner or later."

"And who am *I* saying good evening to?" asked Dante.

"Me."

"And who are you—Santiago or the One-Armed Bandit?"

"We'll talk a bit, and then I'll tell you."

"Do you mind if I sit down?"

"Suit yourself," said the Bandit.

Dante walked over to the easy chair. As he sat down, it seemed to wrap around his body and began rocking him gently. The rocking became a swaying as the chair rose and hovered a few inches above the ground.

Dante felt a grin of pleasure cross his face. "I've wanted to sit in this thing from the first minute I saw it."

"You look comfortable," observed the Bandit.

"I may never get out of it again," said Dante, still grinning. "Okay, I'm ready to listen if you're ready to talk."

"I have a few questions for you," said the Bandit.

"Shoot."

"You tell me there were five Santiagos."

"Right. The last one died when the Navy destroyed Safe Harbor."

"Did all five die violently?"

"I won't lie to you," said Dante, the grin gone. "Yes, they did."

"What was their average age?"

"I don't know as much about the first two as I should. I really couldn't say."

"It's not important anyway. The real question is: what was their average tenure as Santiago?"

"Maybe ten or twelve years. Less for the last one."

"And these were the best men the prior Santiagos could find, and they each inherited a massive organization." It was a statement, not a question.

"Except for the first," noted Dante. "He had to create it—and the legend, and the misdirection—from scratch."

"And even with those organizations, none of them lasted fifteen years, not even a man as accomplished as Sebastian Cain."

"That's right."

The Bandit frowned and fell silent. After a moment he turned and looked out at the street again.

"You're not afraid of dying in ten or twelve years, not with the odds you face almost every day," said Dante. "What's the real reason you're being so hesitant?"

The Bandit turned and faced him. "I don't know if I can accomplish enough before they kill me," he said. "You might be better off with some criminal kingpin or even a disgruntled military commander, someone who's already got an organization in place."

"Is *that* what this is all about?" asked Dante, suddenly relieved.

"I don't want to be the Santiago that failed," said the Bandit. "Is that so hard to understand?"

"I'm sure every Santiago had his doubts."

"Do you really think so?"

"I'm certain of it," answered Dante. "If you say yes to our offer, you'll become not only the most feared man in the galaxy, but the most hated as well. And you won't be hated just by the Democracy. You'll be hated by every decent, law-abiding, God-fearing colonist that you're trying to protect. You'll be hated and envied by the men and women who work for you, and most of them will be the scum of the galaxy. You'll only be able to leave your head-quarters—I won't use the word 'hideout,' but that's what it'll be—if you're heavily disguised. You'll send decent men and women to their deaths. The Democracy will put a huge price on your head, and it'll get higher ever month. You won't even be mourned when an underling or a bounty hunter finally kills you, because we can't let anyone know that Santiago is dead." Dante paused. "Don't you think the other Santiagos had their doubts?"

The Bandit sighed heavily. "When you put it that way, I guess they must have."

"Of course they did," said Dante. "And each of them thought the cause was worth it." He stared at the Bandit, studying his face. "You do a lot of good, and you're a hero." The Bandit was about to interrupt, but Dante held up a hand. "No, don't deny it. You're an authentic, bona fide hero. What we're asking is for you to do ten times, a hundred times as much good—and be thought of as a vil-lain for the rest of your life. In the end, that's what it boils down to. Which is more important to you—being a hero or doing good?"

"You don't pull your punches, do you, Mr. Alighieri?" said the Bandit wryly.

"I'm asking you to become the most feared and hated man in the galaxy," replied the poet. "I don't know how to make it sound like anything other than that." He paused. "And there's something else."

"What?"

"If I *had* to couch it in diplomatic terms, then you're not the man we're looking for."

"Oh, I'm the man, all right," said the Bandit with another deep sigh. "I just wanted to make sure I knew what I was getting into, because there's no turning back."

"You're right about that. Once you're in, you're in for keeps." Dante paused thoughtfully. "Have you got any family?"

"Not much. A brother somewhere. I haven't kept in touch. Maybe a distant cousin or two. My parents are dead, and my sister died in the same battle where I lost my arm."

"No wife, no kids, no romantic attachments?"

The Bandit shook his head. "I never found the time for it. I always planned to someday."

"Forget about it. To you they'd be a wife and kids; to millions of men and women, they'd be targets."

The Bandit nodded thoughtfully. "Yes, I can see that."

"How about your arm?" continued Dante. "Does it need servicing?"

"Never has yet. Why?"

"We couldn't let your doctors know, or even guess, that they were working on Santiago."

The Bandit frowned. "You'd kill them?"

"Not me," said Dante. "I'm just a poet."

The meaning of Dante's statement was reflected in the Bandit's face. "I see."

"Could you order it done?"

The Bandit stared at him, unblinking. "I'd have to."

"That's right—you'd have to."

"I don't imagine decisions like that get any easier to make over the years."

"Not if you're the man we hope you are," agreed Dante.

"Okay, I've asked my questions," said the Bandit. "What do we do now?"

"Now we meet the members of your organization that are currently on Heliopolis II, and we start making plans."

"There's really an organization?"

"The start of one."

"Are they down in the lobby?"

"No," said Dante. "I told them I'd contact them if and when you committed."

The poet pulled out a communicator, and a moment later had made contact with the four people he sought.

"This is Dante," he said. "We have plans to make. I expect to see you all in"—he paused, then smiled—"in Santiago's room at the Royal Khan in half an hour."

"Santiago's room," repeated the Bandit. "I like the sound of that."

"That's who you are. The One-Armed Bandit ceased to exist three minutes ago."

Dante spent the next few minutes telling him tales of the previous Santiagos, tales he hadn't told the day before. The Bandit was most interested in how they died.

"Violently," answered Dante.

"I know. But *how*?"

"The first was killed during a raid on a Navy convoy," said Dante. "The second one died from injuries he received in prison. The third—"

"They had Santiago in prison?" interrupted the Bandit.

"Yes," answered Dante, "but they didn't know who he was. Many men were tortured to death without telling them." He paused. "The third was killed by a bounty hunter named the Angel. The fourth, who I'm convinced was Sebastian Cain, was assassinated by another bounty hunter, either Peacemaker MacDougal or Johnny One-Note. The last of them, a former thief known as Esteban Cordoba, died when the Navy vaporized his world." Dante paused, almost overwhelmed by the litany of violent deaths. "None of them died in bed."

"Except maybe for the second one."

"It's not a death you'd want. I gather they mutilated him pretty badly."

"There are so many worlds on the Frontier, literally millions of them. I'm surprised none of my predecessors could stay in hiding for as much as fifteen years."

"Probably they could have."

"Then why—"

"Because each of them seems to have reached a point where he decided not to run again." Dante shrugged. "I don't know. Maybe being Santiago affects your judgment after a decade or so. Maybe because you've held off the best killers the Democracy could throw against you, you start feeling that you can't be killed, that you're somehow immortal."

"The first might have felt that way," said the Bandit. "The others had to know better."

"Then you'll have to tell *me* someday. I sure as hell don't have any better explanation."

"I didn't mean any offense, Mr.—"

"*Stop!*" said Dante harshly.

"What's the matter?" asked the Bandit, surprised.

"Two things," said Dante. "Santiago doesn't call anyone *Mister*, and he never apologizes."

"I'll try to remember."

"See that you do," said Dante. "I'm serious about this. Any sign of deference or regret will be viewed as weakness not only by your enemies, but, worse still, by the men who work for you. Santiago bows to no one, he apologizes to no one, he defers to no one. Never forget that, or you'll be long buried when I want to ask you that question a decade from now."

"I'll remember," amended the Bandit.

Dante stared at him for a long moment.

"What's wrong?" asked the Bandit.

"Ordinarily I'd suggest cosmetic surgery, a whole new face, maybe prosthetic eyes that can see into the infrared and ultraviolet and retinas that aren't on record anywhere, but . . ." He let his voice trail off.

"But what?"

"But there's no way to hide or disguise your arm. I don't know that we'd want to, anyway. Once people know what it can do, just threatening to use it may win us a couple of bloodless battles." He got to his feet and started pacing back and forth. "I suppose what we'll have to do is find a sector of the Frontier where you've never been, where no one knows you, and build our organization from there. We'll have to fake the One-Armed Bandit's death, and make it spectacular, so everyone knows about it."

"Why?" asked the Bandit. "Sooner or later they're going to figure out who I am."

"You're Santiago."

"You know what I mean."

"Santiago can't be anyone except Santiago. That's why everyone has to know that the One-Armed Bandit's dead. Perhaps he was Santiago's friend. Maybe he even saved Santiago's life, and Santiago had his real arm removed and this prosthetic weapon installed in its place as a tribute to the Bandit, or because its power and efficiency impressed him. But the thing you can never forget is that Santiago is more than a man. He's an idea, a concept, a myth. He can't be bigger than life if everyone knows who he used to be."

"It sounds like you've considered all this pretty thoroughly," remarked the Bandit.

"I'm as close to a biographer as you're ever going to have," said Dante, "so I have to know everything there is to know about Santiago."

There was a knock at the door.

"Open," said the Bandit.

The door slid back and Matilda, Virgil, Blossom, and Wilbur Connaught entered the room.

"I know you," said the Bandit to Matilda. He turned to Blossom. "I've *seen* you." He gestured to Virgil and Wilbur. "These two I don't recognize at all."

"They work for you," said Dante. "Time for the introductions." He laid a hand on each of their shoulders in turn.

"This is Matilda. This is Virgil. This young lady is Blossom. And this gentleman is Wilbur."

"No last names?" asked the Bandit.

"You'll learn them soon enough," said Dante. He walked over to the Bandit and turned to face the four of them. "And this is Santiago. He has no past, no history. He is a spirit of the Frontier made flesh. That's all you have to know about him, and all you will ever tell anyone else. The One-Armed Bandit is no more, and will never be referred to again until we are free to talk about his untimely and very public death. Is that clear to everyone?"

The four agreed.

Dante turned back to the Bandit. "Dimitrios of the Three Burners has committed to our cause. We'll get word to him that we're ready to have him join us."

"Let him continue to do what he does best," said the Bandit. "When I have an assignment for him, that'll be time enough to meet him."

Dante stared at the Bandit. *You look larger, somehow. Can you possibly be growing into the part right in front of my eyes?*

"Well, let's get down to work," said Dante. "As money comes in, we'll turn it over to Wilbur. He'll have to open his books to me or to Matilda if we request it, but only Santiago can fire him."

"How much are we paying you?" asked the Bandit.

"Three percent of everything I make."

"That seems fair. Wait here a moment." He walked into the bedroom, then returned a moment later with a small cloth bag. "Here," he said, handing the bag to Wilbur. "There are sixty-three diamonds in it. Get what you can for them—probably you'll have to go into the Democracy for the best price—and put the money to work for us. There's no sense having you wait around until we start generating cash. And Wilbur?"

"Yes."

"Those diamonds belong to every underprivileged, abused colonist on the Inner Frontier. If you or they should

disappear, I will personally hunt you down and make you
wish you'd never been born."

"You didn't have to say that, Santiago," said Wilbur in
hurt tones.

"The One-Armed Bandit didn't have to say it," replied
the Bandit. "Santiago did."

By God, you're really him! thought Dante. Aloud he said,
"I think our first duty is going to be to find a headquarters
world, someplace parsecs away from anyone who's ever
seen you in action."

"It makes no difference to me what world we choose,"
said the Bandit. "Any suggestions?"

Dante turned to Matilda. "You're far more familiar with
the Inner Frontier than I am. What do you think?"

"Let me think about it for a day," she replied. "Probably
someplace in the Albion Cluster. You haven't been there,
have you, Santiago?"

"Just once, ma'am, a long time ago—before I lost my
arm."

"I think that's probably long enough," said Dante.

"Besides, his arm's his most distinctive feature," added
Blossom. "It's what people remember."

"Okay, check out the Albion Cluster and come up with
a safe haven by tomorrow." Suddenly Dante smiled. "Well,
now I know how Safe Harbor got its name."

"What can *I* do?" asked Blossom.

"Come to the Cluster with us," said the Bandit. "When
I decide where I want to strike first, I'll send you ahead to
be my eyes and ears until I arrive."

"Now, once we've got a headquarters world, we'll start
building an organization from the ground up," said Dante.
"We'll recruit whoever we need, and we'll come up with
some kind of battle plan." He paused. "Correction: *Santiago* will come up with a battle plan." He looked around
the room. "Has anyone got any questions, or anything else
to say?"

No one spoke up.

"Then I guess that's it," said Dante. "We'll meet again

tomorrow when Matilda has come up with some worlds for our consideration—though again, we can only suggest and advise. It's Santiago's choice."

They began walking to the door, and then the Bandit spoke: "Before you leave, I want to say something."

They stopped and turned to him.

"You've given me an honor I don't deserve, and at the same time you've given me a challenge I can't refuse. From this moment on, I am Santiago, and the only thing that matters to me is protecting the colonists of the Inner Frontier from the Democracy. I realize that we will never overthrow it, and we wouldn't want to if we could—it serves its purpose in a galaxy where we're outnumbered hundreds to one—but we will devote our lives to reminding it with whatever degree of force is required that we of the Inner Frontier are Men, too, and that we are not the enemy." He looked at each of them in turn. "I pledge to you that I will never give you any reason to be ashamed of me."

There was a moment of silence, and then Dante began applauding, and soon all the others had joined in. Finally they walked out to the airlift and descended to the lobby. Matilda, Blossom, and Wilbur all left to go about their business, but Virgil made a beeline to the bar, and Dante joined him a moment later, sitting down next to him.

"You didn't say a word up there," noted the poet. "Not a single word."

"I didn't have anything to say."

"And do you now?"

"Not really."

"No comment on Santiago at all?"

"None," said the Injun. "What do *you* think of him?"

"He's humble, he's decent, he's polite, he's the deadliest man I've met but he only kills when he has to, and he seems to be adjusting to the role he's going to play."

"He only kills when he has to?" repeated Virgil.

"That's why he hasn't wiped out the Unicorns. He could, you know."

"Well, I'll tell you something," said Virgil. "While you

were busy indoctrinating him, I went out and got some facts and did a little math."

"And?" said Dante.

"You know how many people our Santiago has killed?"

"I haven't the faintest idea."

"Thirty-seven men and an unspecified number of aliens, thought to exceed the thousand mark," Virgil paused and looked at the poet. "Do you think they *all* needed killing?"

"If *he* killed them, yes," said Dante sincerely. "Hell, he'd be justified in killing ten thousand Unicorns, the way they attack humans at every opportunity."

"If you say so."

"Listen to me, Virgil," persisted the poet. "This guy is the hero every kid wishes he could be. He's well-mannered. He's humble. He's moral. He's almost too good to be true."

"That's the gist of it," agreed Virgil.

"I don't follow you."

"It's been my experience," said the Injun, "that when you come across something that seems to be too good to be true, it usually *is* too good to be true."

19.

GLORIA MUNDI, BORN ON MONDAY,
GLORIA MUNDI, DIED ON SUNDAY,
GLORIA MUNDI, ROSE ON TUESDAY,
WHICH QUALIFIED AS A BAD NEWS DAY.

NO ONE EVER KNEW HER real name. The betting is that she herself had long since forgotten it. It didn't make any difference. What really matters is not *who* she was, but rather *what* she was.

Gloria Mundi had been a beggar woman, living out her life in squalor in the slums on Roosevelt III—until the day (and yes, it was a Sunday) that she was struck by lightning. It killed her, but because of the thousands of deaths and casualties caused by the Sett War, which had reached the Roosevelt system two weeks earlier, they didn't have time to perform a postmortem or prepare the body for a funeral. They were working around the clock, saving the wounded and trying to identify the dead, so Gloria's body was shunted aside until they finally had time to work on it.

And, miraculously, two days later she woke up, found herself in a room with dozens of corpses, and began screaming. She kept the screaming up for a very long time, until they finally found and sedated her.

When she awoke from the sedative, she claimed to remember what she had experienced while dead. A number of the medics felt she had merely been in a deep coma, that no one comes back from the dead after thirty-six hours . . . but when they checked the records of the medical computers and sensors that had examined her, they had to admit that yes, she really had been dead for a day and a half.

The moment that fact was made public, a number of news organizations offered her millions in exchange for her exclusive story. But before she could choose among them, or even adjust to the fact that she no longer had to worry about where her next meal was coming from, suddenly there were more people out to kill her than ever went after Santiago. And if the would-be killers weren't fanatical priests, ayatollahs, ministers, rabbis, and shamans themselves, then they were in the employ of such men. Publicly they all believed that their religion was the only true one, and that Gloria Mundi would confirm it . . . and privately their first thought was to make sure she didn't reveal any experience she might have had or knowledge she might have gained that would confirm the truth of a rival religion.

As for Gloria herself, she never spoke about what she had experienced. Somehow she eluded her assassins until they finally decided she had died of old age or at the hands of another killer, or their employers gradually lost interest in her.

And so, at age eighty-six, Gloria Mundi found herself on Heliopolis II, temporarily (and, for all she knew, permanently) safe from the men who had tried to hunt her down. Her health was gone—she had just about every disease of the aged except senility, and her brain hadn't functioned all that well since she had revived—but she kept to herself, didn't bother anyone, and seemed likely to live out her few remaining months or years in some semblance of peace.

She was far from everyone's thoughts when they met at the Bandit's rooms the next morning. Matilda had come up with Beta Cordero II, a world in the Albion Cluster, and she was extolling its virtues to the group.

"Standard oxygen, temperate climate, ninety-four-percent Standard gravity. No indigenous sentient races."

"None?" said Dante.

"Well, there were two—one humanoid, one not—but the Navy went a little overboard pacifying them about six hundred years ago. There are a few remnants on other planets who claim ownership of the world, but none of them have returned."

"Why not?" asked the Bandit.

"It only became safe for habitation a couple of years

ago," answered Matilda. "Prior to that there was too much radioactivity. The water just passed inspection five weeks ago, so this is a perfect time to establish a presence there."

"What are the nearest major worlds?"

"The biggest trading world in the sector is Diomedes. There's a military outpost on Jamison V, but it's pretty small. A few nearby farming worlds that supply about sixty mining worlds within, oh, perhaps five hundred light-years."

"It sounds promising," said Dante. "Has the Democracy staked any legal claim to it?"

"No," answered Matilda. "I'm sure they'd claim it was within their sphere of influence, but there are no ownership claims."

"When was the last time the Democracy or its representatives set down on it?"

"They sent a drone ship thirty-two days ago to test the radioactivity level. As far as I can tell, no member of the Democracy has actually set foot on Beta Cordero II in more than six hundred years."

"Sounds good to me," announced the Bandit. "We'll set up shop there as soon as we can."

"Fine," said Dante. "Now we'll need a name for it."

"It *has* a name," replied the Bandit. "Beta Cordero II."

"That name's on every star map created during the past millennium, maybe longer," explained Dante. "We need a name to give to our agents, a name that if overheard won't tell the Democracy where we are."

"That makes sense," agreed the Bandit. He lowered his head in thought for a moment, then looked up. "We'll call it Valhalla."

"Valhalla it is," said Matilda.

"When shall we leave?" asked Blossom, speaking up for the first time.

"Not much sense going there until we've got some shelter," said Dante. "We'll have to send some people ahead to build us whatever we need—once Wilbur can raise some money. In the meantime, I guess we'll stay here."

"That's unacceptable," said the Bandit. "It's time to start making a difference."

"Well, I suppose there are still some buildings standing, but after six centuries, I don't know . . ."

"We're not going to use ancient buildings that are probably ready to collapse the first time someone sets foot in them, if indeed they're still standing," said the Bandit firmly. "And we're not going to wait for Wilbur to work his magic with the diamonds I gave him yesterday."

Good, thought Dante. *You're showing us what Santiago is supposed to do and be.*

"I don't see what you're getting at," said Blossom.

"Santiago is the King of the Outlaws, isn't he?" replied the Bandit. "And this is a mining world, run by the Democracy. What better place for us to announce that Santiago is back?"

"You're going to rob the assay office?"

He shook his head. "I'd just get a few diamonds they hadn't transferred to the bank yet, and then we'd still have to wait for Wilbur to convert them into cash." He paused. "Santiago is going to rob the Heliopolis branch of the Bank of Deluros VIII. We'll pick up a few million credits in half a dozen currencies, money we can use immediately." He turned to Matilda. "Valhalla hasn't been worked in more than half a millennium. I think rather than posing as a farmer, perhaps I should be a reclusive sportsman, or maybe a trapper."

"I'll check and see if any animals are left on the planet."

"If there are, maybe they've mutated into something worth hunting," said Dante.

"No one has a problem with this?" asked the Bandit.

There were no responses.

"You," he continued, indicating Virgil. "You never speak. Why not?"

"I've got nothing to say," answered the Injun.

"There have been times when you couldn't shut him up," added Dante.

"If your silence is disapproval," said the Bandit, "now's

the time to cut and run. I won't hold it against you. But once Santiago makes his presence known, I won't tolerate disloyalty."

"I'll stick around," said Virgil.

"You approve of Santiago, then?"

"I couldn't care less about Santiago," said the Injun. "My fate is tied to the poet's."

"In what way?"

"He's Dante, I'm Virgil," said the Injun, as if that explained everything.

"I don't understand."

"Neither do I, really," admitted Virgil, "but I know that it's my destiny to lead Dante through the nine circles of hell to the promised land."

"I don't know what you're talking about."

"What difference does it make? I serve the poet and he serves you, so therefore *I* serve you."

The Bandit considered his answer for a moment, then nodded his approval. "Okay," he said at last. "I can accept that."

"When are you going to hit the bank?" asked Wilbur.

"We need the money, so I might as well do it right now."

"I don't know," said Dante.

"What's your problem?" asked Matilda.

"We can't stay on Heliopolis once he robs the bank, but nothing will be ready for us on Valhalla."

"So we'll make our way there in slow, easy steps, while I send a crew ahead to prepare our headquarters for us."

"The Democracy's not going to pursue us in slow, easy steps," said Dante.

"The Democracy will be looking for Santiago," said Matilda. "What do *you* think he looks like? What are his identifying marks? How big is his gang?"

"Point taken," said Dante.

"Can I help?" asked Blossom.

"Are you any good with a burner or a screecher?" asked Dante.

"No."

"Then you might as well stay here, where you'll be safe."

"If you want to come, you can come," interrupted the Bandit. "There will probably be enough loot that we'll need all the help we can get just to cart it away."

"How will you carry it from the bank back here without being seen?" asked Matilda.

"We won't," answered the Bandit. "We'll summon transportation to take us right from the bank to the spaceport."

I don't know how well thought out this is, thought Dante, *but you're the boss. Let's see what happens, and if you're making a blunder, at least you're making it on a minor world and not on Binder X or Roosevelt III.*

"I'll handle the fighting," said the Bandit. "Whoever's with me is just there to cart out the money. I don't want to have to keep an eye on you once the shooting starts, so stay well behind me. Are there any questions?"

"Back in the Democracy," said Dante, "it's standard operating procedure for one or more of the bank's employees to have an implant that reads their blood pressure and adrenaline and is tied in to the bank's computer."

"What if the clerk is just reacting to a pretty girl?" asked Virgil.

"If the reading goes more than ten percent above normal, the teller's computers will register it. Then he's got about ten seconds to disable it, which means it *was* a pretty girl, or an insect sting, or something like that. If he *doesn't* disable it in ten seconds, it sends a signal to the police station."

"I didn't know that," said the Bandit.

"You've never robbed a bank before," said Dante with a smile. "I have. There's no reason to believe the technology hasn't spread to the Frontier. We can still do the job, but we'll have to act *fast*."

Silence.

"All right, then," continued the Bandit. "I'll give you each an hour to collect whatever you plan to take along to Valhalla and load it into your ships or mine." He gave them the location, ID number, and computer code to his ship.

"Mine is big enough to carry all of us, but if we split up we should be harder to spot, in case anyone gets a good description of us." He turned to the Grand Finale. "Wilbur, you might as well leave right now. If we come away with cash, we won't need you to convert it for us, and if you wait a day or two, security at the spaceport will be much tighter and they'll almost certainly find the diamonds I gave you." He paused. "Meet us on Valhalla. We'll probably get there first, so radio us before you land and we'll give you coordinates. If we come away with some diamonds as well as cash, we'll turn them over to you and send you back into the Democracy with them."

Wilbur nodded his agreement. "Good luck," he said, and left the room.

"Okay," said the Bandit. "I'll see you at the bank in exactly two hours."

He sat down and lit up a smokeless cigar.

"Aren't you taking anything out to your ship?" asked Blossom.

"Just me. Anything I take might be too easy to identify."

"That makes sense," said Dante. "If this holdup works, we can all afford to buy whatever we need. If not, it won't matter anyway."

He sat down next to the Bandit.

"Well, if everyone feels that way, we might as well get started," said Blossom.

"Sit," said the Bandit.

"Why?"

"We've got to give Wilbur time to collect the diamonds, get out to the spaceport, and take off."

"Shit!" she exclaimed. "I hadn't thought of that."

"It's not your job to think of that," said the Bandit.

"What if they alert the spaceport after we're on our way there?" asked Blossom.

"Then we'll improvise," said Dante.

"They won't alert the spaceport," said the Bandit with such conviction that no one challenged him.

The five of them waited in silence for almost two hours. Finally the Bandit got to his feet.

"It's time," he announced.

The others got up and followed him to the door. They took the airlift down to the main floor, then were about to walk out through the airlock when Dante stopped by the desk, spoke in low tones to the clerk, allowed the cashier to scan his retina and then rejoined the party.

"What was that all about?" asked Matilda as they emerged into the hot, oppressive Heliopolis day.

"I paid for the Bandit's room for another month."

"That was stupid," said Virgil. "He's leaving today, and who cares who knows it?"

"If two Democracy soldiers hang around waiting for him to come back, that's two less that'll be on our trail once we leave Heliopolis," answered Dante. "As for the money, I'll take it out of what we steal from the bank, or I won't need it anyway."

"I approve," said the Bandit. "That's good thinking, Rhymer." He turned to Matilda. "Are you sure you want to be part of this, ma'am? You can wait in the ship if you prefer."

"If things get rough, she'll be more help to you than I will," Dante assured him.

The Bandit shrugged. "Your choice."

The bank was two hundred yards away. The Bandit walked with an easy spring to his stride, as if he was walking down a thoroughfare on Deluros VIII or Earth itself. The others struggled to keep up with him.

"It might be best for you four to wait outside," he said when they finally arrived at their destination.

"Not unless you make it an order," said Matilda.

"It was just a suggestion. The only order is: stay behind me, and make sure none of you gets between me and anyone else."

They entered the bank, the Bandit first, then Dante and the two women, and Virgil bringing up the rear. It was a small building, tightly bonded titanium beneath a wood veneer. There were a couple of coat closets, a huge water bubbler, a quartet of chairs carved from some alien hardwood, and holograms of the bank's founders on the walls. There were three tellers—two human, one robotic—behind a counter, and a well-dressed executive in a glassed-in office. Six customers were lined up at the windows, five miners and a small, wiry, eighty-six-year-old woman—Gloria Mundi.

The Bandit waited until one of the tellers' windows was open, and then approached it.

"Yes, sir?" said the clerk, a middle-aged man. "What can I do for you?"

"You can start by emptying out the drawer in front of you," said the Bandit calmly.

"I beg your pardon?"

"This is a holdup. Give me all the money you can reach without moving your feet. Then we'll go to work on the rest."

"I know who you are," said the clerk nervously. "You work *for* Men, not against us. This is some kind of joke, right?"

Disable him now, thought Dante. *Your ten seconds are almost up!*

"Give me your money," repeated the Bandit. "I won't ask again."

Suddenly lights started flashing and alarms began ringing. Metal bars appeared where open doors and windows had been. Two screechers suddenly appeared in the robot teller's hands. The clerk whose adrenaline readings had precipitated all this ducked down behind the counter, completely out of sight.

The Bandit whirled and sent a laser burst into the robot teller. It knocked the robot back against the wall, melting one of its arms, but didn't totally disable it. Another burst took the robot's head off its body, and it collapsed to the floor.

The Bandit then fired through the barrier where the clerk was hiding, and the man's body fell over with an audible thud. Next came two holo cameras and the third teller. A

laser blast just missed him, and the Bandit turned and
pointed a deadly finger at the executive.

"You'll never get away with—" yelled the executive, but
the Bandit's lethal arm fired again and his sentence ended
with a moist gurgle.

The Bandit looked at the carnage. No one was left alive
except two customers, a man and a woman.

"Get in that corner," he ordered, indicating where he
wanted them to go. Finally he turned to his confederates.
"All right," he said. "Start collecting the money—fast!
Concentrate on Far London pounds, Maria Theresa dollars,
New Stalin rubles, and other Frontier currencies. Only take
credits that haven't been bundled; there are too many ways
for the bank to have marked the others."

Dante and the others quickly went to the tellers' windows, removing large wads of cash from them.

Two police officers burst into the bank. The Bandit fired
at one, killing him instantly. Virgil straightened up and shot
the other with a screecher, firing through the teller's window.

"Where the hell's the safe?" asked Matilda, staring at the
blank wall behind the windows.

Dante looked around. "It's got to be in the office." He
raced into the room and couldn't spot it.

"It's a bank—it *has* to have a vault!" said Matilda.

"Of course it does," said Dante. "Let me think." He examined the office. "Something's wrong here. No one has
two coat closets, not on Heliopolis II." He opened the first.
Nothing but a fresh white shirt. Then he tried the second—
and hit pay dirt.

"Santiago!" he called out.

"What is it?" answered the Bandit.

"Got a helluva complex lock here," said Dante. "It'll take
me the better part of twenty minutes to break the code."

"Step back," said the Bandit, entering the office.

Dante stepped away from the safe. The Bandit made a
swift adjustment to his arm, and then he fired—and the

door to the vault simply vanished amid a cloud of acrid smoke.

"Get to work!" said Dante, racing into the vault just ahead of Matilda and Blossom.

Dante found a pair of cloth bags and tossed them to the woman. Then he quickly rummaged through the office until he found a briefcase and began filling it with cash. After about two minutes they'd emptied the vault of all its cash.

"Where are the safety-deposit boxes?" asked Matilda.

"Don't bother with them," said the Bandit.

"We need all the money we can get!" she objected.

"There's a Democracy garrison four miles east of town. It's almost certainly tied in to the alarm. They figure to be here any second. It's time to leave."

Matilda ceased her objections instantly, and raced to the door.

"No vehicle," she announced.

"I put in a call for one," said the Bandit.

"Let's hope it arrives ahead of the soldiers," said Matilda.

Dante took a quick look out the door. "No such luck."

"They're here already?" asked the Bandit, more surprised than alarmed. "They were faster than I thought."

"What are we going to do?" asked Blossom.

"Stay calm," said the Bandit. "I'll handle this."

He waited until the two military vehicles that were approaching the bank pulled to within fifty yards, then made another quick adjustment to his arm and pointed it at them—but just as he was about to fire, the male customer launched himself at the Bandit's legs, knocking him to the floor. The Bandit brought his real hand down on the back of the man's neck, a killing blow that resulted in a loud *crack!* Then he got to his feet, stood in the doorway, pointed at each vehicle in turn, and calmly blew both of them away.

"That should discourage anyone from playing the hero before our transportation arrives," he announced.

"How will they know what happened or who to blame?" asked Blossom.

"We'll tell them," answered the Bandit. He pointed at the wall behind the cashiers and carved out the name SANTIAGO with a laser beam.

"That should do the trick," agreed Dante.

The old woman spoke up for the first time. "That will fool no one," said Gloria Mundi. "I know who you are."

"I'm Santiago," said the Bandit.

"You're the One-Armed Bandit," she replied, "and I'll tell everyone I know who you are. Santiago's been dead for more than a hundred years."

"I'm sorry you feel so strongly about that, ma'am," said the Bandit regretfully. He turned to her and pointed his finger between her eyes.

"Wait!" shouted Dante,

"What is it?" asked the Bandit.

"Santiago doesn't go around killing old ladies!"

"Santiago doesn't leave witnesses who can identify him."

"She's a crazy old woman who thinks she saw God once," persisted Dante. "No one will listen to her!"

"She's a threat to our continued existence," said the Bandit. "She's got to go."

"I agree," said Matilda.

"Is that how you want it to begin?" demanded Dante. "With Santiago killing a half-crazed beggar woman?"

"How do *you* want it to begin?" she shot back as the empty airport transport pulled up, avoiding the smoking shells of the two Democracy vehicles. "With a description of each of us on file with every soldier and bounty hunter on the Inner Frontier? We need the Democracy to be searching for clues *here* while we're setting up shop in the Albion Cluster."

"This isn't the way we're supposed to start," said Dante bitterly.

"We're in the revolution business," replied Matilda. "This is a war. There are always civilian casualties."

"What war?" croaked Gloria Mundi. "You're a bunch of

bank robbers, working for the One-Armed Bandit!"

"That's it," said Matilda. "We have no choice. She has to die."

"What if she promises not to tell the authorities what she saw?" asked Dante.

"Would you believe her if she *did* promise it?" asked Matilda, staring at Gloria Mundi.

"No," admitted Dante, his shoulders slumping. "No, I wouldn't."

"Well, then?"

"Damn it, Santiago doesn't kill helpless old ladies!" repeated Dante.

"I hope you don't think I *want* to do this," interjected the Bandit. "But it was you yourself who pointed out all the unpleasant choices Santiago would have to make and all the unsavory things he would have to do."

"I didn't mean *this*."

"We both know Santiago will have to do far worse things before he's done," said the Bandit.

Suddenly they heard a humming sound and turned to see the source of it. Virgil Soaring Hawk had just aimed a burst of solid light between Gloria Mundi's eyes and left a smoking hole in the middle of her forehead.

"Enough talk," said the Injun. "Let's get the hell out of here."

Not an auspicious debut, thought Dante as he stepped over the old woman's corpse and carried his briefcase out to the vehicle. *Not a promising start at all.*

20.

CANDY FOR THE BILLFOLD, CANDY FOR THE
   NOSE,
CANDY FOR THE CLIENT, AS THE BUSINESS
   GROWS.
CANDY BY THE BUSHEL, CANDY BY THE TON;
THE CANDY MAN SUPPLIES IT, COME AND
   SHARE THE FUN!

IF HE HAD A NAME, no one knew it. If he had fingerprints,
they had long since been burned off. If he had a retinagram
on file, it was rendered meaningless when he replaced his
natural eyes with a pair of artificial ones, which had the
added advantage of being able to see far into the infrared.

They say he began his career out on the Rim, and later
moved to the Spiral Arm. No one knew how many addicts
he had created, and no one knew how much money he had
made, but estimates of both were astronomical.

He began with cocaine and heroin, both grown on his
own farms on the Rim, then moved to more and more exotic designer drugs and hallucinogens. He finally stopped
when he got to alphanella seeds, but only because there
was nothing more addictive—and expensive—in the entire
galaxy.

There were warrants for the Candy Man all across the
Outer Frontier, up and down the Spiral Arm, and throughout the Democracy, so it made sense that he eventually
turned up on the Inner Frontier, the one place where there
was no price on his head.

That lasted about three Standard months. By then he'd
taken over a rival drug lord's territory, and had killed three
of the enemy and a pair of the Democracy's undercover
agents. There was no place left to run to, so instead of
running he surrounded himself with a quasi-military oper-

ation. Only the very best, the very wealthiest clients ever got to see the Candy Man face-to-face. He rarely did his own selling, and even more rarely did his own killing. (He *did* do his own accounting, and no one in his employ ever got to see his data files.)

He divided his time among half a dozen worlds, and even his most trusted underlings never knew when and where he'd show up next. He owned an impregnable mansion on each world, and three meals a day were prepared for him at each of them, just to confound any potential assassins. As an ambitious young man on the way up, he'd taken all kinds of chances; now that he was no longer poor and no longer in such a hurry, he saw no percentage in taking any chances at all.

The Bandit and his party had never heard of the Candy Man when they touched down on Beta Cordero II. They had spent a leisurely month getting there, approaching it by a wildly circuitous route to give the crews Matilda had hired time to build what appeared to be a large, luxurious private hunting lodge. There was no way the casual, or even the acute, observer could spot the three subspace antennae, or the generator that not only supplied light and power for the lodge but for its underground computer complex. There were three guest houses; two were what they seemed, and the third was an arsenal, currently four-fifths empty but soon, they hoped, to be filled with whatever weaponry Santiago needed to accomplish his goals.

The Bandit walked quickly through the lodge, ignoring the huge living room with the four-way fireplace crafted out of shining alien stone, checked his sleeping quarters, and declared it acceptable. He then summoned Dante and Matilda to the cozy paneled room he had claimed as his private office.

"I don't see any reason to waste time," he announced. "We might as well get to work."

"Have you something in mind?" asked Dante.

"There's no sense building an organization when we can simply take one over," answered the Bandit. "Find the biggest drug and smuggling rings in the sector."

"They might not be anxious to join us," said Dante.

"They won't have a choice. You just find them; I'll handle it from there."

"Whatever you say, Santiago," replied Dante.

"You don't need me for that," said Matilda. "I think I could serve you better by contacting some of the people I know and recruiting them."

The Bandit nodded his approval. "Keep in touch," he said, dismissing her. She left the room and he turned back to Dante. "Will you need to spread any money around to find out who's in charge of each ring?"

"Almost certainly."

"Take whatever you think you'll require. We're going to get it back anyway."

"You're going to kill the leaders?" It wasn't really a question.

"My job is protecting the citizens of the Inner Frontier," replied the Bandit. "They are preying on *my* people."

"We might be able to buy them off, get them on our side," suggested Dante.

The Bandit stared at him expressionlessly. "We don't want them on our side. They're parasites, nothing more."

Which is precisely what we'll become when we take over their organizations. I wonder how you rationalize that—or does Santiago just not consider such things?

"Killing their leaders will be an object lesson to the rank and file," continued the Bandit. "No one rises to a position of authority in such an organization without being totally ruthless. This will convince them that Santiago is an even more ruthless killer. That should impress them and keep them on our side."

Why do I feel uneasy about this, wondered Dante. *This is exactly what Santiago is supposed to do, so why does it worry me when you talk about doing it?*

"That's all," said the Bandit, dismissing him. "Let me know when you have the information."

"Yes, Santiago," said Dante, getting up and leaving the office.

Matilda was waiting for him in the corridor. "Well," she said as they walked past a number of holograms of savage alien animals to the living room, "what do you think?"

"About what?"

"About *him*," said Matilda. "He's growing into the role exactly as we'd hoped."

"If you say so."

"You don't think so?"

He shrugged. "I don't know."

"What's bothering you?" she asked.

"I can't put my finger on it," said Dante.

"He was right to want to kill the old woman, you know," said Matilda. "It would have been suicide to have left her behind."

"There were alternatives."

"What? Take her along for a month and then turn her loose? She'd still have betrayed us."

"Nonsense," he replied irritably. "All he had to do was turn to me or Virgil, address us as Santiago, and ask if we wanted him to do anything else."

She stared at him, surprised. "Hey, that's not bad."

"Yeah—but *he* didn't think of it."

"Not everyone's as devious as you are."

"You asked, I answered." He paused. "Also, he really gets into giving orders. The 'misters' and 'ma'ams' vanished pretty fast."

"He's Santiago. It's his job to give orders."

"I know, I know—but good manners ought to last a little longer."

"He's adaptable. And he's a born leader. Look at his decision to rob the bank, and burn Santiago's name into the wall. Look at the other ideas he's had." She paused. "What does he want you to do?"

"Find the biggest smugglers and drug runners in the sector."

"Whom he'll then proceed to kill?"

Dante nodded. "And take over their operations."

"Isn't that precisely the kind of thing that Santiago is supposed to do?"

"I suppose so. I just don't like it."

"That's why you're the Rhymer and he's Santiago."

"Probably you're right," he said.

"Then let's get going," said Matilda. "We both have work to do."

Dante sought out Virgil and handed him a wad of credits and Maria Theresa dollars.

"What's this for?" asked the Injun.

"The best drugs you can buy."

"That's my job?" asked Virgil with a happy smile. "I could really get into working for this guy."

"Just buy them, don't take them," said Dante.

"I'm ambidextrous," said Virgil. "I can do both."

"You heard me," said Dante firmly. "Buy it, and see if you can find out who sells it."

"The guy I buy it from."

"Find out who he works for, as high up the line as you can go."

"But I can't take any of the drugs?"

"That's right."

"This fucking scheme was a lot better when it just had *me* thinking about it," muttered Virgil.

"And let me know where you're going, so we don't visit the same worlds."

"You're buying drugs too?"

"That doubles our chances of finding the headman."

"Do you get to take any?"

"You can have mine when this is all over and we've got our man," said Dante disgustedly.

Virgil grinned. "That's more like it!" he said, and headed off toward the newly poured slab that housed all their ships.

Dante stopped by his room, packed a small bag, made sure he had enough money left, and then walked to the tiny landing slab. He fired up the pile on a one-man ship, climbed into it, had the navigational computer throw up a globe of the sector and its populated worlds, and decided on Alabaster, about sixteen light-years distant. He radioed his destination to Virgil to make sure they didn't both visit the same planet, and then took off. He hit the stratosphere about ninety seconds later, then jumped to light speeds.

He slept through most of the voyage, and awoke when the ship's computer told him he was in orbit around Alabaster. The world was almost totally covered in the fleecy white clouds that gave it its name. The ship turned over control of its functions to the spaceport's landing tower, and touched down without incident.

Dante emerged, passed through Customs, and caught a subterranean monorail that took him into the underground city of Snakepit. There were too many cyclones and tornadoes on the surface, so Man had built this commercial outpost where none of the planet's weather could bother him.

Snakepit extended about two miles in each direction. Since the planet had never been inhabited by a sentient race, the alien quarter—the exclusive domain of offworld non-Men—was a little smaller and more upscale than usual. There were a number of banks—all far more heavily guarded than the one on Heliopolis II—and the usual array of traders, assay offices, hotels, brothels, casinos, restaurants, subspace stations, holo theaters, and permanent residences.

Dante checked into a hotel and then decided to take a look around and get the feel of the place. The first building he passed was a grocery selling fruits from Pollux IV, vegetables from Greenveldt and Sunnyblue, mutated beef from Alpha Bezerine IV, even some wine from distant Altagore.

He continued walking, came to a grubby bar, and entered it. He studied the faces he found there. These weren't the hard men who traveled the Frontier, living by their wits and their skills. These men weren't traveling anywhere, and such skills as they had once possessed were long gone.

You're the bottom of the food chain. There will be too many connections between you and the man I'm after.

He turned and left, ignoring the catcalls that followed him, then began looking into store windows until he found one that sold formal wear. He went in, purchased the finest outfit they had, waited while the robot tailor shortened the sleeves and took in the waist, then returned to his hotel and napped until dinnertime.

Then he donned the formal outfit, changed some of his larger bills at the hotel desk so that his roll of money would look even bigger, and had the desk clerk direct him to the most expensive restaurant in Snakepit. He wasn't very hungry, and found the food mediocre and overpriced, but he stayed long enough to be seen by a goodly number of people. Then, after he paid his bill with cash, flashing his huge roll of money, he went off to the Golden Flush, the most expensive casino in town.

He made quite a production of peeling bills off his roll to bet at the craps table, broke even after half an hour, then wandered over to the *jabob* table (the one alien game that had taken hold in the Frontier's casinos), and dropped a quick fifty thousand credits.

Next he went to the men's room, ostensibly to rinse his face off, actually because it was the most private spot in the casino and the one where he was most likely to be approached. And sure enough, a blond man with almost colorless blue eyes followed him in.

"I saw you at the tables," he said.

There was a long silence. Dante wasn't going to make it any easier on the man. He'd sell harder if Dante offered him no encouragement.

He hadn't asked any questions, so Dante offered no reply.

"You look like a man with money to spend," continued the man. "You ever spend it on anything besides the tables?"

"From time to time," replied Dante.

"How about tonight?"

Dante finished wiping off his face, then turned to the

blond man. "The only thing I buy is seed, and I don't buy it from flunkies."

"I'm no flunky!" said the man angrily.

"Bullshit," said Dante. "I can smell a flunky a mile off. You go tell your boss I'll make a buy, but only from him."

The man seemed to be considering his answer, and whether to admit that he even had a boss. Finally he said: "He doesn't deal with the customers."

Dante pulled his wad out. "I've got two million credits here. I have another million Maria Theresa dollars back on my ship. I'm going to spend it on seed. Now, I can spend it with your boss, or I can buy it from someone else, it makes no difference to me." He paused. "But it'll make a difference to you, because I'll pass the word that you're the reason I went elsewhere."

"Maybe I'll just kill you and take your money," said the man menacingly as he stepped closer and loomed over the much smaller Dante.

"Just how dumb do you think I am?" said Dante, allowing his contempt to creep into his voice. "See this diamond stickpin I'm wearing? It's a miniaturized holo camera. Your face, your voiceprint, everything you've said since you came in here are already in half a dozen computers."

It was a lie, but told with utter conviction, and the blond man hesitated uneasily. "Why should I believe you?" he demanded.

"Because we're alone in a bathroom on your turf, and if it wasn't true I'd be inviting you to blow me away. Is everyone in your organization as stupid as you?"

"You call me stupid once more and I'll kill you, camera or no camera!" snarled the blond man.

Don't push it too hard. These guys shoot first and ask questions later.

"Okay, we're at an impasse. I've got millions to spend, your boss has millions to unload. You know I won't deal with anyone else. Do you take me to him, or do I spend my money somewhere else? It's getting late; I need a decision."

The blond man frowned. Finally he said: "It may take a while to reach him."

"That's not my problem. All he has to know is that my name is Dante Alighieri, and I'm staying at the Cheshire Hotel. He can find me there." He walked to the door, then turned back to the man. "I'm leaving in the morning. If I don't hear from him by then, I won't be back."

He walked out of the men's room without waiting for a reply, kept walking past the bar and tables of the Golden Flush, and didn't stop until he reached his suite at the Cheshire a few minutes later. Then he considered his situation. By now they'd checked out his identity and his ship's registration. They wouldn't be able to find out where he got his money, but they'd be able to assure themselves that he was who he said he was, that he wasn't a Democracy undercover agent. It would take a few hours for the man to round up some muscle and come to the hotel. He had time to get out of his uncomfortable formal outfit, take a quick Dryshower, and get into his regular clothes.

He finished dressing and had spent the next two hours hovering a few inches above the floor on a form-adapt chair, staring out his window at the city, watching the artificial lights play on the rough underground walls, when the Spy-Eye alerted him that he had visitors and showed him holograms of the seven humans who were standing at the door to the suite. He ordered it to open, then had his chair turn until he was facing his visitors.

The muscle entered first. What surprised him was that the muscle that seemed to be in charge were both women. They were hard-featured, hard-muscled, hard-eyed, and heavily armed, one with long auburn hair, the other with short blond hair, otherwise almost identical. They and the four men spread out and began searching the suite, examining it for hidden microphones, hidden cameras, hidden killers. Finally, satisfied, they stood aside and a stocky man entered with them. He was dressed in colorful silks and satins out of a previous, more spectacular galactic era, and he wore a hat with a huge feather in it, which he soon took off, revealing a colorfully tattooed bald head.

"Allow me to introduce myself," he said, showing no inclination to offer an exquisitely gloved hand. "I am known as the Candy Man."

"Pleased to meet you," said Dante.

"Are you really?" asked the Candy Man. "In fact, why are you meeting me at all? You were told I don't deal directly with the customers."

"And I told your man I don't deal with flunkies."

"Of course you do. Every single time."

"And yet here you are."

"You act like a rich, foolish man, Mr. Alighieri, and yet based on what my associate told me, you are not foolish at all. Since you seem to be pretending to be something you are not, I thought we should meet. I just happened to be on Alabaster today"—he stared hard at Dante—"or did you already know that?"

"All I know is that I came here to buy some seed. How much can you supply?"

"Subtlety is not among your virtues, Mr. Alighieri," said the Candy Man.

I'm glad you think so. I must be a better liar than even I thought.

"I'm in a hurry. Have you got any seed, or any I wasting my time?"

"I have more than you could use in half a dozen lifetimes," said the Candy Man.

"Prime?"

"The best."

"That's what they all say," replied Dante.

"You show me the color of your money, I'll show you the color of my seed."

"Money is my other favorite subject," said Dante. "How much are we talking about?"

"How many seeds are we talking about?" shot back the Candy Man.

"Fifty now, more later."

"You'd better go easy on them, Mr. Alighieri. Use them

up in less than half a Standard year and there won't be any later."

"How I use them is *my* business," said Dante irritably. "Yours is selling them to me, and you can't do that without naming a price."

"For fifty? Are we talking credits, or New Stalin rubles, or . . . ?"

"Whatever you want."

"Most of my clients use credits," said the Candy Man. "Fifty seed will cost you two and a half million."

"You've got to be kidding!" exclaimed Dante.

"Do I look like I'm kidding?"

"I can get fifty prime seeds for an even million on Beta Cordero II!"

"Nobody lives on Beta Cordero II."

"Somebody does now."

"And they're selling seed at fifty for a million?" demanded the Candy Man.

"Right. Are you going to match their price, or am I going to walk?"

"Walk if you want, Mr. Alighieri, but I guarantee you won't be dealing with anyone on Beta Cordero II."

"Why not?" said Dante.

"Because I don't take kindly to people poaching in my sector. When I'm done with them, Beta Cordero II will be unpopulated again."

"Maybe this guy is thinking of coming to Alabaster and taking over *your* operation," said Dante. "It makes no difference to me, as long as I get my seed."

The Candy Man threw back his head and laughed. "I like your sense of humor, Mr. Alighieri! I'm so well protected that not even Santiago himself could lay a finger on me."

Dante returned his smile. "Not even Santiago?" he repeated. "That's must be a comforting thought."

He was still smiling when the Candy Man went off to plot his next move against his newest rival.

21.

ONE IS THE BLADE, ONE IS THE KNIFE,
ONE TAKES YOUR MONEY, ONE TAKES YOUR
  LIFE.
THEY'RE NEVER ALONE, THEY'RE NEVER APART,
STAY ON YOUR GUARD OR THEY'LL CUT OUT
  YOUR HEART.

DANTE FOLLOWED THE CANDY MAN'S female bodyguards—one tall and auburn-haired, one tall and blond—
down the streets of Snakepit until they stopped at an elegant
restaurant. He waited to make sure they were there to eat
rather than extort money or perhaps meet their boss, and
then he entered and approached their table.

"Good evening," he said. "We met briefly at my hotel
last night. May I join you?"

Their expressions said they'd just as soon kill him as
look at him.

"I just want to talk to you for a few minutes," he said.
"Tell you what: if you don't like what I have to say, I'll
pay for dinner."

They exchanged glances, and then the auburn-haired one
nodded her assent.

"Sit," she said.

"Thank you." Dante pulled up a chair and sat down.

"What do you want?" said the blonde.

"I told you: I want to talk to you."

"You'd better make it good," said the blonde. "You've
already lied to the Candy Man."

"Me?" said Dante, surprised. "About what?"

"You've never chewed a seed in your life."

"Why would you say something like that?" asked Dante
with mock indignation.

"Because they were delivered to you this morning, and

you're still clear-eyed and clearheaded," she said. "No seed chewer in the galaxy could go all day without chewing one, and once they do that, they're in their own world for days."

"I have excellent self-control."

A waiter approached, and the blonde waved him away. He bowed obsequiously and went off to serve a table at the far end of the restaurant.

The auburn-haired woman suddenly laid a screecher on the table next to her fork. "If you lie one more time, Mr. Alighieri, I'm going to kill you right here, right now. I assure you this is not an idle threat. Now tell us why you are here."

"What makes you think—?" he began, and her hand closed on the sonic pistol. He stopped and sighed. "I followed you here because I want to talk a little business with you."

"And you've never chewed a seed, have you?"

"No, I never have."

"All right, Mr. Alighieri," said the blonde. "You have a business proposition for us. We're listening."

"If we don't like what we hear," added the auburn-haired one, "we can always kill you later."

"Just relax," said Dante. "You're going to want to thank me, not kill me."

"I hope so for your sake," said the blonde.

"Before I begin, I'd feel much more comfortable if I knew your names," said Dante. They exchanged glances again. "How can it hurt?"

"I'm the Knife," said the blonde. She gestured to her partner. "She's the Blade. That's all you have to know."

"Interesting sobriquets," commented Dante.

"Get on with it," said the Blade impatiently.

"All right," said Dante. "Let me begin by saying that the Candy Man has an impressive organization, not the least of which are you two."

"Flattery will get you nowhere," said the Blade.

"Except an early death," chimed in the Knife. "Now either tell us what you came to tell us or we'll kill you."

He stared at them. They had lovely faces, but there was no compassion in them, no trace of mercy at all. These ladies were not ambivalent about killing.

"As I was saying, the Candy Man has a good organization, as well he should. He's the biggest fish in a small pond—but a bigger fish has come to the Frontier. Not to put too fine a point on it, your boss's days are numbered."

"Explain," said the Knife.

"Santiago has set up shop in this sector. It's as simple as that. Your boss is a walking dead man."

"Santiago?" repeated the Knife, frowning. "What are you talking about?"

"Santiago has been dead for centuries!" added the Blade.

"A popular misconception," replied Dante. "He's alive, he's nearby, and he will not tolerate any competition. His organization dwarfs what the Candy Man's set up, and he's getting more powerful every day. You wouldn't believe some of the people who've joined him."

"Like who?" said the Knife dubiously.

"Like Waltzin' Matilda. Like Dimitrios of the Three Burners. Like the Rough Rider." He paused after each name for it to sink in, then added the clincher. "Like the One-Armed Bandit."

The Blade looked impressed. The Knife looked dubious. "If he's got all that firepower, why did he send *you*?" she demanded. "In fact, why are we still alive?"

"That's what I'm here to discuss with you."

"Why we're alive?"

"Why he's allowing you to live," said Dante. "There's a reason. Would you like to hear it?"

"We're listening," said the Blade.

"Santiago's got his fingers in a thousand pies on ten thousand worlds," said Dante. "He can't be bothered with the day-to-day operation of one obscure little drug ring that only covers half a dozen systems."

Suddenly the Knife's eyes widened.

Good, thought Dante. *You've figured it out.*

"Are you suggesting he wants *us* to take it over?" she said.

"He prefers to promote from within," said the poet. "Who knows the clientele and the routes better than you? Who can defend it better while he's occupied elsewhere?"

"Why doesn't he try to buy off the Candy Man?"

"Because it would be a demotion for the Candy Man, a step down no matter how you cut it. He couldn't help but be resentful, and a resentful partner isn't a loyal one. Santiago demands absolute loyalty from his partners." He paused while the words sank in. "But it wouldn't be a step down for you two. There'd be more money, more authority, more autonomy."

There was a moment of silence.

"What's he offering?" asked the Blade at last.

"Half—which is a hell of a lot more than you're making now," Dante pointed out. "I should add that we have a man who will audit you regularly. Santiago has no use for people who try to cheat him."

"Half?" repeated the Blade.

"Half," agreed Dante.

"Just for standing aside while Santiago kills the Candy Man?"

"He's going to want a little more than that as a token of your good faith," said Dante.

"Oh?" said the Knife suspiciously.

"He wants to know that you're fully committed to him and his organization," said Dante.

The Knife looked blank, but not the Blade. "Are you telling me he wants *us* to kill the Candy Man!"

"That's right."

"What's to stop us from killing the Candy Man and *not* splitting with anyone?" asked the Knife.

"You wouldn't live out the day," said Dante, amazed that he could lie with such absolute conviction. He leaned forward. "You're looking at it all wrong. Join him and you'll be millionaires within a Standard month, and you'll have the protection of Santiago's galaxy-wide organization if

you should ever need it. As long as you're Santiago's partners, no outsider will ever be able to do to you what you're
going to do to the Candy Man."

"What about insiders?" asked the Blade. "There will be
people who already work for the Candy Man who may
think *they* should be running things."

"This is a test of your leadership abilities," said Dante.
"If you can take this organization over and run it success-
fully, Santiago will help you go on to bigger and better
things."

The Blade picked up her screecher and tucked it back in
her belt, then stood up.

"We have to discuss this. In private."

"I can wait outside for you," said Dante.

"That won't be necessary." She turned to her blond companion. "Come on."

The Knife got up and followed her to the women's bathroom while Dante ordered a Cygnian cognac. He had just
about finished it when they returned and sat down opposite
him.

"All right," said the Blade. "It's a deal."

Dante looked at the Knife. "Yeah," she said, "it's a deal."

"Fine. I think you've made a wise decision. You'd gone
as far as you could with the Candy Man. You'll advance
much farther with Santiago."

"So now you'll tell Santiago we're in business?"

"No."

"No?" demanded the Blade.

"He'll know it when he hears that the Candy Man is
dead," said Dante.

They finished the meal, and Dante returned to his hotel.
The next morning the entire city was abuzz with the news
that the Candy Man had been murdered.

Dante paid for his room, went to the spaceport, and was
soon on his way to Valhalla. He contacted the Bandit en
route and told him what had transpired.

"Amazing!" said the Bandit.

"What are you referring to, sir?"

"They actually believed you, without any proof to support what you said. You must be one hell of an accomplished liar."

"Well, I *am* a poet, sir," replied Dante.

22.

JACKRABBIT WILLOWBY, LIGHTNING FAST,
BUILT AN EMPIRE MADE TO LAST;
SOLD HIS SOUL FOR WORKS OF ART—
FAST HE WAS, BUT NOT TOO SMART.

JACKRABBIT WILLOWBY HAD NEVER ACTUALLY seen a
jackrabbit. In fact, he'd never been within sixty thousand
light-years of Earth. But he knew that the jackrabbit was
one of the very few animals that wasn't extinct more than
three millennia after the dawn of the Galactic Era, and that
it survived because of its fecundity. Willowby himself had
forty-three children from thirty-six mothers, all of which he
neglected, and took his name from that prolific animal.

He didn't have an abundance of virtues. He was an agent
of the Democracy, in charge of monitoring the black market
in a fifty-world sector than included Beta Cordero II. He
was in charge of close to a thousand men spread across
those worlds, ready to respond to his commands.

In most cases, those commands were exactly what the
Democracy wanted—but in a few cases they were not. Willowby and a handful of carefully chosen confederates were
happy to look the other way for a consideration, which
averaged some twenty-five percent of the black marketeer's
take. They afforded the very best protection, and no one
who dealt with them ever had cause to regret it. Similarly,
those few that they approached who chose not to deal with
them soon found themselves serving long jail terms or else
were mourned by their friends.

Willowby developed a taste for expensive works of art,
which led him to expand his operation, reaching more and
more worlds, even those not officially under his control,
finding new routes for contraband material, and protecting
those routes with the full force of the Democracy. Before

too many years had passed he was worth tens of millions of credits, and none of his employees had any cause for complaint. He understood the need to keep them all happy—and loyal—and while his crew was far from the most honest on the Inner Frontier, they were unquestionably the wealthiest and most contented.

He had only one rule: no one retired. He wanted his team to work in the shadow of the gallows until the day each of them died. He never wanted any to lose contact, or feel they could make their own deal with the Democracy and supply evidence against their confederates. You could get filthy rich working for Willowby, but that was the price you paid—there was no end to it. Most of his employees had no problem with that. The few who did didn't live long enough to cause any serious complications.

Dante had heard rumors about Willowby, and he knew it was just a matter of time before he showed up and made his pitch. The sudden death of the Candy Man could only hurry the day, and Dante was anxious for the meeting to take place.

"We don't want anything to do with him," said the Bandit when Dante brought up the subject. "He works for the Democracy. That makes him the enemy."

"True," answered the poet. "But this one has a ready-made organization that could bring in fifty times what we're going to make from the Candy Man's operation."

"If we deal with enough Democracy members, we'll be no different than they are," insisted the Bandit.

"I think you're looking at it all wrong, sir," said Dante. "If we can put Willowby to work for us, or somehow take over his organization, we'll be plundering him of millions every week, money that would eventually be spent or invested in the Democracy. Think of the good we could do with that money! Think of the hospitals it could build."

"You're getting ahead of yourself," said the Bandit. "First we need a Frontier-wide organization. *Then* we'll worry about hospitals and everything else."

"Even the original Santiago didn't have that big an organization," said Dante. "He just made it *seem* like he did."

"What good are hospitals and schools and whatever else you want if I can't defend them?"

"It's not what *I* want," protested Dante. "It's what *we* want. And it's not just hospitals and schools. Hell, there's two hundred alien races living in fear and poverty out here on the Frontier. They need our help."

The Bandit stared at him, seemed about to reply, then decided to remain silent.

"So can I tell the Knife and the Blade to send Willowby here if he starts making any inquiries?" continued Dante.

"Yes," said the Bandit.

"Alone, I presume?" said Dante. "Or just with his personal muscle?"

"Whatever makes him happy," said the Bandit. "It makes no difference to me."

Dante leaned back and relaxed. He'd been half afraid that the Bandit had planned to kill Willowby, and while he had no moral problem with killing the enemy, it made a lot more sense to coopt this one and leave him in place. The Candy Man worked just a handful of systems, really just six planets, and the Knife and the Blade knew all of his contacts. But from everything Dante had been able to learn, Jackrabbit Willowby's organization encompassed hundreds, perhaps thousands, of worlds, and if they killed him, there'd be no way they could keep his organization intact, or even find out who belonged to it.

Dante spent the next two days working on his epic, reworking the verses, honing the language, making lists of the colorful characters he'd heard about that he wanted to meet and include in the text.

Then Virgil checked in, stoned out of his mind. He'd found the drugs, which was admittedly the easy part of his assignment, but he couldn't remember where he'd gotten them or who he'd purchased them from. Dante checked the computer log of Virgil's ship, found out that the Indian had visited Nestor III, Lower Volta, and New Waco, and decided to send Blossom off to see if she could find out where

Virgil had purchased his drugs, and from whom.

"And don't be a hero," he cautioned her. "We've already got one, and he'll handle any dangerous situation."

"We're *all* heroes, Rhymer," she said adamantly. "Everyone who fights the Democracy is a hero."

"Let's keep it to ourselves," said Dante. "The less people who think we're heroes, the less often we'll have to prove it. Remember: what we're doing only works as long as the Democracy thinks we're outlaws. Once they figure out what we're really about, that's the end of Santiago and everyone who has anything to do with him . . . so just make some *very* discreet inquiries, try not to call any attention to yourself, and then come back with whatever information you can get."

"Why should I listen to *you*?" she demanded. "I work for Santiago."

"And I speak for him," said Dante.

"I thought you were supposed to be a poet."

"I am. Don't make me write about how you turned Santiago down the first time he needed you."

She considered his remark, and finally nodded her assent. "But next time I want to hear it direct from *him*."

"All right, next time you will."

She left, and Dante spent another half hour working on his poem until he was summoned to the Bandit's office.

"What's up?" he asked upon arriving.

"I just heard from the Blade. Jackrabbit Willowby is on his way to Valhalla."

"Alone?"

The Bandit smiled. "Hardly."

"What is that supposed to mean?"

"He's coming with a little display of force to impress me."

"How little?"

"Twenty men, maybe twenty-five."

"I'm impressed already," said Dante. "Where do we put them all?"

"I'll meet them outside," answered the Bandit. "I might as well show them I have nothing to hide."

"You can meet them there, but you'll want to deal privately with Willowby in your office. You don't want anyone else to hear your negotiations. You might have to get tough with him."

"Don't worry," said the Bandit. "I just want them all to see me, since they're going to be dealing with me from now on."

Dante shrugged. "Okay, if you're sure that's the way you want to do it."

"I'm sure."

Dante waited in his quarters until he heard Willowby's ship approaching the landing strip. He looked out a window as it came into view and soon settled gently on the slab.

Twenty men emerged from the ship and formed two lines. Five more climbed out, went to the end of the lines, and fanned out, ready to handle trouble from any direction.

Then, after a wait of perhaps three minutes, Jackrabbit Willowby came out of the hatch and climbed down to the ground. He was a short man, elegantly dressed, and he moved with an athletic grace. Dante couldn't spot any weapons on him, but then, with all those bodyguards, he didn't need any.

Dante noticed that everyone's attention was directed toward the lodge. He turned and saw that the Bandit had walked out the front of the compound and was approaching Willowby.

Six of Willowby's men moved to form a living wall between them. The Bandit came to a stop and looked expectantly at Willowby.

"Good day, sir," said Willowby, parting the men with his arms and stepping forward to stand between them. "To whom do I have the pleasure of speaking?"

"You know who I am," said the Bandit.

"They told me your name was Santiago, but that is either a joke or a lie."

"I'd be careful who I called a liar, Jackrabbit Willowby."

"You see?" said Willowby. "You know *my* name. It's only fair that I should know yours."

"You do," said the Bandit. "My name is Santiago."

One of the men walked over and whispered something to Willowby.

"I'm told that you are actually the One-Armed Bandit."

"You've been misinformed. I am Santiago." The Bandit stared at his visitor. "Are we going to spend all afternoon arguing about my name, or do you have some reason for being here?"

"You're a very brave man, to speak to me like that when I'm surrounded by my men."

"You haven't answered me."

"Of course I have a reason for being here," said Willowby. "You deal in contraband materials. I work for the Democracy."

"So you're here to arrest me?"

"Putting you in jail won't do either of us any good," replied Willowby easily. "I'm here to negotiate a fine with you."

"A fine?"

"If I put you out of business, someone would just replace you next week or next month, the jails would have one more mouth to feed, and what purpose would be served? Let's be totally honest: there is a continuing demand for the goods you sell. *Someone* is going to satisfy it; it might as well be you."

"I'd call that very reasonable of you," said the Bandit.

"I can see we understand each other," said Willowby with a smile. "How does twenty-five percent sound to you?"

The Bandit seemed to be considering the offer for a moment. Finally he shook his head. "No, that's not enough."

Willowby looked confused. "Not enough?" he repeated.

"I think a third makes more sense."

"You'd rather pay me a third than a quarter?"

"No," said the Bandit. "*You're* going to pay *me* a third."

"What are you talking about?"

"I want a third of your business. Give it to me and you can leave here alive."

"Are you crazy?" snapped Willowby. "I've got twenty-five men with me!"

"You mean these men?" asked the Bandit, waving an arm in their direction. As he pointed, a laser beam shot out of his finger and mowed them down before they knew what was happening. The last seven or eight had time to reach for their weapons, but the beam was replaced by an exploding energy ball, and an instant later Willowby was the only member of his party still standing.

"Who *are* you?" he demanded.

"I told you: my name is Santiago. And you are a member of the Democracy. That's all I need to know."

The Bandit pointed a deadly finger at him, and an instant later Willowby fell to the ground, dead.

"That was stupid!" yelled Dante, rushing over to join the Bandit. "I told you—we needed his organization!"

"He worked for the Democracy," said the Bandit calmly. "The Democracy is our enemy."

"You were always going to kill him, weren't you?"

"That's what Santiago does to his enemies."

"Yeah, well, Santiago could use his brain every now and then!" snapped Dante. "You've cost us billions. *Billions!*"

"I don't deal with the enemy."

"Then next time let me!"

The Bandit turned to him, and for just an instant Dante thought he was going to aim his lethal arm at him.

"You're a poet. Go write your poems. I'm Santiago. Let me handle my business in my own way—and don't ever stand between me and the enemy." He turned to one of the men who had run out of the house. "One of them is still alive. The fifth from the left."

"You want me to finish him off, Santiago?" asked the man.

"No," said the Bandit. "If I'd wanted him dead, I'd have killed him myself. Treat his wounds, drop him off on some colony world, and make sure he knows that it was Santiago who did this. Let him pass the word about what happens to anyone who stands against me." He turned to Dante. "Does that meet with your approval?"

"Hell, no!" said the poet bitterly. "What the fuck does *he* know about running an organization that spans a hundred worlds?" He tried to control his temper. "If you were going to let someone live, why not Willowby? He'd have been just as impressed as that poor bastard."

"Yes, he would have," agreed the Bandit. "And next time he'd have sent two hundred men, or five hundred, or a thousand, and he'd have stayed away until it was over. He'd never give me another chance at him once he knew what I could do, and he couldn't let me live after I'd grabbed a third of his empire. If he'd shown any weakness of resolve, his own men would have been dividing the rest of his business."

"You could have negotiated," complained Dante. "Ten percent would still have been worth hundreds of millions."

"You don't negotiate with officers of the Democracy," said the Bandit coldly. "You kill them."

"But he was a *corrupt* officer, damn it! We could have reached an accommodation."

"They're *all* corrupt," said the Bandit, turning and heading back to the compound. "This conversation is over."

Dante watched him walk away.

Maybe you're right. Maybe you can't deal with representatives of the Democracy, even thoroughly corrupt ones. But damn it, you sounded a lot more reasonable when you were still just the One-Armed Bandit.

23.

COME INSIDE THE BLIXTOR MAZE;
SPEND YOUR MONEY, SPEND YOUR DAYS.
NAMELESS PLEASURES LIE IN WAIT—
COME ALONG AND MEET YOUR FATE.

THE BLIXTOR MAZE WAS THE brainchild of an alien architect named Blixtor. No one was quite sure what race he belonged to. Some said he was a Canphorite, but others said no, the Maze wasn't rational enough to have been created by a native of Canphor VI or VII, that he must be a native of Lodin XI. Still others said it was actually created by a human, but that his computer had crashed and he'd given up on the project, and other races built it based on what they could reconstruct from his shattered modules and memory crystals.

This much is known: no one ever succeeded in mapping the Blixtor Maze. It was said that parts of it went off into the fourth dimension, and other parts were so complex that not even a theoretical mathematician could explain them. It was approximately one mile square. No one knew how many levels there were. The only thing that was certain was that no one had ever walked from one end to the other in less than a week, and even homing wolves, those remarkable domesticated creatures from Valos XI, were unable to retrace their steps.

It took four centuries to build the Maze on the isolated world of Nandi III. Legend has it that the original Maze was to be four miles on a side, but two crews got lost and starved to death. Nobody believed it—until they tried to find their way out of the Maze. There were some who felt the Maze was constantly moving, or rotating in and out of known dimensions, because you could wander into an antiquarian chart shop or a drug den, and when you walked out the same door nothing was where it had been. Further, if you had left something behind, you could turn and attempt to go back and retrieve it, only to find that the establishment you thought was two paces behind you was nowhere to be seen.

There were no warning signs as you approached the Maze, because the authorities operated on the reasonable assumption that you wouldn't be on Nandi III if you didn't have business there. Far from banning weapons, visitors were encouraged to enter the Maze heavily armed, since no lawman or bounty hunter was likely to respond to any entreaties coming from within the Maze. All laws were suspended the moment you took your first step inside the Maze. Murder was no longer a crime; neither were any of a hundred other actions that could get you executed or incarcerated in the Democracy, or the half dozen that were still illegal across most of the Inner Frontier.

Dante was unsurprised to learn that Virgil was guilty of at least three of them. He was contacted by Blue Peter, who explained that Virgil was being held inside the Maze, that a group of permanent residents had him under what passed for house arrest, and that it was going to take a guide to find him and a lot of money to bail him out.

"How did *you* get out?" asked Dante over the subspace radio.

"The Maze spit me out," answered the alien. "It didn't want me."

"It spit you out?" repeated Dante.

"Come to Nandi," said Blue Peter. "It'll make more sense once you see it."

Two days later the Bandit's ship touched down at the Nandi spaceport. He and Dante passed through Customs—both used false IDs and passports—and took a room in a run-down hotel that was fifty yards from the entrance to the Maze.

Blue Peter was waiting for them.

"I'm glad you got here," he said. "Who knows what they're doing to him?"

"Whatever they're doing, he's probably so grogged up on bad booze and worse drugs that he's totally unaware of it," said the Bandit.

"Shouldn't we go get him?" asked Blue Peter as the Bandit walked into the hotel's restaurant.

"First we'll eat dinner," answered the Bandit. "We'll leave our gear here, get a good night's sleep, and go after him in the morning." He paused. "And tonight, before we're through eating, you'll tell us what you know about the Blixtor Maze."

"Nothing," said the alien. "Well, almost nothing."

"How could it spit you out?" asked Dante.

"That might be the wrong term," admitted Blue Peter. "I hid in this warehouse right across street from the jail where they were holding Virgil. I planned to wait until it was dark and then see if I could break him out." He paused. "When the sun set, I waited an hour and then I stepped out, ready to cross the street—and somehow I wasn't facing the jail. In fact, I wasn't even in the Maze. I was standing on the road that borders the north side of the Maze. I looked for the door I'd come through, but there was nothing but a solid wall for hundreds of yards." He smiled an odd alien smile. "The Maze didn't want me. That's when I knew I'd have to contact you if he was ever to get out of there."

"I can see the entrance to the Maze from the front of the hotel," said the Bandit. "Can you find him if we go through it?"

"Yes," said Blue Peter. Then, "No." Finally, "Maybe."

"Explain."

"It's never the same twice," said the blue alien. "If it's the way it was the last time Virgil and I entered it, and nothing inside the Maze has changed, I can find it—but the odds against that are thousands to one. I've been in the Maze a dozen times, and it's never been the same twice. I've talked to people who live in the Maze, who have been there for years, and they never know what they'll see when they walk out their front door."

"How do they keep finding their front door when it's time to go home?" asked Dante.

"Oh, if the Maze wants you to find something, you will," Blue Peter assured him. "It might even move things around just to accommodate you."

"You make it sound sentient."

"It's not sentient—I mean, how could it be?—but it's tricky as hell."

The Bandit stared at him for a moment, then walked to a table and called up the menu. The other two joined him, and they ate the meal in total silence.

"I'll see you in the morning," said the Bandit when he was through. He got to his feet. "Sunrise, right here."

He left and headed toward the airlift as Dante turned to Blue Peter.

"Just what the hell was Virgil doing that got him incarcerated?" asked the poet. "From what I know of this world, I'd have thought nothing was illegal. Certainly it couldn't just have been drugs."

"It wasn't."

"Well, then?"

The alien looked at him for a long moment. "I don't think I'm going to tell you."

"Why not?"

"Because you will want to work with him again, and if I told you, you might leave him here forever."

"It was that bad?"

"Let us say that it was that *unusual*."

"Were you involved?"

"I think I've told you everything that I'm going to tell you," said Blue Peter. "Good night, Rhymer. I'll see you in the morning."

"What's your room number?"

"This hotel is for humans only," said the alien with no sign of bitterness. "I am staying a few blocks away."

"See you in the morning, then," said Dante as Blue Peter left the restaurant and walked out the front door of the hotel. He spent a few minutes sitting at the table, staring at

his empty wineglass and trying to imagine what new per-
version Virgil had discovered. Finally he got up and went
off to his room.

His bed woke him gently just before sunrise, as he had
instructed it to do, and he showered and dressed quickly,
then went down to the restaurant. He decided he couldn't
stand the smell of food that early in the day, so he sat in
the lobby and waited for the Bandit to finish. Blue Peter
joined him a moment later, and the two of them sat, half
asleep, until the Bandit emerged from the restaurant.

"Okay," he said. "Let's go get him."

The three of them went out into the cool dry air of Nandi
III, turned right, and rode the slidewalk past a row of low
angular buildings to the entrance to the Maze.

"This is it?" asked the Bandit.

"That's right," said Blue Peter.

"If everything moves around, how are we going to find
him?" asked the Bandit.

"We'll hire a guide."

"A guide? You mean someone knows his way around
the Maze?"

"It's not that simple," began Blue Peter.

"Somehow it never is," interjected Dante dryly.

"There is an alien race, almost extinct now, that can usually find what you're looking for. Not always, but usually.
Rumor has it that they were imported to Nandi III centuries
ago to help build it. These are their descendants. No one
knows what world they originally came from."

"Can they find their way back out?" asked the Bandit.

"Frequently."

"How do we make contact with one?"

"We'll just enter the Maze," answered the alien. "They'll
start contacting us."

"What do they look like?"

"They're humanoid," said Blue Peter. "Perhaps four feet
tall. Covered with fur. Their colors differ markedly from
one to the next."

"Has the race got a name?"

"Probably," said Blue Peter. "I mean, all races have names, don't they? Inside the Maze, though, we call them Lab Rats, since they're the only ones who can find their way around with any degree of accuracy."

"Lab Rats?" said Dante with a smile.

"Your face just lit up," said Blue Peter. "You're going to use them in your poem, aren't you?"

"How could I not write about a race known as the Lab Rats?" responded Dante.

The Bandit stared at the entrance, which was a broad archway.

"We just walk in, right?" he asked.

"That's right."

"Okay, let's get on with it."

He strode forward, and Dante and the alien fell into step behind him. Ten feet into the Maze he stopped and looked behind him.

"The entrance is still there," he noted.

"Yes, it is," agreed Blue Peter.

"Maybe you were exaggerating a little bit?"

"I wasn't," said the alien adamantly.

They followed the street for fifty yards, until it dead-ended against a large modular triangular building built of imported alien alloys.

"Let's try the left," said the Bandit, walking off in a new direction.

They followed him. The street narrowed until the buildings were so close together that he couldn't fit through the opening.

"So much for that," he muttered. "All right, let's go in the other direction."

He turned and backtracked, but when they came to the triangular building, everything seemed different.

"Something's wrong," he muttered, looking around.

"What is it?" asked Dante, who was bringing up the rear.

"That alley," said the Bandit, pointing. "It wasn't there before." On a hunch, he turned to his right, toward the entrance. It was gone. "Okay, so you weren't exaggerating."

Suddenly a creature the size of a child emerged from the shadows and approached them. It was covered by dull gray fur, and its face was long and angular, with wide-set green eyes and a broad purple nose.

"Need a guide?" it hissed in a sibilant whisper. "Need a girly-girly house? Need a trip to Dreamland? Like to make a bet? I take you anywhere you want for 20-credits-20."

The Bandit tossed a coin to the Lab Rat. "Tell him," he ordered Blue Peter.

"I'm looking for a friend," began the alien.

"No blue girly-girly houses in the Maze."

Blue Peter shook his head. "This is a human friend. He's been locked up. His name is Virgil Soaring Hawk. I want to find him."

"I must search," said the Lab Rat. "I tell you soon."

"Should we wait here?" asked the Bandit.

"Go wherever," said the Lab Rat. "When I am ready, I find you."

He shambled off and scuttled around a corner.

"No sense following him," said Blue Peter. "When you get to the corner and look for him, he won't be there."

"Then let's walk around and see what the Maze is like, as long as he says he can find us," said Dante.

The Bandit agreed, and the three of them set off. The farther into the Maze they got, the stranger it became. Streets ended inside buildings, or curved and twisted back onto themselves. Buildings were all shapes; some seemed to blink in and out of the men's dimension, though when they approached them they seemed solid enough. There were doorless, windowless buildings from which peals of human laughter emanated, and stores that sold objects that were totally unfamiliar to Dante. There were brothels showcasing males and females of a dozen different races, and gambling dens with long, winding, seemingly endless tunnels leading to individual games. They followed a corridor, found a room with aliens playing *jabob*, retraced their steps, and found themselves inside an alien shrine that featured an altar stone still wet with blood. They walked out the exit, and found themselves blocks from the gambling den, on a four-level avenue covered by a building that rose from the ground on both sides of the street, leaned toward the middle, and joined about ten feet above the top level, forming a huge triangular arch.

"This gets weirder and weirder," said Dante.

"This is the ordinary part," said Blue Peter. "It gets really weird about three blocks from here."

Another Lab Rat, this one light tan with large black spots on its fur, approached them. *"Psst!"* it hissed.

"Go away," said Blue Peter. "We've already got a guide."

"Psst!" it repeated. "Your guide has deserted you. I will never do that. I offer the unusual, the exotic, the bizarre. All for only twenty credits."

"Not interested," said the Bandit.

"For you, fifteen credits," said the Lab Rat. It pulled its thin lips back in a distorted smile. "Eat at Joe's."

"If we want a restaurant, we'll find one without your help," said Blue Peter irritably.

"Not like Joe's," said the Lab Rat. "Your meal is lightly basted and still alive. You can listen to it scream as it slides down your gullet."

"Forget it."

"It is forgotten," said the Lab Rat. *"Psst!* Girly-girly house of cyborgs, only twelve credits."

Their own guide suddenly appeared. He stared at the other Lab Rat and growled deep in his throat. The new Lab Rat hissed at him. A moment later they were roaring and screeching, jumping up and down and making threatening gestures. Finally, as the noise reached a crescendo, they both stopped at the same instant, and the new Lab Rat raced away.

"Do not let my brother disturb you," said their guide. "I will kill him later."

"He's your brother?" asked Dante.

"Probably" was the answer.

"Did you find Virgil Soaring Hawk?" asked the Bandit.

"Ah, the unfortunate Virgil," said the Lab Rat. "Yes."

"Why 'unfortunate'?" asked Dante.

"He is guilty of sins for which they have not yet created any names," replied the Lab Rat. He turned to Blue Peter. "You helped."

"Take us there," said the Bandit.

"They will not release him."

"That is not your concern," said the Bandit, tossing him another coin. "Just take us there and then leave."

"If I leave, you will never find your way out."

"That is *our* concern," said the Bandit.

"You will die of old age here, all but the blue one," warned the Lab Rat.

"Why not me?" asked Blue Peter.

"The Maze finds your presence offensive. It will throw you out."

"How do you know?"

"The same way I know how to find Virgil Soaring Hawk," replied the Lab Rat, as if that answered everything.

"But—" began Blue Peter.

"Shut up," said the Bandit. He turned to their guide. "No more talk. Take us to Virgil."

The Lab Rat stared at him, gave a shrug that rippled down its entire body, and headed off down a dank, twisting alley. The Bandit and his companions fell into step behind the furry creature, following as it turned one way and then another, seeming to follow no rational course—but they noticed that while they were constantly backtracking, they never passed the same street or building twice.

Finally the Lab Rat ascended two levels, walked a block, climbed back down to the pavement, and waited for his party to assemble.

"Here we are," he said.

"*Where* are we?" said the Bandit.

"You wanted to find Virgil Soaring Hawk, didn't you?"

"Yes."

The Lab Rat pointed to an unmarked door. "Just walk through there."

"There are fifty identical doors on this block," said the Bandit. "How do you know it's this one?"

"Because."

"All right. Open it."

"I am done. You are not paying me to stay."

"I paid you to find Virgil Soaring Hawk. You're not done until I know he's inside."

The Lab Rat turned to him. "Have I ever lied to you?"

"You haven't said five sentences to me."

"There. You see?"

"Open the door."

"I weep at your distrust."

"You'll do more than weep if he's not in there."

The Lab Rat stared at him for a long moment. "This door," it said, walking to a door next to the one it had originally indicated.

"I thought it was the other door."

"I changed my mind."

The Bandit opened the door and turned to Dante. "Keep an eye on him until I make sure that Virgil's here." He entered the building.

"What's behind the first door?" asked Dante.

"Open it," said the Lab Rat.

"Just tell me."

The Lab Rat forced his lips into another smile. "That would spoil the surprise."

"I notice your Terran has become a lot more fluent since our first meeting," noted Dante.

"That's because it is noon in the Maze."

"It gets better or worse depending on the time of day?"

"And the weather."

Dante was about to reply when the door opened and the Bandit reappeared.

"Okay, let him go and follow me."

Dante turned to tell the Lab Rat to leave, but it was already gone. He walked forward and entered the building, followed by Blue Peter. They walked down a narrow arched corridor that curved to the left, and after a moment came to a lighted room. There was a strange multi-level desk with a small, olive-skinned man seated behind it.

"This gentleman," said the Bandit, indicating the man, "seems to be in charge of the place."

"I *am* in charge."

"It's not a jail and it's not a stockade, right?"

"That is correct."

"And yet you freely admit that you have incarcerated Virgil Soaring Hawk here."

"The Maze is used to aberrant behavior," said the man. "It is used to perversions that I hope you cannot begin to imagine. And yet your friend has performed acts that offend not only the inhabitants of the Maze but the Maze itself."

"And the Maze told you that, did it?" asked Dante.

"Not in so many words, but if you live here long enough, you know how to interpret its moods."

"I am sorry our friend has offended you," said the Bandit. "Tell me how much we owe you for damages, I'll pay his tab, and we'll be on our way."

"The same perversions, performed on another world, will be no less offensive," said the man.

"But since you won't know about them, they won't offend *you*," the Bandit pointed out.

"The Maze says he must stay. He will not be harmed, he will be well treated—but he will be confined alone for the rest of his life."

"He belongs to me," said the Bandit. "I'm taking him away with me."

"Do *you* indulge in similar sins?" demanded the man.

"What I do is no one's business but my own."

"And I suppose you're going to tell me that what Virgil Soaring Hawk does is no one else's business?"

"That's right."

"That's wrong. Two men and a female Tellargian have been taken to a psychiatric ward after spending less than half the night with him."

"What the hell did he do to them?"

"We have no idea, but it is our duty to make sure that he never does it again."

"Enough talk," said the Bandit. "Name your price and I'll pay it. Just turn him over to me and we'll leave."

"That's out of the question."

"Nothing is out of the question for Santiago. Now, where is he?"

"He's quite safe, not only from his own urges, but also from delusional intruders who think they're Santiago."

"I'm only going to ask once more," said the Bandit. "Where is he?"

The olive-skinned man glared at him and offered no response.

The Bandit looked around the room, turned to the wall at the far end of it, and pointed his finger. A laser beam shot out, and soon cut a doorway through it.

"Rhymer," he said, purposely avoiding mentioning Dante's name, "go see if he's there."

Dante stepped through and found himself in what seemed to be a haberdasher's storehouse. He stepped back into the room.

"No, there's nothing there."

The Bandit turned back to the olive-skinned man. "I'm going to count to five," he said, "and if you haven't told me where I can find Virgil Soaring Hawk, I'm going to melt one of your fingers to putty. Then I'll count again. When we run out of fingers and toes, I'll melt more vital things. Look into my eyes and tell me if you think I'm bluffing."

The man stared into the Bandit's eyes and swallowed hard. "You're not bluffing."

"Then save yourself a world of pain and tell me what I want to know."

"I'll take you there," said the man with an air of defeat.

He got up and led them back down the corridor through which they had come, but instead of letting them out into the street, it dead-ended at a metal door.

"He's in there?" asked the Bandit.

"Yes."

"Open it."

The man uttered a code that was half mathematical formula and half song. The door vanished and Virgil, who had been lying on a floating pallet, got to his feet.

"Well, fancy meeting you here," he said.

"Shut up and get out of there," said the Bandit.

The Injun quickly exited his cell.

"Made my bail, huh?"

"So to speak." The Bandit turned to the olive-skinned man. "How do we get back to the street?"

"You don't."

The Bandit pointed a deadly finger between the man's eyes. "Do we have to go through all this again?"

"I'm not kidding. The Maze doesn't want him freed."

"The Maze doesn't have a vote," said the Bandit. "We're leaving this planet."

"You can try," said the man.

"Let's start by going back to your office."

The man led the way, but when they arrived, it was no longer an office, but a stone cell with iron bars on the windows. A heavy door slammed shut behind them.

"I told you," said the man. "The Maze will never let you leave."

"Don't bet every last credit you own on it," said the Bandit. He made a slight adjustment to his artificial arm, then stepped back and pointed at the wall with the iron bars. A pulse grenade shot out and exploded when it hit the wall, and a moment later there was a huge gaping hole.

The Bandit stepped through it, followed by his party. They found themselves in a walled courtyard, and the Bandit shot another grenade at a wall.

The Maze responded, entrapping them again, and it became a battle of attrition. The Bandit would explode or melt any barrier the Maze created, and the Maze would use all its resources to find a new way to imprison them.

After an hour the Bandit turned to Dante. "I don't have

unlimited supplies of energy or ammunition," he said. "I'm going to have to put an end to this."

"What are you going to do?"

"Watch."

He made one more adjustment to his arm, then pointed to the sky. Something shot out, something small and glowing with power. It reached its apex at a thousand feet, then whistled down at the very center of the Maze. There was no explosion, no sense of heat, no tremors of the ground beneath their feet—but suddenly the Maze began to vanish, starting at its core and radiating outward. Buildings disappeared, streets and sidewalks vanished, thousands of Men and aliens popped out of existence without a sound.

Dante thought whatever the Bandit had precipitated would gobble them up as well, but it stopped about thirty yards away.

"What the hell was that?" asked the poet, trying to keep his voice calm and level and not succeeding very well.

"A little something I commissioned a Dinalian physicist to create for me," answered the Bandit. "It works on the same principle as a molecular imploder, but it creates a chain reaction."

"You could have killed us!" said Blue Peter.

"I know its physical limits," answered the Bandit.

"As it was, you probably killed a few thousand Men and aliens," said Dante.

"They would have stopped us if they could," said the Bandit. "That makes them our enemies."

"Bullshit!" snapped Dante. "Ninety-nine percent of them didn't even know you were here and couldn't care less."

"Then this will add to the legend. Try to understand: Santiago has no friends in the galaxy, just enemies and hirelings."

"So we're just hirelings?" demanded the poet.

"I didn't mean you, of course."

"The hell you didn't!"

"I saved your life. This is no time for an argument."

"You saved my life at the cost of thousands of the lives you were *created* to save."

"It was a value judgment," said the Bandit. "Don't make me decide I made a mistake."

"It wasn't an either/or situation," said Dante. "There were half a dozen alternatives. Santiago—a *real* Santiago—would have found one!"

The Bandit turned to the olive-skinned man, who had been listening intently, and burned a deadly hole between his eyes.

"What was *that* for?" shouted Dante.

"It was your fault," said the Bandit angrily. "You implied that I wasn't Santiago. I couldn't let him hear that and live to pass it on."

"So you killed him, just like that?"

"*You* made it necessary."

"How the hell did you get so warped?"

"There's nothing warped about it," said the Bandit. "It goes with the job."

Dante snorted contemptuously.

"What do you know about it?"

"What do *I* know?" repeated the poet. "I *made* you!"

"You *found* me," replied the Bandit. "There's a difference."

Dante was about to reply, but something about the Bandit's expression convinced him to keep silent. A few days earlier he had told the Knife and the Blade that everyone in Santiago's organization was expendable, but he never really believed it.

Until now.

24.

DANTE NEVER WROTE A VERSE about the Madras 300. He tried several times, but it never came out right.

But then, neither did the Madras 300.

It began a week after their experience in the Blixtor Maze. Dante, who had felt uneasy ever since they returned, was sitting alone in the dining room very late at night, sipping a cup of coffee, when Virgil Soaring Hawk approached him.

"What are you doing up?" asked the poet.

"Couldn't sleep."

"Why not?"

"Probably because you're using the strongest stimulant on the planet," said the Indian with a grin.

"I'm not interested in your habits or your perversions," said Dante.

"That's what I want to talk to you about."

"I just told you: I'm not interested."

"Neither is Santiago."

"Is that supposed to mean something to me?"

"It should."

"Virgil, it's halfway through the night and I don't know what the hell you're talking about," replied Dante. "I'm not in the mood for guessing games, so if you've got something to say, say it."

"I just did."

"Go away."

"You're not paying attention," said Virgil.

"I must not be, so spell it out for me."

"Look, Rhymer, I know why you came after me in the Maze. We're joined at the soul, you and I."

"The hell we are."

"It's an historic inevitability. Dante has to have his Virgil. But why did *he* come along?"

"You work for him," said Dante. "We all do."

"All I've done is buy drugs for him," said Virgil. "That's hardly an indispensable job."

Dante stared at him. "You think he *shouldn't* have come after you?"

"Maybe so, maybe not. But I know what I am and what I've done, and he at least knows some of it. So why did he destroy the Maze and maybe kill a couple of thousand people just to free me? I'm probably just going to get arrested again on the next world I visit for crimes against God and Nature. You know it, I know it, *he* knows it."

"Let me get this straight," said Dante, frowning. "Are you telling me you wanted him to leave you there?"

"I didn't *want* him to. I want to be free! But what kind of Santiago frees one lone redskin pervert at the cost of all those lives?"

"He's reestablishing the legend," said Dante uneasily. "He has to let people know how powerful he is."

"By killing the people he's supposed to protect? Hell, *I* could do that. He's supposed to do something better."

"I don't know what you want."

"It's not what *I* want," said Virgil. "I work for you—"

"You work for *him*," interrupted Dante.

"No!" said Virgil firmly. "Everyone else around here works for him. I work for *you*—and it's my job to tell you that I think you put your money on the wrong horse."

"And you reached this conclusion because he saved your life at the expense of others?"

"How much more honest can I be?" retorted Virgil.

Dante finished his coffee and sat in silence.

"So what do you think?" persisted the Indian.

"He's only been Santiago for a few weeks, and we're redefining the job."

"That's no answer."

"It's the best I've got," said Dante. "Hell, *he's* the best I've got."

"You found him very fast. Maybe you should have looked a little longer."

"Maybe I should have. I don't know. But the Frontier needs him *now*."

"It needs *help* now," agreed Virgil. "That doesn't mean it needs *him*."

"What do you suggest?" said Dante irritably. "Who has the authority to fire him? Who has the skills to kill him?" He sighed heavily. "Hell, he's doing what he thinks is right. Who am I to challenge that? I'm just a small-time thief turned poet. I don't have a monopoly on right or truth."

"All right," said Virgil. "You're the boss."

"I'm *not* the boss, damn it!"

"You're *my* boss. I won't bring it up again."

The Indian turned and left Dante alone with his thoughts and his doubts. By morning he had convinced himself that both of them were wrong, that this was a century and a half after the original Santiago and different times called for different approaches.

Then came the Madras raid.

Word came from an informant that a small Navy convoy was shipping gold bullion to their base on Madras IV, a mining world some 132 light-years distant.

The Bandit knew he didn't have the firepower to take on the Navy in space, so he waited until they landed and most of the ships departed. Then he touched down on Madras with Dante, Virgil, and three new hirelings.

The moment they emerged from their ship they were captured by an armed patrol. The Bandit meekly surrendered, the others followed suit, and shortly thereafter they found themselves incarcerated in an otherwise-empty stockade, surrounded by a sonic barrier that became intensely painful every time anyone got within four feet of it.

"I wonder how long they plan to keep us here?" mused one of the new men.

"Not long," said the Bandit. "They'll want to know what we're doing here."

"Well, it *is* a mining world," said Dante. "We could say we're here to consider investing in one of the mining complexes."

"We'll tell them the truth," said the Bandit.

"That we're here to rob them of their bullion?"

"That's right."

"You could save a lot of ammunition that way," said Virgil dryly. "Given our position, they just might laugh themselves to death."

"You mean this cell?" asked the Bandit. "I can leave it whenever I choose to."

"Then what are we doing here in the first place?" continued Virgil.

"Wasn't this easier than searching the whole planet for their headquarters?" said the Bandit.

"Now that you've found their headquarters, why are we still incarcerated?" persisted the Indian.

"So far all we've seen are the guards. I assume we'll be questioned by someone higher up the chain of command, someone who might know exactly where the bullion is."

"You know they're probably monitoring every word we say," put in Dante.

"So what?" replied the Bandit. "Sooner or later they're going to have to talk to us—and if it's too much later, I'll destroy the stockade and initiate the conversation myself."

"I don't know why you didn't do it in the first place," muttered Virgil.

"If I'd just walked in and blown them away, no one would know who was responsible. I plan to answer all their questions honestly, especially who I am, and let them inform the Democracy exactly who it was that robbed them."

"Isn't this a little early in the game for that?" suggested Dante. "Shouldn't we accumulate a nest egg and some more manpower before we start taunting the Democracy?"

"How much is enough?" replied the Bandit. "The sooner we begin our mission, the better."

A quartet of armed guards suddenly appeared, flanking an officer with a chest full of medals.

"So you want the Democracy to know who you are?" said the officer. "I think we can arrange that."

"I am Santiago," said the Bandit.

The officer laughed in amusement. "Can you spell 'delusional'?"

"I'm here for the bullion," continued the Bandit. "Where is it?"

"I admire your sense of humor," said the officer. "I can't say as much for your grip on reality."

"I'm only going to ask you once more. Where is the bullion?"

"In a safe place," said the officer. "We've run retina scans on all of you. You're the One-Armed Bandit. This one here is Virgil Soaring Hawk, the one on your left is a thief and murderer called Danny Briggs, the one directly behind you is—"

"I am Santiago," repeated the Bandit.

"We've got a holo recording of your intention to rob the bullion," said the officer. "You can be the One-Armed Bandit or Santiago or Peter Pan, for all I give a damn. You might as well call yourself Methuselah, because you're going to spend one hell of a long time in this stockade."

"You've had your chance," said the Bandit. He waved his arm at the officer and the guards, and a moment later all five lay dead on the shining, multicolored floor.

Then he stood back, pointed to the tiny control panel on the far wall, and melted it. The sonic field vanished, and they walked out.

"If it was that easy, why are any of the rest of us here?" asked Virgil.

"Four of you are here to carry the gold, and the Rhymer's here so he can chronicle my exploits," said the Bandit. "The stockade is at the far end of the compound. As we were brought in, I saw a barracks, a mess hall, and an office. I'll handle the opposition. You search every inch of the compound until you find the bullion."

The Bandit didn't wait for them to respond, but walked out the door and straight to the barracks. Dante heard some screams, and then all was silent. He went to the office and began to search through it. There was a safe with a complicated computer lock that took him almost thirty minutes to disable, but there was no bullion in the safe, nor even any money, just a handful of coded crystals that presumably showed the disposition of Navy ships in the sector.

"Any luck?" asked Virgil from the doorway.

"Not yet," said Dante, sitting at a computer and examining the crystals. "How about you?"

"Not a thing."

"Wait a minute!" said Dante, sitting at a computer and examining a decoded crystal. "Hey, Santiago—I've got it!"

The Bandit appeared in the doorway a moment later.

"What did you find?"

"There's a school about four miles from here. The bullion is hidden there."

"Why?" asked Virgil.

"Probably to safeguard it against what just occurred," said the Bandit. "Did it give the bullion's location at the school?"

"No, just that it's there."

"There were some vehicles out front," said the Bandit. "Let's go."

A moment later they were racing toward the school. It turned out to be a boarding school, with a pair of dormitories and a large cafeteria.

"No guards," noted Virgil.

"Guards would call attention to the place," replied Dante. "This way no one will assume there's anything here that *needs* guarding."

The Bandit got out of the vehicle. "Unload the airsleds," he instructed Virgil. "The bullion's going to be heavy."

"I wonder where it's hidden?" said Dante. "This is a pretty large complex."

"Let's find out," said the Bandit. He pointed at a window,

and a second later it crashed into a hundred pieces. Ten more windows, chosen at random, followed.

Suddenly a number of adults—obviously teachers—burst out of the school's entrance.

"What the hell is going on?" demanded one of them, a gray-haired woman who seemed to be in charge.

"This is a robbery," said the Bandit calmly. "We're here for the bullion."

"Bullion? What are you talking about?"

"Please don't waste my time by feigning ignorance. We have just come from the military compound. We *know* that they stored their bullion here."

"We don't have any bullion!"

"I told you not to waste our time," said the Bandit. "I tell you now that if you don't immediately agree to produce the bullion, I will take out the east wing of your school, regardless of who might be in it."

"You wouldn't dare!" said the woman. "There are three hundred children in that wing."

The Bandit turned and pointed toward the east wing.

"No!" yelled Dante, hurling himself at the Bandit's arm and trying to hang on to it.

The Bandit shrugged and Dante went flying through the air. By the time he'd hit the ground, there was a deafening explosion and the east wing was no more.

"The bullion," said the Bandit calmly, "or the west wing goes next."

"Don't!" cried the woman. "I'll show you where it is!"

The Bandit nodded at Virgil and the three other men. "Follow her and bring it back out."

As they disappeared inside the school, the Bandit turned to Dante, who was still sprawled in the dirt.

"I will not tolerate another display of disloyalty," he said coldly.

"Goddammit to hell!" spat Dante. "Do you realize what you've done?"

"I got us the bullion."

"You killed three hundred kids!"

"They were Democracy children," said the Bandit with an unconcerned shrug. "Why wait until they grow up to exterminate them?"

Dante stared long and hard at his handpicked Santiago. *My God—what have I done?*

PART IV

SILVERMANE'S BOOK

25.

THERE ARE THOSE WHO WILL SWEAR HE'S A
   HERO,
BORN TO FULFILL MANKIND'S DREAMS.
BUT LISTEN TO THOSE WHO NOW ARE HIS
   FOES:
SANTIAGO IS NOT WHAT HE SEEMS.

THE DOOR OPENED AND MATILDA entered her room.

"Lights," she said, and instantly the room was filled with
light.

She turned to walk to a closet, then jumped as she saw
Dante Alighieri seated in a chair by her desk.

"What the hell are you doing here?" she demanded.

"We have to talk."

"I've spent two weeks on the road recruiting members
for the organization. I'm tired. We'll talk tomorrow."

"Now," he said, and something in his voice convinced
her to sit on the edge of her bed and face him.

"All right," she said, staring at him. "What's up?"

"We've made a terrible mistake."

"What are you talking about?"

"The Bandit."

"You mean Santiago?"

"He's no more Santiago than I am," said Dante. "He
never was."

"Just because he doesn't fit your image of—"

"Shut up and listen!" snapped Dante.

Again she stared at him. "Just what the hell did he do?"

"What would you say if I told you he killed three hundred kids for no reason except that someday they'd grow
up to be members of the Democracy?"

"Did he?"

"Yes. On Madras IV."

"He must have had some reason."

"I just gave it to you."

She frowned. "Three hundred children?"

"In cold blood." Dante paused. "You and I can argue about whether he should have killed that crazy old lady back on Heliopolis. After all, she was a witness to a crime and could describe Santiago. But these were just kids. They never saw us, we never saw them."

"That doesn't seem like him."

"The hell it doesn't. He killed a couple of thousand people in the Blixtor Maze. This isn't the same guy we knew three months ago—or if it is, then we were terrible judges of character."

"Of course he's the same man. We didn't set out to select an angel."

"We don't want an angel," agreed Dante. "But we want someone who can discriminate between a Democracy officer or bureaucrat and a child who lives in the Democracy."

"Maybe we defined the perameters of the job wrong," suggested Matilda. "Maybe he thinks—"

"You're not paying attention," interrupted Dante. "Fuck the definitions. Do we want a Santiago who'll wipe out three hundred kids for any reason at all?"

She sighed deeply. "No," she said at last. "No, we don't."

"Part of it is my fault. I told him to lose the 'sir's and 'ma'am's, and never to apologize, that Santiago didn't do that. But he's gone overboard. I should have known it would happen before we ever set foot on Madras."

"How could you?"

"Virgil's helped me out of some tight spots, and introduced me to some people I wanted to meet . . . but let's be honest: he's a lying, drug-addicted killer who's probably sent half a hundred bedmates to the psycho ward. Whatever he is to me, he's nothing to Santiago—and yet thousands of men and aliens died in the Blixtor Maze just so the Bandit could set him free. That's not loyalty; that's out-and-out crazy."

"All right," said Matilda. "When you put it that way, I can't disagree with you."

"I don't know where it started going wrong," continued the poet. "I never met a more decent, more humble man than the One-Armed Bandit. He practically reeked with concern for his fellow man. How could just calling himself Santiago change him so much?"

"You can ponder that for the next few years," she answered. "The more immediate question is: what do we do about him?"

"I don't know," admitted Dante. "We certainly can't take him out by ourselves. I've seen him wipe out twenty hired guns without working up a sweat." He paused. "Besides, there probably aren't half a dozen men on the Frontier who can kill him. Do you want someone that formidable, that potentially uncontrollable, to become our Santiago? We'd just be replacing one problem with another."

"If we can't tolerate him and can't remove him, just what do you propose to do?" demanded Matilda.

"I don't know. That's why we're talking."

"I suppose we can wait until there's an opportunity . . ." began Matilda.

"To do what?"

"To kill him, of course," she replied. "He doesn't have any reason to suspect we're turning against him. Sooner or later he's got to drop his guard, relax, turn his back, do *some*thing to give us a chance."

"And then what?"

"Then we find another Santiago, or you go back to writing your poem without him and I go back to being the best thief on the Frontier." She stood up and began nervously pacing back and forth across the room. "Hell, I just wanted a Santiago so the Democracy would have a bigger target than me. If I can't have one, I can't have one. I was doing just fine before I met you, Rhymer; I can do fine again."

"It's more than my poem," said Dante. "The Inner Frontier needs Santiago. Hell, the human race needs him."

"Even if he kills three hundred innocent children?"

"He's not Santiago."

"He is now. Just ask him. Or your ladyfriends from Snakepit. Or the survivor from Jackrabbit Willowby's little army. Like it or not, Santiago is abroad in the galaxy once more, all thanks to us."

"We created him," agreed Dante. "We have to find some way to uncreate him."

"Short of finding an even better killer, I don't know what we can do," said Matilda. "We've given him an organization. We've set him up in the drug trade, and robbed millions from a bank. We've supplied him with Wilbur's services, and that's probably doubled his money already. We've hired two dozen guns, and we've got a couple of ladies like Blossom who'll do anything, no matter how perverse, if it's for the good of the cause. We did more the create him; we made him successful."

"Some of them might leave if we give the word," said Dante with more conviction than he felt.

"Name one, besides Virgil," she challenged him.

He grimaced. "I can't."

"I know."

"Still, we have to do something. Somehow, in his mind, he's equated being against Santiago with being *for* the Democracy. The originals knew the difference. They didn't expect anyone to thank them, or to understand what they were doing. Santiago didn't get to be a myth that's lived for over a century by killing children and old ladies."

"You really feel you can't reason with him?"

"He's armored in his . . . I was about to say his ignorance, but that's not it. He's armored in his *righteousness*—and it's been my experience that there's nothing more difficult to reason with than a righteous man."

"So what do we do?"

"We keep in touch, we talk whenever we're alone, we try to keep him from doing any more harm until we can come up with a solution, and we hope we don't cause even more unnecessary deaths by waiting." He paused. "I know this started out as a way for me to add to my poem and you to get the heat off you—but it's much more than that now. He'd still be killing Unicorns back on Heliopolis if it wasn't for us. I don't even blame him; he can't help being what he is, and Lord knows he didn't apply for the job. It's our fault he's here, doing what he's doing, and we've got a moral obligation to put an end to it."

"I never thought I'd hear you argue in favor of moral obligations," she noted wryly.

"Neither did I," he admitted. "I certainly don't think of myself as a moral man. But we've unleashed something very dangerous, something uncontrollable, and I think it's our duty—mine, anyway—to do something about it."

At that moment the door burst open and three recently hired men entered the room, burners in their hands.

"What the hell's going on?" demanded Matilda.

"He wants to talk to you," said one of the men. He turned to Dante. "To *both* of you."

"Who does?" asked Dante.

The man looked amused. "Guess."

Dante and Matilda walked out of her room, down the corridor to the living room, and then to the office. The Bandit was sitting at his desk.

"That will be all," he said to the three men. "You can leave now."

"Are you sure, Santiago?" asked the spokesman.

"I am quite capable of protecting myself," he said in a voice that brooked no opposition.

The three men left without another word, and the door slid shut behind them.

"What do you want?" asked Matilda.

"Yeah," said Dante. "We were just about to get romantic."

"Spare me your lies," said the Bandit.

"Who's lying?"

"Just how stupid do you think I am? I heard every word you said."

"What are you talking about?" said Matilda.

"I had both your rooms bugged."

"Why?"

"How can you ask that when I just told you I've been listening to you since Matilda entered her room?" said the Bandit irritably.

"All right, you heard us," said Dante, deciding that further denials were futile. "Now what?"

The Bandit looked from one to the other. "I thought you were more perceptive than you are," he said at last. "You have absolutely no concept of what Santiago is, what I must do if I am to succeed. We don't live in a humanistic universe. There is absolute good and absolute evil abroad in it. The Democracy is the evil, and we can never compromise with it, can never appease it, can never show it any more mercy than it would show to us if it were given the opportunity."

"You're talking about the Democracy, and I was talking about the three hundred kids you killed," said Dante. "How evil were *they*?"

"Can't you understand?" replied the Bandit. "That's three hundred armed men who won't be coming after us in fifteen years."

"That's three hundred kids who might have grown up to be doctors, who might have saved a million lives, including some right here on the Frontier."

"They belonged to the Democracy. They would have been trained to be the enemy."

"That's a crock," Dante shot back. "For all you know, it was a religious school, training ministers to come out to the Frontier."

"No more word games," said the Bandit. "My problem is not what to do with members, however young, of the Democracy. It is what to do with *you*." He paused. "I should kill you, as you would kill me if you had the chance. That is the only logical course of action, do you agree?"

Dante and Matilda stared at him, but made no reply.

"Well, at least you don't disagree." The Bandit rubbed his chin thoughtfully with his real hand. "On the other hand, I wouldn't have become Santiago without you. I owe you something for that."

"If you can solve this moral problem, you can solve others," said Dante. "Maybe there's hope for you yet."

"Shut up," said the Bandit, making no attempt to hide his annoyance. *Not anger*, noted Dante. *We're not important enough to arouse his anger. He's just annoyed, as if we were insects that were bothering him on a hot summer day.*

The Bandit was lost in thought for another moment. Finally he looked up at Dante and Matilda. "I know I can never again trust you, that you will kill me if you are given the opportunity. By the same token, I can't trust anyone you recruited; I don't know where their loyalties lie. So this is my decision: I will give the two of you, as well as Blossom and Virgil, one Standard day to get off Valhalla. If you are still here when the day is over, I'll kill you. I will contact Wilbur and tell him to transmit all my money to an account of my choosing, and that if he doesn't do so within that same Standard day he's a walking dead man."

"Maybe he can't do it in a day," suggested Matilda.

"He'll find a way, or he'll wish he had." The Bandit got to his feet and faced them. "One day and one second from now, we are at hazard. If you don't act against me, I won't seek you out—but know that starting tomorrow, I will kill each and every one of you the next time we meet."

26.

THEY SAT IN THEIR SHIP—Dante Alighieri, Waltzin' Matilda, Virgil Soaring Hawk, and the Flower of Samarkand—half a dozen light-years from Valhalla, and discussed their situation.

"I don't believe you've told me everything," said Blossom angrily. "What did you do? Why has he turned against us?"

"He hasn't turned against us so much as he has turned against Santiago," said Dante.

"You keep saying that," protested Blossom. "How can he turn against Santiago? He *is* Santiago!"

"No," said Dante. "He's a man we've been calling Santiago. There's a difference."

"Maybe he had a point about those children," she said. "At least they won't be gunning for him in ten or twelve years."

"Are you saying that if he had the ability to kill every child in the Democracy, he should?" asked Matilda.

"No," said Blossom. "But there are billions, maybe hundreds of billions, of children. He killed three hundred. Is that any reason to turn against him?"

"If he'd killed one, that would be reason enough," said Dante.

"Didn't all the other Santiagos kill people?" she demanded. "Innocent people as well as guilty?"

"Yes, they all killed people," answered Dante. "And sometimes innocent bystanders were killed. That's the fortunes of the kind of war Santiago has to wage. But no

Santiago ever went out of his way to kill innocent bystanders when it could be avoided."

"How old are you?" said Blossom. "Thirty? Thirty-five? How do you know what Santiago did more than a century ago?"

"I know what he was."

"That's no answer!"

"It's the best you're going to get."

"Which is a roundabout way of saying that you don't know for a fact whether or not any Santiago killed innocent children."

"If they did," said Dante, "then we're going to improve upon the originals."

"Who made you the arbiter of what Santiago does and doesn't do?" continued Blossom. "You're just a poet."

"Not even a very good one," admitted Dante.

"So?"

"I'm carrying on the work of a very good one," said Dante. "In the cargo hold of this ship are thousands of pages of his manuscript. I've studied it until I damned near know it by heart, and that means I know what Santiago did and what he meant to the Frontier. The One-Armed Bandit is no Santiago."

"Where does it say that he has to be? That was *your* idea, not his."

"It's his now," said Dante. "But he doesn't understand the concept. He's made it too black and white. He's the good guy and all the members of the Democracy are the bad guys—but it's not that simple. It never has been. Most members of the Democracy are just men and women who are trying to get through each day without rocking the boat or hurting the people they love. Not only don't they have any interest in the Democracy's abuses, they don't even have any knowledge of them. As for the Democracy itself, we don't want to get rid of it; it's all that stands between us and a hostile galaxy. What we want to do is limit its abuses, and remind it who it's supposed to be protecting out here on the Frontier. The Bandit would destroy it; Santiago just wants to straighten it out. Neither will ever succeed, but the Bandit will kill more innocent people with each passing day, and eventually bring down destruction on all the people he's fighting for, because he's going to commit some abuses that the Democracy can't ignore."

"Santiago committed abuses," said Blossom. "That's why he was King of the Outlaws."

"Santiago committed *crimes*," said Dante. "That's why the Democracy put a price on his head and left it to the bounty hunters to find him. If he'd gone to war against innocent Democracy citizens, the whole goddamned Navy would have come out to the Frontier, two billion ships strong, and blown away every world they came to until they found him. *That's* what the Bandit's asking for."

Blossom sighed deeply. "All right. Maybe you're right, maybe you're not—but it's all academic now anyway, since he's banished us and plans to kill us on sight. So what do we do now?"

"I don't know," said Dante. "Find the true Santiago, I suppose."

"While this one's killing people right and left and telling everyone Santiago's to blame for it?" asked Virgil.

"What do you suggest?" said Dante.

"Kill him."

"Who's going to do it?" Dante shot back. "You? Me? Matilda? You've seen him in action. Even Dimitrios of the Three Burners wouldn't stand much chance against him."

"There must be someone out there."

"So you find a better killer," said Matilda. "Then what?"

"Then you hope he's more reasonable than the Bandit," replied Virgil.

"We're going about this all wrong," said Dante. "Santiago is more than merely a competent killer. We chose the Bandit not just because of his physical abilities, but because we thought he was a moral man."

"He is," answered Virgil. "Too moral. Sometimes that can be as much a fault as not being moral enough."

Dante turned to Matilda. "Have you got any suggestions?"

"He's not an evil man," she began.

"But he's done evil things, and he's almost certainly going to do more."

"Let me finish," she said. "He's not an evil man. He's wrongheaded in some respects, but he's willing to put his life on the line for the cause—as he perceives it—every day, he's willing to be hated and feared and mistrusted by all the people he's trying to defend, he's willing to do everything required of Santiago. The problem isn't that he's a shirker, but that, because of his misconceptions, he's willing to do too much, not too little."

"What's your point?" said Dante.

"I think it's more practical to educate him than replace him," she said. "After all, he's already set up shop as Santiago. Even if you found a way to kill him, there's no guarantee that the next one would be as moral, or as self-sacrificing."

"How are we going to educate him if he's going to shoot us on sight?" demanded Dante in exasperation.

"*We* aren't," said Matilda. "That much is obvious."

"So . . . ?"

"So we find someone who can."

"You're saying we get someone to join his organization and try to influence him?" asked Dante. "That strikes me as a pretty slim hope."

"Do *you* want to kill him?"

"You know we can't."

"Anyone can be ambushed. We're smarter than he is. It wouldn't be that hard—especially now, before he builds a truly formidable organization." She stared at him. "Now answer my question."

"No," he admitted. "No, I don't want to kill him."

"Then we have two choices: we can hope someone else kills him, or we can try—by proxy—to change the way he looks at things."

"Do you have anyone in mind?"

"Not yet."

"I don't want to cast a pall of gloom here," volunteered Virgil, who looked only too happy to do so, "but you're the guys who chose the Bandit in the first place. What makes you think you'll do any better this time around?"

"If we don't find a replacement, who will?" asked Dante.

"Me."

"You have a candidate in mind?"

"Yeah. I figure the easiest way to make the Bandit accept our candidate is to send him someone with a reputation, someone with bona fides, so to speak—but a freelancer, not someone who proposes to share his business out of the blue."

"All right," said Dante. "Who is it?"

"You ever hear of the Black Death?"

"He's a killer for hire?"

"Everyone's a killer for hire," said the Injun. "The difference is the he don't make any bones about it."

"And what makes you think he can influence the One-Armed Bandit?" asked Matilda.

"He owes me a couple of favors."

"Sexual, of course," said Dante distastefully.

"Personal, anyway," said Virgil noncommittally.

"Can you trust him?"

"Probably."

"Just 'probably'?" asked Matilda, frowning.

" 'Probably' is as high a rating as I'd give the Rhymer here," retorted Virgil, "and he and I are connected at the soul."

"The hell we are!" snapped Dante.

Virgil grinned. "You see? My closest friend in the galaxy, and he's pissed that I cherish our friendship. One of these days he'll sell me out for thirty pieces of silver."

"Two pieces of lead alloy would do it," muttered Dante.

"Get back to the point," said Matilda. "Can we trust the Black Death?"

"As much as you can trust anyone," answered Virgil.

"*Can* he kill the Bandit if he has to?"

"Hell, *I* can kill him when his back's turned. How many times did he turn his back on you in the past month? A hundred? A thousand?"

"So your friend shoots people in the back?" said Dante.

"Not really, though I'm sure he'd have no serious objection to it." Virgil lit a smokeless cigar. "His job is killing people. He doesn't care if you subtract points for form."

"Where can we find him?" said Dante. "I'll want to talk to him before we agree to this."

"Not a good idea," said Virgil.

"Why not?"

"He doesn't like being hemmed in. Let me talk to him one-on-one."

"Not a chance," said Dante.

"Why not?"

"Not to put too fine a point on it, you're a moral dwarf compared to the Bandit. I don't want you telling anyone how we want the Bandit to behave."

"You really know how to hurt a guy, Rhymer," said Virgil with an obvious lack of sincerity. "Say that in public and someone might think you disapproved of my lifestyle or my ethics."

"There's nothing wrong with either that castration and a couple of decades in solitary confinement wouldn't cure," said Dante. "Now tell me where we can find this Black Death."

"He's not like the Tyrannosaur," replied Virgil. "He doesn't have his own world, and he doesn't stand out in a crowd—at least, not the way you'd think. He's a freelancer. It might take me a few days to track him down."

"Start."

"Start how? We're eight light-years from the nearest inhabited planet."

"Get on the subspace radio. Ask your contacts. Pass the word that you've got a lucrative job for him."

"I'll ask around, but you don't want me to lie about a paycheck. He might take it as an insult."

"Just get your ass over to the radio and do what you have to do," said Dante irritably.

Virgil started to say something, thought better of it, and went over to the subspace radio, where he tried to track down the Black Death.

"We can't just sit around and hope this works out," said Dante. "If I know Virgil, this Black Death is more likely to kill for the Bandit than persuade for us."

"So what do you want us to do?" asked Blossom, who had been silent for the past few minutes.

"I'm glad to see you're talking to me again," said Dante dryly. "And to answer your question: we'll keep looking."

"For what?"

"I wish I knew. Some way to educate or depose the Bandit." He stared at her for a long minute. "If we can't come up with something, maybe we'll send you back."

"He'll kill me!"

"What if you contacted him and convinced him that we made you leave against your will, that you believe in him and everything he's doing and you want to come back?"

"Which probably isn't too far from the truth," commented Matilda.

"He won't care about the truth," said Blossom. "You know how rigid he is. He's already said he'll kill us. He never changes his mind."

"Well, it's something to keep in reserve," said Dante.

"Fuck your reserve!" snapped Blossom. "I believed in him, and now you've fixed it so he'll kill me the next time he sees me! I want out. The next planet we touch down on, you go your way and I'm going mine."

"I can't stop you," said Dante.

"You're damned right you can't," she replied. "You're a fool, you know that? You've got a saint on Valhalla, and that's not good enough for you. You want a god."

"I just want Santiago."

"The *real* Santiagos were killers and thieves. You want yours to walk on water!" She got to her feet. "I'm going to my cabin. Leave me alone until we land."

She walked through the galley to the cabins and entered the nearest of them.

"Well, I handled that with my usual aplomb," said Dante bitterly. "Virgil, the Bandit, and her." He grimaced. "Sometimes I wish I'd never found that goddamned poem."

"Sometimes I wish I were Queen of the Universe," replied Matilda. "Tell me when you want to stop talking drivel and get back to business."

"I think you'd make a rather nice queen."

"You heard me."

"I heard you. I just don't see any viable options." He sighed deeply. "Maybe the kids were an aberration. Maybe he'll work out after all."

"Maybe he will."

"Except it wasn't just the kids," complained Dante. "It was all those people in the Maze. And the old lady at the bank, too—and the fact that he couldn't think his way out of it, couldn't come up with a lie that would allow him to let her live."

"I know," she agreed. "At first I thought he was right, but after I heard you explain how we could have avoided killing her, could even put her to use explaining that we all worked for Santiago, I knew he was wrong." She paused. "He's just not very quick on his mental feet."

"Most fanatics aren't," said Dante.

Suddenly Virgil stood up and turned to them. "It's all arranged," he announced. "Lay in a course for Tosca III."

"What's on Tosca?" asked Dante.

"The Black Death."

27.

THE BLACK DEATH COMES, THE BLACK DEATH
  GOES,
THE BLACK DEATH CAN BE BELLICOSE.
SO FRIEND, BE ON YOUR GUARD TODAY—
HIS BLOOD IS UP, HE LIVES TO SLAY.

AS DANTE BECAME MORE COMFORTABLE with his epic, he began using poetic license here and there. The first time was when he wrote of the Black Death.

He was writing about heroes and villains so big they blotted out the stars, so memorable that children would be telling their stories decades after he wrote them, and once in a while he came across such an aberration that he felt free to embellish or, in this case, to out-and-out falsify.

Not that the Black Death wasn't every bit as deadly as Dante said. In point of fact, he was even deadlier. Not that he didn't deserve the three verses Dante gave him, or that he wasn't feared wherever he went—once he was recognized.

The interesting fact is that he was almost never recognized.

Until it was too late.

The name itself conjures up fantastic images. A tall, muscular black man clad in muted colors, plain blazers or screechers in worn holsters, shopworn shoes or boots.

Or perhaps a slender man, looking like Death itself, wearing a black frock coat, his clothes and his drawn skin absorbing all color and reflecting only the total absence of color.

You can picture an unforgiving face, cold lifeless eyes like those of a shark, a thin-lipped mouth that never smiles. Some kind of hat or headpiece so that the sun never illuminates that death-mask countenance.

Expensive gloves that never slip off the handles of his weapons, that leave no fingerprints, that never expose his surprisingly delicate fingers to prying eyes.

That's the image of a man called the Black Death—and yet the only thing it had in common with the *real* Black Death was the gloves.

His name was Henry Marston, hardly a name to roll off frightened men's lips. And he wasn't black. He was a pale, chalky, sickly white; what pigment his skin had once possessed was almost totally gone.

He stood five feet seven inches, when he was strong enough to stand. His weight varied between 110 and 125 pounds; it had never in his life been more than 136.

His clothes were nondescript, wrinkled, a bit faded. The left elbow was patched, the right cuff frayed. He wore no primary colors; everything was neutral.

The only belt he wore held his loose-fitting pants up. It housed no weapon of any kind. There were no telltale bulges pinpointing hidden knives or pistols anywhere on his body. His boots were so old they were past the point of holding a polish, and the large toe of his left foot poked out through a crack in the inexpensive material.

And there were the gloves.

They went halfway up his forearms, totally functional, totally unstylish.

There was also the mask. It was transparent, and covered his face from the bridge of his nose down to his Adam's apple, then all the way around to the back of his head.

If there was ever a man who looked less than formidable, it was Henry Marston.

So it was probably God's little cosmic joke that he was the deadliest man alive, far more dangerous than Dimitrios or the One-Armed Bandit or Tyrannosaur Bailey, with a sobriquet that was more accurate than most.

"No matter what you think," Virgil told his companions as they waited patiently to pass through Customs at the Tosca III spaceport, "he's everything I've said he is."

"Why shouldn't we believe you?" asked Dante.

"Well, he doesn't make a good first impression," admitted Virgil. He paused thoughtfully. "Come to think of it, his second and third impressions aren't much of an improvement."

"We came here on your say-so," said Dante angrily. "If you've been wasting our time, maybe you'd better tell us right now."

"Everything I said about the Black Death is true," said Virgil. He spat on his hand and held it up, palm out. "I give you an Injun's solemn oath on that."

"There's something you're not telling us," continued Dante.

"It'll probably be better if you find out for yourself."

"Why?"

"Because if I tell you any more about him, you won't want to meet him."

"He's that ineffectual?" asked Matilda.

Virgil smiled. "I told you: he's the deadliest killer out here—at least the deadliest I've ever seen."

"Then why won't we want to meet him?"

"You'll be afraid to."

Dante glared at him. "Just how much seed have you been chewing today?"

"None," Virgil assured him. "I'm depressingly sober."

"Then shut up," Dante ordered him. "The more we talk, the angrier I'm getting with you. Just take us to meet this Black Death and let's get it over with."

"You're the boss," said Virgil. They passed through Customs without incident. "By the way," added Virgil as they walked to a hovering limo, "call him Henry."

"Why?"

"Because that's his name. And he hates being the Black Death."

"You mean being *called* the Black Death," Matilda corrected him.

"That, too," agreed Virgil.

The limo took them into Red Dust, the nearest of Tosca's three towns. The buildings showed the effects of the wind constantly blowing the dust against them, and two of the slidewalks were closed for repairs, also owing to the omnipresent dust.

The limo announced that they had reached the municipality of Red Dust and asked for a specific destination.

"Take us to the Weeping Willow," said Virgil.

"Done, sir," replied the limo so promptly and formally that Dante decided that it must be frustrated at its inability to offer a snappy salute.

The Weeping Willow was a nondescript tavern, small and unimpressive, filled with secondhand and oft-repaired chairs and tables. There was no back room for gambling, no upstairs rooms for sex, nothing but a small selection of mediocre liquor from various points on the Inner Frontier, an unused alien dart game hanging on one wall, and a much-dented metal bar in addition to the tables.

Dante glanced around the tavern. A small, sickly-looking man sat at a table in the corner. Two oversized women, smoking alien cigarettes and drinking alien whiskey, sat at another, playing a complex game using hundreds of cards with unfamiliar markings. The only other person in the place was the tall, muscular bartender, who looked hopefully at them when they entered, then lost interest when he saw they weren't there to drink.

"Your information was wrong," said Dante. "He's not here."

"Yes he is," answered Virgil calmly.

Dante looked at the small man with the transparent mask and the long gloves. "Is this some kind of joke?" he demanded.

"Why don't we talk to him, and then you can tell me if it's a joke or not," said Virgil, approaching the small man's table.

Henry Marston looked up and tried to smile at Virgil. It was evidently too much of an effort, and the smile froze halfway across his face, then vanished a few seconds later.

"Hi, Henry. It's been a while."

"Hello, Virgil," said Henry, stifling a cough. "What brings you to a little dirtball like Tosca?"

"I'd like you to meet two friends of mine—Dante and Matilda."

"I hope you'll forgive me if I don't get up," said Henry in a weak, hoarse whisper.

"I heard you were on Tosca," said Virgil, pulling up a chair and motioning for his companions to do the same. "Got a job to do here?"

"It's done," said Henry.

"Then why are you still here?"

"I was paid to kill her," was the answer. "I have to stick around and make sure she died."

Wonderful, thought Dante. *The old man's such a lousy shot he doesn't know if his victim will live or die. Why are we wasting our time here?*

"Excuse me for interrupting," said Dante, frowning, "but are you really the man known as the Black Death?"

"It's not a name of my own choosing," said Henry.

"I mean no disrespect, but you look like you're half dead yourself."

"I am."

Dante turned to Virgil. "And this is the guy you think can take out the Bandit?"

"If he has to," said Virgil. "But I thought the plan was for him to ride herd, to kind of redirect him."

"Ride herd?" repeated Dante. "No offense, Henry, if that's your name, but he can barely sit up in his chair. What the hell got into you?"

Virgil chuckled. "Nothing got into me. That's why I'm still alive."

"I think your friend deserves an explanation, Virgil," said Henry.

"Yeah, I suppose so," agreed Virgil. "Too bad. I just love to watch him when he's confused."

"Is one of you going to tell me what this is all about?" said Dante, trying to control his temper.

"It's *him*," said Matilda, nodding her head toward Henry.

Henry smiled. "You're very perceptive, my dear."

"I'm getting really annoyed!" growled Dante. He turned to Matilda. "What do you know that I don't know?"

"You're not the Black Death at all," said Matilda, staring at Henry. "That may be what they call you, but that's not what you are. You're its carrier."

"What are you talking about?" demanded Dante.

"Look at him," said Matilda. "That mask isn't there to protect him from unfiltered air. It's to protect *us* from *him*. Look at his gloves. You can't touch him and he can't touch you." She paused. "What disease are you carrying, Henry? *Ybonia*?"

"*Ybonia* takes weeks to act," replied Henry. "I'm a carrier for *Bharzia*."

"How fast does it act?"

"If I touch you, you're dead within an hour. If I breathe on you, it could take up to two days. They are not days you would wish on anyone."

"I've heard about *Bharzia*," said Dante. "There's no cure for it."

"Not yet," agreed Henry. "Maybe in another ten or twelve years."

"I thought it killed everyone that was infected," continued Dante. "That once it showed up on a planet it decimated the whole population. How come you're still alive?"

"No one knows," said Henry. "Genetic sport, probably. I haven't had a healthy day in two decades, but I don't die. There are days, oh, thousands of them, when I *wish* I was dead, but it never happens."

"How did you decide to become the Black Death?" asked Matilda.

"I figured that if God has such a vicious sense of humor that He'd leave me alive when all I wanted to do was die, the least I could do was even the score by killing men and women He wanted to live."

"An interesting philosophy," commented Dante.

"What do you do with your money?" asked Matilda.

"What *can* someone like me do?" responded Henry. "I

spend some of it on moral lepers like Virgil, who allow me to vicariously experience some very out-of-the-ordinary things. And I donate millions to research. Without me, they'd be thirty years from a cure."

"It doesn't sound like much of a life."

"It's the only one I've got."

"Maybe you'd like to do something meaningful with it," said Dante.

"Are you suggesting that killing hundreds of men and women isn't meaningful?" said Henry sardonically.

"I'm being serious."

"All right, let's be serious," said Henry, staring back at him through watery eyes. "Who do you want me to kill?"

"Hopefully no one."

Henry looked amused. "My only skill is killing people. If you want me to let them live, that could run into real money."

Dante was silent for a long moment, studying the old man. Finally he spoke. "I'm sorry for wasting your time, Henry. You're not the man we want."

"I don't even know what the job is," complained Henry.

"It doesn't matter," said Dante. "It requires a man with a stronger moral compass than you possess."

"I resent your drawing moral and ethical judgments on my character before you've had a chance to know me," said Henry.

"Okay, you resent it," said Dante. "What are you going to do—take off your mask and breathe on me?"

"It's a possibility."

"That's why we can't use you," said Dante. "Killing the man in question was a last resort . . . but killing seems to be your *only* resort."

"You do what you're good at," replied Henry bitterly. "This is what *I'm* good at."

"I don't mind that it's what you're good at," said Dante. "I mind that it's *all* you're good at."

Henry stared at his gloved hands for a long moment. "Just out of curiosity, what would the job have paid?"

"I don't know."

"You don't know?" repeated Henry unbelievingly.

"It's too complicated to explain. You'd have been working for someone else."

"The man you wanted me to kill?"

"The man I hoped you wouldn't have to kill."

"This is getting very complicated," said Henry. "I'm a simple man. Show me who you want dead and I'll kill them. Show me who you want to live and I'll leave them alone. Black and white makes sense to me. I don't like grays."

"That's the problem, all right," said Dante. "I'm sorry to have bothered you."

"No bother at all," said Henry. "Leave two hundred credits at the bar."

"Why?"

"For my time. I didn't ask for this interview."

Dante considered it, then nodded his agreement. "Fair enough."

"If you ever decide what you really want, come on back and we'll talk some business," said Henry.

"If you're still alive," said Virgil with a smile.

"Oh, I'll be alive," Henry assured him. "If God wanted me dead, the son of a bitch would have taken me out twenty years ago."

"Well, I'll see you around," said Virgil, as the three of them got to their feet.

Henry was about to reply when a single gunshot rang out. The old man fell over backward in his chair, a bullet buried deep between his eyes.

Dante turned to the door to see who had fired the shot, then blinked his eyes very rapidly and shook his head. Maybe it was simply because Henry has been referring to the deity, but for just an instant it seemed to the poet that he was looking at God Himself.

28.

HE'S A MASTER OF EACH WEAPON, AND HE'S
   GOT A LION'S HEART.
HE TURNS MAYHEM INTO SCIENCE, AND THEN
   SCIENCE INTO ART.
HE'S SILVERMANE THE HERO, AND THERE ISN'T
   ANY DOUBT:
IF YOU GO AND BREAK THE LAW HE WILL
   SURELY CALL YOU OUT.

HE WAS THE MOST BEAUTIFUL man Dante had ever seen. Not beautiful in a feminine way, but rather every-feature-perfect, the kind of beauty Michelangelo had striven for and never quite achieved.

He stood six feet eight inches tall, but so balanced were his proportions, so catlike the grace with which he moved, that he seemed smaller. His eyes were a clear and brilliant blue, his nose straight, his teeth porcelain smooth, his jaw firm without being overly square. His shoulders were broad, his waist and hips narrow, his legs long and lean.

His most distinctive feature was his hair. He had a huge thick shock of it, and it was silver in color—not black streaked with white to form a bright gray, but actual silver, every strand the purest color. It hung down his back, the longest section of it reaching his waist, and gave the impression of a huge, heavily maned lion.

He wore a matched set of projectile pistols, and the belt that supported his holsters held perhaps a hundred bullets. A knife handle peeked out from the top of one of his polished boots. His clothes were black and silver, and fit him as if they'd been designed by the finest tailor back on Deluros VIII. He wore no jewelry of any kind, not even a ring.

A thousand of the best commercial artists over the eons

had tried to capture his likeness on the covers of adventure books and magazines, and had never succeeded. Heroic statues had always fallen short of the mark. Dante had a feeling that when women thought of their ideal man, they would have traded whatever their imaginations came up with for the man standing in the doorway of the tavern, putting his pistol in his holster.

The man stared at Dante and his two companions curiously, as if expecting a reaction.

"You know who that was?" said Dante at last.

"The Black Death," said the man in a strong, clear baritone.

"You meant to kill him?"

"I hit what I aim at."

Dante moved his chair away from Henry's corpse. "Well, you might as well pay the insurance."

"Pay the insurance?" repeated the man, frowning.

"Put a bullet in his ear, just to be on the safe side."

"I told you: I hit what I aim at."

"You never miss?"

"Never." The man noticed that a trickle of blood had rolled down the side of Henry's head and was moving slowly toward Dante's boot. "I'd move if I were you. His blood is probably as deadly as the rest of him."

Dante quickly stood up and walked a few steps away. "Thanks. Are you a bounty hunter?"

The beautiful man shook his shaggy silver head. "No."

"The law?"

The man smiled. "There isn't any law out here."

"Let me guess. You just didn't like the way he looked?"

"You don't strike me as a fool," said the man. "Don't say foolish things."

"I'm just trying to find out who you are and why you killed the man I was talking to."

"Then you should ask."

"Consider it done."

"My name is Joshua Silvermane, and I killed that man because he didn't deserve to live."

"Silvermane," repeated Dante. "I've heard of you. Dimitrios thinks very highly of you."

"Dimitrios of the Three Burners?" asked Silvermane.

"Yes."

"He's right."

"He never mentioned your modest streak," said Dante sardonically.

Silvermane stared at him without making any reply, and suddenly the poet became very nervous. Finally the tall man spoke. "I don't trade witticisms."

"I know why *I* think the Black Death deserved to die," said Dante, quickly changing the subject. "Why did *you* think so?"

"He killed a woman who had never done him any harm, a woman who was far better than he was."

"Your lover?" asked Matilda.

"I never met her."

"Someone paid you to hunt him down and kill him," concluded Dante. "That's pretty much like bounty hunting."

"No one paid me anything."

Dante frowned. "Then I don't understand."

"She had just married a friend of mine. A very bitter and unsuccessful suitor commissioned the Black Death to pay her a visit."

"And you hunted him down for your friend?" said Dante. "I'd call that a noble thing to do." He paused. "What do you do when you're not hunting down killers for your friends?"

"I right wrongs."

"For whom?"

"Sometimes you don't worry about that. Sometimes you just see something that's wrong, and no one is doing anything about it, so you have to."

"Why you?"

"Because someone has to."

"That's not much of an answer."

"When I was seven years old," said Silvermane, his perfect face reliving the event, "I was walking down the street of a Tradertown on Majorca II with my father. There was a fight in a building we were passing, and a stray laser beam caught him in the neck. He dropped to the ground, bleeding profusely, and for an hour I begged people to help him while they just walked around him or crossed the street and ignored him. He died before anyone helped get him to a doctor, and I swore that I would never walk past someone who needed help, would never be one of the ones who looked away."

"A not-for-profit avenger!" said Virgil, amused. "How do you pay your bills?"

"Sometimes people pay me out of gratitude," said Silvermane. "I've never asked for money, and I've never felt bitter or cheated when it wasn't given—but it comes often enough to feed and clothe me, and keep me in bullets."

"Why bullets?" asked Virgil. "I haven't seen half a dozen projectile pistols in my life."

"They make a bang," said Silvermane. "People aren't used to the noise, and it sometimes freezes them into immobility for a second or two. That's usually more advantage than I need. Also, my pistols never run out of power. I know how many bullets I have left in each and in my belt, and I don't have to constantly check my power packs."

"You know," said Dante, staring at him curiously, "Sebastian Cain used bullets, too."

"Never heard of him."

"He died a long time ago," said the poet. "I think you may have a lot in common with him."

"Interesting," said Silvermane with no show of interest whatever. He turned to the bartender. "Find me a waterproof groundsheet or something else that's airtight and doesn't leak and I'll take the body off the premises."

"Coming up," said the bartender.

"Have you got a burner?" continued Silvermane.

The bartender reached beneath the bar and produced a small laser pistol.

"Good," said Silvermane. "After I get the body out of

here, take that thing and fry every drop of blood you can find on the floor."

"Was something wrong with him?" asked the bartender.

"More than you can imagine. Just do it."

"Right." He disappeared into a back room, then returned a moment later with the requested groundsheet, which he carried over to Silvermane.

"Have you got a trash atomizer out back?" asked the tall man.

"Yeah," said the bartender. "Just walk around the building. You can't miss it."

"I'm going to use it," announced Silvermane, bending over and wrapping Henry Marston's body in the blanket while being careful not to touch it with his bare hands, then hefting it to his shoulder as if it weighed almost nothing. "Even dead, this fellow is too dangerous to bury."

"Be my guest," said the bartender, as Silvermane walked out the front door.

Dante turned to his companions. "Are you thinking what I'm thinking?"

"I don't know," said Matilda, a troubled expression on her face. "We've been wrong once already."

"And the Bandit seemed a lot more tractable than this guy," added Virgil.

"But the Bandit's a fanatic," said Dante. "We couldn't know that up front."

"And this guy travels around the galaxy risking his life righting wrongs for free," Virgil pointed out. "Doesn't that seem a little fanatical to you?"

"Maybe," said Dante. "Maybe it's noble." He signed deeply. "It's almost as if Black Orpheus himself is telling me that this is the one. He uses bullets, just like Cain did . . ."

"But four other Santiagos didn't," said Matilda.

"I know," said Dante.

"Now why don't you admit the real reason you're considering him?" continued Matilda.

"And what is that?"

"The same reason *I'm* considering him," she replied uncomfortably. "He's the first man we've seen who might actually have a chance against the Bandit."

"What if he wins?" asked Virgil. "Are you really sure you want to replace one fanatical killer with an even more formidable one?"

"I don't know," said Dante. "I've just got this feeling."

"Take deep breaths and think pastoral thoughts," said Virgil. "It'll pass."

At that moment Silvermane reentered the tavern and approached their table.

"The three of you are witnesses to a killing," he announced. "If you're going to report it, let me know, and I'll stick around and give my side of it. I don't intend to be a fugitive."

"Report it to *who*?" asked Virgil.

"I don't know," admitted Silvermane with a shrug. "I just got here half an hour ago. I don't know if they have any local law enforcement."

"My guess is that they don't even have any local laws," said Dante. "Anyway, we're not reporting anything. The man you killed was scum and we all know it."

"Good," said Silvermane. "Then I'll be on my way."

"I'd like to buy you a drink first," said Dante.

"I know you would," said Silvermane.

"You do?"

"Of course. You could only have one reason for talking to the Black Death, and now he's dead." He turned to the bartender. "Bring me a beer. A cold one." Then it was back to Dante. "Who did you want him to kill, and why?"

Dante uttered an embarrassed laugh. "I wasn't ready for such bluntness."

"There's a lot of evil abroad in the galaxy, and life is short," said Silvermane. "I have no time to waste. Who's your target?"

"It's not that easy."

"It never is—but I can't help you if you don't tell me what you want."

"I want someone to stand up for people who can't stand up for themselves," said Dante.

"That's what I do best," said Silvermane.

"So you say."

"Who's the enemy?"

"The Democracy."

Silvermane stared long and hard at him. "You don't look like a traitor."

"I'm not."

"Continue."

"There's a difference between being a traitor to your race and being opposed to the excesses of your government," continued Dante.

Silvermane stared at him and offered no reply.

"Well?" said Dante, uneasily breaking the silence.

"Well what?"

"What I said. Does it sound like something that might interest you?"

Silvermane continued staring at him. Finally he spoke. "Do you seriously expect me to believe that you were recruiting the Black Death to go to war with the Democracy?"

"No. I was interviewing him about eradicating a mistake—but he wasn't the man for the job. We were just about to leave when you showed up."

"What is the mistake?"

Now it was Dante's turn to stare in silence for a long moment, as he tried to decide how much to tell the tall man. "We chose the wrong man for the job."

"The job you're offering me?"

"The job I'm willing to discuss with you. I'm not offering anything yet."

"All right. Who did you choose originally?"

"A man known as the One-Armed Bandit."

"I've heard of him."

"Everyone has," Virgil put in.

"I heard he vanished from sight a few months ago," continued Silvermane. "I assumed he'd been killed. Eventually that happens to just about everyone in our line of work."

"The One-Armed Bandit is no more," said Dante. "But the man who *was* the One-Armed Bandit is still around."

"Oh?"

"These days he calls himself Santiago."

"The King of the Outlaws," said Silvermane. "If he wanted to attract attention, he couldn't have chosen a more obvious name. Tell me about it."

"We convinced him that it was time for Santiago to return to the Inner Frontier, to walk among Men again, to harass and harry the Democracy."

"The way I heard it, Santiago harassed and harried everyone for profit," said Silvermane.

"That's the way he *wanted* people to hear it," said Matilda.

Silvermane didn't have to be force-fed the proper assumption. "Okay, so he was a revolutionary. He didn't get very far. We've still got a Democracy."

"We need the Democracy," said Dante. "No one's trying to overthrow it."

Again the tall man surprised them with the speed with which he could assimilate what was being said. "So he was trying to lessen their abuses out here, and of course he had to convince them he was an outlaw. Even Santiago couldn't have held off the Navy."

Dante and Matilda exchanged looks.

He's awfully fast on the uptake. Maybe, just maybe . . .

"That's it in a nutshell," said Dante.

"And what's the problem with the One-Armed Bandit?" asked Silvermane. "Has he gone overboard on the outlaw part?"

"I wish it was that easy," admitted Dante with a grimace.

"What is it, then?"

"We were on Madras a couple of weeks ago . . ." began Dante.

"That was *him*?" said Silvermane. "That made the news everywhere on the Frontier, as well as the Democracy. More than three hundred kids slaughtered."

"That was him."

"What the hell got into him?"

"He says that's three hundred kids that won't grow up to be three hundred members of the Democracy."

"He's a fool," said Silvermane. "Ninety-nine percent of the Democracy is just like the men and women who walked past my father when he was dying. They're not heroes or villains, they just don't want to get involved. Hell, they're what the Democracy's there to protect. If you've got a problem with the Democracy, eventually you emigrate and come out to the Frontier." He paused. "You've got yourself a real problem, and of your own making. I assume that without you, there'd be no Santiago."

"I was part of it," interjected Matilda. "It wasn't just him."

"We've been a century without Santiago," said Silvermane. "A trillion people have been born and died in that time, maybe more. Why is it that you two have decided to resurrect him?"

Matilda gestured to Dante. "He's the new Black Orpheus."

"Self-appointed?"

"I've got the original's manuscript," said Dante. "That's how I was able to find out what Santiago really was. I'm continuing his work—and if it's to be about anything besides a handful of misfits and losers, if there's to be any balance in the galaxy, then we need a Santiago."

"So you want me to become Santiago because it'll make a satisfying poem," said Silvermane noncommittally. He turned to Matilda. "What about you?"

"I'm his great-granddaughter."

"You want me to plunder the Frontier and then die so you can claim your inheritance?"

"It's simpler than that," she answered. "I need Santiago to take the heat off me, to give the Democracy a bigger target."

Silvermane smiled. "I was wondering if we'd ever meet, Matilda."

"I haven't told you my name."

"You didn't have to. I heard that Waltzin' Matilda was traveling with the new Black Orpheus. And you just told me as much yourself: if only Santiago can draw the Democracy's attention away from you, you have to be Waltzin' Matilda." The smile vanished as he stared at her. "I've been hearing about you for years. Given your accomplishments, you're younger than I expected."

"I started early."

Silvermane turned to Virgil. "What about you?"

"I'm with him," said Virgil, jerking a thumb in Dante's direction.

"Why?"

"It's too complicated to explain—or maybe too simple."

"Try."

"He's Dante. I'm Virgil."

"How many circles of hell have you led him through so far?" asked Silvermane.

"Sonuvabitch!" exclaimed Virgil, obviously impressed. "You've read it!"

"It seems to me there's an awful lot of poetry going on around here," said Silvermane. "But it seems that these days even poets wind up relying on the sword."

"Maybe the two aren't mutually exclusive," suggested Dante. "Maybe it's the pen that must direct the sword."

Silvermane patted his pistol. "Maybe I'm writing history with my own pen."

"Are you ready to write an epic?" asked Dante. "Or are you going to keep writing little unrelated pieces that will all be forgotten?"

"I'm happy curing the ills of the Frontier one by one," said Silvermane. "I don't know how I'd feel about trying to cure them wholesale."

"I can't make you," said Dante. "I just want you to think about it."

"You say that, but what you mean is that you want me to think about killing the One-Armed Bandit—who, I should point out, wouldn't need killing if you hadn't chosen *him* to be your secret hero."

"I really don't want him killed if it can be avoided, if we can find some other way."

"How many deposed tyrants are walking around these days?" asked Silvermane. "If he's got the bit between his teeth, if he believes in what he's doing, there's only one way to replace him, and we both know what that is."

"You're a cold son of a bitch, you know that?" said Dante irritably.

"I'm in a cold business."

"You're not in a business at all. You don't demand pay for what you do." Dante paused and studied him carefully. "How do we know you won't be as much of a fanatic as the Bandit is?"

"You don't."

"What do *you* think?" said Dante.

"I have no idea," admitted Silvermane. "I don't think I'm a fanatic, and I don't think I can be corrupted—but until you give me a cause I'm willing to die for and combine it with absolute power, how can I answer your question with any certainty?"

"You just did," said Dante. "I trust you."

"I thank you for your trust, but I haven't said I'm interested in the job yet."

"I know. Take some time and think about it. We'll explain how we're setting up an organization, what connections we've established so far." Dante paused. "But don't take too long. If he goes and slaughters another three hundred kids, I'll have to take him on myself, and I don't have the chance of a snowball in hell."

"Then why do it?"

"Because he's my responsibility," answered Dante. "Because those kids would be alive if it wasn't for me."

"If I agree to become Santiago, I think we're going to get along just fine," said Silvermane.

"When do you want to learn about the operation?"

"The first thing you'd better tell me about is the One-Armed Bandit," said Silvermane. "On the not-unreasonable assumption that he has no intention of resigning, he's the first obstacle, and if he can't be overcome, none of the rest matters. I've heard about that prosthetic arm of his, but I don't really know anything about it. Just how lethal is it?"

"Depending how he's using it, he can pinpoint a target no bigger than a coin at six hundred yards, or he can take out a city block."

"Is he inclined to shoot first or talk first?"

"Once upon a time he talked first," said Dante. "These days I don't know."

"Left arm or right?"

"Left."

"Any vision problems?" asked Silvermane.

"Not to my knowledge."

"Okay, I'll think about it."

"Where will we find you?"

"I'll be leaving for New Patagonia in an hour. That's about sixteen light-years from here. You can find me at the Jong Palace."

"That's a casino?"

Silvermane smiled. "A hotel."

"With Henry—that's the Black Death—dead, we have no reason to stay here. We might as well go to New Patagonia with you."

"There's no room in my ship."

"I meant that we'll leave Tosca when you do."

"All right. I'll see you there." He walked to the door, then turned back to them. "If I decide to do it, you won't regret asking me. I'll be the best Santiago I can be." Then he was out in the street.

"Jesus, I hope so!" muttered Dante.

29.

SIMON TEN BROEK LOVES TO DRAW
   ATTENTION;
SIMON TEN BROEK SPENT YEARS IN BLEAK
   DETENTION;
SIMON TEN BROEK, WITH CRIMES TOO VILE TO
   MENTION;
SIMON TEN BROEK WON'T LIVE TO SEE HIS
   PENSION.

NEW PATAGONIA WAS EVERYTHING THAT Tosca was not:
green, temperate, pleasant, crisscrossed by rivers, framed
with snowcapped mountains. It had been developed into a
resort world by the cartel that had laid claim to it. They
erected a ski lodge atop the snowiest mountain, then leased
out the rest of the range, until the place was dotted with
ski facilities. Next they expanded downward, building half
a dozen fishing camps along the meandering rivers. Soon
a quartet of towns sprang up, and before long the secluded
little world was actually bustling with permanent and tran-
sient populations.

The largest of the towns, quickly approaching city status,
was Belvidere, and it was there that Dante and his companions found the Jong Palace. After registering for a room,
Virgil immediately went off by himself in search of a little
professional love, hopefully from a different species, and
Dante and Matilda sat down in a corner of the lobby while
a small furry alien loaded their luggage onto an oversized
airsled and carefully guided it up to their rooms.

"Have you done any further thinking about it?" asked
the poet when he was sure no one could overhear them.

"That's *all* I've been thinking about," answered Matilda.

"Me too."

"And what have you concluded?"

"If the Bandit goes out and kills more innocent bystanders, kids or adults, it makes no difference. We'll have to stop him, and like it or not Joshua Silvermane is the only weapon we've got."

"I keep thinking that if we found the Bandit and Silvermane in less than four months, maybe we could find the perfect Santiago in a year or two," said Matilda.

"Maybe we could," admitted Dante. "Or maybe we found him already."

"Silvermane?"

"Maybe."

Matilda frowed. "Surely you're not referring to the Bandit?" she said.

"I don't know. Maybe I was a little too full of myself when I thought this thing up. What special insight do *I* have into what it takes to be Santiago? Hell, maybe killing them off before they grow up to be soldiers and cops and bounty hunters is the right way to go about it."

"You don't believe that for a moment," she said firmly.

"I don't know what I believe anymore," he admitted. "Except that maybe it was a bit presumptuous, trying to force my will on the history of the Inner Frontier. No one told the first Santiago that it was time to become Santiago. He wasn't manipulated. He just did it, because it was his destiny." He sighed deeply. "Hell, I don't even know what *my* destiny is. Why am I screwing around trying to tell them theirs?"

She stared long and hard at him. "I don't like it when you're like this."

"Like what?"

"Full of self-doubt," said Matilda. "From the outset, you've always known what you wanted to do, and how you planned to do it. This isn't like you."

"I stood back and took a good look at what I've done," he replied. "A lot of people are dead who wouldn't be if it weren't for me."

"You didn't kill them."

"They're dead just the same. Not just the children,

though that's the worst of it—but I killed the Candy Man and Jackrabbit Willowby just as surely as if I aimed the weapons and pulled the triggers."

"They deserved to die."

"I'm not arguing that," said Dante. "But the fact remains that if I'd stayed on Bailiwick and never come to the Frontier, they'd still be alive. I'm the reason they're all dead, maybe the only reason."

"So are you quitting?"

"No, I'm not quitting. But I've got to be *certain* this time. I can't keep choosing the wrong man and turning him loose on the galaxy."

"It just means you care, and that you're giving it a lot of thought."

"It means I've got a lot to make amends for." He looked at her. "And it means that I can't make any more mistakes."

"If it was anyone's mistake, it was *mine*," she protested. "Don't forget—I'm the one who got you to come to Heliopolis to meet the Bandit in the first place."

"And I'm the one who approved him."

"There's enough guilt to go around," said Matilda.

"Yeah, I suppose so," agreed Dante. He got to his feet. "Come on. I'll buy you a drink."

"You're on," she said, relieved that the conversation was over.

"In fact," he continued, "instead of going to the hotel bar, why don't we go out for that drink and take a look around town? I've never been to New Patagonia before, and I'll probably never come back. It'd be a shame not to spend at least a couple of hours getting the flavor of the place."

"Sounds good to me," said Matilda, taking his arm and walking out into the street with him.

"It's really quite a lovely world," said Dante approvingly. "Fishing, skiing, skating—they probably even have hunting safaris."

"And even though there's snow surrounding us, it's still very pleasant down here in the valley," she added.

"Let's walk up and down the street and see what kind of shops they have."

"What are you looking for?"

"Anything I can steal." She looked annoyed, and he smiled at her. "Oh, don't worry, I won't—but a lifetime's habits are hard to lose. I still like to look."

They walked down the block, reached a corner, and were about to cross to the other side of the street when Dante heard a familiar voice behind him.

"Hi, Danny boy," it said. "You've led me one hell of a merry chase."

"Shit!" muttered Dante, freezing.

"Turn around very slowly," continued the voice, "and keep your hands out from your body."

Dante did as he was ordered. "You're a long way from home, Commander Balsam," he said when he finally was able to face his antagonist.

"It's just plain Balsam now," said the big man, aiming his burner between Dante's eyes. "Things got so dull back on Bailiwick after you left that I quit my job and became a bounty hunter." He paused. "You've been a busy boy, Danny. I've been on your tail for months now, but all I keep finding are dead bodies."

Matilda began edging away from Dante, and suddenly Balsam trained his weapon on her. "That's far enough."

"You want *him*, not me," said Matilda.

"You're with Danny Briggs," said Balsam. "That's enough for me. You're going to stay with us until I find out if there's any paper on you." Dante took a tentative step toward him. "Watch it, Danny. You're wanted dead or alive. It makes no difference to me which way I bring you back."

"You've really been following me since I left Baili-wick?" asked Dante.

"A few weeks later," said Balsam. "You leave an awful easy trail to follow."

"I'd totally forgotten I was wanted back in the Democracy," admitted Dante. "I've had more important things on my mind."

"Always thinking—that's my Danny." He paused. "Where's the Indian?"

"What Indian?"

"Don't play stupid, Danny. It's unbecoming, and it doesn't fit you at all." Balsam looked around. "My information says that you usually travel with an Indian."

"I don't see one," said Dante. "Do you?"

"No, but after I take possession of that poem you're supposed to be writing, I'll figure out who he is and find him." He smiled. "Am *I* in it?"

Dante shook his head. "I only write about interesting people."

"You cut me to the quick," said Balsam with mock pain. Suddenly he laughed. "Hell, I'll write myself into it after I take it away from you."

"You're not touching it," said Dante firmly.

"We'll see about that," said Balsam. Suddenly he grinned. "You're only worth sixty thousand credits this month, Danny. How much is it worth to you if I let you keep your damned poem and you go deeper and deeper into the Frontier?" He paused. "I'm not saying I'll never come after you again, but I'll give you a sixty-day head start. How does that sound?"

Dante looked past Balsam and saw Joshua Silvermane exit a restaurant and step out into the street. The tall man stopped and surveyed the little scene calmly, an armadillo watching ants bickering.

"You haven't answered me, Danny."

"I don't deal with blackmailers."

"View me as a liberator," said Balsam.

"You don't want to know what I view you as."

"I'm running out of patience, Danny. I can kill you or I can take you back alive or I can let you go—but one way or another I'm going to make myself sixty thousand credits. Now, do I do it the hard way or the easy way?"

"Why not make a trade?" said a strong baritone voice.

"Who the hell are you?" demanded Balsam as Silvermane approached them.

"My name's Joshua Silvermane."

"I never heard of you."

"That's okay," said Silvermane. "I never heard of you, either."

"What kind of trade are you talking about?"

"Just a moment," said Silvermane, walking to the entrance to a drug parlor about forty feet away.

"Where are you going?" said Balsam suspiciously.

"Stay where you are. I'll be right back."

Silvermane vanished into the drug den's interior. A moment later there was a deafening *crash!*, and an instant after that a body literally flew out through a window and landed with a sickening *thud!* on the street, where it lay, twitching feebly.

Silvermane emerged and approached Balsam again.

"That's Simon Ten Broek," he said, not even deigning to give the moaning man a glance. "There's paper on him all over the Frontier. He's worth a hundred thousand credits back on Spica VI, even more in the Roosevelt system."

"What the hell did he do?"

"Rape. Arson. Torture. Murder. Three jailbreaks. You name it, he's probably done it."

"Okay, he's a wanted man. So what?"

"I'll trade him to you for the poet and the lady," said Silvermane. "You'll come out at least forty thousand credits ahead."

"What if I say no?"

"Then I'll kill Simon, and when I'm done, I'll probably kill you too."

Balsam aimed his weapon at Silvermane. "You forget who has the advantage here, friend."

"Put that burner down or I'll take it away and cram it up your ass," said Silvermane with no show of fear or apprehension.

The grin vanished. Of all the answers Balsam had expected, that was the least likely, and it troubled him. "How do I know that's really Simon Ten Broek?"

"How do I know you're really a licensed bounty hunter?" Silvermane shot back.

"This is ridiculous!" snapped Balsam, his courage slipping away in the face of this totally confident stranger. "I've wasted enough time! You want a trade? All right, we'll trade! Just take them and get the hell out of my sight."

"You've made a wise decision," said Silvermane. He turned to Dante and Matilda. "Come on."

They fell into step behind him as he began walking back to the Jong Palace. As they did so, Balsam went over to Simon Ten Broek and delivered a powerful kick in his ribs. "Get up!" he bellowed.

Silvermane was beside Balsam before he realized it. "And *that*," he said, "was a foolish decision." He grabbed Balsam's wrist before he could reach for his weapon. They stood motionless for a moment. Then there was an audible *crack!*, and Balsam screamed. Silvermane released his grip, and Balsam dropped to one knee, holding his wrist.

"I gave you a prisoner, not a toy," said Silvermane sternly.

"You broke my wrist!" snarled Balsam.

"You'll have time to think about abusing your fellow man while it heals."

"Abusing my fellow man? *You* threw him through that fucking window!"

"*I* met him on equal terms," said Silvermane. "You didn't. If I hear he was further abused, I'll come looking for you. You'll live a lot longer if I don't."

Silvermane stood and stared down at the bounty hunter.

"I heard you," grated Balsam.

"Make sure you remember."

Silvermane turned and walked to the Jong Palace, followed by Dante and Matilda.

"Thank you," said Dante once they were inside.

"There's no need," said Silvermane. "I took an instant dislike to your officious Democracy associate. Besides, it makes no difference whether I kill Simon here or they put him to death back in the Democracy. The important thing is that he dies."

"What did he do?" asked Matilda.

"More than I hope a lovely lady like yourself can imagine," said Silvermane.

"He's the reason you came to New Patagonia?"

"He's the reason."

"What will you do now?"

"I haven't decided."

"Have you thought about what we discussed last night?" asked Dante.

"Why else would I save you from a bounty killer?" replied Silvermane with an amused smile.

"And have you reached a decision?"

"I'm working on it."

30.

BILLY GREEN-EYES, BOLD AND BRAVE,
WOULD NEVER BE A HERO.
AND NOW OUR BILLY SEEKS THE GRAVE:
HIS PROSPECTS TOTAL ZERO.

SILVERMANE ANNOUNCED THAT HE HAD one more world
to visit before he made his decision. It was the mining
world of Trentino, the seventh planet in the Alpha Bellini
system, and they had no choice but to follow him in their
own ship.

The journey took three days. Virgil opted for seventy
hours in the Deepsleep pod, but Dante and Matilda chose
to remain awake most of the time, discussing their options,
wondering if they'd found their Santiago or if they could
do better with a little more searching.

"It doesn't really make much difference if there's a better
man out there," said Matilda after they'd gone over the
possibilities for the tenth time. "We have an immediate
problem, or we wouldn't be here. We've got to stop the
Bandit before he kills more innocent people."

"We could hire an assassin if that's all that matters,"
responded Dante. "I think our original idea was right. We
just chose the wrong man."

"Maybe it's not time," said Matilda. "Maybe events
choose the man. You and I are just people, not events.
Maybe it's simply not yet time for Santiago to cast his
shadow across the galaxy."

"How much worse do things have to get?"

"I don't know. But do you ever get the feeling that we're
like journalists who stop reporting the news and start cre-
ating it?"

"I'm not a journalist, and neither are you."

"You know what I mean. Maybe we're not supposed to

handpick a Santiago. Maybe he'll step forward on his own. Maybe until he does, until it's *his* idea to be Santiago, we're being premature about the whole thing."

"I thought you *wanted* a Santiago," he said accusingly.

"I did," she said. "And I got one. And look at what's happened."

"That's because he's *not* Santiago."

"Make up your mind. Is he Santiago because you say he is, or because we set him up in the Santiago business, whatever that is—or is he Santiago because he's an historic inevitability at this time and place?"

"Oh, come on. Next you'll be telling me that only God can anoint him."

"I'm just saying that maybe God is working on a different deadline, and that He might do a better job of choosing a Santiago than we've done."

"We have it within our grasp to do some good, to make a difference," said Dante adamantly. "You don't get more than one or two such opportunities in a lifetime. I'm not turning my back on it."

"It's not a question of turning your back, but of pursuing it too vigorously," replied Matilda.

"Damn it!" exploded Dante. "Whose side are you on, anyway?"

"The Frontier's," she answered. "And I want to make sure that what I do doesn't bring it even more hardship and misery."

He stared at her for a long moment. "It's time. In fact, it's past time. Santiago's reign ended on a fluke. To this day the Democracy doesn't even know they killed him."

"You're absolutely sure you're right?"

He paused for just an instant. "I'm absolutely certain that I hope I'm right."

"Maybe he'll take the decision out of our hands and turn us down," she said hopefully.

"He won't."

"What makes you so sure?"

"I've been watching him. He's not a fanatic, he's no

One-Armed Bandit—but he's got an ego as big as all out-doors. The more difficult we make the job sound, the more we explain that he'll be fighting a holding action, that he can never hope to overthrow the Democracy, the more he'll want to prove that we're wrong, than he can bring the whole thing down."

"And you want that quality in a Santiago?" she said dubiously.

"The odds are a billion to one against him," said Dante. "He's got to be a bit of an egomaniac even to consider taking the job on."

"Well, I've never known you to be wrong about anyone," she said. Then she added: "Except the Bandit. How did you miss what he would become?"

"You don't want to know."

"Yes, I do."

"I let your opinion influence me," said Dante.

"Bullshit!"

"You vouched for his character, so all I concentrated on was his ability. And he *does* have the ability; otherwise we wouldn't be trying to find ways to stop him."

"So the One-Armed Bandit is *my* fault?" she said heatedly.

"No. I'm the one who made him the offer and hired Wilbur and Blossom and set up the drug deal with the two ladies from Snakepit. If I made the wrong decision, and I did, I have no one to blame but myself."

"So what do we do now?"

"Wait. The offer's on the table. The next move is Silvermane's."

"He's almost too good to be true," she remarked.

"Virgil had something very wise to say about things that were too good to be true," said Dante wryly.

"What was it?"

"It's not important." Dante got to his feet. "We'll be landing in an hour. I think it's time to wake Sleeping Beauty."

He went to the Deepsleep pod and spent the next five minutes bringing Virgil to wakefulness.

"How are you feeling?" he asked when the Indian finally climbed out of the pod.

"Stiff."

"That's normal," said Dante. "You haven't moved in almost three days."

"And hungry."

"You haven't eaten in three days either. We'll go back to the galley and get something for you."

"How soon do we land?"

"Less than an hour."

"I'll wait," said Virgil.

"I thought you were hungry."

"There's nothing like the taste of galley food to kill an appetite. I'm an hour from a real restaurant. I can wait."

Dante shrugged. "Suit yourself."

He stopped by the galley, got a cup of coffee, rejoined Matilda in the command cabin, ordered the ship's computer to respond to any questions from the planetary authorities, and relaxed until they touched down.

"Where are we staying?" asked Virgil as they rode the slidewalk to Customs.

"I haven't bothered to reserve any rooms," answered Dante. "The way Silvermane operates, I figure we'll be back on the ship before nightfall."

"He doesn't waste his time, that's for sure," said Virgil. "He could be a little friendlier, though."

"He saved my life," said Dante. "How much friendlier does he have to be?"

"Okay, so I used the wrong word. He could be a little warmer."

"I don't think it's a job requirement."

"Have it your way," said Virgil, losing interest in the conversation.

They reached the Customs station, and found themselves facing a uniformed woman rather than the usual robot.

"Welcome to Trentino," she said. "May I ask the purpose of your visit?"

"Business," answered Dante.

"Precious stones or fissionable materials?"

"Neither."

"Those are our only two industries."

"We're here on personal business," said Dante.

"I must insist that you be more explicit, Mr. Alighieri." She stared at his titanium passport disk. "That's very odd. It's such an unusual name, and yet I could swear I've encountered it before." She frowned, shrugged, and looked back at him. "Why are you here, Mr. Alighieri?"

"To confer with a business associate named Joshua Silvermane, who either landed within the past few hours or will be landing shortly."

"Ah, Mr. Silvermane!" she said, her face lighting up. "What an absolutely beautiful man! And what wonderful manners!" She checked her screen again. "What is the nature of your business with him?"

"I don't believe I'm required to divulge that information," said Dante. "But if you have any doubts that he is expecting us, just contact him."

"That will not be necessary," conceded the woman. She glared at the poet. "You cannot pass through here without purchasing visas."

"What are the shortest visas available?"

"One week. They cost one hundred credits apiece."

"You don't have anything for daytrippers?"

"We don't get daytrippers on Trentino."

Dante pulled the cash out of his pocket and gave it to her. She encoded the visa on each of their passports.

"I am required to warn you that the atmosphere of Trentino is inimical to human life. As you pass through the spaceport, you will emerge into a domed, enclosed area that is approximately one mile long and a quarter of a mile wide. You must be a registered miner to pass beyond the dome, and if you attempt to do so without a protective suit no attempt will be made to hinder you—but the air, such as it is, is eighty-three percent methane, and the temperature is minus ninety-two degrees Celsius, which is to say you will not survive for even a minute." She paused. "I am also required by law to ask you if you understand my warning."

"Perfectly," said Dante.

They had begun walking past her station when a metal bar shot out, stopping them.

"You may not answer for your companions. Each of them must answer for themselves." She turned to Matilda. "Did you understand my warning?"

"Yes."

And to Virgil: "Did you understand my warning?"

"Right. I just didn't care about it."

"Welcome to Trentino," she said with an expression of distaste. "You may pass through now."

The three of them walked past the Customs station, made their way through the spaceport, and soon found themselves outside the facility but still enclosed by the huge dome.

"So where do we go from here?" asked Matilda.

"He wouldn't tell me who he's after," replied Dante. "I suppose we might as well wait here. I mean, hell, you've seen him in action. Can you imagine it'll take him more than an hour or two to find whoever he's looking for and take care of business?"

"That seems so . . . passive," she said. "He's a very distinctive man. Perhaps we should ask around. He's not the kind of man people forget."

"If that's what you want," said Dante. He turned to Virgil. "You wait here by the spaceport entrance, just in case we miss him."

"How will I know you've missed him?"

"He'll come back alone. If he does, tell him we're here and that I want him to wait for us."

"Fine."

"We really have to talk to him," said Dante. "No booze and no drugs, and no fucking any stray pets that pass by."

"What fun is that?" said Virgil with a smile.

"I'm not kidding."

"Neither am I."

Dante was about to say something further, changed his mind, then turned and began walking down the major thoroughfare with Matilda at his side.

"Where do we start?" he asked. "Bars, I suppose."

"You're in a rut," she replied. "For all we know, he's after a stockbroker or an incompetent doctor."

"I can't walk into every brokerage house and infirmary and ask if they've seen this tall silver-haired guy who's here to kill someone."

"Okay," she conceded. "You've got a point."

"If he's looking for someone, and doesn't know anything except that he's on Trentino, I imagine he'd stop at the first bar he came to and ask about him. And if he didn't get any answers there, he'd stop at the next one, and so on down the line."

"Why not drug dens or whorehouses?"

"A man's likely to visit a bar more often than the other two. And if he's chewing seed or with a woman, they may not want to disturb a good client, so they'd lie and say they didn't know him. I think a bar's the likeliest spot."

"I'll give you this much," she said. "You've always got a sensible answer."

"God didn't give me Silvermane's abilities, and medical science hasn't given me the Bandit's, so I have to use what I've got."

They stopped by a bar about half a block away, and Dante described Silvermane. He got as far as the hair and the height.

"Yeah, absolutely, he was here maybe half an hour ago," said the bartender. "Couldn't mistake him for anyone else. He was looking for Billy Green-Eyes."

"Where would we find Billy Green-Eyes?" asked Dante.

"Same place as always. Go two blocks down, turn left, and you'll come to a small park built around a fountain. Check the first bench you come to."

"It sounds simple enough," remarked Dante. He turned

to Matilda. "Let's go. The fireworks should be all over by now."

They followed the bartender's directions. When they turned and approached the park, they saw Silvermane standing, hands on hips, talking to an emaciated man who was seated on the bench.

As they drew near, they could see that the man was horribly mutilated. He was missing his left arm, his right leg, and his left eye. Part of his left ear was gone, burned off by a laser beam. He was dressed in rags, and a cheap pair of crutches were balanced against the back of the bench.

Silvermane looked up and nodded a greeting.

"Hi," said Dante. "Where's Billy Green-Eyes? Have you found him yet?"

"You're looking at him," said Silvermane.

"*Him?*" said Dante, startled. "*He's* what you came to Trentino to kill?"

"He's not quite the man he used to be," said Silvermane with a grim smile. "Are you, Billy?"

The man on the bench muttered something unintelligible.

"What the hell did he do?" asked Matilda.

"About seven years ago a plague broke out on New Damascus, way out in the Belladonna Cluster. Billy-boy here stowed away on the ship that was racing the vaccine to them, killed the crew, and held them up for a few million credits before he delivered the vaccine. Thousands died during the negotiations." He paused. "Sweet man, our Billy."

"So what happened to him?"

"Six of the survivors happened to him," continued Silvermane. "Billy killed them all, but not before they did what you see. He'd blown all his money on seed, and his deeds made him a pariah even among the scum he associated with, so no one would help him or give him money to go back to the Democracy for the necessary prosthetics. Hell, even if he'd managed to borrow the money, they'd have jailed and executed him the second they spotted him.

So Billy has been rotting out here for the past few years, isn't that right, Billy?"

Another unintelligible answer.

"He lives in the filthiest corner of the filthiest warehouse on Trentino. Each morning he comes out to the park and sits here, hat in hand, begging, but of course everyone knows he's the man who extorted millions for the New Damascus vaccine, so he probably takes in about three credits a week, all from newcomers. We've just been discussing his situation, haven't we, Billy?"

Billy glared at him balefully with his one remaining green eye, but said nothing.

You cold son of a bitch, thought Dante. *Whatever he's done, I don't know how you can shoot a helpless old cripple who can't lift a finger to defend himself.*

"And now we're all through discussing it," concluded Silvermane.

"All right," said Dante uncomfortably. "Shoot him and let's get it over with."

"I'm not shooting anyone," replied Silvermane.

"Oh?"

"Four thousand men, women, and children died on New Damascus while Billy was negotiating a price for the vaccine. Killing's too easy for him."

"So what *are* you going to do to him?" asked Dante.

Silvermane stared at the emaciated one-eyed, one-armed, one-legged beggar. "Not a thing," he said. "Have a long life, Billy." He turned and began walking back to the spaceport.

Jesus, you're even colder than I thought, mused Dante. And then: *Still, that's very much like justice.*

"I hope he lives another century," said Silvermane.

"He deserves to," agreed Matilda.

"Still, I'll give him credit for facing those New Damascans. There were six of them, and he stood his ground, for what little good it did him."

"You sound like you admire him."

"I admire the trait, not the man," explained Silvermane.

"I suspect there's a lot to admire about your One-Armed Bandit as well."

"There is," she admitted.

"Seems a shame," he continued. "From what I've heard, he's a moral man doing the best he can."

"His best isn't good enough," said Dante firmly. "He can destroy what we're trying to build."

"I know," said Silvermane. "That's why I've decided to accept your offer."

31.

THE PLYMOUTH ROCKER MOURNS A LOVE
THAT USED TO BE AND IS NO MORE.
HE CURSES TO THE SKIES ABOVE—
A MOST UNHAPPY TROUBADOUR.

BODINI II WASN'T MUCH OF a world. Small, flat, green, agricultural, dotted here and there by impenetrable thorn forests. It had a trio of towns, each with a small spaceport where the local farmers and agricultural cartels brought their goods to ship to the nearby colonies and mining worlds.

It was here that Silvermane took Dante, Matilda, and Virgil when they left Trentino. They passed through Customs without incident and stopped for a quick lunch in one of the spaceport restaurants.

"Couldn't you just send this guy a subspace message telling him to join us?" asked Dante.

"Not the Plymouth Rocker," answered Silvermane.

"And we really need him?"

"He's the one I want."

"What makes him so special?"

"I trust him." Silvermane paused. "There aren't many men I've trusted over the years. He's the best of them."

"I heard a lot about him maybe ten, fifteen years ago," volunteered Virgil. "Not a word since then. I figured he was dead."

"Why?" asked Dante.

"When you stop hearing about people out here, especially people like him, you just naturally assume someone or something caught up with them."

"I heard someone mention him not too long ago," said Matilda. "Dimitrios, maybe, or perhaps the Bandit."

"He had quite a reputation back then," said Virgil. "What happened to him?"

"To *him*?" replied Silvermane. "Nothing."

"The way you emphasized that," interjected Dante, "something happened to *someone*."

"You're a perceptive man," said Silvermane. "I suppose that goes with being a poet."

"So what happened?" said Dante, ignoring the compliment.

"He had a woman," answered Silvermane. "Lovely lady. Mind like a steel trap. Totally fearless. Devoted to him. They made a hell of a team."

"Did she have a name?" asked Dante, pulling out a stylus.

"She had a lot of them, depending on the situation," said Silvermane. "I first knew her as Priscilla, so that's the way I think of her. They did everything together, Priscilla and the Rocker. I don't remember ever seeing them more than eight or ten feet apart. He'd start a sentence and she'd finish it, or the other way around. If you were with them for any length of time, you finally appreciated what the term 'soulmate' really means."

"What did they do?"

"A little of everything. They were actually law officers together back in the Democracy, two of the best. They worked the entire Quintaro Sector, and they put one hell of a lot of bad guys away." He paused thoughtfully. "I think they did a little bounty hunting when they first moved out here. Then they spent a couple of years bodyguarding Federico Bogardus when he was King of New Lebanon. Just the two of them . . . but that was enough to scare off any potential assassins."

"How did she die?" asked Dante.

"What makes you think she died?"

"You said he *had* a woman. Past tense. You don't leave a woman like that—or bury yourself on an obscure little world like this one. Not without a reason."

"You're good, poet. We're going to work well together."

Silvermane paused for a moment, staring sightlessly into the past. "She was quite a woman, that Priscilla. Been dead about a dozen years now."

"What happened?"

"She died," said Silverman noncommittally. "The Rocker left Prateep a few weeks later, and he's spent the last few years on this little backwater planet."

"Is he a farmer?"

"No. He just rents a house from an absentee landlord."

"What *does* he do, then?" asked Dante.

"He hides."

"From what?" asked Matilda.

"From the past. From his memories." The tall man smiled grimly. "They always find him."

"And this is the man you want by your side?"

"Nobody fights by my side," said Silvermane with what Dante thought was just a touch of arrogance. "But this is a man I want for our organization."

"Why should he be willing rejoin the world?" asked Matilda curiously.

"Because I know him better than he knows himself," said Silvermane.

"I still don't see why you couldn't have just sent him a message to join us," said Dante.

"It's been years since he's seen any action," said Silvermane. "I want to make sure he's in good enough physical and emotional shape. A decade of seclusion and mourning can change a man beyond all recognition."

"Well, let's hope it didn't."

Silvermane got to his feet and threw some Maria Theresa dollars on the table. "Let's go find out."

Dante and the others joined him, and a few moments later they were rapidly skimming a few inches above a dirt road in a sleek limo.

"Beautiful country," remarked Dante, looking out across the green fields.

"Dull country," said Silvermane. "Beautiful country has hills and mountains and valleys and makes lousy farmland.

You need an expanse of flat characterless land like this to grow anything in quantity."

"I grew up surrounded by mountains and valleys," said Dante. "We paid a premium for the food we imported." He smiled wryly. "Maybe that's why I appreciate farmland."

"Take a look at *that*!" said Matilda, pointing to a huge cow that stood a good ten feet at the shoulder. Suddenly another enormous cow came into view, then a whole herd of them. "Aren't they remarkable?"

"Mutated," said Silvermane. "Cost a bundle to create them, but once they began breeding true they've more than paid back their cost."

"You sound like you've been here before," noted Matilda.

"Once, about eight years ago."

"You didn't get him to come with you back then. Why should this time be any different?"

"I didn't ask him to come with me then," answered Silvermane.

"What were you doing here?"

"I'd been wounded, and I needed a place to stay while I healed. The Rocker gave it to me."

"He sounds like a good friend."

"He was, once."

"Maybe he still is."

"We'll know soon enough," said Silvermane.

They rode the next half hour in silence, and then the limo came to a halt, hovered for a moment, and lowered itself gently to the ground.

"We have arrived at our destination," announced the navigational computer.

Silvermane climbed out of the limo, then helped Matilda out. When Dante and Virgil had also emerged, he turned and faced the farmhouse a short distance away.

The door irised and a burly man stepped through. He took one look at Silvermane and a broad smile crossed his sallow face.

"Joshua!" he called out. "How the hell are you?"

"Just fine this time," answered Silvermane, approaching him. The man trotted forward and threw his muscular arms around Silvermane.

"Damn, but it's good to see you!" He backed away a step. "Who are your friends?"

Silvermane introduced each by name. "And this is the notorious Plymouth Rocker," he concluded, indicating the man.

"It's been a long time since I was notorious," said the Rocker. Then: "Come on into the house. You must be thirsty after your trip out from the spaceport."

"One of us sure as hell is," volunteered Virgil, stepping forward.

The Rocker took them back to the farmhouse, and a moment later they were inside it. The walls of the foyer were covered with holos of a lovely woman, who Dante knew must be Priscilla. They passed to the living room, which had still more holos, plus a dozen little remembrances of her: a favorite book of poetry, a gold-handled hairbrush, a crystal wineglass that had stood empty for more than a decade.

"It's like a goddamned shrine to her," Dante whispered to Matilda.

"It must be wonderful to be loved the way he loved her," she whispered back.

"Wonderful or stifling," whispered Danny. "Either way, it had to make losing her almost unbearable."

The Rocker brought out beer for everyone, then invited them to sit down on the various chairs and couches.

"So, what brings you to Bodini?" he asked Silvermane when they were all settled.

"You."

"I'm always glad to see you, Joshua," said the Rocker. "But I'm out of the business."

"What business?" asked Silvermane with mock innocence.

"*Any* business."

"You can't bury yourself here forever."

The Rocker pointed to an elegant urn with gold inlays that floated in an antigrav field near his fireplace. "That's what remains of my Priscilla," he said. "When I die, I've left orders to cremate me and then mix our ashes together. I won't have it any other way." He paused. "I don't want to die on some other world and be separated from her forever."

"Whatever you say," said Silvermane.

"*That's* what I say."

"Still, it seems a shame."

"That I can't go killing bad guys with you?" said the Rocker with a smile. "You don't need me. You never did."

"It's a shame," continued Silvermane, as if the Rocker hadn't said a word, "that you can't avenge her death."

"What are you talking about?" demanded the Rocker, suddenly alert. "No one knows who killed her—you know that. How can I avenge her?"

"You've been looking at it all wrong. You don't know which individual killed her. But you know he worked for the Democracy, that he represented it."

"So what?" said the Rocker bitterly. "How do you go to war with the whole Democracy?"

"That's the easy part. You join me."

"Just you and me against the whole Democracy?"

"You and me—and them," said Silvermane, indicating his companions. "And the whole of Santiago's organization."

"How can Santiago have an organization?" said the Rocker in exasperated tones. "He's been dead for a couple of hundred years, if he ever really existed at all. You're not making any sense, Joshua."

"Santiago is alive," said Dante.

The Rocker turned to him. "Another quarter heard from."

"Santiago is more than a man," continued Dante. "He's an ideal, and he changes outfits just the way you and I do. Today he's wearing Joshua Silvermane."

"Well, I'm sure that's very interesting, but it doesn't make any sense," said the Rocker.

Dante was about to explain, but Silvermane cut him off. "It doesn't have to," he said. "All you have to know is that you can punish the Democracy for what they did to Priscilla, or you can stay here and mourn her and never do anything about it. It's your choice."

The Rocker stared at Silvermane for a long moment. Dante thought he was actually going to take a swing at him, but instead he finally got to his feet.

"I'll only come if I can take Priscilla with me," he said at last.

"If that's what you want."

"It's not negotiable. Wherever I die, she's got to be there or they'll never mingle our ashes."

"Have you considered living?" suggested Silvermane.

"Not lately," admitted the Rocker. "But now you've given me a reason to, even if we only last an hour—which, I might add, seems optimistic." He walked to a closet, pulled out a very old pulse gun, and tucked it in his belt. Then he tenderly took the urn in his arms. "Okay, I'm ready. Let's go."

"Don't you want to take anything else?" asked Dante.

"Like what?" asked the Rocker.

Dante shrugged. "I don't know. Some clothes, maybe, or perhaps another weapon?"

"I'll buy 'em when I need 'em."

A few moments later they were racing back to the spaceport, as Dante and Silvermane took turns filling in the newest member of their organization.

32.

THEY DIDN'T ALL LEAVE BODINI II together, since they had
come in a number of ships. Dante, Silvermane, and the
Plymouth Rocker took off first and landed on Brandywine,
a lovely little world in the Spinos system, where Silvermane
had a mountain retreat. He hadn't visited it in close to three
years, but it had a full-time staff—a husband-and-wife
team, plus a groundskeeper—and it was in perfect repair.
Dante left messages to Matilda and Virgil to meet them
there. He wasn't sure how far he could trust Blossom, so
he kept her out of the loop.

"Nice layout," commented the Plymouth Rocker, walking through the rustic retreat. "Build it yourself?"

"I appropriated it from someone who didn't need it any
longer," replied Silvermane.

"Who was it?"

"Nobody very important," answered Silvermane in tones
that made it clear the subject was closed.

"Well, Joshua, what's our next step?" asked the Rocker.

"We're about to decide—and call me Santiago."

"Sorry."

"I've been thinking about it," said Silvermane. "And it
seems to me that there's no reason to build a new organization when it's so much easier to take over the One-Armed
Bandit's. How many men does he have working for him
now?"

"I'm not sure," answered Dante, settling down in an angular chair of alien design that was more comfortable than
it looked. "He has people recruiting all over the Frontier. I
would think he's got between seventy-five and a hundred
by now, maybe even more."

"That proves my point. It could take us months to get

that many men—and then we'd have to go to war with *his* men. Much better to just take over what he's got."

"Won't the One-Armed Bandit have a little something to say about it?" asked the Rocker.

"Not if we work it right," said Silvermane.

"You're not talking about walking right in and killing him?" said Dante. "We don't have any idea what defenses he's installed since I left—not that he needs very many."

"No, I don't plan to confront him on his own world," replied Silvermane. "I may be brave, but I'm not suicidal."

"So the trick is to get him off Valhalla," said the Rocker.

"That's right."

"How?"

Silvermane turned to Dante. "I thought our resident poet might have an idea. It seems that he's never short of them."

"Are you being sarcastic," asked Dante, "or are you really asking for suggestions?"

"Both."

Dante lowered his head in thought for a moment, then reached into a pocket and pulled out a notebook and a stylus and began scribbling something.

"What's he doing?" asked the Rocker.

"I'm sure he'll tell us when he's done," said Silvermane, watching the young poet as he crossed out words, wrote in new ones, and stared off into space, obviously thinking. Finally he looked up.

"Here's how we do it," he announced, and then read aloud:

> *"Women scream and children shake,*
> *Lawmen hide and strong men quake.*
> *The world is turning upside down—*
> *The One-Armed Bandit's come to town."*

"What the hell does *that* have to do with anything?" asked the Rocker.

Silvermane smiled. "You're on the right track, Rhymer."

"Would someone explain what's going on to me?" said the Rocker.

"Dante is the new Black Orpheus," said Silvermane. "He's the reason that Santiago is being resurrected in the first place. The One-Armed Bandit knows this. Do you start to follow?"

"Okay," replied the Rocker. "So the Bandit sees the poem, and he realizes that Dante is telling the Frontier that he's not the hero he's cracked up to be. So what? From what you tell me, he's already going to kill Dante the next time he sees him."

"He's calling himself Santiago these days," said Silvermane. "He's done everything he can to separate himself from his identity as the One-Armed Bandit. He's going to make enough enemies as Santiago; he doesn't need the ones who have reason to kill the Bandit."

"That's not enough," said the Rocker. "Are you telling me he's going to drop everything he's doing and come after Dante here just because he writes one lousy stanza calling the Bandit a villain?"

"Use your imagination," said Silvermane. "This is the opening shot, the Bandit's wake-up call." He turned to Dante. "Am I right?"

"You're right."

"Okay," said the Rocker. "What comes next?"

"I find a remote planet maybe a hundred thousand light-years from Valhalla," said Dante, "and I start printing poems in the classified section of its major newsdisk—and each poem is more explicit. I point out who he deals with, what he looks like, where he lives. I start naming his key people. Then we get a third party to transmit all this to the Bandit. How long do you think it'll be before he comes after me himself?"

"Why wouldn't he simply send one of his killers?" asked the Rocker.

"Because I know too much. He's got to be *sure* he shuts me up, and that means he'll do the job himself."

"And once we know he's left," concluded Silvermane,

"you and I will pay a visit to Valhalla and take over the Santiago business."

The Rocker turned to Dante. "And then you come back from the planet before the Bandit can reach it?"

"I'm not going to it at all. I don't have to be there to put the ads in. We'll have to send *somebody* there, because he'll check to see if they were inserted locally, but I'm the only one he'll recognize, and I'm no more suicidal than Santiago here."

"Okay," said the Rocker. "Now that you've explained it, I don't see any reason why it shouldn't work." He paused. "I'm not stupid, no matter what you think. I'm just not used to dealing with a devious bastard like yourself."

"I'll take that as a high compliment," said Dante, forcing a smile.

He spent the next three days writing the verses that would convince the Bandit to leave his headquarters and travel halfway across the Frontier. In the meantime, Silvermane contacted a friend who owed him a favor and had him to go Hadrian II, a distant, isolated Frontier world that had a large enough population to support a hugely popular newsdisk.

Matilda showed up the day after Dante finished the poems, and Virgil arrived two days after that. Blossom radioed them that she had decided to return to Valhalla and beg the Bandit to take her back.

"Stupid," said Dante.

"Maybe he *will* take her," said Matilda.

"She's signed her own death warrant," said Dante. "If he doesn't kill her, *we* probably will. After all, there's no question now where her loyalties lie."

"You recruited her," said Matilda. "Can't you unrecruit her, just send her back to Heliopolis?"

"She practically worships the Bandit. Do you think she'll just pack up and leave peacefully if we kill him—or if we take over while he's gone and haven't killed him yet?"

"No," she admitted, "I suppose you're right. I'm just sorry about it."

"If I were you, I'd worry about how many more innocent bystanders the Bandit will kill before we depose him," said Dante. "At least Blossom knows the score and made an informed choice. Stupid, but informed."

Even at light speeds it took Silvermane's friend eight days to reach Hadrian. Dante could have sent the poems via subspace radio while the man was en route, but he couldn't be sure the man wouldn't just transmit them on, and the whole purpose was to make certain that if the Bandit or any of his people traced the poems to their source, there could be no doubt that they came from Hadrian II itself.

Finally the man landed on that distant world, the poems were transmitted, and within two days the first four had appeared on the newsdisk, which had a new edition every eight Standard hours.

Then came the question of how best to get the poems into the Bandit's hands.

"It's too obvious to send them directly to the Bandit," said Dante. "I mean, hell, if they come from an 'interested friend,' he might try to find out who the friend is before he races off to Hadrian."

"What do you suggest?" asked Silvermane.

"I've been thinking about that," said Dante. "We'll use Wilbur Connaught."

"Santiago's accountant?" said Silvermane, surprised. "The one they call the Grand Finale?"

"That's the one."

"Why him?"

"Because I can give him a reason for reading the classified section of the Hadrian newsdisk," answered Dante. "He told me once that he used to work for Barioke, one of the major warlords out on the Rim. That was a long time ago. Barioke's probably dead by now; he's certainly not a warlord any longer."

"So?"

"So we run a classified saying that Barioke needs to speak to Wilbur about a very private matter, and that since he's lost track of him he's trying classifieds all over the galaxy." Dante paused. "Then we put the same ad in twenty other newsdisks, but we wait two days to insert it. Since Wilbur has to get into the Democracy now and then to keep an eye on Santiago's investments, he's still got a Democracy ID, which means all of Barioke's messages will be routed to his code no matter what computer he's using. But the one we want him to read will get there first—the others are just to convince him he's not being used—and we'll make sure that it appears right next to the poem. He'll see it, and bring it to the Bandit's attention. The Bandit may make sure the poem originated on Hadrian, but I don't think he'll check Barioke's message, or even read it."

"Sounds good to me," said Silvermane. He looked around. "Does anyone have any objections to it?"

No one did—until Matilda burst into Dante's room three days later, a worried expression on her face.

"What's up?" he asked, looking up from the stanza he was working on.

"You'd better get your ass out to Hadrian II *quick*!" she said. "The Bandit's probably got a half day's start on you. You have to beat him there!"

"What are you talking about?" said Dante. "I'm not going anywhere—and we *want* the Bandit to go to Hadrian."

"You don't understand!" snapped Matilda, tossing a computer cube across the room to him.

"What is it?" he asked.

"The Hadrian newsdisk," she replied.

"The ads are there?"

"Yes."

"Well, then?"

"That's all anyone else read," said Matilda. "But I read the whole damned thing. Do you know the name September Morn?"

"Sounds like a painting, if memory serves."

"Screw memory! She's the poet laureate of the Questada Cluster, and she lives on Hadrian."

"I didn't know they had a poet laureate."

"There are a lot of things you don't know," said Matilda. "For example, I'll bet you don't know that she's won an award for a poem about Santiago."

His eyes widened. "You're kidding!"

"Do I look like I'm kidding?"

"Oh, *shit!* He's going to think *she* wrote it!"

"Almost certainly."

"We'll contact her via subspace and tell her to get the hell off the planet!"

"Do you think the Bandit will stop looking for her if she's gone when he gets there?" asked Matilda.

"No," said Dante. "No, of course he won't. But what the hell do you expect *me* to do if I get there ahead of him?"

"I don't know, but this was your idea. I think you owe it to her."

"To do what?" he yelled in frustration.

"You're the big thinker," said Matilda angrily. "Think of something."

"All right, all right," he said, getting to his feet. "Give me ten minutes to pack some things, and tell Virgil I need to borrow his ship. It's faster than mine."

She nodded her assent. "Anything else?"

"Hell, I don't know." He paused. "Yeah. See if you can contact Dimitrios of the Three Burners and have him meet me there. Tell him I *really* need some help."

Nine minutes later Dante took off from Brandywine, convinced that he probably wouldn't live to see it again.

He turned control of the ship over to the navigational computer and began preparing the Deepsleep chamber.

I don't know how it happened, he thought. *Suddenly everything's falling apart. Three hundred children are dead because of events I initiated. I don't know if Silvermane can beat the Bandit, or even if he's the right man for the job. And now I've endangered a brilliant poet who I didn't even know existed half an hour ago, and if I luck out and find her, then I'm going to become the prime target of the most competent killer I've ever seen.*

He lay down in the pod, and as consciousness left him, he had time for one final thought:

I wish I'd never found that goddamned poem.

PART V

SEPTEMBER
MORN'S BOOK

33.

HE'S NOT WHAT HE SEEMS, HE'S NOT WHAT
  HE CLAIMS,
HE'S AS FAKE AS HIS PHONY ARM.
HE LIVES ON VALHALLA, PLAYING HIS GAMES,
AND HE MEANS YOU NOTHING BUT HARM.

THAT WAS THE SECOND POEM to appear in the Hadrian newsdisk. The first was the one Dante had written while Silvermane was watching him.

The third one made it clear that there was a real Santiago, and that he would soon take his vengeance upon the One-Armed Bandit for impersonating him.

The fourth and fifth named two of the Bandit's most trusted henchmen.

The next half dozen told more details, details the Bandit would gladly have killed to keep secret, and, Dante was sure, would now kill to punish the poet for making public.

By the time the Deepsleep chamber gently roused him from his sleep to inform him that he was in orbit around Hadrian II, twenty-two stanzas had appeared, and there actually wasn't much more to reveal.

Dante lay still for a moment, his brain coming back to life more quickly than his body. Then he sat up, climbed out of the pod, realized that he was starving, and headed off to the galley, where he assuaged his hunger. He took a Dryshower, changed clothes, and finally went to the control cabin, where he found that his navigational computer had already answered all of the spaceport's questions and was preparing to break out of orbit and land.

The radio hummed to life. "May I speak to the captain, please?" said a voice.

Dante took over manual control of the radio and opened a channel.

"This is Dante Alighieri, captain of the *Far Traveler*, registration number R-two-six-S-M-three-six-two, five days out of Brandywine. What's the problem?"

"Your ship is registered to Virgil Soaring Hawk."

"Contact him on Brandywine. He'll confirm that he loaned it to me. In the meantime, let me land, and you can hold the ship until you speak to him."

A brief pause. Then: "Agreed."

"I also need a favor."

"How may we help you, Mr. Alighieri?" said the voice at the other end of the transmission.

"I'm supposed to meet a business associate on Hadrian. If he's already landed, it would surely be within the past six Standard hours. He travels under two names—the One-Armed Bandit and Santiago—and I don't know which he's using. Can you tell me if he's arrived yet?"

"Santiago? He's got a sense of humor."

Dante ignored the comment. "Has he landed?"

Another pause. "Let me check. . . . No, no one of either name has landed."

"All right," said Dante. "I need one more favor. I'm a writer, and I'm supposed to interview one of your local poets, a woman who called herself September Morn. Can you tell me where to find her?"

"We can't give out addresses or even computer ID codes," came the answer. "I can transmit your message to her and have her contact you."

"Tell her I'm staying at . . ." He checked the computer screen. "At the Windsor Arms, wherever the hell that is. And tell her I've got to speak to her at her earliest convenience, and not to make her presence known to anyone else."

"You're making this sound more like espionage than an interview," commented the voice sardonically.

I can't tell you the truth. If you even hint that you know why the Bandit is coming to Hadrian, if you make any attempt whatsoever to protect her, he'll blow the whole spaceport to kingdom come.

"There's a rival reporter coming out to interview her," said Dante, making it up as he went along. "It's the man I asked you about, the one who writes under the pen name of Santiago. If he gets to her first, I could lose my job." He paused. "Please. This means a lot to me."

There was a final pause.

"All right, Mr. Alighieri, we'll do what we can to help you keep your job."

"Thank you," said Dante. "And I can't overstress the need for speed and secrecy."

"You journalists!" said the voice, half amused, half disgusted. "You'd slit each other's throats for a scoop. Signing off."

Dante leaned back and watched the viewscreen as the ship approached the surface. There were six cities spread across the face of the planet, more than usual for a colony world, especially one on the Inner Frontier, where small Tradertowns were the order of the day. He had no idea which city September Morn lived in, but then, neither did the Bandit, and he was getting here first, so with any luck he'd make contact with her first. If nothing else, he was sure the Bandit wasn't subtle enough to fabricate a story about why she should seek *him* out.

He touched down and cleared Customs. To make things go more smoothly he identified himself as Danny Briggs; the ID would check, and no one on the Frontier except the occasional bounty hunter would give a damn if the Democracy had put a price on his head. Finally he hired a limo to skim above the surface and take him into Trajan, the planet's capital city, which was home to the Windsor Arms Hotel.

He stopped at the desk to register, took an airlift up to the eighth floor, found his room, waited for the security system to scan his retina and compare it with the scan he'd just undergone downstairs, and finally entered the room as the door dilated to let him pass through.

The first thing he did was walk across to the desk that

was positioned by a corner window and activate the computer that sat atop it.

"Good morning, Mr. Alighieri," said the computer in a soft feminine voice that startled him. "How may I help you?"

"I need to find a woman named September Morn. I know she lives on Hadrian II," replied Dante. "Check all the vidphone directories and see if she's listed."

"Checking . . . No, she is not," announced the computer. "This means that she either does not possess a vidphone, or else she possesses an unlisted number."

"Tie into the Master Computer on Deluros VIII and access any information it has on her."

"That will be a extra charge of five hundred credits, or one thousand two hundred twenty-eight New Kenya shillings. Press your left thumb against the spot indicated on my screen if you agree to the charges."

Dante pressed his thumb against the screen, then waited almost two minutes for the computer to address him again.

"The only information the Master Computer possesses is that September Morn is a writer residing on Hadrian II, that she has sold four novels and two volumes of poetry, and that her poem entitled *The King of the Outlaws* won this year's Questada Prize for literature."

"Contact her publisher and see if you can get her address, or her ID, if she's got one."

"Contacting . . . It is against their policy to give out such information."

"The local newsdisk must have a morgue with all prior issues. See if you can find any information on how to contact her directly."

"That could take as much as ten minutes, Mr. Alighieri."

"Why so long?"

"They use a primitive filing system, and I will have to reaccess it by year."

"Don't go back more than four or five years. I need current information."

"Understood."

"One more thing. Let me know if a man named either Santiago or the One-Armed Bandit lands at the spaceport."

"Yes, Mr. Alighieri. Is there anything else?"

"No."

"My screen will go blank, and I will not speak until I have finished my assignments, but although I will appear to have shut down all systems, this is not the case, so please do not mistakenly report me as broken or inactive to the management."

"No problem," said Dante. The computer went dead so quickly he wasn't sure it heard him.

He ordered the wet bar to pour him a beer, and had just taken his first swallow when there was a knock at the door.

"Open," he ordered, and the door dilated again to reveal Dimitrios of the Three Burners.

"I got Matilda's message," he said, entering the room. "What the hell's going on?"

"To borrow an ancient saying, we put our money on the wrong horse."

"So he's turned pure outlaw instead of helping the Frontier?" asked Dimitrios.

"It's not that simple," replied Dante. "He's become a fanatic. If it has anything to do with the Democracy, it can't be permitted to survive."

"Isn't that the purpose of the exercise?"

"He just slaughtered three hundred children who might have someday grown up to be Democracy soldiers or bureaucrats."

"Ah," said the bounty hunter. "I see."

"The original plan was for me to lure him out here and never even show up myself—but everything's gone to hell. If we can't find some way to stop him, he's going to kill a woman who doesn't even know he's alive, let alone after her."

"Back up a minute," said Dimitrios, frowning. "Why did you want to lure him here in the first place? What's so special about Hadrian II?"

"It's about as far as you can get from Valhalla and still be on the Inner Frontier."

"Valhalla. That's the planet where he's set up his headquarters, right?"

"Right."

"So what is supposed to happen while he's gone?" asked Dimitrios.

"His successor will move in and take over, and present him with a fait accompli."

"And who is this successor?"

"Joshua Silvermane." Dante couldn't help but notice that Dimitrios grimaced at the mention of the name. "Do you disapprove?"

"He's as good a symbol as you could ever find," began Dimitrios. "He looks like a statue, and he's certainly as good with his weapons as the Bandit."

"But?" said Dante. "You look like there's a 'but.' "

"But he's a cold, passionless son of a bitch," continued the bounty hunter, "and he's so self-sufficient that he doesn't inspire much loyalty, if only because it's apparent he doesn't need it or want it."

"But he's a moral man without being a fanatic."

"He's a man of his word," agreed Dimitrios. "He's so beautiful and so deadly that people will watch him in awe, but I don't know if he's the kind of man other men will follow." He paused. "I guess you'll find out—if the Bandit doesn't go back and kill him once he's done here. Exactly what's drawing him here in the first place?"

Dante explained his plan, and even quoted a few of the poems to Dimitrios.

"Sounds fine to me," said the bountry hunter. "What went wrong?"

"Just a stroke of bad luck," replied Dante. "Of all the goddamned planets on the Frontier, this is the one that's home to a woman who just wrote an award-winning poem about, of all things, Santiago."

"Suddenly things make a lot more sense."

"Her name is September Morn," Dante concluded. "And we've got to find her before he does."

"Well, on your behalf, you couldn't know she'd gone and won a prize for a poem about Santiago," said Dimitrios. "It was a hell of a good idea except for that."

"Thanks," said Dante with grim irony.

"Problem is, you've endangered this woman, and we don't know how to reach her to protect her or warn her off."

"Neither does *he*," Dante pointed out.

"That's one thing in our favor. If we're starting out even, I'll put my money on you to outthink him."

The computer suddenly hummed to life.

"I am sorry, Mr. Alighieri," it said, "but the newsdisk morgue gives no indication of how to contact September Morn. All I could learn is that as of two years ago she resided in Trajan."

"Well, that's a start," said Dante. "What's Trajan's population?"

"One hundred and ten thousand, four hundred and sixty-three at the last census."

"So much for going door-to-door." The poet paused. "Thank you, computer. You may deactivate until I need you again."

"This contradicts your order that I alert you if a man named Santiago or the One-Armed Bandit lands on Hadrian II," the computer reminded him.

"I forgot that," admitted Dante. "All right, do that and nothing more."

"Understood."

The machine seemed to go dormant again, but Dante knew it was monitoring the spaceport.

"So what do you suggest we do?" asked Dimitrios. "I'm at your disposal."

"I asked the authorities to contact September Morn and let her know I had urgent business with her," replied Dante. "And I gave the Windsor Arms as my address. I don't think we should leave the place until I hear from her."

"I haven't eaten today," said Dimitrios. "I saw a restaurant in the hotel, just off the lobby. Let's grab a bite there. If she tries to contact you by vidphone or computer, the hotel can transfer it to our table, and if she shows up in person they can point us out to her."

"I don't see any harm in that," agreed Dante, getting to his feet. "Let's go."

They took the airlift down to the main floor, and were soon sitting in the restaurant. Dimitrios ordered a steak from a mutated beef animal. Dante just had coffee.

"You're not hungry?" asked Dimitrios.

"No."

"Don't be so nervous. We'll find her."

"We'd better."

"Get some calories into you," said Dimitrios. "Maybe they'll get that brain of yours working again."

"All right, all right," muttered Dante irritably. He called up the menu and placed a finger on a hologram of a pastry.

"They have wonderful meat," said Dimitrios.

"You said calories. This has calories."

"What the hell—do what you want," said the bounty hunter with a shrug.

They ate in silence, got up, and were walking to the airlift when Dante glanced out the window and suddenly froze.

"Do you see her?" asked Dimitrios.

"I don't even know what she looks like," replied the poet. "I saw *him*."

Dimitrios walked to the window. "I don't see anyone. The street's empty."

"He's in the hotel right across the street. Probably looking for her."

"Or you."

"Or me. If he sees me here, that lets her off the hook. He'll know I wrote those verses."

"You're not seriously considering walking out there?" demanded Dimitrios.

"I can't let him kill her."

"Are you going to challenge him to a thinking match?" said Dimitrios angrily. "Or maybe a poetry contest? They're the only two things you can beat him at."

"What do you suggest?" snapped Dante. "I don't want to die, but I can't let him find and kill September Morn!"

"What do I suggest?" repeated Dimitrios. "I suggest you step aside and let someone face him who's at least got a chance!"

And before Dante could stop him, Dimitrios had stepped out into the street. He stood there patiently for a few seconds, and then the Bandit came out of the hotel.

"Dimitrios?" said the Bandit, surprised. "It's been a long time. What are you doing here?"

"I'm here on business," replied Dimitrios.

"Who is he? Maybe I know him."

"I'm sure you do. He wiped out a schoolhouse on Madras."

"Forget your business," said the Bandit. "You're a good man, and you're no friend of the Democracy. Go in peace."

"You're a good man, too," said Dimitrios. "But you've gone a little overboard. We should talk, Bandit."

"My name is Santiago," the Bandit corrected him.

"Not anymore. That's what we have to talk about. You can work for him, you can help him, but you can't *be* him."

"Stand aside, Dimitrios. I'm only giving you one more chance to walk away."

"I can't," said Dimitrios.

"I know," said the Bandit sadly. He pointed a finger at Dimitrios. The bounty hunter went for his burners, but never got them out of their holsters. An instant later he was dead, a black, bubbling, smoking hole in the middle of his forehead.

"Shit!" muttered Dante. "He'll kill the whole fucking city if he doesn't find what he's after."

He walked to the hotel's doorway and stepped outside.

"I knew I'd find you here," said the Bandit.

"You killed my friend."

"I'll kill more than your friend if I don't find the woman who writes poems about Santiago."

"She only writes about the *real* Santiago," said Dante. "*I* wrote the ones you read."

The Bandit stared at him. "Why?"

"To lure you out here."

"Still why?" asked the Bandit, frowning and scanning the area for hidden gunmen.

"To get you away from Valhalla. You'll find some changes when you get back." Dante smiled grimly. "Dimitrios was telling the truth. You're not Santiago anymore."

"We'll see about that when I return to Valhalla," said the Bandit, pointing his finger at Dante. "In the meantime, I told you that the next time we met I'd—"

Suddenly he stopped speaking. A puzzled expression crossed his face. He opened his mouth, but only blood came out. Then he pitched forward on the street, stone-cold dead.

As he fell, the figure of a woman was revealed. She was standing behind him, a burner in her hand.

Dante stood motionless, finding it difficult to believe he was still alive.

The woman approached him. "I believe you were looking for me," she said. "I'm September Morn."

34.

SHE SINGS, SHE DANCES, SHE WRITES NOVELS
   TOO.
THERE'S NOTHING THAT SHE ISN'T ABLE TO
   DO.
JUST SET HER A TASK THAT ALL HAVE
   FORSWORN:
OF COURSE SHE CAN DO IT—SHE'S SEPTEMBER
   MORN.

THEY WERE SITTING IN THE restaurant, which management had closed to all other customers. A lone waiter stood in the most distant corner, awaiting their pleasure.

September Morn poured Dante a stiff drink. "Take this," she said. "You look like you need it."

"Thank you," said Dante, swallowing it in a single gulp, then watching as she poured him another. "I owe you my life. If there's ever anything I can do for you . . ."

"You can tell me why he came here to kill me," said September Morn.

"I will," said Dante, looking out the window to where medical crews were removing the two corpses from the bloodstained street. Finally the last vehicle raced away, bearing the Bandit's body, and he turned back to her. "But shouldn't we be expecting a visit from the authorities any minute now? I mean, you *did* kill him out there in broad daylight. I'll testify that you were saving my life, but surely they're going to want to ask us both some questions."

She shook her head. "Don't worry," she said. "They won't bother us."

Dante downed a second drink, and felt the tension finally ease. "Why not? There are two dead men out there."

"It's very complicated," replied September Morn. "Let's

simply say that I'm not without a certain amount of cachet here on Hadrian."

"Oh?" He stared at her, waiting for her to continue, and finally she did.

"I'm the only native who ever won a major award for anything, and they're very proud of that. When I considered moving to the Binder system, they passed a law declaring me a living monument. My mortgage was canceled, all my outstanding debts were paid, and by definition I cannot break the law—within reason, of course." She grimaced. "All that's on the one side. On the other is that I can't leave the system without a military escort whose sole purpose is to see that I return."

"So no one's going to hassle you for shooting the Bandit?" he said.

"*Was* he a bandit?"

"No. That was just his name—the One-Armed Bandit. He lost his left arm years ago. You saw just a minor demonstration of what his prosthetic replacement could do."

"He called himself Santiago," she said.

"I know."

"There has to be a connection. I wrote about Santiago, and he thought he *was* Santiago." She paused. The waiter mistook it for a signal and instantly walked over to their table. She glanced at him and gestured him away. "But even if he was delusional, what did that have to do with me?"

"It's a long story." Dante leaned back, and his chair changed shape to accommodate him. He realized that he could no longer reach the table and eat his food comfortably, and he moved forward again.

"I've got all the time we need," said September Morn. "And it's about my two favorite subjects—Santiago and me."

"All right," he said, sampling a mouthful of mutated shellfish in a cream sauce, and deciding she had good taste in restaurants. "But let me begin with a question. When did Santiago die?"

"No one knows." She learned forward confidentially. "But do you know what I think? I didn't even put it in my poem, but I think there were *two* Santiagos!"

"Do you really?"

"And I'm almost certain the second was a bounty hunter named Sylvester Cain."

"Sebastian Cain," he corrected her, taking a sip of Belarban wine from a crystal goblet. "And he was the fourth, not the second."

"How do you know?" she demanded sharply.

"I've read Black Orpheus' original manuscript."

Her eyes widened with excitement as she considered his revelation. "You've actually *seen* it?"

"I own it."

"How do you know it's authentic?"

"First, because the style of the verses that no one's seen match those that we all know. Second, because everything he says in those verses checks out."

"Checks out how?"

"I know Santiago's great-granddaughter. She's verified a lot of it. Others have verified other parts. And my ship's computer tells me the paper is more than a century old."

She was silent for a long moment.

"So the Songbird was the fourth Santiago!" She looked directly into his eyes. "Do you want to repay me for saving your life? Let me see the poem!"

"It's on Valhalla."

"So what? We'll go to Valhalla."

"I thought you couldn't leave the planet without a bodyguard. Santiago's people will blow them out of the sky if they approach Valhalla."

"For *this* I'll find a way to leave them behind," she said. "Now tell me everything you know about Santiago. There were four, you say?"

"No, I didn't say that," replied the poet. "I said Cain was the fourth. There were actually five. The last one died in 3301 G.E."

"Five?"

"That's right."

"There couldn't have been that many!"

"I can give you names and dates of death for the last three, and I can prove to you that none of them can possibly have been the original Santiago."

"And only you know it?" exclaimed September Morn, her face and her voice reflecting her excitement. "We've got to find a way to make the poem public. All the lost verses, the apocrypha, everything!"

"There's thousands of pages."

"All the better."

"We'll talk about it," said Dante. "But I'm still waiting for you to ask the operative question."

"And what is that?"

"How many Santiagos have there been *since* then?"

"What are you talking about?" she asked, confused.

"After I found the poem, I thought my calling was to continue it, to bring it up to date, to continue describing the adventurers and misfits who come out from the Democracy—and in a way it was. But the more I delved into it, the more I realized that it was time for Santiago to come back to the Inner Frontier, that conditions were ripe for him. The Democracy was still oppressing and overtaxing the colonists out here, aliens were still being treated like animals, rights were being violated, and it was apparent to me that we needed Santiago more than we ever had . . . so it became my mission to find him." *Talk about hubris,* he thought; *listen to me!* He grimanced in embarrassment. "So I went looking for him," he concluded lamely.

"And the One-Armed Bandit was your candidate?"

"We were wrong."

" 'We'?" she repeated. "Then you're not alone in this?"

"No."

"Good. It was too big a blunder for one man to make all by himself." September Morn stared at Dante. "So what will you do now? Go back to whatever you were doing before you found the poem?"

"Not a chance," he replied. "I was a small-time thief with

big-time dreams who was going absolutely nowhere. I'm not going back."

"Then what?"

"Santiago's story isn't over yet," said Dante. "I'll keep writing it."

"What are you talking about?" she said. "He's dead. I just killed him."

"He wasn't Santiago," answered Dante. "He was just the One-Armed Bandit."

Her eyes widened. "You mean you've got another one?"

"Yes. That's why the Bandit was on Hadrian."

"I don't understand."

"We'd built him an organization, a couple of hundred strong. I found him the best financial brain on the Frontier to manage his money. He had a great-granddaughter of one of the original Santiagos helping him. Even Dimitrios of the Three Burners, the man he just killed, was part of the organization."

She placed a hand on the bottle. "Do you want another?"

"No, I'm okay now," answered Dante. "Anyway, there were two alternatives once we knew the Bandit had to go. Silvermane, our new candidate, could meet him face-to-face . . . but you saw what just happened to a top-notch bounty hunter who tried that. One or the other was bound to die, and we couldn't be sure which. The other option was to lure the Bandit thousands of light-years away from his headquarters and take control of the organization before he got back, to make the place impregnable. We felt there was even a slim chance that he might be willing to become the One-Armed Bandit again and work for Santiago. After all, he still believed in the cause."

"All right, I follow you so far," said September Morn. "But what does that have to do with me?"

"He knows . . . knew . . . that I've been continuing Orpheus' work," explained Dante. "I thought the best way to get him out here was to run some stanzas in the local paper that revealed secrets about the organization."

"I never saw any."

"They ran in the classified section."

"I never read the classified ads. Most people don't. So why run them there?"

"It's very complicated, but believe me, it was the surest way to bring them to his attention. I figured when he saw the information was in verse form, he'd know it was me, and he'd come out here to kill me." Dante sighed deeply. "I never planned to come within fifty parsecs of Hadrian. I was going to stay with Silvermane when he took over Santiago's organization. The one thing I never counted on was that there'd be a prize-winning poet on Hadrian II, and that you'd have won your prize for a poem about Santiago. As soon as I learned that, I knew I had to come out here and try to stop him before he killed you for writing the stanzas that *I* actually wrote."

"Now it all makes sense," said September Morn. She stared admiringly at him. "You're a very brave man, Dante Alighieri. You were willing to sacrifice your life for a woman you'd never even seen."

"It was guilt, not bravery," answered Dante, shifting uncomfortably on his chair. "I've been responsible for the deaths of enough innocent people."

"Whatever the reason, you went out there unarmed and faced a man who had just killed a skilled bounty hunter. That's the kind of courage I wrote about in my poem."

"I have to admit I haven't read it. I'm sorry."

"I'll give you a copy," she promised. "It's a Romance, with a capital R. There are heroes and villains, high adventure, Good and Evil in juxtaposition, and a man who isn't without fear but finds the strength to overcome it, which in my opinion is *real* bravery, the kind you displayed."

"What led you to write about him?"

"A feeling that we'd forgotten his values, that in the overpowering shadow of the Democracy we'd conceded one liberty after another for more and more security until we had no liberties left to give, and one day we woke up and found we needed protection from our protectors. I never thought of Santiago as a role model—I mean, whoever thought he might come back again?—but I felt it was time to remind people that the ideals he embodied didn't have to die with him." She smiled. "And here I was, just writing my daydreams about it, while you were actually going out and *doing* something about it."

"An awful lot of people have died because I went out and did something," said Dante grimly. "You were almost added to the list."

"This is real life, not a book or a play," answered September Morn. "Things don't always work out the way men of virtue hope they will, and sometimes the effort is every bit as important as the results."

"It sounds good," said Dante, "but right about now I'd say we need some results."

"It would be nice," she said. "The Frontier could use a Santiago again." A pause. "To tell the truth, *I* could use him more than most."

"Oh?"

"There are some serious disadvantages to being a living monument," said September Morn as the waiter cleared the table and brought them their dessert pastries and coffee.

"So you told me," replied Dante, watching the waiter retreat in utter silence to the kitchen.

"You mean having to stay here?" she said. "That's a minor annoyance."

"What's the major one?"

"When word of my official status got out, it didn't take long for anyone who heard about it to conclude that if they could steal me away, the government of Hadrian would pay quite a ransom to get me back."

"Have there been many attempts?"

"There have been a few. Nothing I couldn't handle." She paused. "Until now."

"Who's after you now?"

"Something even more formidable than your One-Armed Bandit," answered September Morn.

"I don't think there *is* anyone more formidable, except maybe Joshua Silvermane."

"I said some*thing*, not some*one*."

"Exactly who or what is it that's after you?" he asked, curious.

She took a bite of her pastry. "Fabulous stuff," she said. "You should try it."

"I will," he said. "But first tell me what's after you."

"Have you ever heard of Tweedledee and Tweedledum?"

"Dimitrios mentioned them once," said Dante. He chuckled and took a sip of his coffee. "Those names aren't exactly designed to strike fear into one's heart."

"Don't laugh!" she snapped angrily. "Their names may be childish, but there's nothing childish about them. They're the most dangerous creatures on the whole Frontier!"

His smile vanished. "What makes them so dangerous?"

"They conquer whole planets, just the two of them."

Dante frowned. "You're telling me these two aliens can defeat an entire military force?"

"Yes."

"And they're after you?"

"That's the word that's reached the planetary authorities," she replied. "That's why I was carrying the burner. When I heard that both you and the Bandit wanted to find me, I thought one or both of you worked for them."

"They work as a pair, this Tweedledee and Tweedledum?" he persisted.

"Yes."

"What do they look like? What makes them so formidable?"

"I don't know," admitted September Morn. "I've never actually seen them. All I know is what I've heard and read—and based on that, I hope I *never* see them. They conquer entire worlds, just the pair of them, and nobody who's tried to stand up to them has lived to tell about it." Her expression hardened. "And now they're after me."

Dante reached across the table and placed a reassuring hand on hers. "You saved my life," he said. "The least I can do is return the favor. No one's going to harm you."

She looked questioningly at him.

"I'll get Santiago to protect you," promised Dante. "The *real* Santiago."

35.

MONGASO TAYLOR, CHURCHMOUSE POOR,
BITES THE HAND THAT FEEDS HIM.
EMBITTERED MAN, HE WILL NOT SAVE
THE FAMILY THAT NEEDS HIM.

DANTE SAT ALONE IN HIS room, waiting for Silvermane's face to reappear. For almost a minute it had been popping into and out of existence, terribly distorted. Finally the signal came through, and his perfect features took shape.

"I got your message," he said. "I'm sorry about Dimitrios of the Three Burners."

"So am I," replied Dante.

"And the Bandit is really dead?"

"That's right." Dante smiled wryly. "The girl I came here to protect killed him and saved my life."

"I'm almost sorry," said Silvermane. "I was looking forward to meeting him."

"To killing him, you mean."

"If it had been necessary." He paused. "Well, you might as well come back to Valhalla. There's nothing to keep you there now, and I've got plenty of work for you here."

"I can't."

"Why not?"

"The girl," said Dante.

"The one who saved your life?"

"Right. She's in danger."

"Just a minute," said Silvermane, frowning. "I thought you told me the Bandit was dead."

"He is. But—I'm not quite sure how to put this—she's the most important person on the planet. Or maybe I should say the most popular, or the most revered, or—"

"I get the picture," interrupted Silvermane irritably. "What about it?"

"The planetary government would pay any amount to get her back if she was kidnapped."

"Are you suggesting we kidnap her?" asked Silvermane, who didn't look unduly upset by the proposition.

"She killed the Bandit," Dante pointed out, lighting up a smokeless Antarean cigar he had picked up in the hotel's gift shop. "She's on our side. We *owe* her."

"Okay, you're my man on the scene. If you feel we should protect her, go ahead and do it." A pause. "Have you got any idea who's after her?"

"A pair of aliens—I gather they're called Tweedledee and Tweedledum."

Silvermane's expression darkened noticeably. "You're sure?"

"That's what she tells me."

"Get off the planet right now."

"I don't know if I can do it that quickly," said Dante. "She's been declared a living monument, whatever the hell that means, and there's all kinds of red tape, and—"

"I'm not talking about *her*!" said Silvermane sharply. "Get your ass off Hadrian II right now!"

"I can't."

"Trust me, you're not in their league, Rhymer," said Silvermane. "You can't even protect yourself from them, let alone your ladyfriend."

"Then send help."

"I'll send someone. Just get the hell out of there."

"Not without her," said Dante, fighting back a surge of frustration. "She stood up to the Bandit and saved my life. I can't desert her."

Silvermane sighed deeply. "All right," he said at last. "I can't argue with that kind of loyalty."

"Thanks."

"And arguing with that kind of stupidity hasn't gotten me anywhere," he added sharply. "Where are you staying?"

"The Windsor Arms Hotel."

"I know a man who's not too far from Hadrian, a man who owes me a favor. He's probably not up to taking the aliens either, but at least he'll buy you some time. I'll have him leave for Hadrian today; he should be there in two days' time, maybe sooner."

"Has he got a name?"

"Mongaso Taylor."

"I've heard that name before. I think maybe Dimitrios mentioned him."

"Could be," said Silvermane. "He used to be a hell of a commando for the Navy, back when he lived in the Democracy. They dropped him behind enemy lines on Cyrano IV during the Sett War. He took out eighteen of the purple bastards and blew an ammunition dump all by himself."

"He sounds like he should be all we need."

"He hasn't got a chance," said Silvermane. His voice began crackling with static. "He'll buy you some time, that's all. Do your red tape or whatever's necessary, but get off the planet before Tweedledee and Tweedledum show up."

"It's difficult to take them seriously with those names," remarked Dante.

"Don't let the names fool you," said Silvermane. "I was eager to go up against the Bandit. I've no desire to ever find myself in the same sector with those two."

"Your picture's breaking up," said Dante. "Is there anything else?"

The hologram vanished before Silvermane could reply.

Dante went over to the bathroom, muttered "Cold," rinsed his face off in the flow of water, ordered the blower to dry him, ran a comb through his hair, and prepared to leave the hotel room.

"Open," he said as he approached the door.

The door remained shut.

"I said open."

The mechanical voice of a computer answered. "I must bring to your attention the fact that you have not shut off the water in the bathroom, and that if you leave it will continue running until you return. If that is your desire, say so and I will instruct the servo-mech not to disrupt the flow when it cleans the room. If it is not your desire, I will be happy to shut it off."

"Shut it off and let me out of here," said Dante.

He heard the water stop flowing as the door dilated and he stepped through to the corridor. He took the airlift down to the main floor, then climbed into a robotic rickshaw and had it take him to September Morn's house on the outskirts of town.

It was an old stone building that had a couple of additions grafted onto it, obviously signs of her success in the world of letters. The gardens were carefully tended, filled with flowers he had never seen before. Avian feeders abounded, and several leather-winged little creatures watched him curiously as he approached the front door. He answered a series of questions from the security system, and finally the door dilated. He entered the living room, where September Morn was waiting for him.

The walls were covered with holographic prints of pastoral artworks by human and alien artists alike. One small section held some holos of September Morn accepting various honors. There was a false fireplace, and the mantel was lined with trophies and awards.

"Where are all the books?"

"I actually have very few books," she replied. "They cost too much. My library consists mostly of disks and cubes."

He held up the thin book he'd been carrying. "I wonder if you'd autograph this for me."

"What is it?"

"*The King of the Outlaws*. I bought it last night at the hotel's gift shop."

"I'll be happy to," she said, producing a stylus as he carried the book over to her. "What did you think of it?"

"It depressed me terribly," said Dante.

She looked concerned. "Oh? What didn't you like about it?"

"I liked everything about it," said Dante. "I realized about three pages into it that the wrong person is trying to be the new Black Orpheus." He paused. "I envy the way you use words. I just write these little stanzas. You create textures and tapestries than I can only marvel it."

"I'm flattered. But what I write is far removed from the way Black Orpheus wrote. The person who carries on his work should write in his style."

"That's generous of you to say so, but you can write rings around me in any style you choose and we both know it." He took the book back and looked at the autograph. "I'll cherish this. It's one hell of a piece of work."

"I don't know how many times I can thank you before it starts sounding false," she said with an embarrassed smile. "So please stop praising me."

"All right."

"Besides, we have more important things to discuss."

He nodded. "I spoke to . . . Santiago."

"And?" said September Morn.

"He can't come himself, but he's sending help."

"Good."

"But he wants us off Hadrian as soon as possible."

"This is my home," she replied adamantly. "I'll leave it when *I* choose, but I won't be threatened or frightened into running."

"You're sure?"

"If I run once," said September Morn, "I'll run every time I'm threatened, and then every time I think I *might* be threatened, and one day I'll look around and realize I've spent most of my life running away *from* things rather than *to* them. That's not a life I care to live."

"All right," said Dante. "If I were a little bigger and a little stronger, maybe I could tie you up, sling you over a shoulder, and carry you to my ship. But one thing I know is that I'm not about to win an argument with the wordsmith who wrote the poem I just read."

"Thank you," she said. "And for what it's worth, you couldn't tie me up and carry me off even if you were twice your size."

"Probably not," he admitted.

"So I'm staying right here. I'm a crack shot, and I'm not

afraid. I know how dangerous they are; they have no idea how dangerous *I* can be. My sister and I will be safe here."

"Your sister?" said Dante.

"Yes."

"I didn't know you had one. It's not in your bio," he said, holding up her book. "Does she live here?"

"Sometimes." He looked at her curiously, and she continued: "We don't get along very well. I suppose a lot of siblings are like that. But when push comes to shove, blood is thicker than . . . than whatever those aliens have coursing through their veins. She'll stand up and be counted if they come after me."

"Well, that's you, me, your sister, and Mongaso Taylor," said Dante. "Maybe it'll be enough."

"I doubt it," she said.

"So does Santiago."

"But even if we can't beat them, maybe we can convince them that kidnapping me is more effort than it's worth."

"We can try," agreed Dante.

"All right, we've covered that about as thoroughly as we can until your man Taylor gets here," she said. "Make yourself at home. I'm going to get us some drinks, and then you're going to spend the rest of the day telling me about Santiago—*all* the Santiagos."

It was a pleasant afternoon, and the next morning she showed him around the town of Trajan. They had just finished lunch at a local restaurant when his hotel paged him and told him he had a visitor.

"That's got to be him," said Dante. "Go home and lock all your doors, and don't let anyone in unless he's with me."

"You're overreacting," said September Morn. "They might be twenty systems away from here."

"And they might be twenty minutes away," answered Dante. "It doesn't hurt to play it safe."

"All right, I'll do what you say," she replied. "But I won't *keep* doing it. I value my freedom too much to stay locked up in my house."

"It's your freedom we're trying to protect," he said, getting up and walking out of the restaurant.

He reached the Windsor Arms in five minutes, and looked around the lobby. Standing by the artificial fireplace, his back to the desk, was a tall, slender, almost emaciated man dressed in muted shades of gray. There were a pair of telltale bulges under his tunic.

Dante approached him. "Mongaso Taylor?" he asked.

The man turned to face him. His face was long and lean, like the rest of him, and he had a thick handlebar mustache. "You must be Dante . . . Dante something. I've forgotten your last name."

"It's not important," said Dante. "The important thing is that you're here."

"I *had* to come," said Taylor bitterly. "I needed the money."

"Silvermane's *paying* you? I thought he told me you owed him a favor."

"I don't owe him a big enough favor to put my life on the line without money—five thousand credits up front, twenty more when I'm done."

"Well, that's between you and him. I'm just here to lay out the situation for you."

"You can buy me a drink in the bar while you're talking."

"I thought he just paid you five thousand credits," said Dante with a smile.

"That's more than I've seen in two years," said Taylor. His eyes became unfocused, as if he was looking back across the last few years. "You back out of one goddamned fight . . ."

He fell silent, and while Dante was curious, he decided it would be best not to ask any questions at present. He led Taylor to the bar and let the newcomer order for both of them.

"A pair of Dust Whores," Taylor told the bartender. "Light on the smoke." He turned to Dante. "Okay, I'm paid and I'm here. Who does Silvermane want me to kill?"

"Hopefully no one. But there are two sisters who live on the edge of town, and one of them seems to have become a prime kidnap target."

"You got to have more information than that," said Taylor. "I can't just hang around until some local makes a move. It could take months."

"We're not worried about locals."

"Offworlders?"

"Aliens," said Dante.

"Lady must be worth a bundle," said Taylor, rubbing his chin thoughtfully.

"Don't even think of it. You don't want Silvermane after you."

"You've got a point," admitted Taylor with a sigh. "So who are the aliens—Canphorites? Lodinites?"

"I don't know what they are. I've never seen them, and I don't think the ladies have either."

"Have you got *anything* I can go on?"

"Just their names—Tweedledee and Tweedledum."

Taylor didn't reply for a full minute. Finally he downed his drink, placed the empty glass on the bar, and turned to Dante.

"Nice to have met you," he said.

"What do you mean?"

"I mean I may be poor, but I'm not crazy." He reached into a pocket and pulled out a wad of banknotes. He counted through them, and placed a pile on the bar. "That's three thousand credits. You tell your boss I'm keeping the rest for expenses. If he doesn't like it, he can try to take it back."

"You can't just leave!"

Suddenly Dante was looking down the barrel of a screecher. "Are you gonna stop me?" asked Taylor softly.

"No, but—"

"Then get the hell out of my way."

And with that, he was gone.

Wonderful, just wonderful, thought Dante. *I've got a woman who's too proud to leave and a gunman who's too scared to stay. What the hell do I do now?*

36.

THE LITTLE SISTER, FORTUNE'S BANE,
WISHES SHE HAD NOT BEEN BORN.
FILLED WITH RAGE AND HATE AND PAIN,
THERE SHE SLINKS—OCTOBER MORN.

"HE DID WHAT?" DEMANDED SILVERMANE'S image.

"You heard me," said Dante, sitting in the pilot's seat of his stationary ship and staring at the hologram that appeared just above the subspace radio. "That's why I'm not transmitting from my room. I don't think anyone's watching me, but if they are I don't want this to be overheard."

"He can't get away with this! I don't give a damn about the three thousand he returned."

"I don't care about the money either," replied Dante. "I'm still here with a woman who's a target for these two aliens. What are we going to do about it?"

"Get off the planet," said Silvermane. "I told you that the last time we spoke."

"And I told you that it's not that easy."

"If she's still there when I get there, *I'll* convince her to leave," said Silvermane confidently.

"Then you're coming to Hadrian?" said Dante, relieved.

"Eventually. First I have to hunt down Mongaso Taylor and make an example of him, or others will think they can break their word to Santiago."

"Goddammit!" shouted Dante. "He's nothing but a has-been killer who's lost his nerve! *I'm* the one who made you Santiago, and I need your help right now!"

"Nobody *made* me Santiago," answered Silvermane coldly. "You merely pointed out the fact of it."

"And nobody made your fortress on Valhalla and presented you with two hundred loyal men and women, and nobody killed the Bandit for you!"

"You didn't kill the Bandit," was Silvermane's calm reply. "*She* did."

"And now she needs your help."

"Everything in its proper order—first Taylor, then Hadrian."

"What do we do in the meantime?"

"You're the bright one," said Silvermane. "Use that brain of yours."

Dante broke the connection, cursed under his breath, then left the ship and returned to his hotel. Once there, he tried to raise September Morn on the vidphone. There was no answer.

"Damn it!" he snapped to her holo-message tape, making sure his face looked properly grim. "I told you not to leave your place without me!"

He went out, had lunch, and returned to his room, where he tried again without success to contact her. He checked his timepiece; it was only an hour and a half since his first attempt. He left another message about staying put, then lay down and took a nap.

He awoke in late afternoon and called September Morn a third time. The result was the same.

He went down to the lobby, had the desk clerk summon a robotic rickshaw, and took it out to her house.

The door was missing.

Not broken, or melted, or shattered. Missing. As if it had never been there.

He wished he had a weapon of some kind. He looked cautiously into the interior, took a tentative step inside, then a second and a third.

The place was as neat as ever. Nothing was out of place. There were no signs of a struggle. There were no messages, written or transcribed.

And there was no September Morn.

He spent half an hour scouring the house for clues. There weren't any. Finally he sat down on a chair in the living room to consider his options.

He'd been sitting there pondering the situation for perhaps five minutes when he heard footsteps approaching the house.

"Who's there?" he said.

Suddenly the footsteps began retreating. He jumped to his feet and raced to the door, just in time to see a feminine figure racing away.

"September Morn!" he shouted. "Wait!"

The figure kept running, and he took off after her.

"Damn it! Wait for me!"

The figure kept ahead of him for perhaps two hundred yards, then began slowing noticeably, and finally he was able to reach out and grab her by the arm.

"Stop!" he snapped. "What the hell is—?"

He stopped in midsentence as the girl turned to face him. There were similarities to September Morn—the same high cheekbones, the same light blue eyes, the same neck, the same rounded shoulders—but this girl had a stronger jaw, a broader mouth, and was between five and ten years younger.

"You're the sister," said Dante. It was not a question. "Why did you run away?"

"I wasn't sure who you were."

"Who did you think I might be?"

She wrenched her arm free. "I don't have to talk to you!"

"You have to talk to me now or Santiago later," he lied. "I'm a lot more pleasant."

She glared at him without answering.

"What's going on?" continued Dante. "You saw that the door was gone. That didn't frighten you. *I* frightened you." Still no reply. "But I'm not a frightening guy—at least not until you know me better—and besides, you didn't see me. You were frightened by who you *thought* I was." He gripped her arm harder. "Suppose you tell me who you were expecting?"

"No one!"

"Let me reword that. I know you expected to come home to an empty house. But if it wasn't empty, who did you think would be waiting for you?"

"None of your business!" she snapped, trying to pull her arm free.

"I told you: it's Santiago's business, and he has very unpleasant ways of getting what he wants."

"Fuck off! He's been dead for a century!"

"The king is dead, long live the king. He's back, twice as big and three times as deadly. If you don't tell me what I want to know, I'll turn you over to him." He paused. "You won't enjoy it, take my word for it."

"Why should I believe you?"

Dante shrugged. "Okay," he said, pulling her by the arm. "We'll wait for him at your place."

"Stop pulling me!"

"Stop dragging your ass."

She stared at him. "He really exists?"

"I just told you he does."

Another paused. Then: "All right, I'll tell you what you want to know."

Thank God for that. I don't know what I'd have done if we got to the house and you hadn't given in.

"Let's start with names," he said. "Mine is Dante. What's yours?"

"It depends on who you talk to."

"I'm talking to you."

"It's Belinda—but ever since my sister got famous, they call me October Morn."

"I take it you don't like the name?" said Dante.

"I hate it!"

"You don't like her much either, do you?"

"That's an understatement."

"She likes you," said Dante.

"She told you that?"

"In essence."

"Then she's an even bigger fool than I thought," said Belinda.

"Next question," said Dante. "Why did you run from the house?"

"I thought it had been broken into."

"One more lie and you can tell your story to Santiago." He continued pulling her toward the house. "Why did you run?"

"I thought they had come for me."

"They?" asked Dante.

"The aliens."

"Tweedledee and Tweedledum?"

"Yes." She came to a stop.

"Why would they come for you?" he asked. "Your sister's the one who's worth all the ransom money."

"I thought she had tricked them," said Belinda.

"Explain," said Dante, taking her hand and once more leading her to the house.

"I told them where we lived, when she was likely to be home, what she looked like, and—"

"You sold your sister out to aliens?" Dante interrupted.

"I didn't take any money!"

"Then why—?"

"Because I hate her!" yelled Belinda as they reached the house and entered it.

"Okay, you hate her and you gave her to the aliens. Why did you run?"

"She's smart, smarter than anyone suspects," said Belinda bitterly. "I was afraid she'd convinced them that she was me and I was September Morn. When I realized someone was inside the house, I was afraid they'd come back for me."

"Where would they have come back from?" asked Dante.

"I don't know."

"How did you contact them?"

"Through an intermediary."

"Who?"

"I can't tell you," she screamed, panic reflected in her face. "He'll kill me!"

"And I'll kill you if you don't," said Dante harshly. "I'm a lot closer to you at the moment than he is. I want you to consider that very carefully."

"If I tell you who, you've got to protect me from him!" whimpered Belinda.

"The way you protected your sister?" he asked.

"She never *needed* any protection or any help! She was always the smartest and the prettiest and the most popular and . . ." Her words trailed off into incoherent sobs.

"She needed protection from the aliens," said Dante coldly. "It may have been the only time in her life she needed help, and you betrayed her." He stared contemptuously at her. "I think Santiago and I are going to let you live, just so your sister can take her own revenge on you."

"If my sister isn't dead already, she will be soon."

"Don't bet on it," said Dante. He paused. "We're going to rescue her."

"Why?" asked Belinda, the tears suddenly gone. "What did she ever do for you?"

"She saved my life."

A look of fury crossed Belinda's face. "That figures. She's just the type."

"It's an admirable type," said Dante. "Certainly more admirable than an overgrown petulant brat who sells her sister out to aliens."

Belinda glared at him but made no answer.

"I'm still waiting," said Dante after a moment.

"For what?"

"The name of the man who can contact Tweedledee and Tweedledum."

She considered the question. "You'll protect me?"

"I'll let you live," said Dante coldly. "That's enough of a bargain."

She seemed torn, and finally slumped in resignation. "It's Moby Dick."

"Moby Dick?" he repeated. "Someone's really walking around with that name?"

"Yes."

"You know what will happen to you if you lie to me?"

"Yes, goddammit!" she snapped.

"Where do I find him?"

"The Fat Chance. It's a casino."

"Where is this Fat Chance in relation to the Windsor Arms?" asked Dante.

"A block north, two blocks west."

"Does Moby Dick work for the aliens?"

"He works for himself," said Belinda.

"What does he look like?"

"You'll know him when you see him."

"All right," said Dante. "I'm off to find him." He checked his timepiece. "You've got two hours to clear your stuff out of here."

"This is my house too!"

"You forfeited your right to it. I want you and all your possessions gone today, and I don't want to see you back here. If you disobey me, you'll have to answer to Santiago. Is that understood?"

No answer.

He took a step toward her. "Is that understood?" he repeated ominously.

"Yes," she muttered.

"Then get going."

"I wish you as much luck with Moby Dick as Ahab had!" she said as he turned and headed off to the Fat Chance.

37.

HE'S BIGGER THAN BIG, HE'S WHITER THAN
   WHITE,
HE'S GOT AN IQ THAT'S PLUMB OUT OF SIGHT.
MOBY DICK IS HIS NAME, AND HIS TALENT IS
   VAST:
HE CHANGES THE FUTURE AND TOYS WITH THE
   PAST.

THE FAT CHANCE WASN'T LIKE any casino Dante had ever
been in. There were no craps tables, no roulette wheels, no
poker games in progress. All but a handful of the customers
were aliens—Canphorites, Lodinites, Mollutei, plus a few
species he'd never seen before—and all the games were of
alien origin.

There was a long, polished metal bar, manned by two
robot bartenders. Given the clientele, Dante hated to think
of what was in all the oddly shaped containers displayed
behind the bar.

The poet stepped further into the casino, looking around,
and finally he saw the man he knew had to be Moby Dick.
He was a big man, big everywhere—he stood almost seven
feet tall, and weighed close to five hundred pounds. The
wild part, decided Dante, was that he'd be willing to bet
there weren't twenty-five pounds of useless fat on the man.
He was huge, but he was hard as a rock, and despite his
weight he somehow managed to look fit.

His eyes were a dull pink, his lips were thick, his ears
small, his head almost bald. When he opened his mouth,
he revealed two rows of shining gold teeth.

But the thing that drew Dante's immediate attention,
even more than all his other features, was the fact that the
man was an albino. It wasn't hard to see how he'd come
by his name.

The man sat alone at a table, a drink in front of him, watching the action at a nearby *jabob* pit. Dante approached him slowly, and came to a stop a few feet away.

"You gonna stand there all day?" asked the albino. "Or are you gonna sit down and tell me why you've come looking for me?"

"I'll sit," replied Dante. The huge man snapped his fingers, and a chair floated over and adjusted to the poet's body. "And I'll have something to drink, too."

"Do I look like a bartender?"

"No," said Dante. "You look like a white whale."

Moby Dick smiled. "Most people are afraid to say that, even though it's true." He paused. "I like you already."

"Good," said Dante. "I wouldn't want anyone your size taking a dislike to me."

This time Moby Dick laughed. "Okay, you've ingratiated yourself enough. Now tell me why you want to see me— and don't deny that's why you're here. No human comes to the Fat Chance to gamble."

"Then why are *you* here?"

"I own the place."

"A casino just for aliens?"

"My own race doesn't go out of its way to make me feel wanted," said the albino. "So I repeat: why are you here?"

"I need some information," said Dante. "My name is Dante Alighieri, and—"

"How divine is your comedy?" interrupted Moby Dick.

"I beg your pardon?"

"Never mind. You're not the same one."

"But I chose his name for my own."

"Do you write poetry?" asked Moby Dick.

"After a fashion."

"Then it's a fine name for you. Unlike Herman Melville, I don't write epics about whaling. But I'm a whale among men, I'm whiter than any of them, and I'm ready to kill any one-legged man named Ahab." He smiled again. "Haven't found one yet."

"Maybe you'd like to go hunting more dangerous game?" suggested Dante.

The table glowed, and the albino stared at a holocube. "That's his limit," he said to it. "No more credit for him until he makes good his losses." He turned back to Dante. "Why do I think you have someone in mind?"

"Maybe because I haven't got a poker face."

"Go home, Dante Alighieri," said Moby Dick. "You don't want any part of them."

"Any part of whom?"

"We've finished the social niceties," said the albino. "I'd really appreciate if you didn't play stupid with me."

"All right," said Dante. "October Morn told me you can contact Tweedledee and Tweedledum."

He chuckled. "The little bitch would love to see them kill the pair of us."

"Probably," agreed Dante. "But was she telling the truth?"

"Yeah, I can contact them," said Moby Dick. "But you don't want me to."

"Why not let me be the judge of that?"

"Because you've never met them, and your courage is born of ignorance" was the reply. "Believe me, no sane man wants to mess with them."

"The man I work for does."

"Then the man you work for's not long for this plane of existence," said the huge man.

"Nevertheless."

One of the *jabob* pit bosses, a Lodinite, waddled up and showed a slip of paper to Moby Dick. He grunted, signed it, watched the alien waddle away, and then looked at Dante. "Maybe I should talk to your boss myself."

"He'll be here in a few days' time," said Dante. He paused. "His name is Santiago."

Moby Dick seemed amused. "Why not Caligula or Conrad Bland, while he was at it?"

"Because he *is* Santiago."

"Somebody's been feeding you a fairy tale, Dante Alighieri," said the albino. "Santiago died seventy or eighty years ago, maybe even longer than that."

"A galaxy that can produce you and Tweedledee and Tweedledum and some of the aliens walking around this casino can produce a man who doesn't age and die like other men. I work for the King of the Outlaws."

Moby Dick was silent for a long moment, analyzing what he'd heard. Finally he spoke. "If he really is on his way to Hadrian, I'd like to meet him."

"I thought you didn't believe in him half a minute ago," noted Dante.

"I don't necessarily believe in him now," said Moby Dick amiably. "All the more reason to want to meet him."

"In the meantime, can you set up a meeting between the two aliens and me?"

Mody Dick shrugged. "I can ask. What should I tell them you want to talk about? The lady poet?"

Dante considered his reply for a moment. "Tell them Santiago's coming to kill them, but I might be able to bargain for their lives. I might be able to convince him to take September Morn and hold her for ransom if they'll turn her over peacefully."

"They can't laugh," said Moby Dick. "They're physically incapable of it. But if they could, they'd laugh in your face."

"Just deliver it."

"You're bluffing, of course," said the albino. "Or out-and-out lying. It won't work. They don't understand bluffs. They'll believe what you say."

"I want them to."

"No you don't," said Moby Dick. "I keep telling you: you don't want any part of them. Neither does your boss, whoever he is."

"How is it that you alone know how to contact them?" asked Dante, changing the subject.

"Lots of people know how. I might be the only one currently on Hadrian, or the only one the little bitch sister knows, but there are lots of us."

"Why are you and this small handful of men and women so favored?"

"There are only two of them in the whole damned universe," answered Moby Dick. "There's just so much they can do, so they rule through handpicked men and women."

"And they picked you?"

The huge man shook his head. "Do I look like a ruler? I'm just a supplicant. If things work out, they may toss me a couple of crumbs someday."

"Would I be correct in assuming one of those crumbs will be Hadrian II?" asked Dante.

"Why not?" Moby Dick shot back. "They can't live everywhere. They can't *be* everywhere. Someone has to bring order to their empire."

"How many planets do they control right now?"

"Maybe eight or nine."

"That's not much of an empire. The Democracy controls about a hundred and fifty thousand worlds, and they influence at least that many more."

"It's a start. Even Man started out with just one world, you know," said Moby Dick.

"So you're going to fight for them?"

"They may never ask me to, and if I do it'll be without much enthusiasm," answered Moby Dick. "Show me a better side to fight for."

"I intend to," said Dante. "Order something to drink. This is going to take a while."

For the next two hours, Dante filled the huge albino in on what had been transpiring for the past few months, about the poem, and Matilda, and the Bandit, and Silvermane, and—always—the ideal of Santiago. When he finally finished, Moby Dick stared at him for a very long time, and then spoke:

"It's an interesting idea," said the albino. "If you had the right Santiago, I'd join up this minute. But you don't."

"You haven't even met him."

"I don't have to. You've described him. That was the giveaway."

"The giveaway?" repeated Dante, puzzled.

"Yeah. You described his gun and his bullets, you told me how tall and graceful he is, you told me that he looks like some artist's dream, you told me about his silver hair. You told me almost everything I need to know about him—except who and what he is."

"I told you: he's Joshua—" began Dante.

"You described a very beautiful and efficient killer," interrupted Moby Dick. "And except for being very beautiful, I don't see much to differentiate him from your last killer, the Santiago you and September Morn . . . ah . . . deposed right here on Hadrian II."

"He's *totally* different," said Dante. "For one thing, he's not a fanatic. For another, he really does understand what being Santiago means, what's required of him."

"I don't know," said Moby Dick. "I think they're both dead ends."

"Would you care to explain that?"

"Sure. But first let's generalize a bit. What causes a species to evolve?"

"What are you talking about?" asked Dante irritably.

"You heard me," said the huge albino. "What makes a species evolve?"

"How the hell do *I* know?"

"You would, if you were using your brain. If you don't, you're just like them."

Dante stared at him, but made no reply.

"The answer," continued Moby Dick, "is that evolution is a response to environmental need. Are the branches of a tree too high? Grow a long neck. Is the sun too bright? Grow bigger eyes and better ears and sleep all day. Are you too small to kill prey animals? Develop opposable thumbs and a brain, and learn to make weapons."

"You *are* going to get to the point sooner or later, aren't you?"

"The point is obvious. You found two of the most efficient killers on the Frontier, maybe *the* two best. But because they've always been able to get anything they wanted with their weapons and their physical skills, why should they develop social skills, or be adept at teamwork, or inspire loyalty when they've never required any help before? I'm sure your Silvermane is a dangerous man, and I'm sure he wants to be Santiago—but based on what you've told me, I don't think I'd be inclined to lay down my life for him, or to follow him into battle if the odds were against us."

"You wouldn't be asked to risk your life—or lose it— for *him*," said Dante, "but for the cause."

"The two should be indistinguishable," answered Moby Dick. "And I get the distinct impression that neither of your Santiagos could describe the cause in terms that would make people willing to die for it."

"All right," said Dante. "So you won't join us. Will you at least help us?"

"You really want me to contact them, even after what I've told you?" asked the albino.

"She saved my life. I owe her."

"Noble," commented Moby Dick. "That's not a trait I see much of out here—nobility."

Another pause. "Then you'll do it?"

"I'll do it. Where can I reach you?"

"The Windsor Arms."

"Wait for me there. I'll be in touch."

Dante got up. "Thanks."

"It's a pity," said Moby Dick.

"What is?"

"I like you, Dante Alighieri. You're a little too noble for your own good, but I really like you. I hate to send you and your boss to your deaths."

"I've got to at least *try* to save her," answered Dante simply.

"I know."

Dante turned and left the casino, window-shopped his way back to the hotel, and took the airlift up to his room, where he found a message from Virgil waiting for him.

"I'm on Laministra IV, encouraging a couple of drug

dealers to voluntarily join our network of freedom fighters"—a nasty grin—"and I realized I'm just a hop, skip, and a jump from Hadrian, so I thought I'd pop over there and take my ship back if you're through with it. See you in the morning."

Dante wiped the message, waited a few minutes for Moby Dick to contact him, and finally lay down on the bed and closed his eyes.

He didn't know how long he'd slept, but his computer awoke him by gently repeating his name over and over. Finally he sat up groggily.

"All right, I'm awake," he mumbled. "What is it?"

"A Mr. Dick is attempting to communicate with you, Mr. Alighieri."

"I don't know any—" Suddenly he straightened up. "Put him through!"

Moby Dick's image flickered into existence above the computer.

"I've contacted them," he announced, staring straight at him.

"And?"

"As I told you, they can't laugh—but they *did* seem amused."

"Will they meet with me?"

"No. I gave them the message, exactly as you worded it. They'll meet only with Santiago."

"Where?"

"Kabal III."

"Never heard of it. How far away is it?"

"Perhaps ten light-years."

"Is it an oxygen world?"

"Yes," replied the albino. "That's their only concession to Santiago."

"Concession?" repeated Dante, surprised. "Don't they breathe oxygen?"

"I'm not aware that they breathe anything at all," answered Moby Dick.

"Why would they choose this particular world?"

"It's a deserted colony world, with a couple of empty Tradertowns. There won't be anyone there to interfere."

"Which means they'll have time to booby-trap every inch of it."

"They won't need to," said Moby Dick. "Try to understand: these are aliens who conquer entire worlds with no help from anyone. You have no conception of their powers, no idea what they're capable of."

"So tell me."

"I don't know the specifics. I just know that time after time they accomplish the seemingly impossible with no visible effort."

Thanks for nothing, thought Dante. "I want you to get back to them and tell them Santiago will only meet them on a world of our choosing."

"If you insist, but . . ."

"But what?"

"But *they* have September Morn. It would seem to be a seller's market."

"Tell them anyway. If they don't know what a bluff is, they might think Santiago won't come under any other conditions. I mean, hell, he's never even met her. He has no reason to walk into a trap to try to save her."

"Whatever you say. Stay there."

Moby Dick broke the connection, and contacted him again twenty minutes later.

"Well?" demanded Dante.

"No deal. They may not know how to tell a lie, but they know how to spot one. They'll only meet him on Kabal III."

"At least we tried."

"What now?" asked Moby Dick.

"It's obviously a trap. We can't let him go there alone." Dante did some quick mental calculations. "I can have half our men here in six days' time. Let's set the meeting for then."

Moby Dick's expression said it was a hopeless request,

but he agreed to pass it on. He was back in communication
with Dante ten minutes later.

"Big mistake," he said. "We gave them a time frame.
Now they say that if Santiago's not on Kabal III in one
Standard day, they'll kill September Morn rather than con-
tinue holding her for ransom."

"*Shit!*" muttered Dante. "She's going to die, and it's my
fault! If I'd left it alone, the goddamned government would
have come up with the money!"

"Don't blame yourself too much," replied Moby Dick,
not without sympathy. "You didn't know who or what you
were dealing with."

"Excuse me, Mr. Alighieri," said the computer, "but
there is a priority communication coming in from a Mr.
Santiago."

"No problem," said the albino. "I'll talk to you tomorrow. You can let me know what he said then."

He cut the connection, and an instant later Silvermane's
visage replaced his.

"I found him," he announced.

"Mongaso Taylor?"

"That's right." Something in his manner precluded any
questions about what had happened. "I should reach Hadrian II in about thirteen Standard hours. I'll meet you in
Trajan just before noon." He paused. "Did you talk any
sense into the lady poet?"

"We have to talk about her. I'll go to my ship and get
back to you in half an hour."

"I'm getting tired of that," said Silvermane. "Do you
have any reason to think someone is monitoring this?"

"No, I'm just trying to be safe."

"Then talk to me now."

Dante sighed deeply. "The aliens kidnapped her."

Silvermane seemed unsurprised and unconcerned. "I *told*
you to get her off the planet." He sighed. "Well, they'll pay
the ransom and that'll be that. I hope you learned your
lesson."

"It's not that simple."

"Oh?" asked Silvermane, suddenly alert.

"I made a terrible blunder," said Dante. "I tried to bluff them, to scare them with your name."

"Tell me about it."

Dante filled him in. "And their last message is that they've got her on Kabal III, and they'll kill her if you don't show up tomorrow."

"What are they asking for her?"

"You're not seriously thinking of going there?" demanded Dante. "It's a trap!"

"Of course it's a trap."

"I'm glad we agree on that," said Dante, relieved.

"I don't think my pistols will be much good against them. I can stop by Hadrian on the way to Kabal. Can you hunt up a molecular imploder by tomorrow morning?"

"What the hell are you talking about?" shouted Dante at the holographic image. "They're waiting there to kill you, and it's *their* world! They know every inch of it!"

"You don't seem to understand. They've called me out."

"So what?"

"This goes with the job, poet," explained Silvermane. "If I back down now and get away with it, I'll be tempted to back down again and again. What kind of Santiago would I be then?"

"A live one."

"Don't bury me just yet," he said wryly. "I plan to make a hell of a fight of it—and I've never lost."

"You told me once that you didn't ever want to be in the same sector with them," Dante reminded him.

"That was Joshua Silvermane talking," said the image. "I'm Santiago."

"Surely there's something I can say, something I can do . . ." said Dante.

"There is," replied Silvermane. "Make sure you have the imploder ready for me."

He broke the connection, though Dante stared at the spot where his image had been for a full minute before turning away.

He's going to die, and there's nothing I can do to prevent it, he thought miserably.

He walked over to a mirror and stared at the face that confronted him, searching for all the hidden flaws that he knew must be lurking there.

We're going to lose another Santiago, and it's going to be my fault again, just like the last one. I don't understand it. I try so hard to do the right thing. Why am I as good at getting them killed as I am at finding them?

PART VI

SANTIAGO'S BOOK

38.

HE'S PROUD AND HE'S ARROGANT, FEARLESS
   AND BOLD;
IF YOU TRAVEL WITH HIM YOU'LL NEVER GROW
   OLD.
THOSE WHO OPPOSE HIM HAVE DRAWN THEIR
   LAST BREATH:
HE'S THE KING OF THE OUTLAWS—HIS
   PARTNER IS DEATH.

MOBY DICK STOOD IN THE corridor, waiting for the security system to identify him and inform Dante of his presence. Finally the door dilated and he stepped into the poet's room.

"Did you get it?" asked Dante anxiously.

"No problem."

"No problem?" repeated Dante disbelievingly. "Molecular imploders are outlawed on almost every planet in the galaxy, including out here on the Frontier."

"I am not without my connections," answered the albino with a smug smile.

"So where is it?"

"Back at my casino," replied Moby Dick.

"But I told you that Silvermane needs it this morning!"

"He'll have it—but I'm coming along with it."

Dante stared at him sharply. "Why?"

"Because I agree with you that it's time for another Santiago, and I want to see how this one measures up."

"We're not holding auditions," said Dante. "He's *it*."

"Right now he's just a name, and I don't follow names. If I'm going to join your crusade, I want to see just who it is I'm joining."

"I don't know if he'll let you come along," said Dante.

"He will if he wants that imploder," said Moby Dick.

"He's going to be hard-pressed enough without having to protect you as well."

"I don't need any protecting. They won't bother me. I've dealt with them, remember?"

Dante shrugged. "Have it your way. It's his decision anyway, not mine."

"Good," said Moby Dick, approaching the largest chair in the room. It expanded to accommodate his bulk, then wrapped its arms partway around him and began rocking very gently. "When it's all over, I'll let you know how it went."

"You won't have to," said Dante. "I'm going."

"Didn't you just tell me that he likes to fight alone?" asked the albino.

"I'm not fighting. I'm there to write it up, and hopefully bring back September Morn."

"He could bring her back himself, you know."

"He's never met her," said Dante. "What if they've got twenty women imprisoned there?"

"Then he'll bring back all twenty and you'll tell him which one she is."

Dante listened politely, then uttered a two-word response: "I'm going."

The security system blinked. Moby Dick began laboriously to lift his five-hundred-pound bulk from the chair, but Dante gestured him to stay seated.

"It's not him," he announced.

"Who is it, then?"

"The friend whose ship I borrowed."

"Are you sure this is a hotel room and not a public meeting place?"

Dante smiled. "Not as sure as I was fifteen minutes ago." He muttered a code to the door and it irised, allowing Virgil to step through it.

"How are you doing, Rhymer?" said the Indian. "You don't look any the worse for wear." A pause. "So the Bandit is really dead?"

"Really and truly."

"You know, I didn't believe it when I first heard the news. I didn't think anyone or anything except maybe Silvermane could kill him." He chuckled. "So it was the lady poet that shot him down?"

"That's right."

"Doesn't sound to me like the kind of woman who needs rescuing," said Virgil.

"She need it from *these* captors," said Moby Dick.

"Yeah, that's what everybody who knows them says," agreed Virgil. He stepped forward and extended a hand. "Virgil Soaring Hawk. Pleased to meet you."

"Moby Dick."

"Not the Moby Dick who used to live in the Carnasus system?" said the Indian.

"No, that was another one," replied the albino. "He was the wrong color, but the right mutation. The way I hear it, he was born with gills, and he could breathe in the water just as easy as in the air."

"I didn't know whales could breathe water," said Virgil. "Of course, there ain't been any around for a couple of thousand years, so what do I know?"

"They can't breathe water," agreed Moby Dick. "But my namesake could."

"He still alive?"

"I don't think so."

"Someone harpoon him?"

Moby Dick shook his head. "Got shredded by a pleasure craft's motor, or so I heard."

"Serves him right for spending all his time in the water when he could have been chasing the ladies—or the gentlemen, for that matter," said Virgil with his usual single-mindedness. He turned back to Dante. "Silvermane hasn't shown up yet, I take it?"

"Not yet. And call him Santiago."

"Yeah, I know—I keep forgetting."

"How did things go on Valhalla?" asked the poet.

"Pretty smoothly since word reached them that the Bandit wouldn't be coming back." He paused, then smiled.

"Matilda's put together a team she calls the Thieves' Carnival."

"Catchy name. Any reason for it?"

"There's half a dozen of them, they work together, and she sent them to Calliope."

"That's the carnival planet, isn't it?"

"That's the place," said Virgil. "Ten million vacationers any given day, all of them with money. You couldn't ask for a better world for Santiago to pick up operating funds." He glanced out the window. "When's he due here?"

"He's late already," answered Dante. "I expected him right after sunrise."

"Maybe he's not in such a hurry to die," offered Moby Dick.

"Are you saying he won't show up?" demanded Dante heatedly.

"What's the point? He can't defeat them. Whole armies have tried and failed."

"Anyone can be defeated," said Dante. "It's just a matter of coming up with the right strategy."

"Nonsense," said Moby Dick. "You're a minnow. I'm a whale. You can't defeat me. All you can do is escape to live another day."

"That's a defeat of sorts," answered the poet. "And if I tell all the other minnows how, and we all escape every day, you might find yourself growing a little weaker and a little slower, which will make you weaker and slower still, until you starve to death."

"By God, I *knew* I liked you!" said Moby Dick with a sudden laugh. "Santiago's got himself a hell of a biographer, young Dante Alighieri."

"I'm not his biographer," answered Dante. "Well, not exactly. Not primarily. I'm just carrying on what Black Orpheus started."

"Isn't it about time you stopped kidding yourself?" said the albino.

"What are you talking about?"

"From everything I can tell, just about the only thing

you've done since you found that poem is try to find a new Santiago."

"What the hell do *you* know about it?" said Dante irritably. "I've written hundreds of verses, and I've spent days and weeks honing and revising them."

"What's more important to you?" asked Moby Dick. "Writing your poem or making sure that there *is* a Santiago?"

"What's more important to you—eating or breathing?" Dante shot back.

Virgil grinned. "Do you still like him?" he asked Moby Dick.

"Hell, yes!" said the albino. "He's as good at evading questions as answering them. That's a rare talent."

"Flatter me any more and I might take an axe to you," said Dante. "Or worse still—I might lock you in here with Virgil and not come back for a day or two."

"Promises, promises!" muttered the Indian.

Dante was about to reply when the security system told him that Silvermane was at the door. He commanded it to dilate, and the tall man, immaculate as usual, strode into the room.

"Who are you?" he demanded, staring at Moby Dick.

"And I'm pleased to meet you too," said the albino.

Silvermane did not look amused, and Dante immediately stepped between them. "This is Moby Dick," he said. "He's the one who's supplying the imploder."

"Then I thank you," said Silvermane sternly. He looked around. "Where is it?"

"It's in a safe place," said Moby Dick.

"Get it. I don't have any time to waste."

"Once we reach an agreement."

Silvermane glared at him. "How much?"

"No money."

"Then what?"

"I'm coming along."

"I won't protect you," said Silvermane.

"I don't need protecting," said the albino.

"Against these two, *everyone* needs protecting."

"Not me," said Moby Dick. "I have an arrangement with them."

Silvermane looked at the huge man as if he was the lowest form of life, but he made no reply.

"Well, we *don't* have an arrangement," interjected Dante. "Maybe we could use some help." Silvermane turned to him. "This whole planet loves September Morn, practically worships her. Give me a few hours. I'm sure I can gather a few hundred men and women to come along and—"

"Santiago doesn't beg for help," said Silvermane.

"But he doesn't have to turn it down if it's freely offered," urged Dante.

"They didn't challenge Hadrian II. They challenged *me*."

"That's your final word?"

"It is."

"At least let *me* come with you," said Dante. "You don't know what she looks like. If they have more than one captive and they've done them any damage, you won't know which one's her."

Silvermane frowned. "Just how stupid do you think I am? I've pulled up a dozen holograms of her from the local newsdisk."

"Then consider this: if you're good enough to kill the aliens—aliens she felt could not possibly be defeated—she may find you so terrifying that she won't want to put herself in your power."

Silvermane considered what Dante had said for a moment, then nodded his head almost imperceptibly. "All right, you can come." He looked at Virgil. "But not the Indian. I don't like him."

"I go where he goes," said Virgil.

"You're staying here."

"I'm not one of your sycophants," said Virgil. "I don't take my orders from you. I work for the poet."

Suddenly Virgil was looking down the barrel of Silvermane's pistol.

"When I tell you to do something," began Silvermane, "you'll do it!"

"Stop!" yelled Dante, so suddenly and so loud that everyone froze. "Is this the way Santiago treats his allies? I thought you saved your bullets for your enemies."

Silvermane looked uncertain for just a moment, then holstered his gun.

"All right," he said to Virgil. "But stay clear of me, in the ship and on the planet." He turned to Moby Dick. "I've wasted enough time. Let's get the imploder."

He walked out the door, followed by Virgil.

"Four heroes off to slay the monsters," said Moby Dick to Dante, so softly that the other two couldn't hear him. A sardonic smile crossed his face. "I wonder how many of us will still be alive when we get there?"

39.

OH, TWEEDLEDEE AND TWEEDLEDUM,
THE PARTS ARE GREATER THAN THE SUM.
THEY SEND THEIR FOES TO KINGDOM COME,
DO TWEEDLEDEE AND TWEEDLEDUM.

KABAL III WAS A DARK world, considering how close it was to its yellow sun, dark and bleak and gray. Rocky surfaces with jagged edges covered the surface. Undrinkable water created small canyons as it wound through the landscape. Opaque clouds crawled slowly across the sky.

"I don't like the looks of this place," said Dante, studying the viewscreen as the ship took up orbit around it.

"Nobody asked you to come," answered Silvermane, who sat in the pilot's chair, meticulously oiling and cleaning his pistols and checking his ammunition.

"I've never seen them," said Virgil, "but based on all the stories I've heard, you're wasting your time. The most a bullet or two will do is make 'em angry."

"Probably," agreed Silvermane. "But if the imploder doesn't function or doesn't work, I need fallback protection."

"Mine would be: run like hell," said the Indian.

"That's why I'm Santiago and you're not."

Dante hadn't taken his eyes off the screen. "Seven degrees Celsius, one-point-one-seven times Standard gravity, not much oxygen." He sighed deeply. "So you can't use your speed, you can't stand a sustained battle, and you're not going to be able to work up a sweat. Are you sure you don't want to wait until I can mobilize some of the people on Hadrian?"

"If *I* can't defeat them, *they* can't either."

"I see that being Santiago is not necessatily conducive to modesty," noted Virgil wryly.

"They've destroyed entire armies," shot back Silvermane. "There's no reason to believe two hundred yokels
from Hadrian will turn the tide of battle. I'm the best there
is. Either I can beat them or I can't." He turned to Moby
Dick. "It's about time you told me what you know about
them."

"I know they're undefeated," said the albino.

"So is every man out here who carries a weapon."

"They don't carry weapons."

"Oh?" said Silvermane. "What did they do to get you to
work for them?"

"Nothing."

Silvermane's face mirrored his contempt. "You gave in
without a fight?"

"They didn't conquer me," answered Moby Dick. "They
dealt with me."

"And you dealt with the enemy."

"I thought the Democracy was the enemy," said Moby
Dick. "Or is the enemy whoever you're mad at this week?"

"You're here under sufferance," said Silvermane coldly.
"Don't forget it."

"Fine," said the albino. "Give me back my imploder and
I'll leave."

Silvermane stared coldly at him but made no reply.

"Got it!" said Dante, still looking at the screen. "Increase
the image and sharpen it," he commanded, and suddenly a
small fortress came into view. It was made of local stone,
poorly constructed, unimpressive from any angle. "Bring
that up in three dimensions, and give us a three-hundred-
and-sixty-degree view of it, then give us an overhead."

"That doesn't look like it'd keep anyone out," remarked
Virgil, studying the image.

"It won't," said Moby Dick.

"Then what—?"

"They have hostages," interrupted the albino. "It was
built to keep *them* in."

"Computer, take us down," commanded Silvermane.

"Land us four hundred yards due south of the fortress that's on your screen."

"The terrain is too uneven," replied the ship. "There is a flat area that will accommodate my bulk four hundred and twenty-seven yards south-southeast of the fortress. Will that be acceptable?"

"Do it."

The ship broke out of orbit and headed toward the planet. A few moments later it touched down on the precise spot the computer had pinpointed.

"Computer," said Silvermane, "I want you to analyze the area immediately surrounding the ship."

"Done."

"I oxygenated my blood just before we took off from Hadrian II, and I have injected adrenaline into my system. I've let you take readings of both. Is there anything else I should do to prepare myself for extreme physical exertion on the planet's surface?"

"Please wait while I scan you. . . . Done. I recommend the following vitamins and amphetamines . . ." The computer reeled off a small catalog of pills.

"Get 'em ready," said Silvermane, getting up and walking toward the galley. A small packet of pills appeared and he swallowed them all, washing them down with a mouthful of distilled water.

Then he turned to his three shipmates.

"I didn't want you here," he said, "and I won't waste any effort protecting you. If you have any survival instincts at all, you'll remain on board." He looked at each in turn. "I can't force you to behave intelligently. Just know that if you climb down onto the planet's surface, you're on your own—and I don't want any of you near me."

"Agreed," said Moby Dick.

"I got no problem with that," added Virgil.

Dante was silent.

"I'm waiting, Rhymer," said Silvermane.

"If there's a chance to rescue September Morn, I'm going to try."

"No."

"That *is* what we're here for," insisted Dante.

"We're here for me to face the aliens."

"Only because they kidnapped September Morn," said Dante. "There's no other reason for you to be here or to have ever contacted them."

"I'm here because no one challenges Santiago."

"Yeah," said Dante, unimpressed. "Well, *I'm* here because they've kidnapped the woman who saved my life."

Silvermane stared at him for a long time. It was a stare designed to make him back off. Dante stared right back, unblinking.

Finally the tall man shrugged. "Have it your way," he said, breaking eye contact. "Just make sure you don't get between me and them."

"I don't intend to."

Silvermane turned back to Moby Dick. "And there's nothing more you can tell me about them?"

"Their conquests are a matter of record. I didn't require any demonstrations."

"Maybe you should have. Then at least I'd know exactly what I'm going up against."

"Well, if I'd known you felt that way," replied the albino, "I'd have asked them to level Trajan so I could tell you what to expect."

Silvermane glared at him. "You're not much help."

"I gave you the imploder," Moby Dick shot back. "Show me anyone else who's helped you as much."

Silvermane made no reply. Instead, he picked up the molecular imploder, checked his pistols one last time, then commanded the hatch to open, and ordered the stairs to transport him to the planet's surface.

Dante was about to follow him when he felt Moby Dick's hand on his arm.

"Let him get a few hundred yards ahead of you," cautioned the albino.

"Then you *do* know what their powers are!" said Dante accusingly.

Moby Dick shook his head. "No, I truly don't. But if they're formidable enough to conquer an army, you really don't want to be standing next to him."

"I'll be careful," Dante assured him. "I'm not here to fight anyone. I just want to rescue September Morn."

"You may not have any choice once you leave the ship."

"If Santiago risks his life, how can his followers do any less?"

"That man's not Santiago," said Moby Dick with absolute conviction.

"He's got to be," said Dante. He gave the albino a weak smile. "We're all out of candidates." He turned to Virgil. "Are you coming?"

"It all depends," said the Indian.

"On what?"

"On you," replied Virgil.

"On me?" said Dante, surprised.

"*Him* I don't follow; *you* I do."

"He's *my* leader," said the poet. "I'm going out."

"Then I guess I'm going out too," said Virgil unhappily.

"Then I guess you are," said Dante. He turned to Moby Dick. "How about you?"

"They won't harm me. I work for them, remember?"

"Then let's go."

Moby Dick looked out. "He could have set it down closer. That's a long way to walk in *any* gravity."

"What are you talking about?" said Dante. "We're only a quarter of a mile away."

"When you're built like me, a quarter of a mile is too much even at Earth-Standard gravity," muttered Moby Dick unhappily. "I should have brought a gravity mat."

"It's too late now," said the poet.

"You two go ahead," said the albino. "I'll follow along at my own pace."

Dante and Virgil stepped through the hatch, waited until the top stair gently lowered them to the ground, looked around to get their bearings, and spotted Silvermane walking toward the fortress. The poet wasn't inclined to wait until the tall man got there before starting to cross the planet's surface, so he headed off to his right on the assumption that he'd be just as safe, or unsafe, two hundred yards to Silvermane's right as two hundred yards behind him.

There was no sign of life in the fortress, and Dante began wondering if it was a trap.

He must have said it aloud, because Virgil responded: "Of course it's a trap. I just don't know what kind. If the place is as deserted as it looks, it could be rigged to blow up the second Silvermane sets foot in it."

"His name's Santiago," muttered Dante, never taking his eyes off the fortress.

And suddenly, standing in front of it, was a large blue being, some ten feet tall, vaguely humanoid in shape, very broad and heavily muscled, totally nude. Its eyes were large and glowed a brilliant yellow, its nose was a quartet of horizontal slits, its mouth seemed to be filled with scores of brownish, decaying teeth, its ears were shaped like small trumpets. It wore no weapons.

"Where the hell did *that* come from?" whispered Virgil.

"It just materialized."

"So is it Tweedledee or Tweedledum?"

"How the hell do I know?" snapped Dante.

Silvermane took a step closer. "You wanted me," he said. "I'm here. Where's the woman?"

The creature made no reply, and suddenly the imploder was in Silvermane's hands, aimed at the blue being. Its lips still didn't move, but the four humans seemed to hear a deep voice within their heads.

"I am the Tweedle," it said. *"You have intruded upon my world."*

"There are two of you," said Silvermane, looking around. "Where's the other one?"

"He is here when I need him," said the Tweedle.

"Turn over the woman, or you're going to need him pretty damned soon," said Silvermane.

"You think to impress me with your talk?"

"No. I think to kill you with my weapon."

"*Alone, I am a target,*" said the Tweedle. "*But I am never alone.*"

And suddenly it seemed to split right down the middle. An instant later there were two identical Tweedles, both confronting Silvermane. They moved a few feet apart as they spoke, silently but in unison, with similar though not identical telepathic voices.

"*I am the last of my kind,*" said the Tweedles. "*All the others died in warfare or of disease or old age. I alone have survived, for I alone have learned how to release my doppelganger, and by freeing him I have freed all the powers that lay dormant within myself and every other member of my race. Together there is nothing we cannot do. Does the terrain hurt your tender feet? Then behold.*"

The Tweedles moved their left arms in a theatrical gesture, and suddenly the ground between the fortress and the ship was totally flat.

"*Do you peer in the darkness with dilated pupils?*" continued the Tweedles.

Suddenly the area was bathed in light, so bright that the humans had to squint to adjust to it.

"*Perhaps you shiver with the cold.*"

Another gesture, and suddenly the temperature was a pleasant 22 degrees Celsius.

"*We would change the gravity and the atmosphere, but it would deleteriously affect you after the various medications that we see you have taken into your body.*" They smiled at him. "*Do you still wish to match your strength and skills against ours?*"

"All I've seen are some parlor tricks," said Silvermane, trying his best to sound unimpressed. "You could have rigged them all before we arrived. But if you will produce the woman and turn her over to me, and promise never to bother her or her planet again, I will leave in peace."

"Is he crazy?" whispered Virgil to Dante.

"He's bluffing," answered the poet just as softly.

"You can't bluff these two," said Moby Dick, who had

just joined them seconds ago. The albino was panting heavily from his exertions.

"You are a very courageous being. But we have killed courageous beings before."

"You've never faced Joshua Silvermane before," said the tall man.

"Moby Dick was right," muttered Dante. "He'll never be Santiago."

"Makes no difference," whispered Virgil. "They're going to kill him no matter what name he gives them."

Silvermane aimed the imploder at the being on his left. The weapon hummed with power, but had no effect.

He instantly dropped the imploder, drew his pistols and began emptying them, one into each of the Tweedles.

The bullets didn't pass through them, for the Tweedles weren't transparent images with no substance. The bullets entered them, left discernible entry holes, but had no more effect that the imploder. Their bodies simply absorbed whatever he threw at them.

Then each of the beings slowly raised an arm. Nothing more than that. But Silvermane dropped to his knees, obviously in agony. The pistols dropped from his hands and clattered noisily on the rocky ground.

The one on the left made a sudden gesture, and blood began pouring out of Silvermane's ears. He staggered to his feet to face his attackers. The one on the right slowly closed his hand into a fist, and Silvermane clawed at his chest, as if the alien were squeezing his heart.

Finally, with one last effort that took all his remaining strength, Silvermane pulled a knife out of his boot and hurled himself at the creature on his right—and froze in midair, his body suspended four feet above the ground, his knife hand extended, his perfect face filled with hatred. The two creatures made one final gesture in unison, and Joshua Silvermane fell to the ground, headless. His head wasn't severed; it simply vanished. His body twitched once or twice, then lay still as bright red blood gushed out of it.

"Jesus!" muttered Dante. "Did you ever see anything like that?"

"Only during bad trips," answered Virgil, unable to tear his eyes away from the scene.

Moby Dick stepped forward. "I tried to warn him," said the albino.

"That is because you are a rational being, and hence a coward. It stands to reason that you could not dissuade this Silvermane, who was a brave and hence irrational being, from confronting us."

"That's not quite the way I would have worded it," said Moby Dick.

"How you would have worded it is of no interest to us." The creatures turned toward Dante and Virgil. *"Who are you, and why are you here?"*

"I am a friend of September Morn," said Dante. "I want to be sure that she is in good health, and is being well treated."

"I'm with him," added Virgil.

"She is healthy."

"May I see her?"

"No. We will permit you to gather your companion's body and leave Kabal III with it. You may not return."

"Before we do, I have a question," said Virgil.

All eyes turned to him.

"Which of you is Tweedledee and which is Tweedledum, and how can I tell you apart?"

"We did not choose those names."

"I'd like to know anyway, just out of curiosity."

"Your curiosity is of no concern to us."

And, as quickly and easily as they had split in two, they now joined in a fraction of a second and became simply the Tweedle once more.

"What do you propose to do with September Morn?" persisted Dante.

"We will give Hadrian II twenty Galactic Standard days to ransom her for five billion credits."

"That's a lot of money," said Dante. "What if they can't come up with it?"

"Then we shall kill her."

40.

HE FELT THE CALL TO SERVE HIS GOD,
HIS INDISCRETIONS QUICKLY CEASED.
NOW SINNERS ALL ARE THREATENED BY
DEUTERONOMY PRIEST.

"DO YOU GET THE FEELING we're back where we started?"
asked Virgil, as he sat in the Fat Chance with Dante and
Moby Dick, sipping a drink and watching a trio of Can-
phorites squabbling over the result of a nearby *jabob* game.
"We don't have a Santiago, we don't have September
Morn, Dimitrios is dead, and who the hell knows where
Matilda is? Maybe we should have anointed Tyrannosaur
Bailey and let it go at that. Look at the time we could have
saved."

"Shut up," said Dante.

"Every time I've opened my mouth since we got here
you've told me to shut up," complained Virgil.

"I'm thinking."

"Leave him alone," said Moby Dick. "Your friend's at
his best when he's thinking."

"I don't notice that thinking's done us any good," said
Virgil.

"That's because you're a fool," said the albino.

"Could be," agreed Virgil. "But what gives you the right
to say so?"

"You've still got an organization. You've got millions of
credits. You've got a couple of hundred operatives. And
from what I can tell, you've eliminated two unsuccessful
candidates for the top job. That's not bad for six or eight
months, or however long the poet's been out here."

"We're not in the business of eliminating Santiagos,"
said Virgil. "We're trying like all hell to find one."

"One will manifest himself," said Moby Dick. "And if

not, you can still plunder the Democracy six ways to Sunday."

"That's more or less my own line of thought," said Virgil. "We're been spending too much time searching and not enough plundering."

"Shut up," said Dante.

"Just what the hell is your problem, Rhymer?" demanded Virgil angrily.

"We need a diversion," said Dante to no one in particular.

"What are you talking about?"

"September Morn."

"Forget her. You saw Tweedledee and Tweedledum. There ain't no way you're going to get her back without five billion credits. Either the planet antes up or she's dead meat."

"Shut up."

"Fuck you!" snapped Virgil. "Now that I know what you've been thinking about, I don't feel any need to kowtow to you. Even if you steal her back, all you've done is sign a death warrant for the whole goddamned planet."

"You're a fool," said Dante.

The Indian looked annoyed. "Maybe you should talk to the whale here, since that's all either of you can say to me."

"Do you really think you can rescue her without catastrophic repercussions?" asked Moby Dick.

"Of course," said Dante distractedly. "Avoiding repercussions is the easy part."

"No more drinks for him," said Virgil. "He's had enough."

"Shut up," said Moby Dick.

"Are you guys brothers?" said Virgil disgustedly.

"Go out back and molest one of the servo-mechs," said Moby Dick. "I'll let you know if you're needed."

Virgil stared at him. "You're kidding, right?"

"Am I smiling?" replied the albino.

"I never had a servo-mech before," said Virgil. "How does one . . . ah . . . ?"

"You're a creative sort of pervert. You'll figure it out."

Virgil got to his feet. "Talk some sense into him while I'm gone." He headed off toward the back door, and a moment later was out of the building.

Moby Dick ordered his chair to glide closer to Dante's. Once there he laid a hand on the poet's shoulder. "Take a break, Rhymer. All you're going to do is give yourself a headache. There's no way to beat the Tweedle."

"Oh, I know how to do that," said Dante distractedly. "It's the other details I'm having trouble with."

The albino stared at him. "You *really* think you know how to defeat them?"

"Yeah—but I have to go to Kabal III first."

"Go back? Why?"

"I've got to get September Morn off the world before I do anything else." Dante paused, still staring at his untouched drink. "*That's* the tricky part. Everything else follows from that."

"If you know how to kill Tweedledee and Tweedledum, kill 'em first and then get the girl."

Dante shook his head. "I can't."

"I don't suppose you'd care to tell me why?"

"Wait until I work it all out," said Dante. "Damn! I wish Matilda was here. She can spot the flaws in a scheme quicker than anyone."

"So send for her."

"It'll take her seven or eight days to get out here, and if I'm wrong, we don't have time to come up with a different scheme. They gave Hadrian twenty days to come up with the money—and that was two days ago."

"You can talk to her on the subspace radio," suggested Moby Dick.

"I will, once I work out all the details."

"Just how the hell many details are there? Either you can rescue her or you can't."

Dante finally looked up, as if paying attention to him for the first time. "You don't understand," he said at last.

"Enlighten me."

"Rescuing September Morn is just the first step."

"And killing the aliens is the last, I know."

Dante shook his head. "No, that's just another step along the way."

"What the hell are you talking about?" asked Moby Dick.

"I came out here to accomplish something," said Dante. "I've been so busy trying to do it piecemeal that I lost sight of the whole."

"All right," said Moby Dick. "I know better than to argue with a genius when he's working."

"I'm no genius," said Dante. "I'm just a guy who doesn't want to go back to being Danny Briggs."

"Who's Danny Briggs?"

"An unimportant thief who never did a memorable thing in his life."

There was a brief silence.

"You mentioned a diversion before," said the albino. "What kind of diversion? Is there some way I can help?"

"I need something or someone that can entice the Tweedles a few hundred miles from their fortress," replied Dante. He grimaced. "That's going under the assumption that they can't teleport. If they can change locations instantaneously, then I can't save her."

"Or kill them."

Dante looked annoyed. "Killing them is the easy part."

"There are a couple of million corpses strewn around the Frontier that would disagree about killing them being the easy part," said Moby Dick.

"They went about it wrong," said Dante. "If I can get them three hundred miles away, maybe they won't see me land. Even if they *can* teleport, they have to have a reason to do so. If they're far enough away, they won't have one."

"We can fly low and drop some explosives three hundred miles away," said the albino. "Or five hundred, or eight hundred, if that's what you want."

Dante shook his head. "Then they'll come after the ship. I have to get them to leave the fortress and give me time to get September Morn out."

Suddenly Moby Dick smiled. "I think I've got the solution to your problems."

Dante looked at him expectantly.

"Did you ever hear of Deuteronomy Priest?" continued the huge man.

"No."

"He preaches all over the Inner Frontier. Last I heard, maybe three weeks ago, he wasn't too far from here. I think I can have him on Hadrian in two Standard days, maybe less if his preaching has taken him in this direction."

"Then what?"

The albino grinned. "Then we turn him loose on Kabal III."

"There's got to be more to it than that," said Dante. "Tell me about this Deuteronomy Priest."

"He's a hellfire-and-damnation preacher the likes of which I'll wager you've never seen. Used to be a male prostitute, of all things. Then he got the call, and now no sinner is safe from his ministrations, which mostly take the form of rather unpleasant predictions about the particularly nasty afterlife awaiting you if you don't repent." Moby Dick paused. "And since almost no alien has ever been baptized, they've become his special project."

"Let me get this straight," said Dante. "He's a preacher. He's not a bounty hunter, like legend says Father William was. He doesn't carry weapons, just invectives?"

"You got it," said Moby Dick. "If we land him next to the fortress, they'll probably kill him before his ship touches down. At any rate, you won't be able to sneak in." Suddenly he grinned again. "But what if we program his ship to land a thousand miles away, give it a state-of-the-art communication system, something that'll carry his voice a hundred miles or more, and tell him to start preaching?"

"The Tweedle would want to see what the hell's going on," continued Dante excitedly. "And once he got there, he'd probably be more curious than deadly. He'd want to know what this guy is carrying on about before he kills him." He closed his eyes, did some quick calculations, then looked at the albino. "Even if the Tweedles can get there in five minutes, if Priest can keep them amused or interested or even just curious for another five minutes before they kill him or leave him alone, that's bought me a quarter of an hour. If we monitor them, I can land when they're halfway to Priest. The fortress isn't that big. I'll bring sensors, she can yell, one way or another I can find her in a couple of minutes, and I can blast her out of any cell she's in." Suddenly he frowned. "Only one problem. Will the Tweedle show up on our ship's sensors? Is he so alien that it won't be able to read where he's at? After all, Silvermane's ship didn't find any sign of life when we landed."

"I didn't think of that," admitted Moby Dick.

"It's not your job to," said Dante. "All right, we'll just have to assume the Tweedles become aware of him almost as soon as he lands. Now, will they go there immediately, or will they stay put and see if he's waiting for allies?"

"They don't worry about losing battles," said Moby Dick. "I think they'll go right away."

"I agree," said Dante. "If they can't teleport, how soon can they get there?"

"The planet's got a heavy atmosphere. Whatever kind of vehicle they're using, if they go too fast they'll burn up. Let's land him a thousand miles away and give them six minutes to get there. Maybe it'll take them an hour, but I sure as hell doubt it."

"Okay, I'll just have to assume they act like rational beings and show a little curiosity."

"And if they don't?"

"Then I'll have to do some mighty fast talking when they ask me what I'm doing there," said Dante.

"Is there anything else?"

"Lots," replied the poet. "But let's see if your preacher's available first."

"Let me get to the radio and I'll contact him," said Moby Dick, relaxing as his chair gently changed shapes and helped lift his huge bulk onto his feet.

Dante suddenly realized that he hadn't slept the night

before, that he'd been sitting here at the table for almost twenty hours working out all the ramifications of his plan. Suddenly he could barely keep his eyes open, and he went back to his room at the Windsor Arms. He didn't even bother taking his clothes off or climbing under the covers. He just collapsed on the bed, and was asleep ten seconds later.

When he awoke, he felt like he'd just come out of the Deepsleep pod. All his muscles ached, and he was starving. He looked at the timepiece on his nightstand: he'd been asleep for twenty-two hours.

His mouth felt dry and sour, and he wandered into the bathroom, drank a glass of cold water, threw some more on his face, took a quick shower, rubbed a handful of depilatory cream on his face, climbed into the robe the hotel had supplied, and went back to the bedroom. He put on fresh clothes, and was considering having breakfast delivered to his room when the security system told him he had visitors. The moment he saw that one of them weighed in excess of five hundred pounds, he commanded the door to dilate.

"I trust you slept as well as you slept long," said an amused Moby Dick, stepping into the room.

Accompanying him was a pale, thin, almost emaciated man with piercing blue eyes, an aquiline nose, and thin lips above a pointed chin. He was dressed all in black, except for a glowing, diamond-studded silver cross that hung around his neck.

"Dante Alighieri, allow me to introduce you to Deuteronomy Priest," continued the albino.

"Pleased to meet you," said Dante, staring at the strange-looking man.

"More pleased than this fucking alien will be, I can promise you that," said Deuteronomy Priest in a vigorous voice that seemed much too powerful for his body. "The blue bastard will never be the same. Once I convert the fuckers, they *stay* converted!"

Dante looked at Moby Dick with an expression that seemed to say: *Is this a joke?*

Moby Dick grinned back so happily that Dante knew it wasn't a joke at all, that this was the person September Morn's—and his own—life depended on.

"You got anything to drink?" asked the preacher, looking around the room.

"Sorry," said Dante.

"What the hell kind of hotel doesn't supply booze for its guests?" groused Deuteronomy Priest. He looked up. "How about drugs?"

"I don't have any."

"What the hell are you good for?" muttered the preacher. He walked to the door. "I'll be back in the casino. Let me know when we're ready to read the riot act to this alien bastard."

And with that, he was gone.

"I wish you could see your face right now!" chuckled Moby Dick.

"Is this guy for real?" said Dante.

"He's perfect for the job," answered the albino. "Nothing in the world can shut him up or scare him. Once he touches down, he's the one person you can be sure won't be tempted to cut and run when the Tweedles confront him. Hell, he might actually convert them!"

"Just keep him sober enough to stand up and talk once he gets there."

"When are we leaving?"

"Not for a week, maybe even a bit longer."

"That long?"

"We've got a lot of work to do first."

"We do?"

"Matilda and I have built a formidable organization. In Santiago's absence, I'm going to put it to work—and you're going to help."

"Just who are you going to war with, besides the Tweedle?" asked Moby Dick.

"No one. The key to survival is avoiding wars, not fighting them."

"Then what are you going to do?"

"Arrange a war between two other parties," answered Dante.

41.

HE KILLED A MAN BY ACCIDENT, THEN TWO,
   THEN SIX, THEN TEN.
HE'S GOT TO WHERE HE LIKES IT, AND LONGS
   TO KILL AGAIN.
HIS NAME IS ACCIDENTAL BARNES, HE
   CANNOT LOSE THAT YEN—
HIS WEAPON IS THE CROSSBOW, HIS GAME IS
   KILLING MEN.

DANTE ARRANGED FOR THE HOTEL to give Deuteronomy Priest the presidential suite, and put Moby Dick in charge of him. Then he went back to his own room and raised the Grand Finale on the subspace radio.

"Well, hello, Rhymer," said Wilbur Connaught's image as it flickered into existence. "I haven't heard from you in a while. How are you?"

"I'm fine, thanks," replied Dante.

"What's all this I hear about someone called Silvermane taking over?"

"Forget it. He's dead."

"Then I still report to the Bandit?"

"He's dead, too."

Wilbur frowned. "Who's left?"

"Until we find another Santiago, you'll report to me," said Dante. "But that's not what I'm contacting you about. You've been operating inside the Democracy for a few months now. Have you got three or four men or women, also within the Democracy, that you can trust?"

"Four for sure. Maybe five."

"Stick to the sure ones."

"Okay," said Wilbur, lighting a smokeless cigar. "What do you want them to do?"

"I want them to spread out, thousands of parsecs from

each other. And I want each of them, independently, to report to the Navy that an alien entity that calls itself the Tweedle was responsible for slaughtering all those children in the Madras system, that it's been bragging about it all across the Inner Frontier."

"Didn't the Bandit do that?"

"That's one crime Santiago doesn't need the credit for," answered Dante. "Once the Democracy has someone to blame, they'll be out in force."

"Okay, so we'll lay the blame on this alien. I assume you have a reason?"

"I do. Now listen to me, and capture and save this conversation, because if you mess up the details you've killed me." Dante paused. "Are you ready?"

"Shoot."

"I want you and each of your people to inform the Navy, all independently of each other, that no one knows where the Tweedle lives, but they know it will be on Kabal III, on the Inner Frontier, six days from now, for a payoff. It's a very cautious creature, and it travels with its own army. It will arrive at a fortress that's at latitude thirty-two degrees, seventeen minutes, and thirty-two seconds north, and longitude eight degrees, four minutes, and eleven seconds east. It will show up exactly two hours after sunrise at the fortress—my computer tells me that's 1426 Galactic Standard time, keyed to Deluros VIII; make sure you tell them that—and it'll be gone ten minutes later. The planet is uninhabited. The only way to defeat the Tweedle is to pound the whole fucking planet until there's nothing left of it."

"You're giving yourself an awfully small window, Rhymer," noted Wilbur.

"Any earlier and they'll kill me and someone who's working with me. Any later and the Tweedle almost certainly *will* be gone, and I hate to think of what it'll do to Hadrian if it gets away from Kabal."

"I'll take your word for it."

"Can you convince the Navy to do it?" asked Dante. "Everything depends on that."

"Probably. I'm not without my connections—and you haven't been back here since Madras. It's still in the news every day. They've been looking for the culprit ever since it happened. Our pal the Bandit didn't leave any clues."

"I'll be in touch with you in five and a half days. I can still call it off then, if you don't think the Navy's bought your story."

Dante broke the connection, then left the room, took the airlift down to the main floor, and took a slidewalk over to the Fat Chance. Moby Dick was sitting at his usual table, and Dante quickly joined him.

"Is your preacher going to hold up for six days?" he asked by way of greeting.

"He's been abusing his body with bad booze and worse drugs for the better part of thirty years now," answered the huge albino. "I don't imagine another few days will make much difference."

"I hope you're right," said Dante. "I've got another job for you."

"What is it?"

"Find me an engineer. I want to be able to operate Priest's ship from a thousand miles away."

"What's the matter with autopilot?"

"Nothing, once he's taken off. In fact, I want it programmed to take him to some uninhabited world—but I have to be able to make it take off when *I* want it to."

The albino frowned. "Why an uninhabited world?"

"If my plan goes wrong, the Tweedle is going to be chasing one or the other of us, and I don't intend for either of us to lead them to Hadrian or any other populated world."

Moby Dick grinned. "He's gonna be that pissed, is he?"

"That's a pretty fair assessment," agreed Dante.

"I take it you're really going to go back for September Morn?"

"That's right."

"How much time do you think you'll have before the Tweedle knows you're there and tries to stop you?"

"I don't know. Five minutes. Ten at the outside."

"Then I want you to take a friend of mine along."

Dante looked sharply at him. "Oh?"

"He's as brave as they come, he can help you look for her, and if it gets rough, he'll be another distraction. It might just buy you the extra few seconds you need."

"I'll be taking Virgil."

"Take my friend, too," urged the huge man. "You're telling me you've only got five minutes. The more people you have trying to find where he's stashed her, the better."

"I hope *you're* not going to volunteer, too," said Dante with a smile. "It'd take you ten minutes just to get from the ship to the fortress, even if I land right next to it."

"I know my strengths and I know my weaknesses," said Moby Dick. "I'm staying right here."

"All right. Who's your friend?"

"Did you ever hear of Accidental Barnes?"

"It sounds like a joke."

"There's nothing funny about him."

"It's the name that's amusing."

"He killed his first man by accident," said Moby Dick. "He killed his next thirty on purpose. If things get nasty, you'll be glad you've got him with you. He's certainly more use than that goddamned Indian." He grimaced. "You know, none of my servo-mechs have worked since yesterday."

Dante chuckled. "I seem to remember you suggesting that he pay them a visit."

"Only because I never thought he'd do it!" snapped Moby Dick. Suddenly all the alien gamblers stopped what they were doing and stared at him. "Go back to your games," he said in a more reasonable tone of voice. "Nothing's wrong." He turned back to Dante. "I don't know why you let him hang around. He's useless."

"That useless man may possess some tastes that you and I disagree with," answered Dante, "but he's as deadly a killer as Dimitrios was. And he's totally loyal to me. If there's a better reason to let him hang around, I can't think of it."

"Point taken," acknowledged Moby Dick.

"Now, where is this Accidental Barnes?"

"He's staying at your hotel. He arrived while we were off visiting the Tweedle."

"What's he doing here?"

"Gambling," said the albino. "He doesn't need the money, but he enjoys the challenge."

Dante looked around. "So why isn't he here?"

"This casino is for aliens."

"Nobody's ever stopped me from entering."

"He can enter it any time he wants, but we don't have any human games, and he prefers them." Moby Dick signaled to a Mollutei, which ambulated over and stood in front of him. The albino spoke in an alien tongue for a moment, and then the alien left the casino. "I've just sent for him. He should be here in a few minutes."

They waited in silence, and five minutes later a short, stocky man with spiky blond hair and a bushy beard, blond but streaked with white, entered the casino. He looked around, spotted Moby Dick, and walked over.

"Dante, this is Accidental Barnes, the man I was telling you about."

Dante extended a hand, which Barnes accepted.

"Got a job for you," continued Moby Dick. "How would you like to ride shotgun on a rescue mission against Tweedledee and Tweedledum?"

"Tweedledee and Tweedledum?" repeated Barnes. "Nice to know you're not thinking small. What's it pay?"

"Nothing if we fail, bragging rights if we win," said Dante.

"You're asking me to go up against the most dangerous pair of aliens on the Frontier," said Barnes. "And I didn't hear any mention of money."

"You're not going to. They've kidnapped a woman. I plan to rescue her. We'll be in and out in five minutes, or we're dead. Moby Dick volunteered you. I don't *need* your help, but I'd like it."

"And you're not paying anything at all?" said Barnes.

"The woman is September Morn," said Moby Dick.

Barnes's entire demeanor changed. "Why didn't you say so in the first place? I'm in."

"You know her?"

"She's as close to royalty as this sector has produced," answered Barnes. "If the Inner Frontier ever gets civilized, it's going to be because of people like her, not you and me."

"The question is whether we *want* it to be civilized," interjected Moby Dick. "Most of us came out here to get away from civilization."

"We came here to get away from the Democracy, which isn't the same thing," replied Dante.

"I agree," said Barnes. "And whether the whale here likes it or not, sooner or later we *are* going to get civilized." He turned to Dante. "Where are Tweedledee and Tweedledum keeping her, and when do we strike?"

"I'll tell you the planet as soon as I know where it is," said Dante. "We'll leave in four or five days."

"Count me in." Barnes got to his feet. "Nice meeting you. You can find me at the Windsor Arms."

Barnes left the casino.

"Why didn't you tell him she's on Kabal III?" asked Moby Dick.

"You heard him. He thinks she's royalty. He wanted money until he found out we're after September Morn, and now he's willing to risk his life for free. If I tell him where she is, I don't think he'll wait until I'm ready."

"So what if he goes early?"

"He'll get us all killed," answered Dante firmly.

"Are you sure this is going to work?" asked Moby Dick.

"No," said the poet. "If everyone does what I tell them to do, I'm sure it *ought* to work, but that's not the same thing."

Dante went back to his room, contacted a few more peo-

ple he knew and trusted in the Democracy, and gave them
the same instructions he'd given to Wilbur.

He then spent four days trying not to think about what
was coming. He arose each day, ate breakfast, and took
long drives through the countryside, avoiding Virgil, Moby
Dick, and Accidental Barnes whenever he could, and just
trying to relax and ease the tension that was gnawing at his
stomach.

Finally, on the morning of the fifth day, he contacted
Wilbur again.

"How are we doing?" he asked.

"So far so good," answered the accountant. "I had to
spread a little money around, just to be on the safe side.
As things stand now, they'll blow the whole fucking planet
at exactly 1435 Standard time. You got any more instructions?"

"One very important one," said Dante. "I'm flying a four-
man Silver Meteor, registration GF-five-three-one-four-GL.
I want you to alert the Navy that I'm the guy who located
the Tweedle, and that I'll be taking off like a bat out of
hell just a minute or two before they're due to strike. I don't
want them jumping the gun while I'm on the planet, and I
don't want them mistaking me for the Tweedle and blowing
me out of the sky while I'm racing away from Kabal. Can
you do that?"

"Easy."

"I want you to be very sure, Wilbur. If you screw this
up, you'll kill me."

"Trust me," said the accountant. "I haven't let you down
yet, have I?"

"So far all you've done is make money. This is a little
more important to me."

"I'll take care of it, Rhymer."

"If you don't, I'll haunt you from the grave."

"If I don't, there won't be enough left of you and your
ship to put in a grave."

"All the more reason to do it right," said Dante. "Oh,
one more thing. There's another ship that will be leaving

when mine does. It belongs to a preacher named Deuteronomy Priest, and they're not to fire on it, either. I'll get back to you with the registration number later today. Over and out."

He walked over to the Fat Chance and roused Moby Dick from his formfitting support chair.

"Get the preacher over to the spaceport," he said. "His ship is programmed to land on Kabal, one thousand miles due south of the fortress, at exactly 1408 Standard time. It won't activate the communicators until then." He paused. "I know your engineer gave me a remote control for his ship. Is there anything I need to know about it?"

"Just press the yellow button," said the albino. "Easy as that."

"Okay, get him onto his ship."

Moby Dick went to the hotel to pick up Deuteronomy Priest, and Dante allowed himself the luxury of one last breakfast at a real restaurant before he was reduced to eating the food from his ship's galley.

Then he contacted Virgil and Barnes and told them to meet him at his ship. When they arrived Dante stared at Barnes' weapon.

"What the hell is *that*?" he demanded.

"A crossbow."

"I thought they were obsolete four or five millennia ago," said Dante.

"That was before we were able to create bolts with nuclear devices in their tips," said Barnes, lovingly patting his quiver.

"Okay, bring it aboard."

They took off a few minutes later, and came to a stop when they were half a light-year from Kabal.

"Let me check one last time and make sure everything's on schedule," Dante announced. He contacted the Grand Finale and his other agents, received positive reports from them, and finally shut down the radio. He ordered the ship to resume flight, and instructed the navigational computer to land as close as possible to the fortress at precisely 1416

Standard time—ten minutes after the preacher landed, and ten minutes before the Navy arrived. He considered arming himself, but decided any weapon he could carry would be useless against the Tweedle.

The three of them spent the next hour with their eyes glued to the chronometer. Finally the ship began descending to the planet's surface. Dante had the sensors try to pick up any form of life other than Deuteronomy Priest, who had landed six minutes earlier, but nothing showed up.

"You'd better be right about where they are and how fast they can travel," said Virgil, also staring at the sensor panel.

"If I'm not, we'll know it soon enough," answered Dante, passing out communicators. "Make sure to keep in constant touch with each other. We haven't got much time."

The ship touched down fifty yards from the fortress, precisely on schedule.

"Well, at least he's not perfect," commented Dante.

"What do you mean?"

"We're right next to the fortress," he said. "Last time we were here he leveled the ground just to impress us, and he's forgotten to let it revert to its natural jagged surface."

He stepped through the hatch, waited impatiently for his companions to join him, and let the platform lower them to the ground.

"I'll take the west side. Virgil, you take the east. Barnes, you're riding shotgun, just in case there's something waiting for us. If there's nothing there, walk straight through and check the north end."

They entered the fortress, half-expecting to bump headfirst into the Tweedle. It seemed deserted.

"September Morn!" he yelled as he turned to his left and entered a darkened corridor. "If you can hear me, speak up!"

No answer.

"It's Dante Alighieri!"

Silence.

"I'm in a corridor on the east side," said Virgil. "There aren't any doors."

"No opposition," said Barnes, checking in. "I'm heading to the south wall."

Dante continued walking, afraid to spend too much time examining his surroundings and simultaneously afraid that if he went too fast he could go right past September Morn.

"Virgil here. Still nothing."

"Ditto," said Barnes.

"Damn it!" said Dante. "We've only got seven or eight minutes left."

"I'm going as fast as I can," said Virgil. "It's not exactly a maze, but I still can't find any doors."

"Me neither," said Barnes. Then, suddenly: "Wait a minute! I think I've got something!"

"Where are you?" demanded Dante.

"About eighty feet from the west wall, and ten feet from the north wall. In the open—there doesn't seem to be a roof here."

It took Dante almost a minute to find it. Virgil arrived a few seconds later. Barnes was trying to move a circular slab of rock from where it sat on the ground.

"It's too perfect a circle," grunted Barnes. "Nature never made anything like that on a world like this."

Dante knelt down next to him. The two men strained to no avail, and then Virgil lent his strength, and finally the rock moved a bit, revealing a darkened chamber beneath it.

"Thank God!" said September Morn's voice.

"Hang on!" said Dante. "We'll have you out in a couple of minutes."

"Better make that less than a minute," said Virgil, his face flushed with the effort he was putting forth on the slab. "I've been counting."

The three men finally moved the slab about two feet. Then Virgil, the tallest of the three, lay on his belly and extended his arm down.

"Can you reach my hand?" he asked.

"I can't see," she said. "My eyes haven't adjusted to the light. Let me feel around."

There was a moment of tense total silence.

"Got her!" said the Indian suddenly. He began pulling her up, and suddenly stopped. "Give me a hand. I can't pull her any higher."

"Just don't let her go!" said Dante sharply, as he and Barnes stood over Virgil and slowly pulled his torso up until September Morn's hand was visible. Than Dante grabbed it and pulled her the rest of the way out, and a moment later she was standing next to them, a little weak and wobbly on her feet.

"I didn't think I'd ever see a human again," she said. Suddenly she smiled. "I'm too relieved even to cry."

"Are you strong enough to run?" asked Dante. "We haven't got much time."

"I don't know."

"Then I'll have to carry you." He picked her up. "Barnes, lead the way! Virgil, protect my back in case anything comes after us!"

"Where's the Tweedle?" she asked as Dante began running toward the ship.

"Let's hope he's hundreds of miles away," said Dante, as they raced out of the fortress.

When all four were inside the ship, he ordered the hatch to close, and then took off. He counted to thirty and pressed the yellow button that would lift Deuteronomy Priest's ship off the surface if it still existed.

"How did you manage it?" asked September Morn, still trying to focus her eyes.

"Mostly luck," answered the poet.

"Won't they be coming after us?" she asked.

"Not if things go according to plan," said Dante. "Computer, show us Kabal III on the viewscreen." He turned to her. "Can you see it?"

"Yes. My pupils are finally adjusting. I'd been down there a long time."

"Then keep an eye on the planet," said Dante.

And no sooner had he spoken than the Navy bombarded it with all the terrifying power at its disposal, and suddenly Kabal III was nothing but a spectacular light show. When the Navy left a few minutes later, nothing remained but a cloud of swirling dust.

"Is the Tweedle dead?" she asked.

"He's got to be."

"I wish I could believe that, but I don't know . . ." she said, shuddering at the thought of the creature. "It could be invulnerable to all that. For all we know, it's floating in space, already planning its revenge."

"He's dead," said Dante.

"How can you be so sure?"

"He had nostrils," said Dante. "I don't think any living being could stand up to that pounding, but even if he could, his nostrils mean he has to breathe. There's no planet, which means there's no atmosphere. He's dead, all right."

"I never thought of that!" said Virgil.

"Of course not," said September Morn, staring at the poet with open admiration. "You're not Dante Alighieri."

42.

HIS MOTHER WAS A COSMIC WIND,
HIS SIRE AN ION STORM.
HIS ARMY CHARGES STRAIGHT FROM HELL,
A FILTHY OBSCENE SWARM.
HIS SHOUT CAN LEVEL MOUNTAINS,
HIS GLANCE CAN KILL A TREE,
HIS STEP CAN CAUSE AN EARTHQUAKE,
HIS BREATH CAN BOIL THE SEA.

SEPTEMBER MORN WROTE THIS VERSE, because Dante Alighieri was much too busy to work on the poem. She imitated his style and rhymes, which were much more austere than her own lush, rich, metaphor-filled poetry, but she wrote an eight-line stanza to differentiate it from his work.

They had been back on Hadrian II for less than a day when word reached them that Wilson Tchanga, the Rough Rider, had been robbed and killed on his farm on Gingergreen II. Dante immediately sent for Virgil, who showed up in the poet's room a few minutes later.

"What's up?" asked the Indian.

"The Rough Rider's dead—murdered."

"Big deal," said Virgil. "From what I hear, he was over the hill anyway."

"As sensitive as ever," said Dante sardonically.

"I never met him" was Virgil's explanation.

"I don't care," said Dante. "I want you to get your ass out to Gingergreen II."

"What's on Gingergreen II?"

"That's where he lived."

"It's a waste of time," said Virgil. "Whoever killed him is long gone."

"Shut up and listen," said Dante. "I want you to go to Gingergreen and spread the word that Santiago robbed and killed the Rough Rider. I'm going to have Wilbur send you a hundred thousand credits, and I want you to bribe or buy three or four men who will swear they saw Santiago making his getaway from Tchanga's farm."

"What did Santiago look like?" asked Virgil. "Artificial arm or silver hair?"

"One of your men will swear he was tall, thin, and bearded. The second will say he was short, fat, and clean-shaven. And the third will claim he was an alien, eleven feet tall, with orange hair." Dante paused while Virgil assimilated his instructions. "If the locals won't put up a reward, put up one yourself. Make as much noise as you can, and when you're done on Gingergreen, hit every neighboring world with the story and the offer of the reward."

"How much should I offer?"

"It doesn't matter. Nobody's going to claim it."

"I don't understand any of this," complained Virgil.

"You don't have to understand it," sand Dante. "You just have to do it."

"How soon do I leave?"

"As soon as you can get to the spaceport."

"Well," said the Indian, "you usually know what you're doing. I suppose this will make sense to *some*one."

He turned and left.

Dante had a cup of coffee, then went down to the lobby and had the desk clerk summon a robotic rickshaw, which he took out to September Morn's house.

"Hi," he said, when she ordered the door to dilate and let him pass through. "How are you feeling today?"

"Much better, thank you," she replied. "I had to buy a new door, but otherwise the house seems intact." She paused. "My sister seems to have packed up and left. Would you know anything about that?"

"I seem to remember her expressing some interest in seeing the galaxy."

September Morn smiled. "You're a lousy liar."

"Let's hope you're a good one," said Dante.

"What are you talking about?"

"I notice that Trajan has a police department. Do they have a Neverlie Machine?"

"I suppose so. Most police departments do," said September Morn. "Why?"

"I want you to submit to it, turn it up to lethal, and make a holodisk of yourself swearing that Dimitrios was killed by Santiago."

"You're crazy!" she said. "It'll fry me in an instant!"

"No it won't," he corrected her. "You'll be telling the truth. The Bandit *was* Santiago when he killed Dimitrios."

A look of comprehension crossed her face. "He was, wasn't he?"

"Right. Can you do it?"

"I'll do it twice. Once at minimum voltage, so it just gives me a little jolt if it thinks I'm lying. Once I'm convinced that it's safe, I'll do what you want."

"Good. I'll send Accidental Barnes with you, to make sure none of the police play any games with the machine while you're in it."

"I assume there's a reason for this?"

"Just bring me the holodisk when you're done."

"All right."

He left and went back into town. Before the day was out, a huge man, taller than Silvermane and almost as broad as Moby Dick, wandered into the Fat Chance, looked around, spotted Dante sitting at a table with the albino, and approached them.

"You've come a long way and accomplished a hell of a lot, Rhymer," he said in his booming voice. "I've been hearing about you all the way back on Devonia."

Dante jumped to his feet. "Tyrannosaur Bailey!" he said. "I never thought I'd see you again."

"I never thought I'd leave Devonia—but when I heard that you killed Tweedledee and Tweedledum, I decided that you actually did what you set out to do and found Santiago, and the time had come to take a stand. You point him out to me, and I'll sign up to follow him."

"I can't," said Dante. "We've had a couple of unsuccessful candidates. But the organization is intact, and we could sure use you on our side."

"There's no Santiago?"

"At the moment."

Bailey shrugged. "What the hell—I'm here."

"Then you'll join us?"

"Yeah, I'll join you. Truth to tell, I was starting to feel a little claustrophobic back on Devonia." He paused. "So what do I do now?"

Dante stared at him for a long moment, then spoke.

"Do you really want to help?"

"I said I did."

"Then I want you to go back to Devonia—"

"I just left!" interrupted Bailey.

"Just for a short time," continued Dante.

"And what do I do once I get there?"

"Burn your tavern down."

Bailey stared at him as if he was crazy. "Do *what*?"

"You heard me. Burn it down."

"Just go home, burn it down, and leave?"

"And tell everyone who will listen that Santiago did it, and you want his head." Dante paused. "I especially want you to tell that to any member of the Democracy, or anyone who might soon be traveling to the Democracy. Can you do it?"

"Of course I can do it!"

"Good. Can you leave tonight?"

"I just got here. I plan to eat, shower with real water, and sleep in a real bed. I'll go back in the morning."

"Fair enough."

"What about you?" asked Moby Dick after Tyrannosaur Bailey had gone off in search of a meal. "You're sending everyone else off on missions. What do *you* do now?"

"Go back to Valhalla, I suppose, and see what needs taking care of," said Dante. "Matilda and the Plymouth Rocker are still there, and they probably need some help." He paused. "You might as well come along."

"Me? I've got a business to run right here."

"It'll get by without you, and we may need you to use your alien contacts on our behalf."

"For how long?"

"I don't know. A few days. Maybe a week."

"All right," agreed the albino. "I don't suppose there's any sense backing out now that we've already beaten the Tweedle."

"We'll leave in the morning."

"How about tonight?" said Moby Dick. "I've got nothing better to do. We might as well get started."

Dante shook his head. "I want to stick around to make sure Bailey leaves for Devonia. Then we'll go."

Moby Dick shrugged. "You're the boss."

"In the meantime, get hold of Deuteronomy Priest and convince him that Santiago is the Antichrist."

"And then what?"

Dante smiled. "Then turn him loose."

They took off in midmorning. During the flight, Dante contacted Wilbur Connaught and had him transfer half the money he'd raised to a numbered account on Far London. Then he climbed into a Deepsleep pod—Moby Dick was already ensconced in one—and didn't wake up until they'd broken out of orbit around Valhalla and were about to touch down.

Matilda was waiting for him, as were the Plymouth Rocker, Accidental Barnes, Blue Peter, Virgil Soaring Hawk, and dozens of other members of the organization. Even Tyrannosaur Bailey, possessed of a faster ship, was there.

"I hear you've been a busy man," said Matilda. "You look like you've lost a little weight."

"I'm lucky that's all I lost," he replied.

"The Rhymer's done pretty well to hang on to his life when so many men and aliens were trying to relieve him of it," agreed Moby Dick.

Dante introduced the albino to the assembled group, then went off to the office with Matilda, who'd gotten a description of Silvermane's death and the destruction of Kabal III but wanted all the details.

"I just love the fact that you had the Navy kill the Tweedle!" she said when he was done.

"I think it was an elegant solution," replied Dante. "They were the only ones with sufficient firepower to destroy the planet—and not only did they do our dirty work for us, but the one crime we didn't want laid at Santiago's door has been officially blamed on the Tweedle."

"And now you're getting Santiago blamed for crimes he *didn't* commit."

"We lost sight of that along the way," said Dante. "He's got to be a criminal, important enough for the Democracy to be aware of his activities, and yet not enough of a threat for them to go after him with the full force of their military might."

"The Bandit was right," said Matilda.

"About what?"

"You've got a wonderfully devious mind."

"Thank you," said Dante. "I think."

Nine days later, word filtered back to Valhalla that Devonia had posted a 500,000-credit reward for Santiago. Gingergreen II upped it to 750,000 credits the next day, and a week after that September Morn showed up, having eluded her bodyguards, with word that the Hadrian system was offering a million credits for Santiago, the killer who had murdered Dimitrios of the Three Burners in the streets of Trajan.

Before the month was out, the Democracy itself announced a reward of two million credits for the notorious Santiago, dead or alive.

"Well, everything seems to be working out," announced Dante to the rest of them at dinner that evening. "Now all that remains is to actually find our Santiago."

Moby Dick laughed.

"What's so funny?" asked Dante.

"He's right here," said the albino.

"What are you talking about?"

"Santiago," added Matilda. "He's been here all along. We've just been too blind to see it."

Dante looked around the table curiously. "Tyrannosaur?"

"How can you be so foolish when you're so smart?" said September Morn.

"You think better, risk more, and work harder than anyone," added Matilda.

"Me?" said Dante with an expression of disbelief.

"They're right, you know," said Virgil. "It's always been you."

"Always," echoed Matilda.

43.

HIS NAME IS ONLY WHISPERED,
HIS FACE IS NEVER SEEN,
HE'S KING OF ALL THE OUTLAWS,
HE'S HUNGRY AND HE'S LEAN.
NOTHING EVER HINDERS HIM,
AND NOTHING EVER WILL—
FOR HE IS SANTIAGO,
AND HE LUSTS FOR MONEY STILL.

DINNER HAD BEEN OVER FOR almost ten minutes, yet no one had left the table. They were all waiting for Dante, who had not moved or uttered a word, to speak.

Finally he looked up.

"You're all wrong," he said, looking at all of them. "I wish you weren't, but you are. I'm a poet, and not even a very good one at that."

"*I'm* a poet," said September Morn, "and you're right— I'm a damned sight better than you'll ever be. Starting today, I'm going to be writing the poem."

Dante was about to object, but he found that he agreed with her. She *was* a much better poet. Which meant he was out of a job.

"We discussed this among ourselves before you arrived," said Matilda, "and the conclusion is obvious. We just didn't see it until now."

"I appreciate your confidence," he said, "but I'm just a thief. I've never done anything worthwhile in my life."

"You saved me," said September Morn.

"And me," said Virgil.

"And you found a way to kill the Tweedle," added Matilda.

"Anyone could have done that," he said with a self-deprecating shrug. "You're not paying attention. Santiago is a leader of men. No one will follow me."

"I will," said Moby Dick.

"Me, too," chimed in Barnes.

"And me," added Bailey.

And suddenly he was overwhelmed by a dozen more pledges of allegiance.

"I've only been on the Frontier for a year," he protested. "I don't know anyone. I wouldn't begin to know who to contact."

"You've done pretty well so far," said the Plymouth Rocker.

"I'll be your liaison," offered Matilda.

"And I'll act as your go-between with the aliens," said Moby Dick.

He stared at them for a long minute. "You're sure?"

"We're sure," said Matilda. "You've changed every one of our lives, and always for the better. Who but Santiago could have done that?"

"All right," he said, feeling an almost tangible warmth flowing from them to him. "I'll give it my best shot."

"That's all anyone's asking," said September Morn.

Late that night he was sitting in the office, going over the figures Wilbur had transmitted to him, trying to decide the best way to put the money to use, when Matilda appeared.

"It's late," she said. "You don't have to do it all your first night on the job."

He sighed deeply. "There's so much work to do. I've got to get started."

"If I can help, let me know."

"You can tell me this isn't all some cosmic joke," he said.

"I don't understand."

"An unimportant little thief is leading an army made up of a foul-mouthed preacher, an Indian whose goal is to copulate with every race in the galaxy, an albino who's so huge he needs help just to get on his feet, a prize-winning poet, a killer who uses a crossbow of all things . . ." He shook his head as if to clear it. "What the hell kind of army is that?"

"Exactly the kind Santiago would have," she said.

"You think so?"

"Of course I do," said Matilda. "You're Santiago, aren't you?"

"Everyone seems to think so." He paused. "If I am, then when did I become him?"

"Like I told you: you always were."

Just before he went to bed, he looked into the bathroom mirror and studied the face that confronted him. For the first time, he noticed the tiny lines of character, the firm set of his jaw, the openness with which the image stared back at him.

"Well, I'll be damned," he said to the face that no longer bore any trace of Danny Briggs, and was fast losing the look of Dante Alighieri. "Maybe she was right."

EPILOGUE

HE'S BACK FROM THE DEAD,
HE'S BACK FROM THE GRAVE;
HE'S CLEVER, HE'S CUNNING,
HE'S RUTHLESS, HE'S BRAVE.
FEAR IS UNKNOWN TO HIM,
MERCY IS TOO.
HIS NAME'S SANTIAGO—
AND HE'S COMING FOR YOU!

THERE WAS A LOT OF work to do, a lifetime or more, and they soon got busy, each in his own way—for as Santiago explained, everything that had been done up to this point merely put the pieces in place. It would be years before the Democracy truly realized that the King of the Outlaws was back, defying them at every turn.

September Morn never returned to Hadrian II, but remained on Valhalla, where she added another two thousand stanzas to the poem, while still writing her own works.

Moby Dick opened a chain of Fat Chance casinos all across the Inner Frontier, each catering exclusively to aliens, and spent most of his time covertly helping Santiago.

Deuteronomy Priest spent the rest of his life warning anyone who would listen that Santiago was the devil in disguise, and that as long as he remained in human form, he was fair game for any God-fearing Christian with a weapon and a strong sense of moral outrage.

Accidental Barnes and Blue Peter crisscrossed the Inner Frontier, quietly recruiting human and alien foot soldiers for a ragtag army whose existence would always remain a secret from the Democracy.

The Plymouth Rocker did what he was told, went where he was sent, and proved to be every bit as good a major-domo as Silvermane had predicted.

The Blade killed the Knife and took over the Candy Man's operation, but continued to send Valhalla its percentage.

Tyrannosaur Bailey led the first successful raid on a Navy convoy in more than a century. And the second, and the third.

Wilbur Connaught never left the Democracy to live on his beloved Inner Frontier again, but he channeled tens of millions of credits to the organization that fought in secret to defend that Frontier.

Virgil Soaring Hawk realized that he no longer had a Dante to lead through the nine circles of hell. He stayed on Valhalla for a time, but eventually he wandered off to satisfy his unholy appetites, and was never seen again.

Waltzin' Matilda continued to practice her criminal trade, at which no one was better, but this time it enriched the coffers of her organization rather than her own bank account.

As for a small-time thief named Danny Briggs who had once operated on the world of Bailiwick, he was never seen or heard of again. After a year had passed the Democracy assumed he had been killed, canceled the reward, and closed his file.

And that is the story of how Santiago came back to the Inner Frontier.